FIVE

WAYS TO

DISAPPEAR

FIVE
WAYS TO
DISAPPEAR

B.C. BLUES CRIME

R.M. GREENAWAY

DUNDURN
PRESS

Publisher: Scott Fraser | Editor: Allister Thompson
Cover designer: Laura Boyle
Cover image: woman: shutterstock.com/ShotPrime Studio

Library and Archives Canada Cataloguing in Publication

Title: Five ways to disappear / R.M. Greenaway.
Names: Greenaway, R. M., author.
Series: Greenaway, R. M. B.C. blues crime novel.
Description: Series statement: B.C. blues crime
Identifiers: Canadiana (print) 20200380850 | Canadiana (ebook) 2020038094X | ISBN
    9781459741560 (softcover) | ISBN 9781459741577 (PDF) | ISBN 9781459741584 (EPUB)
Classification: LCC PS8613.R4285 F58 2021 | DDC C813/.6—dc23

We acknowledge the support of the Canada Council for the Arts and the Ontario Arts Council for our publishing program. We also acknowledge the financial support of the Government of Ontario, through the Ontario Book Publishing Tax Credit and Ontario Creates, and the Government of Canada.

Care has been taken to trace the ownership of copyright material used in this book. The author and the publisher welcome any information enabling them to rectify any references or credits in subsequent editions.

The publisher is not responsible for websites or their content unless they are owned by the publisher.

Dundurn Press
Toronto, Ontario, Canada
dundurn.com, @dundurnpress ✔ f ⊙

To my brothers, John and Rafael,
with love
and
To my mentors, Holley Rubinsky and Deryn Collier,
with gratitude

PART I
CROSSWINDS

ONE

WHIRLWIND

March 15

BEAU GARRETT LAY damning the devils that were trying to kill him. They had been at it again through the night, sitting on his lungs, binding his bowels into knots. Jabbing and twisting spikes into knuckles and knee joints. Hard to catch a breath. He rolled over on his mattress. He worked his oversized hands into fists and thought, *What if I die here in bed? What about the kid?*

With the shifting of his body he was able to fill his lungs. He looked around his room. The white ceiling had a dark-blue hue, not even a streak of dawn light yet. He turned his head and could just pick out the forget-me-nots in the forget-me-not wallpaper and the clutter of pill bottles on the window sill casting shadows. If he could only fall asleep again, that would be a good thing. But his mind was working now. Wondering.

What had he dreamed?

About ghosts from his past, that's what. Evvy, his wife, Sharla, his daughter. Only natural he'd be dreaming about the two of them pretty steady since they'd each shown up at his doorstep just lately. Two separate visits, each stirring up the mud of his past, disturbing him with dreams that made no sense.

In all the dreams he'd ever had of Evvy, she was young, like when they were first married. There were no fights in his dreams. No violence. No fun, either. They'd be in strange places talking about things he couldn't remember on waking. Sometimes Sharla would be there in the background, a little girl instead of the dumpy fifty-something woman she'd become.

Sometimes Sharla wasn't even a girl, but a dog, cat, bird. One time she'd been an eel. He didn't like dreams. Didn't trust them. On waking he'd have to remind himself that the years had rolled on, and Evvy was no longer twenty-five like in his dreams, or thirty-five like when they'd split up. No, she'd be a seventy-nine-year-old bag of bones now, much like himself. Old and tired and full of pains of her own.

Or so he'd been telling himself till she'd shocked the living hell out of him early yesterday morning by appearing on his doorstep, banging on the front door, in spite of the sign telling visitors to go to the back, the back door being easier for him to deal with. And when the knocking had become insistent he'd made his way through the living room, out through the little porch with its clutter of old furniture, and opened the door to find a nice-looking older woman standing there, who he'd realized after just a flash of confusion was Evvy. Not a tired bag of bones at all. At seventy-nine she was looking as fit as a fiddle and not a whole lot different from the day she'd thrown him out and they'd told each other good riddance so loud the neighbours had called the cops.

Her attitude hadn't changed a whole lot, either. Still antsy like he was about to deal her a blow, but still ready to give as good as she got. And down roadside sat a car, idling in the mid-March chill. The balding guy in glasses sitting behind the wheel was looking through the driver's side window, staring up at Beau. Probably her new boyfriend, here as backup in case the abusive ex got ugly.

The meeting on the doorstep had been brief. Evvy said she was looking for Sharla, who'd up and left her Chilliwack home without warning, taking her grandson Justin with her. Had Beau seen her at all?

To that question Beau had flat out lied, and he still wasn't sure why. Probably spite. But lie he did, telling Evvy he didn't know what the hell she was talking about and shutting the door in her face. Watched the car spit dust and drive away.

Truth was Sharla had come by just three days before that. Like Evvy, she'd ignored the sign and knocked on the front door till he opened up. Unlike Evvy, he didn't recognize her, his own daughter. Nor did he know the little boy she'd had with her. Both of them were loaded with backpacks and suitcases and shopping bags and what looked like a fish tank half full of water. The woman had addressed Beau as Dad straight off, then more or less pushed her way in as he worked out that this was the daughter he hadn't seen since she was nine, and had only spoken to once since then.

That phone call had been about twenty years ago, first day of the new century, as a matter of fact, her in her thirties wanting to reconnect, him not having much to say. And now she was back, standing in his living room, snapping words at him, saying how hard it was to track him down, *wow, isn't family great.* Beau had never been able to keep up with fast talkers, and most of what she said went in one ear and out the other. The boy was Justin, she said. Her grandson, who she'd been taking care of for a couple of years. Since Justin's mother, Kim, had died.

"Kim," Beau had said, getting a word in edgewise.

"Kim, my daughter, who I told you about when I phoned," Sharla had said. She gave him a little glare, too, and looked something like Evvy. Then she said meanly, "Kimmie was three then. Day one of the new century and I gathered up the nerve to get in touch. Thinking you might want to see us. You said you did but I could tell you didn't. So why bother. Well, you'll never see Kimmie now, as she's dead. Leaving this little guy, who's your great-grandson, which is why you should be happy to get to know him a little. Bloodline, right?"

Beau had stood looking down what seemed like a mile at the shrimpy white-haired child, who had only stared right back at him.

Sharla then said something about going south with a guy she'd met who was into hedge funds or something, and she was leaving Justin for just a couple days as she didn't trust Evvy to use it against her in some kind of custody thing they were having over the boy. *Just a couple days, here's his stuff,* Sharla had more or less said, and then she'd left without so much as a please or thank you for taking care of Justin, in spite of Beau saying he could do no such goddamn thing.

That's what the dreams were all about. After years of living alone, these people were back, littering up his thoughts. Evvy most of all. Showing off that her life had carried on without him just fine, thank you. New boyfriend and all. Nice car, too. Older model, but good set of wheels. A Buick.

His thoughts cycled back to the questions he'd been asking himself. The old question that didn't bother him much: *What if I die here in bed?* And the new one, which did: *What about the kid?*

He knew he'd die one of these days. The pain told him so, coming on pretty much the day he'd moved here to the North Shore. He wondered if the house was cursed. Except he didn't believe in curses. He'd gone to the doctor, but didn't believe in doctors any more than he believed in curses, and sure enough the pills had helped a little but bothered his stomach, so he'd quit them. And quit doctors, too.

Serve them all right, he thought. *I die here in bed and they come back to find the kid has starved to death.* He pictured them all in tears. Then he pictured the kid waking up and looking for breakfast, and when breakfast didn't come, finding his great-grandpa laid out here stiff as beef jerky, mouth an open suck-hole for moths and flies.

No. Mustn't do that. Get dressed, put the teeth in at the very least, give the kid instructions about going to the nosy neighbour, Louise, when the time came, then he could damn well die in style. He pushed himself up. Puckered his eyes, had a bit of a coughing fit. Then he set his feet on the floor and cranked himself upright. The bridge no longer fit so good, but damned if he'd go back to that maniac who called himself a denturist.

Maybe because he was dying, Beau felt like he was watching himself from above as he went about his daily routine. He watched himself select his best clothes and pull them on. Watched his big knobbly hands fight with buttons and zippers. Watched himself shuffle down the hall to the bathroom, duck the doorway, wash his face and comb his silver-black hair. Wanted to be cleanish as they packed him up and shipped him off to hell. He saw himself peering at the mirror and knew what he was: a train wreck of a once-strapping old man who'd never been anything to look at, not in the best of times, now going through the motions of living a life he had never been good at.

Why was he feeling so grim? So angry? The fantasy was blown, that was it. Fancying that Evvy missed him. Imagining her attending his funeral and remembering the good times, realizing what she'd missed out on, all full of regret and mourning.

Now he knew. She wouldn't mourn him one bit. She'd celebrate. She'd get the house, sell it, go off on some world cruise with the new boyfriend.

Fit as a fiddle. Laughing in the sunshine. Like a girl again.

He'd get his revenge. He'd put off dying for a while. Live, get fit himself. No chance he'd find a new woman to show off back at her, but — it struck him now, a genius plan — he'd do one better. Connect with the child who she was fighting over with Sharla. That's what he'd do.

Justin would call him Grampa — *Great-Grampa* being too much of a mouthful. And once this visit was over, the boy would beg to go visit Grampa. Prefer seeing Grampa Beau over Gramma Evvy. She'd always been a jealous bitch. The kid preferring him over her would drive her apeshit.

With hair combed flat with water, Beau lifted his chin to glare at the mirror. Not so bad. What had attracted Evvy to him in their teens was his size. He saw his young self through her young eyes, such a big, broad-chested powerhouse. The flesh had withered now, but the frame was still intact. Just needed to get out more, build up the muscles and work out the kinks. That's what the doctor had said. Exercise is a must.

Come to think of it, he hadn't been outside in over a month. Least not out walking. Just the cab ride for groceries a couple times, and taking out the garbage.

He'd do it. Go for a goddamn walk.

He returned to the living room and got his bearings. The sky was still dark, the room a mess of shadows. He noticed the goldfish in its little tank, filter burbling. Shook some flakes into the water. Then looked in on the boy, down the hall in the small bedroom not much bigger than a closet, no furniture really but crates for clothes and a mattress on the floor. The kid was sound asleep like a little pale-haired chipmunk curled up against the cold, blankets all a mess around him. Now that it was springtime and the days warmed up pretty quick, Beau kept the thermostat right down. So it gets cold at night? That's what sweaters and blankets are for, he'd told Justin.

The kid had talked back some, but only in four-year-old gibberish before doing as he was told, putting on a sweater and carrying on playing. He seemed like a happy enough kid, considering what a disaster his family had turned out to be. Mom dead, grandmother Sharla running off with some guy and abandoning him with an old fart who was no better than a stranger.

Back soon, don't get up to any trouble, Beau told the boy, but only in his head. How do you make a kid like you? Buy 'em things. *We'll get you a proper bed soon as I can figure out how. A bed shaped like a firetruck, how's that?*

He wedged his feet into his size-thirteen boots. Pulled on his fake sheepskin coat. Left the house out the back, heavy rubber-tipped cane in hand. He moved stiff-legged down the wooden steps. Any dawn light that might have come through was smothered in clouds, and he could hardly see the path before him. A brisk wind came and went, and it brought wetness. He now remembered the umbrella but couldn't face climbing the stairs to fetch it.

He made his way around the house to the road and started downhill. Walking was always a chore — downhill easier on the lungs but harder on the joints — but he was on a mission now of getting fit and being a lovable grampa. There was a spot he liked, about a half-hour walk when he was feeling his best, and something like an hour coming back uphill. He imagined taking the boy for walks to that special place, telling him his life story as they went. His life story wasn't great, but he'd whitewash it. Borrow someone else's heroic acts. They'd even carry on farther, get on the bus and go to town. Get hot dogs and milkshakes and go to the movies.

There was a mist over the ground, a fresh chill in the air. Beau's was the last house on a road that some ambitious pioneer had named Paradise, which went winding up into the foothills of the North Shore mountains. The road petered out into forest above and stretched over train tracks into suburbia below. His property was almost what you'd call "up in the country," because further development had been stopped by city planners some years ago, for whatever reason, as his loudmouth cousin Liz had explained to him on her deathbed.

The inheritance was a huge surprise, as Liz hadn't liked him any more than he'd liked her. Must have lost her marbles when writing up her farewell papers, leaving it all to him. Fancy day that was, getting the letter, back when he was healthy. Few months later found himself moving from a condemned trailer in Mission to this million-dollar property in North Vancouver.

Most would call it a shack, Beau supposed, just a squarish one-storey with hip-roof on a grubby plot of land, paint peeling off its clapboards, but it was the nicest place he'd ever had. And the city tax notice made it plain soon enough it was a lot nicer than he could afford. This particular cloud had what he'd call a grey lining. Paying the property tax, even with the pensioner's reduction, gouged his modest bank account every year like clockwork. A millionaire he might be, but he carried on living like the poor bugger he'd come into this world as.

Should sell and move back to Mission.

Maybe one day.

Across the road his neighbour's house stood silent and dark. A fat hairy cat hunched on the window sill, as always, and a sleek white sedan covered in dew sat in the driveway. Beau knew Louise Maxwell was out of town, as he'd seen her leave in a taxi two days back. Off to Reno, he supposed, because Louise was a gambling addict. She'd told him so back when he'd first moved in and she'd come over with a pie and tried small talking him. At least four times a year, especially in the colder months, she liked to fly to warmer climes and throw away her money. *Dumb cow.*

Beau left her home and his behind. The road curved gently before doing a wild switchback downhill. More houses sprang up on either side, all shut down and asleep. Farther along, much farther than he planned to walk today, the streets were wider and smoother and the townhomes sat shoulder to shoulder. Then there was the main road with the bus stop he sometimes used. When was the last time he'd made it that far? Not for a while. Taking the bus might be a lot cheaper than a taxi, but a lot more of a hassle, too.

Beau's lookout, as he called it, was about halfway down the hill. The houses here were newer and bigger, and all of them blocked the view except one — it was a rancher style, set far back on its property and downslope, so that a person standing on the road could easily see over its grey roof to the spread of mountains and glitter of ocean below. Even now, when the best days of his life were behind him, Beau enjoyed that view. He wasn't one for reminiscing much, but he would stand looking down and thinking about his hot summer twenty-something days. Walking the Stanley Park seawall with Evvy, lounging on Sunset

Beach listening to music. She'd been nice to him then. She'd been the housewife who only wanted to make him happy. She'd been pretty. Prettiest thing he'd ever seen.

Frowning, he saw the bend coming up. He saw the rancher he was aiming for and stopped walking. Did he really want to look over its roof at memories spoiled now by Evvy driving off in that shiny Buick with smug Mr. Four-Eyes behind the wheel?

He frowned harder. There was something different about the fence of the grey-roofed house. The fence glared white in the darkness, where it had once been faded brown. But that wasn't all. In the dawn silence, aside from birdsong and the distant hum of traffic, he could hear a grating noise, even from where he stood. A whirring and clattering that rose and fell with the shifting of the wind.

The noise came from some objects set along the fence. Shuffling closer, he saw that the warped old fence had been taken down and a new one put up, pickets and posts straight as soldiers, and standing along the inside of the new white fence was a bunch of clattering, flickering, multicoloured whatsits. And the flickering things blocked the view that meant so much to him.

He stepped onto the strip of roadside grass to look at the things up close. A cartoon pig was the first in line. A foot tall, stuck upright on a thin metal pole. Cut out of plywood, Beau guessed, and painted shiny like the fence, its skin pink, its coat blue, legs attached with a centre nail so they caught the breeze and pinwheeled.

The others, five in all, were different characters. Some had wings instead of legs. All started spinning whenever the wind picked up.

Beyond the fence, halfway down the lawn, was something else spanking new, also white. A gazebo. It sat on the green grass that rolled downslope, neat as a carpet, toward the house. The house was different than he remembered it, too. Where it had been a soft, bleached pink, its siding was now dark red and sore like a sunburn.

Beau took in all the changes, then looked at the pig again, close enough he could see the nap of its paint strokes, the dab of white to give its eye a gleam. Its legs twiddled, *squeak-a-squeak-a-squeak*. Stuck to the pig was a small square of paper that said $59.99. He poked the end of his cane between the upper pickets to push the animal's laughing face. The pig tilted under the steady pressure of his cane, but sprang back into place when released. Beau pushed with more force.

A car zipped along behind him, then silence. Silence but for the squealing all around him of things spinning, muddling with the distant twitter of birds. The squealing sounded like laughter, like a young woman giggling as her new husband caressed her cheek. Beau shuffled along the length of the fence, passed in through the open gateway. He didn't go down the footpath or long driveway, but doubled back across the lawn, past the line of creatures to get his hands on the pig, the pig like Evvy's new boyfriend, smooth and pink and laughing.

His fingers raged with pain as he grabbed hold of it and pulled. Wasn't as easy as he'd hoped. The pig tilted this way and that, loosening only a smidge with every tug. Down at the sunburned house a screen door whined and thumped. A man stood there, giving an overhead wave. Beau stopped struggling with the pig.

He was more tired than angry now. He leaned on the crook of his cane, eyes narrowed, waiting.

"*Halloo*," the man called as he puffed up the driveway. "Nice to see an earlier bird than me."

The man's face was round and smooth, much like the pig's, much like Evvy's new boyfriend. He was squat, young, in his midforties, wearing a brown cardigan over a T-shirt. Sweatpants and some kind of slippers on his feet instead of proper shoes. Thatch of shiny brown hair lifting and falling like a loose roof shingle in the wind.

"What a day, huh?" the man said. He was close enough to place a hand on the pig, wheezing between words. "So, Porky's your fave? We're not self-serve, actually, but no worries." He focused on the bit of paper taped to the pig and made a show of peeling it off, ripping it in half. "Twenty-nine ninety-nine, early bird special, just for you. And there's lots more in the garage, so come on down for a browse. Not just whirligigs, either. Only forty-nine ninety-five for the blooming gardeners, hand made with love. You got a girl? She'd love one in the old flowerbed." He turned to point. "That's those down by the house, see? Or you got a dog? One ninety-nine ninety-five for the gingerbread dog houses, which are all sold out, sorry, but more in progress if you wanna jump the queue and place an order early. And just between you and me, cash in hand gets you another five percent off." He crossed his arms with a wink.

"You make these?" Beau said.

"Yessir. Set up shop before Christmas. Business is brisk, too. The doghouses were out the door like hotcakes. Word's getting around and they're going fast, so if Porky's your fave —"

"Not planning on keeping these out here like this, are you?"

"Come again?"

"Helluva an eyesore," Beau said. The wind picked up and the creatures squealed, a chorus of chuckles.

The man wasn't smiling anymore. "That all depends on your particular tastes, I suppose. What's more up your alley? You gotta dog? 'Cause like I said —"

"I want 'em out," Beau said, unexpected tears smarting his eyes, maybe from the wind, maybe from all the summers lost and the pretty girl who'd set him adrift. He gestured with his cane across the grey roof toward the ocean and the humps of land he could see in the distance. "I plan to walk by here and look at the view without these damn things glaring at me."

"They're not glaring," the man said. "They're *smiling*. They're *funny*. People drive by here and they point and laugh. Little kids love them. They're made to brighten your day, if you've got any sense of humour at all."

Beau's sense of humour was long dead. And not having a car, he couldn't just drive by like other folk. "They don't brighten my day. I'm asking you nicely to take 'em down so I can see the ocean."

"I'm not taking them down so you can see the ocean. You want to see the ocean, go to the beach."

The man stopped talking and was frowning at Beau. He seemed to be thinking. "Hey," he said. "I know who you are. You're the son of a bitch who poured glue all over them last week."

Beau didn't know anything about glue, and didn't care. He pointed the tip of his cane at the offending pig. "Mister, I'm sick, I'm old, and I want these gone. I'll say it again. Take 'em down."

"Or what?" the man said.

"Or I'll take 'em down myself."

The man laughed. "What d'you think you are, the fucking emperor? You know what country this is, gramps? This is *CA-NA-DA,* where I'm free to do what I want, where I want, with what — *oof...*"

Being tall and heavy, Beau had a cane to match. Solid hardwood, it not only supported his weight but doubled as a tool in a pinch, pushing open doors and batting away aggressive dogs. Or prodding annoying salesmen in the gut mid-sentence.

Maybe it was surprise more than force that criss-crossed the salesman's feet. His arms wheeled as he steadied himself. The squealing whirligigs were laughing with Beau now, not at him, egging him on, and with a grin of satisfaction he took aim at the man's middle and pushed again, harder.

The salesman fell ass-first on the lawn, and Beau's grin died. A voice in his head barked at him to stop making trouble. Leave now. But he had always stuck to his guns when challenged. He'd sworn he'd get rid of this carnival crap, and he'd do so if it killed him.

He turned back to the pig and began wrestling it from the ground. A sharp pain wrenched his guts, punched into his shoulder bones, scorched his lungs, but the spike was coming loose.

A hoarse yell came from behind him. "Bastard!"

Beau looked around. The whirligig man had gotten to his feet and was a stone's throw away, leaning on the gazebo frame. "You better run fast, you crazy old bugger, 'cause I'm calling the cops."

With a final yank, Beau pulled the pig free and turned to gloat, meeting the salesman's eyes. The man seemed to take fright. He pushed off from the gazebo and started hobbling toward the house. Didn't make it far, though, falling to his hands and knees like he was made of rubber and crawling instead.

Beau watched him crawl, and somehow knew his plan of befriending Justin to make Evvy jealous was going to fail. The kid would just get scared off like Evvy and Sharla and the few friends he'd ever made and lost in life. But at least he'd won this small war. Pig spike in one hand, cane in the other, he caught up to the crawling man and gave him a final punishing prod in the ribs, meaning to get his attention. Throw down the pig, make his point, and leave.

Didn't turn out that way.

The final prod toppled the man onto his back, and instead of admitting defeat he clamped both hands onto the cane's end and held fast. Beau dropped the pig to work at pulling his cane free, but the man wouldn't let go. The tip swung side to side, up and down, as both men swore. It bobbed toward the salesman's belly, his shoulder, his throat.

Beau was losing steam. He gave up pulling and pushed instead. Six foot four and dense bodied like a time-hardened two-by-four, he put his weight into the thrust just like he'd put his weight into every backhand blow toward his wife and child, because that was the kind of all-or-nothing man he was, and the cane landed in the soft heavy flesh of the salesman's throat and sank deep. Like magic the grasping hands flew open.

Beau stepped back and stared down at what he'd done. The salesman's eyes were popping. He clawed blindly at the air and was making a horrible screeching noise. Exhaustion and a kind of dull horror caught up with Beau as he leaned on the crook of his cane. He was breathing heavily. He watched the salesman twitch and claw and turn purple. He'd be dead in minutes. Was it Beau's fault, though? Had he forced the son of a bitch to grab his cane?

No. Wasn't his fault any more than the squirrel he'd come across once, spun off a car's tire. The squirrel flipped and flopped, and Beau had put it out of its misery with a rock. Now he bent and picked up the blue-jacketed pig by its spike and raised it up high. The man's eyes were now squeezed shut and he wouldn't see it coming. The red spray was fast and startling. The body bucked. Beau let go of the whirligig and backed away. The pig stayed planted and vibrating, its legs settling back into lazy *squeak-a-squeak* spins as the body settled.

As he caught his breath, Beau felt himself lifted up and swept straight to hell. He stood looking at the sky, knowing he was going to jail for what he'd just done. He'd die there, and serve him right. If he could count on Evvy shedding one damn tear for him, that would be some comfort. But Evvy wouldn't mourn.

Looking down, he saw blood spatter on his good trousers. They'd have to be burned, for sure. He turned and walked out through the gate and homeward, slow as molasses, up Paradise Road.

TWO

RED SKY IN MORNING ...

AT A FEW MINUTES to seven in the morning, the sky was giving Constable Cal Dion mixed messages as he drove uphill to the crime scene. The clouds were an ominous dark grey, but tinged red where the blinding low-angled rays of the rising sun pierced through. The visor failed to block the worst of the glare, and he drove hunched forward and squinting. A squarish vehicle fluttered through the rays at the crest of the hill, became an ambulance and rolled past in silence.

The silence of the ambulance confirmed the radio chatter. Whatever lay ahead on this quiet road was going to be ugly.

After one last hairpin bend a bench of hillside stretched out, woods above, homes below. The road was clogged with vehicles. A fire crew was packing up to follow the ambulance downhill. Parked and empty were two marked cruisers, an unmarked SUV, a police van. Then there were the onlookers, half-a-dozen early risers standing on the sidelines and waiting for the show to begin.

Dion parked on the woodsy side of the road and was met by a brisk breeze as he left his car. Up here, separated from the harbour by altitude, there was more forest in the air than salt. Across the road a dip in the topography allowed for a fine view of the city below, then out across the brilliant sheen of strait waters to the distant mounds of the Gulf Islands. The homes in the area looked relatively modest, but with a view like this they'd be hot on the market. He checked his pockets for pen and notepad as he crossed the road to the subject address. In the driveway stood David Leith, lead investigator, newly promoted to corporal, talking on his cell.

Leith looked chilly, the fabric of his windbreaker flapping and his blond hair dancing. He had noticed Dion's approach but was looking down at the brick-red, grey-roofed rancher at the low end of the lot. Or not directly at the house, but something that stood between, a parade of brightly painted cartoon characters planted on spikes in the lawn just inside the white picket fence. Dion couldn't help but stare at them, too. The characters demanded attention like emergency flashers, with their gaudy colours and whirling legs. And arms. And wings.

With an effort he looked away from the gizmos to take in the scene. Slightly downslope from the fence was a gazebo, also painted glossy white, and near the gazebo a blue polypropylene tent was going up to protect what must be the victim against prying eyes.

And against bad weather, too. A light rain was starting to patter down, even as the sun bloomed into a cloud-shrouded corona. Dion zipped the black leather car coat he'd thrown on over suit and tie, shivering. It was the time of year when rain and sun took turns upstaging each other, and at the moment the sun was losing the battle.

Leith finished his call and turned to greet him. "Oh, hey. You're part of my dream, too, are you?"

"It's that bad?"

"No, Cal. It's worse."

"What are these things?"

In answer, Leith indicated a white sign screwed to the fence. *Whirligigs and More* was lettered in swirly red. Underneath, in swirly blue, was *Follick's Frollicks*.

Dion looked up and down the road. The onlookers, with nothing to look at now that the tent was up, were starting to clear out. Constables stood idle, ready to guide cars past and keep them moving. "Not much traffic."

"Small blessings," Leith said. "Won't last. Soon as the news is out they'll come in droves. They'll bring stepladders, telephotos. Drones. Anyway, we're going to be here a while. We'll set up behind the gazebo, once the grass has been cleared."

Set up a staging area, he meant. A second, larger tent where the team could change in and out of their protective clothing. Or sit down, rest up, make their calls, have a sandwich and coffee in relative peace.

"Deceased is Lawrence Follick," Leith went on. "His wife and daughter are in the house. JD's in there with them. Place is cleared, but I'm told the wife is in shock and refusing to leave, and the daughter won't leave without her mom. I figure we'll talk with the two of them there for starters. Follick works in a brewery over the bridge on Clark Drive. Clean record, far as I can see. The body was reported by a 911 caller about six a.m., by ..." He flipped back a page in his notebook and corrected himself. "At five fifty-five a.m. Anonymous female made the call. Didn't give an address, so first responders had a job finding the body, as he wasn't lying out on the road like they expected. All the caller said was 'A guy's lying here on Paradise Road' and hung up. Which about sums up what we know right now."

"Was this anonymous caller old or young?" Dion asked. "Have we traced her?"

"I haven't listened to the recording, so anonymous female is all I know. She made the call from a mobile, and we'll track down whoever's attached to the number pretty quick. I doubt she's the killer, though, unless she's a body builder. Take a look and you'll see what I mean. No need to suit up, unless you want to get close. Which I guarantee you won't."

Their shadows stretched before them as they left the road and walked down the gravel driveway, keeping within a designated path. They stopped by perimeter tape pegged around the body, close enough to take in the details of the violence. Details that were about as shocking as Dion had seen in his ten years on the force, and Leith was right that whoever had killed the victim had to be bigger and stronger than average.

Lawrence Follick had been heavy-set, not tall. He looked to be in his midforties. He'd been left sprawled supine on the lawn, equidistant between gazebo and driveway and six or so metres downslope from the fence. Mouth open and arms outstretched, he gazed upward at the gently breathing tarpaulin while men and women in their protective suits worked around him, the back of his head resting in a seeping marsh of red ooze.

"Estimated time of death," Leith said, "is between four a.m. and the 911 call at five fifty-five. The wife, Brenda, didn't know anything had happened till the first sirens started arriving."

Dion nodded, eyes fixed on the scene. What took it from shocking to surreal was the weapon itself, almost certainly the cause of death, spiked through the dead man's throat. It was one of the whirligigs, a length of rebar topped like a cocktail garnish with one of the cut-out cartoons. Porky Pig, tipping its top hat. Protected from the breeze by the tent, it wasn't running anywhere, its legs at a standstill.

Done with the pig, Dion studied the dead man once more and the track of blood that had fountained to the side from the weapon's point of entry. The fountain had guttered but the force of its arc was written across the lawn. Blood had flowed from the nostrils down either cheek, too, joining a river of what could only be drool and vomit.

The man's clothing was casual. Slack green jogging pants. A grey-and-blue striped T-shirt rode up to show pale belly flesh. A brown cardigan had come off the shoulders. Mismatched socks on the feet, pale-blue leatherette moccasins knocked or kicked clean off. Dion saw the moccasins some distance away, thrown willy-nilly.

The scene shouted blitz attack, struggle. The last thing the victim expected.

Catching Leith's attention, Dion pointed to an area of lawn just off the edge of the driveway. "The killer stood about there." A blood spatter expert, if called in, would confirm it, but the spear's angle told the story to anyone with eyes. The rebar, taking into account its length embedded in the victim and the lawn below, was maybe six feet end to end, and anybody wielding it would have likely lobbed or plunged it from there. "It looks spontaneous," he added. "He'd have grabbed hold of the pig to pull it loose, so there's a good chance he left prints. Glossy painted plywood, perfect." He looked toward the fence and the five characters that remained there whirling merrily. A Popeye and a mouse in a sombrero, a Bugs Bunny, and two more that looked only vaguely familiar. "So, did this pig come from that group?"

"No doubt. There's a fresh hole in the ground, end of the line, corner of the lot."

"Where?"

"There."

They stood in silence, looking at the comical parade. The rain pattered down more insistently, the sun having thrown in the towel. Leith's hood went up. He said, "I hate to say it, but one motive that jumps out right away is the pig itself."

Dion looked at him. "What d'you mean? A copyright issue?"

"No. I mean it's ugly."

Dion was thinking the scruffy blond beard Leith seemed to be cultivating was ugly. Leith was tall and rangy, in his midforties, and could lose some belly fat, but until the beard had come along he hadn't been bad looking. The whirligigs, on the other hand, were skillfully done and in the right setting would be kind of cheerful, in his opinion. This for sure was not the right setting. "You don't kill somebody 'cause something's ugly," he said.

"You could get into a fight about how ugly it is, and the fight could get out of hand," said Leith with finality. "Anyway, like I said, it took muscle to pull out that pig. We're looking for a big guy. Lotta muscle. Young."

"Why out of the six does he go for the pig? Symbolic? It's the farthest from the gate as well as farthest from the killing, so why not that duck, say?"

Leith gave a shrug that said he wasn't into guesswork at the moment and struck off downslope toward the brick-red house, saying something about now for the fun part. Dion followed.

* * *

The rancher with double garage was maybe forty years old. A plaque on the door read *The Follicks* and another, *Home Swede Home*. The interior was smelly, and Dion thought he could separate out bacon, cinnamon, and the distinct whiff of petting zoo. The decor was a mishmash. Though mid-March, a faux Christmas tree blinked from a dark corner, and on the walls and ledges and tables were arts and crafts he supposed were made by whoever had created the whirligigs.

He arrived in the living room and saw that Leith was trying to corral a thin woman in her forties toward the dining room table. She wasn't cooperating, preferring to pace and plead with some higher power to tell her why. A teenaged girl sat curled up on the sofa, face in hands, next to Serious Crimes Constable JD Temple in plainclothes. Somewhere a radio or TV played. Dion asked JD a silent question — just a glance — if she was getting any useful info from the girl. Her silent answer was *no*.

The pacing woman was no doubt the dead man's wife, Brenda. Leith finally managed to get her to sit, and once they were at the table he went on calming her, bringing her into the moment, asking her to tell him what had happened this morning. Dion listened to her disjointed story. She told of being at the kitchen sink, and then of waking up. Larry was likely down in his workshop, so she thought. Except he wasn't.

"I was at the kitchen sink," she repeated, numbly. "I was pouring water into the coffee pot when I saw a fire truck drive by. Going up the hill. Then it drove down-hill, more slowly. Then it came up again. And then it stopped on the road in front of our house. I called out for Larry to come see. I was sure he was downstairs. But he didn't answer. I thought, *Oh my god.* And then I saw it on the grass, near the gazebo. It was still dark out, and it was a dead animal, I figured. Large, maybe a big dog or something. I didn't know it was Larry. I didn't!"

She really didn't want to know what it was, she admitted. She had focused instead on getting breakfast ready. But when an ambulance joined the fire truck, she knew it was a human being on her lawn, and she'd shut the blinds because she didn't want to know more.

Neither did she want to tell Leith about what had happened next. All she wanted was for him to go away and leave her alone.

At the kitchen sink Dion used the wand to open the venetian blinds. He imagined himself standing here, running water, filling the coffee pot. From here he had a good view on the driveway, the lawn, the gazebo, and what was now a blue polypropylene tent. The neighbour's house to the east was visible, the one to the west hidden by bushes.

He couldn't imagine looking out, seeing the shape on the grass, seeing the commotion of emergency vehicles, and not heading out to learn what was going on. Even in darkness, even if he didn't recognize it was his loved one lying there, spiked to the turf, he would have investigated. As would most people.

He left the window and took a chair at the table with Leith, watching Brenda for signs of guilt. Leith would be watching, too, wondering if the wife was somehow involved in the killing. Too slight to have done it herself, but didn't mean she wasn't complicit. Along with the daughter, possibly. What if they'd cooperated? Tasered Follick, hoisted the rebar, plunged it down, then worked up the crocodile tears.

Or what about a hired hit, Dion wondered, then scrapped the idea. If that was the work of a hitman, it was a hitman from another planet.

"How am I going to live without him?" Brenda was asking Leith.

Leith told her that he didn't know how she'd carry on, but he knew she would. He went on in his best calming voice, speaking about the value of family and friends, about community support services, about how her daughter needed her to stay strong.

It was something Leith excelled at, Dion knew. Comforting people. People who were lost or frantic, whether victims of crime or detainees hauled in kicking, more often than not they'd surrender to Leith when he sat them down and spoke to them in a way that said he cared, that he had all the time in the world for them, that nothing mattered but how they were coping. Maybe it was strategy, because the workaday Leith was more grumpy than kind, more edgy than mellow. Or maybe it was real compassion shining through when he felt the person he was dealing with deserved it.

Dion wondered if the compassionate side of Leith would be there for him, too, if he ever ran up against chain-link with no exit.

Actually, it was *when*, not *if.*

Another of Leith's skills was the segue, which he could do seamlessly, from sympathy to inquiry. "So no one you can think of who might have something against Larry?" he was asking Brenda, who now listened attentively. "Even something that might seem trivial to you. Friction with a co-worker, anything like that? Owes a debt to someone? Argument with a neighbour?"

Brenda shook her head to all three suggestions. "No."

She sounded firm, but Dion thought she had hesitated on the last denial.

"You're sure about that?" Leith asked. "Have there been any conversations with the neighbours? About anything? Complaints, say, about the display out front?"

Brenda fumbled in her pockets for something. Maybe a weapon, Dion considered. But more likely cigarettes. "Somebody tried to sabotage his lawn ornaments last week," she finally admitted, still fumbling. "Put glue in there, in the hinges or joints or whatever, made them sticky so they didn't spin. But Larry cleaned them up and they were okay again."

"Do you know who did it?"

"Kids, probably."

"Generally speaking, how's your relationship with other people in the neighbourhood? Seems like a close-knit area, a get-to-know-you kind of road."

"We get along fine with everyone."

Again, Dion heard something in her voice akin to a lie.

Leith seemed to hear it, too. "The people in the houses next door, either side, d'you know their names?"

The cigarettes materialized, and Brenda asked if anyone minded, then lit one. Her hands trembled. Once she had inhaled deeply she shook her head. She didn't know what their names were. The couple on that side were retired, Chinese, currently out of the country. The others, their name was something Italian, she thought.

Leith directed Brenda away from conflict and asked for some of her own family background, and Brenda spoke of a move from Haney to North Van last year, how they preferred Haney as it was more laid back, but were getting used to this place okay. Larry was happy anywhere he went, so long as he had his workshop and tools.

"Wherever Larry is happy, so am I," she said, defying the past tense.

Dion had a feeling she would defy the past tense for as long as she could manage. But she knew. She'd have no choice as the days went by. Missing the aroma of fresh-sawn wood, the stink of paint, the sound of his voice as he joined her at the breakfast table, the weight of his arm across her shoulders. The reality was going to hit her, over and over. And just when she thought she'd accepted he was gone, she'd wake up with a jolt and blink into the darkness ...

She gave in to tears, and Dion looked away. Leith reached to take the forgotten cigarette from her fingers and extinguished it in the ashtray. Over on the sofa the daughter was crying, too, but in a quiet and controlled way, knuckling her mouth, eyes squeezed shut.

"You know what," Leith told Brenda, rising from his seat. "You just sit here and take it easy. I'll ask Mosie a question or two, and then we'll see about getting you into some comfortable accommodations."

In the living room JD Temple stood up from the sofa next to Mosie, and Leith took her place. Dion stood beside JD, ready to take notes. Leith introduced himself to the girl, told her how sorry he was, and asked if there was anything she could tell him about what had happened this morning.

Mosie shook her head. "No. I woke up and it was all just craziness. Mom said Daddy's dead. I don't understand."

"D'you know anybody who might want to hurt him? Looking back, anybody at all, even if it seems unlikely?"

Instead of shaking her head no, as Dion expected, Mosie thrust a stiff arm toward the front window. "That shithead," she said. "He always wants to get in my pants, and him and Daddy got in a big fight about it. *He* killed my Daddy."

Leith, Dion, and JD looked in the direction of the girl's accusatory index finger, across the low fence that divided the two properties to the shadowy form of the house next door. Dion looked at JD, hoping for a bonding moment that might help to heal the rift between them. A solid lead like this one, right out of the gate, was a gift to the team and a reason to high-five, at least telepathically. But there was no high-fiving of any kind with JD lately.

Still, she was pleased, he could tell, that the killer could be placed under arrest within the hour. So was he. Only Leith seemed less than thrilled. But one way or another, trouble was definitely brewing for the possibly Italian neighbour.

THREE

JANGLE

LEITH HEAVED A SIGH. Who relished interviewing traumatized children? He was a father, had a young girl of his own, Isabelle. Izzy was only three, but that wasn't so far off from thirteen, like the young victim of crime he had just questioned. He knew first-hand the impact that words and actions could have on the young. Three was about the age when a person begins to get it, that the perfectly clear and understandable world is actually rife with bullshit. By thirteen, many were jaded.

It was the adult's job, as Leith saw it, to mark a clear path for the children they're responsible for. Guide them through mixed messages and moral confusion till they could find their footing and create their own maps. He only hoped he had the trailblazing skills, as a parent and as a cop. There were times he had his doubts.

As in his interview with Mosie, asking her about the father she had loved and who had just been so savagely murdered. Careful, solicitous, but still he'd made her cry.

After half an hour she was able to provide some details to her accusation, but the story remained questionable, at best. Sometime last month the neighbour had groped her. Whereabouts had this happened? On the sidewalk outside her home as she was returning from school. She'd stumbled and he'd rushed to help her upright, fondling her chest as he'd done so. She'd told her dad about it. He had gone over there and given the neighbour a thrashing. No, she hadn't actually witnessed the thrashing, but her dad had told her about it, and she believed him.

Leith had her story, and now would have to get the other. Once arrangements were made to have Brenda and Mosie transported elsewhere so the house could be forensically searched, he and Dion walked up the driveway and down Paradise Road to the next house over, the pale stucco with its no-doubt fabulous view of the valley from its backside, Leith guessed, and its less fabulous view at the front of the roadside whirligigs battling the wind.

"It's offset," he pointed out, indicating the position of the Italians' home, which sat closer to the road than the Follick residence, its southern flank exposed to the their yard, nothing between them but a low fence. "And look at that picture window. If that's their living room, imagine the view. No wonder the blinds are shut tight."

Dion didn't reply. He could be mind-bogglingly canny, Leith knew, but mind-bogglingly naive, too. At the moment he was being naive in his outright rejection of Leith's perfectly sound clash-of-aesthetics scenario, placing his bets instead on the unlikely motive of angry dad versus pervert neighbour. And all based on the hearsay of a dead man. Maybe it was true Larry had exchanged words with the neighbour over the alleged Mosie incident, but an actual thrashing? Unlikely.

"So what do we do?" Dion asked, when they reached the Italians' doorstep. "Put the Mosie issue to them right off?"

"Depends who opens the door," Leith said, pressing the bell.

A slim, middle-aged woman greeted them, her slenderness emphasized by a black leotard and clingy sarong. Loud swing-style music accompanied her, the blare of trumpets, the swish of cymbals. She inspected their ID cards and gave her name as Sylvia Romano. Dion asked her if she was aware of the incident next door, and she stared out past him and sidelong to what was visible of the commotion, police vehicles lining the road, the group of techies and a corner of the blue tent erected beside the gazebo, partially blocked by a conifer.

"Good grief," she said. "What's going on? I thought I heard a siren go by earlier, but wasn't sure. I had the music up." She paused and added sourly, "Should have gone to take a look, but I avoid the windows on this side of the house these days, if I can help it."

"There's been an incident next door," Leith explained. "All right if we come in and ask a few questions?"

They were invited into a living room that he saw was minimally and tastefully decorated. Not a single clash of colour. "You know your neighbours pretty well, do you?" he asked Ms. Romano.

"Well, I know they're *artistic*," she said, laying the irony on thick. "You can't miss it, as it's all over their signage." She gestured toward the roadway, referring to the board painted in circus colours, swirls of red and blue, attached to the fence. "She's Brenda and he's Larry. Brenda and Larry Follicle. I mean Follick."

She aimed a sunny smile at Dion, who was jotting notes, maybe hoping the misspoken name would go down for posterity in a police file.

"Sounds like you don't care for your neighbours, Mrs. Romano," Leith put to her.

"No," she said. She dropped the pretense and spoke flatly. "And you wouldn't, either. They move in, and first thing they do is tack up that sign and set up a parade of flapping monsters, so now every time you want to sit down with a cup of tea outside and enjoy nature, which is what we moved up here for, you find yourself staring across at those *things* instead, a bunch of Mickey Mouses and Tasmanian Devils. And even if you shut your eyes, you can hear them. You see the fence dividing our place from theirs? It's been perfect all these years. Now it's *way* too low."

"Did you or your husband try to do something about it? Take some action?"

She looked bewildered. "Of course we spoke to them about it. Futile. He shifted the things over a few feet, and made it clear he thinks we're stuck up and have no sense of humour. Love thy neighbour."

"Any further action. More extreme?" On the low end of extreme Leith was thinking glue; on the high end, murder.

"Not a lot we could do," she said. "Dale looked into the zoning laws, hoping we could shut them down as a commercial enterprise in a residential area. But no luck."

"Who's Dale?"

"My husband."

"Is Dale at home?"

"No, he's at work," she said. "So what's this all about? How serious is this incident? Did Larry cut off all five fingers of his right hand on the scroll saw? I mean, what are the chances, but one *can* hope."

Wow, Leith thought. These neighbours were the worst match, and he wouldn't care to have either one living next door. "No, ma'am," he said. "It was a fatality."

Her brows lifted. "A fatality? Like, as in death?"

"Like, as in death."

She was shocked, genuinely. Or a genuinely good actor. "God," she said. "Was it him? Or Brenda? I hope not the child."

"It was Lawrence Follick," Leith said. And now her mood was diverted, he saw. Dammed, actually. Unfortunate to lose the stream, but interesting to see where it would flow.

"Well," she said. "I'm sorry. No, in spite of what I just said, I really am. Sorry, I mean. What on earth happened?"

"I can't get into that right now."

"Did Brenda finally snap?"

It was her idea of a bad joke, but vaguely spoken. Leith wondered if she had somehow switched to auto-pilot, if her thoughts were racing along another line altogether.

Dion asked, "Where does your husband work, Mrs. Romano?"

She fixed her gaze on him. "Davis Long and Associates. Why?"

"What's Davis Long and Associates?"

"Graphics, drafting, computers." Her tension had surfaced, her voice gone brittle. "He's a graphic artist. Why does it matter?"

Leith said, "We have to go through the neighbourhood, see if anybody knows something or saw anything out of place. So we can figure out what happened. That's all."

"Well, it might be helpful to us potential eyewitnesses if you explained what you know of what did happen and when, mightn't it?"

"That might be a good idea," Leith agreed. "About all I can say at this point is it happened early this morning, sometime before six. This is a quiet neighbourhood, so things stand out. Mainly what we're looking for is any sightings of strangers in the vicinity, cars, pedestrians, in the last day or so. Or even if you've heard anything unusual."

He watched her pretend to scour her memory and decided she was processing the idea that there was a crime involved. And seriously regretting all those cruel things she had said about Follick. Possibly she was tracing the possibilities back to her husband, too, a man with an axe to grind.

"No," she said. "I can't remember anything out of the ordinary. Dale and I watched a movie until about midnight, then went to sleep. We both get up fairly early as a rule. He had a bite, jumped in his car, and went straight off to work. We didn't see anything, hear anything, no. Nothing. Sorry."

"He leaves by way of the front door or the back?" Leith asked. "I'm just wondering what his opportunity was to see anything happening next door as he left the house."

"He wouldn't see much of next door. You go down the back stairs to the carport at the side here, drive away downhill, not past the Follicks'. So, no, he wouldn't be able to tell you anything, I'm sure."

"And what time did he leave this morning?"

She hesitated. "About five."

"Early. Is that his normal departure time?"

"Not always, but sometimes. He's assigned projects, deadlines, works on his own time to meet those deadlines." She tried on a smirk and said, "Now, look, if you're trying to pin something on my husband, whatever it is, don't bother. He may not like our neighbour's sense of chi, but he certainly wouldn't *kill* the guy over it. There are less dramatic solutions. We're looking into building a taller fence, for one. So …"

She faltered, and Leith gave her his most severe gaze, letting her know this was the time to come clean. "Mrs. Romano, has there been any friction between your husband and Lawrence Follick about anything aside from the lawn ornaments? That you know of?"

"No. Other than the *lawn ornaments*, as you put it, we all got along just fine."

"Their daughter, Mosie. Any problems there?"

His words struck a chord, but not one he expected. She looked annoyed. "The girl slipped on ice one day, on the road out front — wearing high-heeled boots in February will do that — and Dale helped her up, and she slipped again, and he grabbed for her arm, and

I guess he brushed her boob as he did so, and next thing you know Larry's shouting over the fence that if Dale so much as looks at his daughter again, he's toast."

"You witnessed this?"

"Yes, I was there."

"What was Dale's reaction?"

"He told Larry a thing or two."

"How did it resolve?"

"They both walked away."

"No further confrontation?"

"None. It was such nonsense. Larry was posturing, probably to prove something to his kid. Few days later he called out good morning to Dale, who was taking out the garbage. Like nothing happened. Did Dale grope her? Of course not. The whole family's mad. Honestly, though, I'm getting a little nervous here. Should I be calling a lawyer?"

Searching her eyes throughout the exchange, Leith had read guilt, confusion, anger, and jangled nerves, but nothing that went above whatever marker he used to hang suspicion on. Him being here, breaking the news, hinting at accusation, it was no wonder she was apprehensive.

Apprehensive, but hardly guilty. Her husband Dale, though, could be another story.

* * *

They clocked the drive from the Romano residence to the firm of Davis Long in the commercial zone just up from the harbour. The graphic design business was set up in one of many flat-faced structures that sat shoulder to shoulder: copy shops and small-scale labs, engineering firms and fabricators. In through a front door that buzzed, past nameless closed doors, up dark narrow stairs. Davis Long's front door was open, pop music thumping out. A young woman worked at a photocopier behind the reception counter, and when Leith finally broke through the hip-hop with a shouted, "Excuse me," she led them down a hall.

They were left standing in a bright studio space lit by skylights. There were drafting boards, computer desks, a refreshment nook, a ping-pong set. A lone worker sat on a stool at a workbench that beamed light into his face. He turned as the men approached. He straightened, blinking.

"Good morning," Leith said. "Mr. Romano? It's Dale, right?"

Romano rose from his seat. He was middle-aged, fit, his thick dark hair and moustache shot with silver, his eyes amiable. He seemed surprised to see them, which was good. It meant Sylvia had likely heeded Leith's request to not alert her husband of this pending visit.

"Yes, that's me."

Leith introduced himself and Dion, showed his ID, explained that they were with the RCMP. Romano looked baffled, maybe afraid. Leith sketched out that an incident had taken place on Paradise Road that they needed to ask about. The colour rose in Romano's cheeks and he occupied himself organizing chairs for them to sit.

Once seated, Leith asked Romano, who seemed to be having trouble breathing, what time he'd left for work this morning. Romano gulped and stuttered. "Five or so," he said. "I'm not sure exactly. Why?"

The majority of people Leith spoke to in the course of business were nervous for one reason or another. He had become pretty good at weeding out atypical anxiety, and Romano's anxiety was definitely off-key. Chances were this case would wrap up in record time. Three and a half minutes after entering the premises he was going to have his confession on a plate and the culprit in handcuffs. He would be bragging about it over beers tonight with the crew. "If you left home at five this morning, that gets you here in your seat at about five twenty. Would that be right?"

"Sounds about right," Romano said.

"It's a twenty-minute drive," said Dion at Leith's side. He, too, was sussing out Romano's fear, and his strategy was to get punchy, fast. Voice raised, handcuffs all but brandished. "We timed it. Why did you leave so early this morning? That's not your usual time for heading to work."

Romano stared at him. "Deadlines," he said. "Had a big one. I left it too late, and now have to work long hours to make it up. Ask my wife. She'll tell you procrastination is my worst enemy." He stuttered badly over the word *enemy.*

Christ, Leith thought. *This is too easy.*

Romano was staring down at his work space, which looked one part physical sketches and technical memorandums, one part Post-it Notes, and six parts gigantic computer screen laid flat. On the screen was a realistic rendering of a beer bottle. The bottle was wet. It looked like it was sweating cold fear.

"Your next-door neighbours," Leith said. "The Follicks. Are you friendly with them?"

Romano's eyes were fixed unblinking on his artwork, and Leith could see the thoughts ticking away in there. Thinking about the neighbour he had just driven a stake through, about the freedom he was leaving behind. Unlike Sylvia, who only suspected something was wrong, guilty knowledge throbbed from Dale Romano. The attack had been spur of the moment, nothing premeditated. There would be evidence on the weapon, microscopic proof embedded in his clothes, on his skin, in his hair. He didn't stand a chance, and he knew it.

"The Follicks," Romano murmured. One eye squeezed shut as if the name only faintly rang a bell. "Larry, next door? No, I don't know him well. They're fairly new in the area, moved in around Christmas." He swallowed and finally looked Leith in the eye. "Why? Did something happen?"

Leith told him some of what had happened to Follick, that there had been a death. "You were up early this morning, and so was Larry. You ran into each other outside, is that right? So what exactly happened out there?"

Romano's brown eyes had been widening since the mention of death, and his demeanour now did a little jig, from anxiety to bewilderment. "What exactly happened? Nothing! Nothing exactly happened."

Leith noted, almost subliminally, Dion's reaction to Romano's statement, betrayed by a slight shift in stance and twist of the mouth. "We know you're not on good terms with the Follicks," Leith pressed on, focusing more on his suspect than the vagaries of his partner's thought processes. The moment was pivotal and Romano was just about at breaking point. Leith pitied him. He had a short supply of sympathy for many killers, but he felt for Dale. The man wasn't a killer, at heart. Whatever he'd done, it was a stumble. An act of passion. "Sylvia's explained the problem, Dale," he added.

Using first names would create a power imbalance, psychologically block the exits.

"Do you want to tell us your version of events?"

"My version of events?" Romano echoed, and something in the echo threw cold water over Leith's daydream of a fast wrap. Like Dion, he was starting to have doubts. The suspect's arms had become tightly crossed. His expression was stony. "I didn't run into him this morning. I didn't see him this morning. How can I have a version of events if I wasn't there?"

The possible killer wasn't going to confess, then. His face tilted upward, a fiery spot marking each cheekbone. He was going to deny it all, Leith realized, and the boxes of exhibits would grow, and the trial would be long and tedious.

Still, in messy cases like this where blood had fountained and trace evidence was everywhere, like confetti at a wedding, the end result would be the same. The forensics team would move in and the case would slam shut.

"I want a lawyer," Romano said.

And though he was clearly trying to contain it, the cork blew and he let out a frightened sob.

FOUR

PURPLE SMOKE

AT THE END OF THE DAY, the record-breaking confession of Dale Romano that Leith had been hoping for didn't happen. There was no fast-tracking to arraignment followed by congratulations all around. After eight tedious hours of interviews, phone calls, consultations, and arguments with legal types, Romano was deemed nothing more than one hell of an annoying red herring and released.

It had been about halfway through the eight hours that Leith had started to get at the truth, that Dale's initial jumpiness had nothing to do with murder and everything to do with small-scale vandalism: sneaking over to the neighbour's fence before work last week with a tube of contact cement and sabotaging an annoying whirligig. A crime that would barely ping the average man's conscience. But Dale was better than average, the kind of guy who followed the rules. The kind of guy who wouldn't ordinarily go messing with another man's property. But he'd been driven to it, when all else failed. And the glue had failed, too, as it turned out.

Adding to the confusion, Dale's horror when he'd been told of the death next door had been authentic. Just as authentic as Sylvia's. Sylvia thought Dale had killed the annoying neighbour, and Dale thought Sylvia had, and once the dust settled it was clear that, for crying out loud, *neither* had.

The day was done, as was Leith. He phoned Alison, told her he'd be home in an hour, and drove back uphill to visit square one, the Follick residence with its gazebo still shrouded in blue polyethylene, its whirligigs now taken away as evidence. He parked his car on the woodsy side of the road and walked to the home's frontage, looking around, trying to get a sense of what had really happened here. The neighbourhood was peaceful now, though crime scene investigators continued their painstaking explorations in and around the property. Otherwise, silence. The press had come and gone, and so had the curious locals. He was blissfully alone.

He stood at the white picket fence, looking out over the house's grey roof toward the sea. A good view from here, thanks to the lay of the land and a gap in the tree line. A view he would have found restful, if he wasn't so tense. He thought about the hell Larry Follick had suffered here on his own lawn early this morning. He channelled himself into that man's body, felt his own throat punctured. He scrubbed at his prickly new beard, hoping death had been quick.

Dion came walking up the driveway and joined Leith on the grassy verge that met asphalt. He had been in the house, he explained, talking to Ident. Wasn't much news to share. Nothing of obvious evidentiary value found within the house or in a wide perimeter around the property. No flags on Follick's computer, no questionable correspondence in his desk drawers.

Leith nodded at the non-news. He told Dion about the drive he had just made up Paradise Road, all the way to its top, where the roadway petered out into dirt tire tracks, then foothill forest. He'd passed barely a dozen homes on the way. At the top he'd had to turn around, as there was no way out, other than this road.

"It's a nice area," he added. "Kind of out of the way, offbeat. No through traffic."

Dion agreed it was nice, and they stood in silence, admiring the view. The evening air was pleasant with the earthy scents of spring, still and clean after a fierce afternoon storm. The skies were dramatic orangey pink as the sun sank into banks of clouds that wreathed the distant island ranges. Too beautiful of a day to be swearing at failure, but Leith swore, anyway.

Swearing was a luxury these days, with a small child at home and being obliged to watch his language soon as he stepped through the door. Meaning it was good to vent in advance. Like now. He swore at fucking Dale Romano, then at Romano's fucking lawyer. He pulled a packet of Belmonts from his jacket pocket. He was down to three a day and aiming for zero, but just the feel of the box in his palm was calming. Even the little inset photo of rotten lungs didn't stop him from feeling better as he knocked out an immaculate white tube and flicked his lighter to its tip, making the tobacco crackle.

"You can't blame Ponce for doing his job," Dion remarked, referring to the lawyer Leith had just maligned. "And you can't blame Dale Romano for raising a bunch of red flags that turned out to be just him being careful not to incriminate himself."

"Not to incriminate his wife, you mean," Leith said. "And vice versa. Which tells me they're both capable of murder. We should arrest them for — I don't know — obstructive conceptualization." He was pleased with his own wit. He sucked in smoke, felt it hit his lungs, loved the sensation, and exhaled sideways. The smoke blew upward and outward to join the clouds above.

"So I checked out the magic show," Dion said.

"The what?"

"Down here, behind Parkgate." Dion produced a piece of paper and unfolded it, revealing a black-and-white Google Earth printout. On the diagram he indicated an open area behind a shopping plaza, apparently a park or field neatly buffered from suburbia by strips of woodland. "A community project. They had a trial run a few years ago, and it was a hit, so they've got ideas of making it some kind of big annual thing that'll draw tourists. This is the amphitheatre, this roundish thing, and they've hauled in an old double-wide classroom and put it about here. They're rigging it up with a stage for indoor performances. Magic is the theme, but there'll be food booths and music, as well. If it makes money this year they'll invest in a bigger and better version for the future."

He had more to say, but Leith cut him off at the pass. "A magic show project. Why are you telling me this?"

Maybe thrown off by the interruption, Dion said nothing, but folded the map and stuck it back in his pocket. It was a fragility Leith had seen in him lately. A symptom of depression, he believed. He thought he knew the source of the depression, too. It wasn't only the funerals marking the passing of Dion's friends and acquaintances and workmates, so many deaths in such a short time. It wasn't the end of romance, either. Recently, the man had gotten back together with an ex-girlfriend, Kate, going into the reunion with high hopes. Even more recently they had broken up, and this time with apparent finality.

It was all that, but more so it was a deep, dark secret that was pulling Dion down. Leith knew more than he wished about the secret. Dion had been not much more than a stranger to him early last year when their superior, Mike Bosko, had asked him to do some off-the-record digging. Rout out the crime Dion was suspected of committing. Bring enough evidence into the light to justify upgrading an unofficial inquiry into a full-blown IHIT investigation.

Leith's half-hearted digging had led to certain conclusions. Yes, there was most definitely a crime, one that led via some disastrous chain of events to the car crash that killed Dion's closest friend and colleague, Luciano Ferraro, a.k.a. Looch. Probably the crime was nothing trite. Probably murder. But to say Leith had enough details to lay charges was a stretch. He might have uncovered more, had he carried on with his excavations. Literally speaking. Instead, without telling a soul, not even his wife, Alison, he had chosen to look the other way. Gone wilfully blind. Didn't want to know what Dion and Looch had pulled that night. Didn't want Dion, who he had since come to like, facing charges, losing his badge, heading to the slammer. This was one criminal investigation he hoped would fail.

Fat chance of that, though, now that a witness had come forward. Early in the year a woman had phoned Mike Bosko claiming she had information that would sink Dion. She wanted to set up a meeting. Hadn't given her name, and neither had she shown up at the time and place specified. But Bosko seemed confident she would try again soon.

All in all, an excellent reason to be yoked by depression. The man's luck was running out, like sand in an hourglass, and he knew it.

"I guess you weren't there when we were running it by Bosko," Dion was saying, still talking about the magic show. His attitude had shifted from a thin veneer of enthusiasm to a not-so-thin veneer of gloom.

"Fill me in, then."

"Lawrence Follick had volunteered to help with the magic show. Publicity or something. It's in the notes. It's something Mosie told JD this afternoon, and JD told me. I asked Bosko about it, and he agreed I should follow up. I went down to the field to see if anybody was around to interview, but no luck, so I'll try again tomorrow. Talk to the magic people, see if Follick was working close with anyone on the project."

Leith was tired. He didn't want to hear of more puzzle pieces that had to be knocked into place. He wanted to forget the dead man viciously spiked to the turf and enjoy what was left of his cigarette. In an effort to cheer Dion up, he said, "Talk to the magic people? Impossible."

Dion arched a brow. "Why?"

"They'd just disappear." He could see the punchline falling flat, but said it, anyway. "In a big puff of purple smoke."

Dion didn't bother working up a smile. Leith sighed and gestured toward the vehicles. "Gotta get going."

As they made their way back to their cars, he asked about one of Dion's more mundane troubles. "So how's life at Joe's?"

In February Dion had given notice at the low-rise where he'd been living, only to learn that the availability of a suite in the Harbourview Towers — the high-rise he for some reason coveted — had been a clerical error. It wasn't vacant after all, sorry. Which left him homeless. Leith had helped out by getting in touch with a friend who had a basement suite sitting empty. Which he thought was a decent stop-gap solution till Dion could find something better. He now waited for a friendly answer to his friendly question. Maybe even a word of gratitude.

Dion's snort of contempt said life at Joe's wasn't good at all.

Leith was hurt. "I thought you liked his place. You said you did, when we looked at it."

"I was being polite. I don't know if I can take it much longer. It's giving me bad dreams."

The two men stood by the cars in the gathering and breezy darkness, not quite parting ways. Headlights flickered in Leith's eyes and skimmed past, a vehicle heading to one of the scant homes upward along Paradise Road.

Homes in North Van tended to be upscale and crowded, but here on the rustic upper fringes of the city he had discovered some quaint bungalows still standing, with peeling paint and room to breathe.

"Actually, nightmares," Dion added. "Like nothing I've had before."

"So that's why you're looking so bagged."

True, Dion wasn't so handsome lately, his dark eyes shadowy and his trim black hair flattened on one side as if he hadn't the wherewithal to lift a comb. "That's not 'cause of the bad dreams," he said. "It's 'cause of the bad sofa bed. It's a really bad, really crummy bed. The worst. I'd get my own furniture out of storage except I'll be out of that dungeon soon as possible. Even if I have to camp under a bridge."

"I'm sorry to hear it," Leith said. "I know it's been lousy days for you. You can always give me a call. You know that, right? Whenever."

Dion nodded a brief thanks before driving the conversation back to the job. "So who hated Lawrence Follick enough to do what they did? Random attack? Had to be somebody super strong. Getting those rods out of the soil wasn't easy. You saw it. Took teamwork to remove the rest of them. So whoever did the pig, he had to be fit."

"Or could be the pig had been pulled out earlier," Leith said. "And it was just lying there, ready to be used."

"You'd still have to be strong to pick it up and use it like a spear. And why would someone want to use it in that way? We're still stuck on that."

"Who knows. Maybe nothing more than a hatred for whirligigs."

Dion seemed suddenly amused, and Leith sensed that underlying the amusement was a barb, and that the barb was aimed at him personally. "What's funny?"

"You're back to the pig as motive, are you? You still think this is murder over an *eyesore*?"

"It's not out of the question. Follick's frollicks gave the Romanos heartburn. Maybe the neighbours weren't the only ones who hated those things."

Dion said nothing, leaving his last word hanging like an unfinished thought as he studied Leith's face. Eyesore. Leith caught the beard-related insult and bit back. "You have a problem with this?"

There was a point to the beard. The point was semi-confidential, and had to do with E division. Leith had been encouraged by certain IHIT members — the Integrated Homicide Investigation Team — to sign up. There was a need for new undercover faces to infiltrate the drug world. Dangerous work, but it would be a feather in Leith's cap. It would shoot him up through the ranks, if all went well. Or get him killed, if all didn't.

But going undercover required a look. And a vibe. *Lose the crewcut*, he'd been told. *Or grow it out. And work on a goatee or something.*

The plan was under wraps for now, just a few emails back and forth, a decision still in the works, and he wasn't ready to tell Dion yet. The younger man shrugged and moved away, lifting a hand in farewell to Leith before climbing into his car and firing it up. *Why should I care what you do with your face?* the shrug said. *We're not that close.* It was a point well taken.

FIVE

BAD DREAMS

DION DREADED SLEEP but couldn't avoid it. His body needed recharging. With sleep would come the sickening dread, coupled with helplessness. The dread would build to a climax before he'd wake, hopefully alive. Waking alive didn't seem likely at times.

He'd dubbed them "the basement dreams," since they'd started the night he had moved into Joe Kent's. They were a whole new breed of nightmare for him. They didn't transport him to strange places, but took his reality and used it against him. He was lying on a crappy sofa bed in an unfinished basement, dreaming he was awake but helpless, suffocating with terror. He would lie awake, so it seemed, staring into darkness, knowing that something was coming and that he couldn't escape it.

Night after night the something would take shape on the ceiling, over there by the hall light. Barely visible. A man-sized cocoon that crept so slowly into view its movements couldn't be tracked. Scary enough when he could see it, scarier still when it would sometimes decide to disappear.

He had a rough understanding of what the thing was. Vengeance. An accumulation of everything that had gone wrong in his life, come for payback. There were bits of Looch Ferraro in that cocoon, along with the bones of the man he and Looch had assaulted that terrible night, along with the screams he could well imagine of Looch's widow, Brooke, when she heard the news. All that badness had become one slimy, bony entity that would crawl into his orifices and kill him from the inside out. He knew it.

From the nearby closet came three thumps, loud, *boom boom-boom,* but he couldn't move. The cocoon slid farther into view, and whatever was in the closet was hitting against the door full force, and a pressure on his chest was beginning to snap his ribs, and just as he lost his breath, he woke.

His eyes were open, and he could feel the air rushing into his lungs. But was he awake, or had he just slipped into another phase of the nightmare? He found he could blink. Move. Clench his fists. He sat upright on the spongy sofa bed, clutching blankets to his chest. His temples were damp, his armpits slick, his nerves vibrating. The bedside clock said 4:35. There was no dripping, shifting corpse up there in the shadows of the ceiling; he confirmed it with an angry glance. He was safe. He was fine.

Upstairs a TV grumbled and chuckled, muted through carpeting. Joe Kent worked at the Hyatt lounge. He got home at 2:30 and didn't hit the sack for an hour or so.

One good thing about Joe was his audible presence in the small hours of the night.

Dion dropped back onto his pillow and tried to count his blessings. What was going to kill him wasn't a monster. It wasn't a dream. It was just stress. The stress of living in a dank, unfinished basement suite while he waited to get back into the Harbourview, and soon as he was there he'd be all good again. It was the familiarity, a critical link with the past. He had lived there before the crash, up on the tenth floor with its gorgeous northwest view, and those were the best days of his life. Being there would dial back the pain and put him in that frame of mind once more. Stabilize him.

Happily, he was at the top of the high-rise's waiting list, and he'd been told a vacancy was pending — and this time they promised to get it right. Apartment-hopping was expensive, so it would be best to stick it out till that day came. Stick it out here at Joe's.

The thought made him want to howl.

The TV upstairs laughed out loud, and the counting of blessings wasn't going anywhere, so he counted stressors instead. Breaking up with Kate last month was a shock, but kind of inevitable. Their relationship had always felt like the perfect fit, but in retrospect, it had been artificial all along. He just hadn't seen it for what it was.

David Leith's scruffy beard was of more immediate concern. Maybe it was just evidence of a midlife crisis, but more likely the man was being courted by E division, the undercover unit that fought crime from the inside.

Which should have been good news, because Leith likely had Dion under surveillance, which meant he was a threat, which meant the more miles between them, the better.

Even so, he didn't want Leith to go.

Same with JD. He didn't want her to leave, either, but she was doing just that. Not physically, but emotionally, giving him the cold shoulder. He wanted to ask her why but didn't have the nerve. Probably he wouldn't like the answer. And the longer he put off asking, the colder she became, till these days they only talked job.

Joe Kent's TV switched off. Footfalls creaked on floorboards, then silence.

This would be the worst part of the night, when Dion rolled back through the deaths he had caused. Starting with Stouffer, the man he and Looch had the bad luck of meeting up with that night. Killing Stouffer had started it all. Pummelling that man's face had sprayed blood onto Dion's, and the blood had never washed off. So to speak.

More bad luck was the witness, a pink-haired girl on a dirt bike. Dion had looked up and seen her there, straddling her bike on the shrubby dunes. With all that Surrey farmland solitude, all those long silent roads, at an hour when most of the world was sound asleep, he had expected the defunct gravel pit would be a safe place to bury the body. Temporarily, till he and Looch could regroup and make the evidence disappear for good. Their chance had never come, and Looch was dead, thanks to the pink-haired girl and what she'd witnessed.

Chasing after her at speed with no real plan in mind, Dion's car had collided with a speeding joyrider, killing that driver, and Looch, and putting himself in a coma. The girl on the dirt bike got away with her knowledge and would haunt him now for the rest of his life. Looch's widow, Brooke Zaccardi, was another ricochet casualty. Dion suspected Looch had made a panicked call to Brooke that night, while Dion alone worked at burying the body. Maybe she knew what he and Looch had done, and blamed him for Looch's death, and maybe she was going to spill, and maybe Constable Ken Poole, Dion's self-appointed guardian angel, had killed Brooke to silence her before offing himself.

So many loose ends. And so many mysteries. Like why hadn't Stouffer's corpse surfaced, after all this time, complete with Dion's DNA smashed into his face? Why hadn't the pink-haired girl reported what she'd seen from the dunes that night? What had really happened to Brooke Zaccardi, found dead of an overdose in the Fraser River last month?

He wondered if JD suspected him, if that's why she was giving him the cold shoulder. He wondered how long it would take before all the suspicions of his teammates and superiors congealed into charges and he would be sat down and grilled. And what he would say when that happened. "What am I going to do, Looch?" he asked the darkness. Of course no answer came.

SIX

WHIRLY-GIRL

March 16

BY 8:00 A.M. DION was down in the park behind the
shopping village where the magic festival was setting up.
The cool air was heavy with the scent of fresh-cut grass.
A crew of seven youths was happily at work on the little
amphitheatre, or bandstand, hammering nails and slath-
ering paint. He spoke to them briefly, told them he was
with the RCMP, General Investigations, and asked if they
knew Larry Follick. They didn't. They directed him to the
double-wide trailer where the event office was set up.

Inside the trailer was one woman, who rose from
her desk and introduced herself as the festival director.
She wasn't happy to talk to a cop — it seemed to Dion
that persons in the arts never were — but she answered
his few questions concisely. She gave him some promo
material. The three-day show was Arts Council funded,
mostly, and was scheduled to open next week, March 25,

to capture kids still on spring break. A volunteer force of eighteen was involved in this leg of the project, including herself. Seventeen, now that Larry Follick, their publicity man, was apparently no more. She did not appear heartbroken over news of Follick's death, and only guardedly curious. "What happened to him?"

"We're not sure at this point," Dion said. "So was he a good publicity man, as far as you're aware?"

"He did those flyers," she said, not quite answering the question. "Prepared the copy for the newspapers. Went on the radio a couple of times, pitching the show. Roughed out a poster and designed the banners."

"How was it he got involved?"

"Volunteered, like everyone else. We'd put a notice in the paper, saying anyone who wants to help out, call this number. He called."

"Passion for theatre?"

"And/or a networking exercise," she said. "He's trying to start up a business. Arts and crafts cottage industry, he said. But he's new on the North Shore and was just finding his niche, I think."

"Did he seem to have any close friends in the crew, or anyone he rubbed the wrong way?"

"Not that I knew of. Friendships and frictions will form, but it's early days yet."

"Otherwise, how were things running? Any tensions between the crew, even slight, that you could detect?"

She didn't think so.

"What was Larry like to work with?"

"Good," she said. "Assertive. He had a sense of humour, of sorts."

"I think that's all. Thanks."

"No problem." She was clearly relieved that it was over. Dion suspected she had emphasized the positive and de-emphasized the not-so-positive, when it came to Larry Follick, but he was satisfied she was simply not wishing to speak ill of the dead. She walked him to the door and said, "Pray for no rain, okay?"

Outside, most of the youths working on the bandstand had departed, but a portable stereo remained, playing the kind of punchy old-style instrumentals that Dion expected to blare from loudspeakers at a lively magic show in full swing. Only two volunteers remained on the stage, a man and a woman who might have been twenty-something. They were no longer working, but fooling around. Or dancing, he guessed, some kind of ad lib ballet set to the music. The sound was bad, buzzing on the high notes, and the dance moves weren't great, either. But sincere. Intense, carefree.

Dion stopped at a distance to take in what he supposed was a rehearsal. The dancers seemed oblivious to his presence. They wore loose blue jeans, and though the morning air was chilly, only short-sleeved T-shirts. The man's T-shirt was purple, the woman's yellow. Purple strutted around Yellow, and she turned with him as if fixed to an invisible spindle, her one-footed hop a parody of a pirouette, their eyes fixed on each other as his arms snaked toward her face. The storyline was obvious: a Svengali and his prey, and this was the seduction.

It's not a rehearsal, Dion realized, riveted by the woman's moves, free-form and uninhibited. *They're just playing.* Feeling like a voyeur, he took a step backward to leave, only halting when the woman swooned backward into her partner's supporting arm.

It was a credible swoon, dead weight, crashing both dancers to the floor, and Dion started forward in alarm when the spell caster shouted something in a foreign tongue, snaked his fingers again over the collapsed girl's face, and both actors sprang back to their feet. Purple spun Yellow, and away she went, whirling to the far wall, then reversed yo-yo style. But she reversed to emptiness, as her Svengali was packing to go, taking his stereo with him.

The boy jumped off the stage and walked away, and the music faded into the distance. Dion expected the girl to follow, but she carried on in silence, covering the wooden stage in leaps and bounds, arms up, down, inexpert and graceless.

He crossed his arms. Why wasn't she leaving with her partner? Who was she performing for? Not him, as she still didn't seem to know he was there. She was on a roll, beautiful and smiling, tripping about to the music in her head, jumping and thudding, striking a dramatic pose, and finally tottering in place.

She steadied herself, breathing hard, and looked across the distance at him without surprise. So maybe he was wrong, and she'd known he was there all along. And now that she was motionless and not smiling, her glow was gone. No longer magical but as ordinary as himself.

"Hi," she called out. "Was that great, or what? I think I've missed my calling!"

"I think you're a natural," he called back. He turned to head toward the path that would take him to his car, but she wasn't done being friendly.

"Don't you want an autograph? What's your name?"

So she wanted to chat, and he knew why. She must have been part of the work crew that he had spoken to earlier, though he didn't recall her face. But she'd been there, heard him asking questions, knew he was a cop, and now wanted the dirt on whatever case he was working on.

He approached the stage, its footlights about chest level, and had to tilt his head to make eye contact. "Cal Dion. What's yours?"

It took her a moment to answer as she scribbled an imaginary autograph and flung it at him. "Bianca." She grinned.

She had a gorgeous smile. She was a kind of modern-day flower child, he supposed. Twenty-five years old, maybe. She had short auburn hair with a messy curl to it, and squinty wide-set eyes, and a loose, shapeless mouth. None of it added up to pretty, in the magazine sense. But he couldn't take his eyes off her. "So you're part of the work crew?" he asked. "Or a magician? Or both?"

"I know some good tricks," she said.

"Making rabbits disappear?"

"Rabbits?" She studied him intensely before turning to look at the heavily clouded sky, storm clouds piling up. "No, I wouldn't make a rabbit disappear. I could vanish myself, though."

He interpreted the comment as a poorly veiled hint that it was time for him to buzz off, and since she would likely have nothing of value to add to the file, he saluted a farewell and prepared to do just that. Buzz off. "Good luck with the show."

"Hey."

There it was again. She was hooking him back, and he was glad to be hooked. Maybe neither of them wanted this moment to pass. He looked up at her through hazy sunlight and smiled.

"You've gotta see this," she said. "C'mere." She was squatting at the edge of the stage, rummaging in a floppy canvas shoulder bag. "I can do card tricks, too. Want to see?"

He didn't, much, but obliged. She had found a deck of playing cards and she went about sorting them, sitting up there on the stage with legs dangling. The trick she eventually pulled off was amateurish at best, and she smirked at all the wrong moments, and the grown-up childishness of her deceit was oddly intriguing. He picked a card, put it back, expressed amazement when she correctly selected the ace of diamonds, and decided to put one question to her, if only to formalize this waste of time. He had already asked her workmates as a whole, but maybe she'd missed it. Did she know Lawrence Follick, or Larry?

She was putting away the cards, considering his words. "No, sorry, I don't. Why? Was he killed?"

That she'd guessed right wasn't a shock, since Dion had introduced himself to the stage crew as a cop with the General Investigations Section, and GIS dealt with the more serious crimes on the North Shore, the assaults and murders. At least until IHIT got involved. Maybe she knew all that and had drawn her conclusions. Maybe she wasn't as innocent as she seemed. He nodded. "Yes, he was killed."

"That's sad. Did he suffer?"

"No," Dion lied. "It was fast." He pondered the directness of her question. Just natural human empathy, he supposed. It was a question he came back to every time he thought of Looch. Had he died on impact? Or had he suffered? "Larry Follick was doing some PR work for the festival," he said. "Signs, advertisements, radio spots. Middle-aged guy, about five foot eight, fairly heavy-set. Doesn't ring a bell?"

When she shook her head, he said, "Okay, good, thanks. Anyway, guess I'd better ..."

"I'll walk you to your car," she said. She slung her bag of tricks over a shoulder. "I've been walking for hours. Time to go home."

He was surprised enough to check his watch. Not even nine in the morning, she'd been walking for hours and was already packing it in? The girl followed a strange schedule. "You're done for the day?"

"I'm what?"

"Finished your painting?"

"Oh, I'm not painting. I was just passing by."

He held out his hand to help her jump down off the stage, and she came to earth, landing with a happy *oomph*. When she straightened he found she wasn't as tall as he'd thought, and it was a relief to look down at her instead of up.

They walked to his car, the glossy black Crown Victoria he had left at the end of a park service road. He stood by the driver's door, hoping she would be impressed by his wheels, but she carried on down the path with barely a backward glance.

Walking for hours, he thought. He called out, "So where's home? Close by?"

"No, it's quite far," she replied. She had paused and turned back to point. "Ridgeway Avenue."

Ridgeway was near the detachment, and had to be ten or more kilometres by road. Possibly she knew shortcuts through the woods, but if she didn't, the alternatives were hazardous. Those would be some busy roads she'd be negotiating. Meaning there'd be nothing strange about what he was about to offer. "Need a lift?"

He waited for her *no thanks*, as she would surely be smart enough to take herself quickly away from this overly friendly stranger to a safely crowded place. But she had no sense at all, as it turned out. She swung her bag higher on her shoulder and walked back to him. She had a nice way of walking, with a confident bounce. She was flushed and smiling as he opened the door for her. "Awesome. Thank you so much!"

She climbed into the passenger seat, and as he swung the door shut a phrase came to mind: *Now you're mine.*

Why had he thought that? Chilled, he climbed behind the wheel and fired the engine. A documentary on serial killers, that's where he'd heard it. A psychopath describing the tacit contract he signed with hitchhikers leading up to the kill.

He chased the thought away. "So what are you doing way out here?"

"I walk a lot, wherever. Wow, look at this." Now she *was* impressed, admiring the imposing complexity of the dash. He watched her profile and wondered if she had dropped to earth out of the blue, landing on that stage to be picked up by the first passerby. "I've never been in a police car before," she said, catching his eye, smiling at him. "Where's the siren button?"

"No siren. Just a light that goes on top in an emergency."

He drove slowly toward the bushy turnaround to exit the park. Winter-dry weeds scratched at the vehicle's underbelly. The field was empty around them, but for some crows at play above, plunging and rising with the currents. Bianca seemed unconcerned by the remoteness of where they were, the peril she was possibly in. Her flagrant innocence both excited and nettled him. He wanted to say to her, *Hasn't your mother ever told you not to talk to strangers?* "I'm a terrible driver," she said. "First time I got into a car I wrecked it. So now the fastest thing I'm allowed to drive is a bicycle. No more Ferraris for me!"

She smiled dreamily. Dion knew she couldn't be serious about driving a Ferrari, let alone wrecking one. It seemed her jokes were as lame as her card tricks. He was at the intersection street now, turn signal ticking. He eased onto the road that would take him to the thoroughfare, looking ahead, with her profile burned on his retinas.

"Beautiful," she said, without explanation, and only to herself.

She's simple, he decided.

Had to be.

SEVEN

WINDFLOWER

THE LITTLE BOY CAME pounding up to Beau, who was sitting at the table having his coffee. Just pounded up fast like he was being chased by demons and stared upward, big grey eyes and straight whitish hair, saying something over and over, barely a word making sense in that gibberish talk of his.

Beau looked down at the thin little face and tried to understand. "Whazzat?"

"I'm Cooyus Joje, Gampa," Justin said. "Cooyus Joje. HAT!"

Hat came in a shriek that made Beau shudder. The boy climbed onto a kitchen chair across from him and jumped up and down with arms flapping, then jumped down just as sudden and was off lickety-split down the hall. A door banged. Silence. Beau went back to his coffee.

He frowned. *Hat.* The kid had said it with arms spread out over his head, like he was showing how big the brim was. An image came to Beau now, taking him back through the years to some drawings in a book. A smiling man. Big yellow hat. And not just the hat was yellow but the whole pansy outfit. *Curious George*, a kids' picture book, one in fact he'd read to Sharla when she was small, in the days when he'd done his best.

Curious George was maybe one of those shiny flat books Sharla had dumped along with her grandson and duffel bag. Some things got passed down through the family in a nice way, funny stories about monkeys getting in trouble. But most got passed down in a bad way, the bruises and bad temper. Beau wondered if Sharla had ever swung a fist at Justin or called him names or locked him in his room for hours and let him cry himself dry.

From the living room the tank burbled, and inside the tank, Lucky the goldfish swam. *Justin's pet*, Sharla had said. *I couldn't leave it in the apartment, could I?* On the day of her unexpected arrival she'd plugged in the aquarium, still sloshing, and told him how to clean it — like that was ever going to happen — and how to feed the fish, and that was that.

How long you planning to go? Beau had asked her, in a bewildered rage. But she hadn't answered. A short visit, a snappy explanation, and her car had belted off. Justin had cried and run after her, and Beau had been obliged to go after him, ordering him back in the house. The boy refused. He'd sat himself down in the middle of the road, right where the next car that came along would flatten him to a pancake, and Beau had no choice but to grab him and pull him kicking and screaming back inside. How could the woman leave a kid crying *Gramma* like that? Just leave him in the middle of the road, crying?

Something in Beau's gut twisted, and it wasn't the arthritis.

Hell, where had she gone, and why had she left the boy with him, the worst possible babysitter in the world? Beau's idea about making Evvy jealous by winning over Justin had died on the vine, following the incident down Paradise Road, an incident Beau was doing his best to forget. For starters, he didn't like kids. Especially this one. Justin had got over his first tantrum fast enough but complained a lot since. And when he got playful he yelled and whooped and jumped. Beau glared at the boy to let him know that if he did one yell or whoop too many, he'd pay with a purple eye. Or worse. As Sharla would know full well. He recalled the fuss of cops arriving and everyone yelling, Sharla's arm in a cast, the jail cell. What he couldn't remember was why the girl had made him flip his lid in the first place. Come to think of it, he couldn't remember much of those days.

If he ever bothered to cast his mind back, all he saw was the ripple of heat waves along the beach sands and Evvy in a swimsuit. Evvy next to him in the pub. Or in the bedroom, showing off a new negligee.

The pain in his wrists throbbed, the right worse than the left. With an effort he picked up the mug in front of him and took a sip. But already the coffee had gone cold.

There came a loud hard triple thump on the back door, *boom-boom-boom,* just feet away from the table where he sat. Last year he had taped that bit of paper next to the front doorbell that read *All Visiters To Back*, because it was a hell of a journey for him getting across the dining room and down three steps and out onto the little front sun porch to answer the bell. The back door was worlds easier, being right here in the kitchen where he spent much of his day.

Another *boom-boom*. Sharla, back to collect her belongings, four-year-old brat, goldfish and all. Beau heaved himself up from his chair and shuffled across to the door. The pain was on high today, the ibuprofen no better than sugar pills. He opened the door, and it wasn't his bleach-blond ox of a daughter, but instead a young male police officer in the full uniform, dark-skinned, cap pulled low so you could hardly see his eyes.

"Hello, sir, sorry to bother ya," the policeman said, from one step down. "Constable Sattar, North Shore RCMP. We're re-canvassing the neighbourhood as there was a serious assault yesterday morning down the road here. It's a bit of a ways, but just in case you heard anything or saw anything unusual, sir, strange vehicles I'm thinking, pedestrians, anything struck you out of the ordinary. This would be very early, between four a.m. and six a.m.?"

He seemed to be done, and angled his head so Beau could see his eyes, and waited, a notebook and pen in hand.

"No," Beau said.

The policeman started writing, a short novel by the looks of it. "Thank you, sir. The detectives came by already, but you weren't home and you musta not seen the card they left, so we're just doing a second run through the neighbourhood. Again, sorry to bother you. Could I have your name, sir, please?"

"Beauregard Garrett."

"Would that be G-a-r-r-o-d?"

"Yeah."

The officer wrote it out, but he wasn't done yet. "The house across the way, nobody's home. We tried a couple times already. Any idea where the resident's at?"

"Vegas, likely."

"Ah, out of town, okay."

He tried to see past Beau, but all he would get a glimpse of was shadows. "Anybody else in the household here, Mr. Garrod?"

"No."

Just me and Curious George.

The officer put away his notebook and touched his cap brim. "Okay, sir, thank you for your time."

So saying, he turned and trotted down the steps in a loose-limbed way Beau envied, swung around the side of the house and disappeared.

* * *

Parked in the detachment's underground parkade after his trip to the magic show venue, engine shut off, something caught Dion's eye. It glittered on the floor mat, passenger side. The possibilities flashed through his mind, barely registering except as a flicker of anxiety. Was it an insect? A listening device? An explosive?

He looked closer and saw it was nothing but a sparkly bit of metal. He leaned over and picked it up. A silver necklace, about the circumference of a young woman's throat, with a pendant attached. It was junk jewellery, a dime-sized flower with white petals, nickel and enamel, each petal tipped by a green rhinestone. The rhinestones represented dewdrops, he supposed. The chain's clasp had twisted open.

Luckily, he knew who it belonged to. He had parked alongside a row of older A-frame homes on Ridgeway Avenue that morning, where Bianca had directed him, and when she'd stepped out of his car, fussing with her bag, hoisting it over her shoulder, she must have somehow snagged the chain, and the necklace had slithered to the floor mat.

Or had she done it deliberately? Like a coyly dropped handkerchief.

If so, should he follow up?

Definitely not. The last thing he wanted was a relationship, especially with a carefree hippie trickster from Mars. Yet he longed for human touch. He'd gone hungry — pretty much — since he'd left Kate. Or since she'd left him. Maybe Bianca wanted nothing but that, too, a one-off night with a stranger, a cure for the pangs.

She didn't give off the usual signals, but she wasn't the most usual person. Would it hurt to find out? And even if she wasn't interested, maybe she could be persuaded.

Persuasion. In his world, it was an ugly word. From the driver's seat under the sickly fluorescent parkade lighting, he studied the flower in his palm. Its dewdrops pulled in drab rays and spat back sparks of colour. He looked in the rear-view mirror, into his own dark eyes, and didn't like what he saw.

EIGHT

FLUTTER

"YOU LIKE TO READ, huh?" Beau said.

Justin was quiet now, sitting in a dim corner of the dining room next to the bookshelf, flipping through some ancient *National Geographic* magazines and muttering to himself. He looked up with one of his dopey *Huh*s.

"Huh?" Beau mimicked.

"Huh?" Justin mimicked back.

"You like to read?" Beau said, louder. "You a good reader?"

"I can read all the books," the boy said. Or some such words, butchered and mashed and only understandable in bits.

"Too bad you can't speak so good."

"All of them," the boy went on. "All of them. I got two hundred and fifty." He asked Beau something then that might as well be Greek.

Beau worked his jaw as he turned the gibberish to English. The boy waited. "More books for children?"

Beau said. "That what you want? Hell no, I don't have any books for children. Think I'm a library or something?"

The boy went back to his *National Geographic*, one from a stack Beau still had from way back when. Somewhere in those faded pages were photographs of naked primitives, he knew, so he said, "You don't want to look at those. Put 'em away."

The boy ignored him, and Beau leaned over — a hell of a job for a man with rheumatoid arthritis — and tried to pull the magazine from Justin's grubby little hand. The hand held tight, but Beau wrangled it free and threw it in the trash can. "Not good for little boys. Bad."

They locked eyes in contest, not their first.

As always, Beau lost. He looked instead at the kitchen range and said, "You must be hungry. Let's see, what do I got? You want a ham sandwich, or some tinned stew, or —"

"Jello?" the boy said.

"No jello."

"Boo!"

"I don't got *any*, blue or otherwise!"

They were at war. The boy flopped back, right where he was sitting on the dining room floor, a floor that was none too clean, and stared at the ceiling. He looked tiny and pale, in Beau's eyes. He looked dead.

"Books, blue jello, what the hell next." Beau swatted the air. He was back at the kitchen table, easing down into his chair. Where was the boy's whore of a grandmother? Why didn't she come and take this creature off his hands? He wished the boy gone, and next time he looked around, his wish had come true.

"Justin," Beau called. It was the loudest he'd raised his voice in a long while, and the noise startled him. He saw movement out of the corner of his eye and turned, cranking himself carefully the other direction. Sure enough, the boy was back, in the living room now, bouncing about as he sometimes did, little jumping-bean bastard. It was play of some kind. Which meant he was happy, and nothing wrong with that, really. It meant there were no hard feelings, even after all that quarrelling over magazines and jello.

Strange as all hell, to Beau. Grudges were for keeps, in his world. Friendship always ended in bad blood. He settled and frowned and watched the boy at play.

In fact, it was kind of satisfying, seeing the little jumping bean hopping here and there. His great grandkid kicked and jumped and flopped on the rug, where he'd strewn sofa cushions so he could sail into the air and crash into them. Picked himself up, talking away about a make-belief world, flopped again with a death shriek, his whitish hair flashing like shiny fabric — and this time even the shriek didn't bother Beau.

Finally pooped, the boy lay on his back on the dirty old carpet, raised both legs in the air and sang a song. Rested his feet and raised his skinny arms rigid as posts, rotated his hands, studied his fingers. The clock ticked away the minutes.

Grandkid, Beau thought, skipping the "great." *My grandkid.* Good looking, too. And smart, a reader of books. Carefully, so as not to aggravate his rusty jaw, Beau smiled.

* * *

The house on Ridgeway Avenue was in need of repair. The front porch was smothered in lilac bushes that needed pruning, and the latticework sagged. A calico cat crouched on the balustrade and stared at Dion with cool interest as he climbed the steps. The main floor windows glowed faintly with light from within, and he thought he heard the yap of a small dog. Otherwise all was dark and quiet. For all he knew, Bianca lived with her parents. Or worse, a boyfriend.

There was a lot of junk on the porch. The clapboard paint was old and flaky. Three mailboxes were affixed to the wall between two front doors. The boxes were labelled A, B, and C, and three doorbells were labelled only with surnames: Riddle, Gillespie, and Stone.

The house was a triplex, then, and he had no idea which surname belonged to Bianca. Had she told him? Already losing nerve, he gambled on the Riddle doorbell, as it was the best fit for the dancer, in his opinion.

No answer. A handwritten sign on one of the doors read, *Doorbell Out of Order. Please Knock Loudly.* He didn't know which name corresponded to the sign. He took a gamble and pressed Gillespie, and after a moment heard thuds on the stairs, and a man of his own age opened the door. The man was tall and thin and looked like a methhead. He wore corduroys and a faded tank top, socks on his feet. Fine blond hair hung to his shoulders and worried blue eyes peered through the fringe of bangs.

"Yes?" the man said.

Bianca's boyfriend, no doubt about it.

"I'm looking for Bianca," Dion said, glad he still wore his working suit and tie, proof that he was an official, merely dropping by to return a lost item. "Sorry, I don't know which apartment she's in."

"She does not live in the apartment marked *Brad Gillespie*," the man said severely. "That's me. Do I look like a Bianca to you?"

"It just says *Gillespie*."

Without apology, Gillespie pointed toward heaven. "Miss *Stone* lives on third. You might as well come in."

He insisted Dion go first as they climbed the stairs, and on the second floor landing disappeared behind a door marked B in brass. Dion proceeded up to an attic landing that was flooded with sunlight from a small window, and knocked on the door marked C.

Another no answer. The dancer had told him she worked a night shift somewhere. A server or janitor, he supposed. But she had told him as well that this was her night off. Which was why he was here, hoping to catch her in.

Now he listened to the silence on the other side of the door, and had his doubts. If she worked nights, her sleep patterns were likely screwy. Maybe she was asleep, and he shouldn't bother her. Or maybe she was out. Deciding to count himself lucky that his mission had failed, he tied the broken necklace into a loose loop and hung it on the doorknob. She'd find it soon enough. The white flower dangled and spun, its rhinestones flashing rainbows behind him as he turned to leave.

He was halfway down the stairs when the door above creaked open. He stopped and looked back, catching a glimpse of her startled face before she ducked out of sight.

"Hey, Bianca," he called out.

She reappeared and stared down at him, by no means like the friendly girl he remembered. She appeared to be either angry or afraid. Or both. Did she even know who he was? She was barefoot and shabbily dressed in joggers and a tank top, her curly hair mussed like she'd just risen. He had woken her, then, and should have known better. There was nothing he could say but sorry, and leave.

"Sorry," he said, and started to point out the necklace slung on the doorknob, his only good excuse for being here, but she interrupted with a cry that startled him.

"Oh my god, you're the policeman! I'm so sorry, I didn't recognize you! What planet am I on?" She beckoned eagerly. "Don't go. Come in, please. It's so nice to see you."

"You were sleeping, weren't you?" he asked, as he joined her at the threshold. "I feel bad. I shouldn't have bothered you."

"No, I was just sitting and reading."

She closed the door behind them and locked it, but not before he had scooped the necklace back into his coat pocket. Now that he was inside her flat he realized he was an ass for showing up in suit and tie, like an urbanized Romeo hoping for a kiss. A tongue-tied awkwardness came over him that he hadn't experienced since coming out of a coma two years ago. He had survived the car crash but woke to find his passenger and best friend, Looch, had died. Truth be told, though, being tongue-tied then had more to do with keeping secrets than head trauma. He was better these days. He knew how to survive a conversation, as long as he didn't get confused. Bianca's reception of him was confusing.

She hadn't been expecting him, clearly, which meant her dropping of the necklace in his car was just that: the dropping of a necklace. Not an offer, not a lure. At the same time she was behaving as if his visit was inevitable, and how did that add up?

Didn't matter. He should now make a small ceremony of returning the item to her possession, earn himself a brief feel-good moment, and say goodbye.

But Bianca was telling him to take off his coat, not to worry about his shoes, to make himself comfortable, and would he like tea or something? Should she put the kettle on? And instead of saying no thanks, as intended, he found himself saying, "Yes, sure, thanks," and smiling at her bright and pretty face.

"What kind?" she said.

"What kind of what?"

"Tea. I have all sorts."

"Oh, any kind," he said. "Thanks."

The apartment was open concept, and Bianca was in a small nook of a kitchen, pouring water into a kettle. Dion removed his coat and draped it over a chair. He started to loosen his tie, but thought it might look presumptuous, and left it snug.

"I've actually just made a salad," Bianca said. "It's kind of fancy, with avocado and pecans and stuff. Would you like some?"

"No," he said. "No, thanks. I was just passing by."

He was surveilling the place, discreetly. Like it was a fresh crime scene, absorbing what he could in a slow sweep. A small bookshelf seemed to be more a display case for knick-knacks than a place for books. He took in the funky kitchen, living room, and dining room all merged, bedroom through that open door — he could see a generous bed — bathroom down a short hallway, and at the end of the hallway a glass-paned door leading out to a wrought-iron fire escape.

Bit of a dive, with badly plastered walls and scuffed fir floorboards, but whimsically furnished and warm with girlish decor. Orange, red, yellow. There was a plush gold sofa loaded with too many throw cushions, a junky armchair gussied up with a flowery fringed throw. A rose scent hung in the air. Expensive looking Indian rug underfoot, though stained and damaged, and some art on the walls that he thought was classy. Hanging from a hook near the window was an empty birdcage of ornate design. The tenant was clearly poor but sophisticated.

"Here's your tea," Bianca said, and he turned to her with a smile of thanks. She held out an old-style teacup and saucer. The steam was chai scented. Dion sat on one end of the sofa, Bianca sat in the junky armchair, and they sipped their beverages like grannies.

"Where's the bird?" he asked, nodding at the empty cage.

"The canary," she said. "I opened the window and it just took off."

Birds would do that, it seemed to Dion. He took another tentative sip. He was no tea aficionado, but even he knew this one was bad. Weak and flat, as if the teabag had been recycled and the water not brought to a full boil. He looked into his cup, wondering how he could avoid it without hurting her feelings. As it turned out, there was no need, as Bianca gave a shout of disgust. "Goddamn it," she said, setting her cup and saucer down on the coffee table with a clatter. She gestured passionately at the ceiling. "It's not rocket science, for fuck's sake. I can't even make a decent cup of tea. You're lucky you said no to the salad, because it's just gross. It doesn't look anything like the picture and it's way too lemony, plus I absolutely slaughtered the avocado and it looks like green guts."

Her passion would have been funny, except her eyes had welled with tears.

Dion stared at her. "Hey, look —"

"No," she told him, taking both cups to the kitchen, her angry voice trailing behind her. "Never mind. I know it's nothing. Just a stupid cup of tea, and we're all dust in the wind. Nothing matters, anyway, does it?"

He could hear her swearing under her breath. He could see her foot-pedalling open a trash can, and knew she was going to exact revenge on the failure of a salad by dumping it. He also knew from experience that many culinary flops could be remedied. He joined her in a kitchen with barely room for two and took in the mess. A recipe torn from a magazine was taped to the fridge, its photo featuring a picture-perfect tossed salad. The massacred remains of vegetables cluttered the counter, along with bottles of oil and bags of assorted herbs, nuts, and dried fruit. The sink was full of dirty dishes and the faucet was dripping. The dancer stood trembling with anger or frustration or self-loathing, standing over the open bin holding a sizeable wooden bowl of green mishmash, nuts, and berries.

Dion tried to fathom her anger. Maybe she was dirt poor. Maybe she'd spent the last of her savings on pricey ingredients. He took the bowl from her and found a clear spot on the counter to place it. "Food never comes out looking like the picture," he told her. "Trust me."

He tasted a lemon-doused romaine leaf, chewed thoughtfully for a moment and said, "Just needs olive oil and salt. We can fix it."

Bianca's trembling stopped as they worked together to salvage what to her had been a world-class disaster. By the time they sat down to eat, she was chatting merrily, and merriness made her beautiful again, just as she had been up on the bandstand, flushed and happy. She was even talking about him staying the night, which filled him with hope. Maybe his luck had turned.

The salad wasn't great, but as he told her, master chefs weren't born overnight. He didn't have the heart to break it to her that the pecans she'd sprinkled over the salad were actually peanuts. She should be told, he supposed. But not now. Maybe tomorrow.

NINE

WILDERNESS

March 17

LEITH SAT AT HIS desk in a patch of morning light and worried about the concept more than the details. A transfer would shift him into the interior of the province, at least for a while. Vernon. Not a huge commitment. One training course and one assignment, after which he could either stick it out or move on. If it worked out, he might find himself on the road a lot, following the path of danger. But also the path to promotion.

It was a super challenge, he thought. A fantastic opportunity. Could he take the stress, though?

He'd never been a big fan of stress, even when younger. He preferred things neat and predictable. He'd been talked into going on a wilderness trek, once, and hated every stinking, sweaty, bug-bitten moment of it. Preferred government campsites and flush toilets. And now that he was getting older, his tolerance was dropping. These days he didn't even like the thrill of a scary movie.

He straightened in his chair and shook off thoughts of decline. He wasn't *old*. He was a healthy forty-four. He only felt like he was on his last legs because of his dad's stroke last month. A minor stroke, but it had caused a great kerfuffle within the clan, and it was Leith's first real wake-up call. *We're all heading to the grave*, he thought, and spun a ballpoint on the desktop as he read a fresh report. The 911 caller on Paradise Road had a name now. Tracy Hildebrandt. Except it wasn't Tracy who had made the call, if she could be believed. Tracy said she'd lost the phone last week. Probably at the supermarket. Hadn't actually noticed till the police got in touch.

"How do you not notice you've lost your phone?" Leith asked JD at her nearby desk. But she was working on a promising lead, as she'd told him, was just nailing down the particulars, and the tilt of her head said she wasn't into answering pointless questions. Or even acknowledging them.

Leith went on to read Tracy's transcribed answer. It sounded reasonable enough. She was in her eighties, not of the cellphone generation, she said. She only had one as her kids insisted she move with the times and be reachable 24/7. Being reachable 24/7 didn't appeal to her, frankly, so when the phone had gone missing, she maybe subconsciously let it stay so.

Did the phone have a passcode? No. Tracy could hardly remember her own name, let alone a bunch of random numbers.

On request, Tracy's account remained active, in case whoever had it — whoever had made the 911 call, supposedly — would use it again and ping their location.

Leith gave the pen another spin, and JD turned to send him a wordless message that he couldn't fail to read: lifting a pen, giving it a little twist, shaking her head, and fixing him with a look that said *don't*.

Instead of reminding her that he now outranked her, he let the pen spin to a stop. JD bowed back into her paperwork. She was in plainclothes, like himself. Plainer than himself, in fact about as plain as a female police officer could get, in a black turtleneck under black blazer over black trousers. No makeup, no bling. Her only concession to womanhood, in Leith's opinion, was she had let her short dark hair grow longer at the front, giving her a stylish swoosh of bangs. Maybe only to better hide her scowl.

Sergeant Mike Bosko had arrived and was making his way over to say good morning, blocking the sunlight. He was younger than Leith, somewhat bigger all round, and a lot further ahead in his career. He wore a nice new suit today, not his signature boring grey, but a summer-weight tan, though the March day promised to be cold and rainy. The tie he wore looked new, too, a metallic motif of diamonds alternating with hearts.

Why was Leith so fixated on clothes today? He'd always been a boring dresser, himself. Plaid shirts and Levis off duty, powder-blue button-ups (as now) and wool-blend trousers (also as now) on duty. He was wondering how he would look in biker duds, if it came to that. "Nice suit," he heard himself say.

"Thanks." Bosko took a chair.

Leith and Bosko had a unique working relationship, linked by their informal investigation into Dion's misconduct. Whenever they talked, Leith expected Bosko to tell him the news. That the witness had rematerialized, that the case was off the shelf and back on track.

Leith hoped it would stay shelved. Ignorance was bliss, and he was starting to believe he would blissfully never know what really happened out in Surrey. He was hoping he could write the whole thing off as a great steaming pile of misunderstandings and that Bosko would let him off the unenviable hook of being asked to snitch on a friend.

"Listen," Bosko said. The word itself could presage either chitchat or red alert, and with Bosko's perpetually pleasant drawl, one never knew which it would be. Leith braced himself. Thankfully, what came next was nothing to do with the walking disaster named Cal Dion. "I've heard there's been a bit of talk going around," Bosko went on. "So I'm kind of in damage-control mode, doing the rounds, letting people know, yes, Sarah and I are getting a divorce. I just wanted to tell you before you heard the rumours. Before the truth got distorted."

"Oh no," said Leith, who had heard all about the divorce last week, distortions and all. "I'm sorry to hear that."

One of the possible distortions he'd heard was that Bosko was already seeing someone new. Hence the fashion makeover? Leith hoped the other rumour wasn't true, that the someone new was Dion's ex, Kate. Leith had spied Kate and Bosko chatting a time or two in the recent past, and they seemed to have hit it off. Wasn't there some rule about not dating your subordinate's ex?

"Happens," Bosko said. "Sarah and I, well, we haven't been terribly close for a while. It's partly geographical. She has her heart set on Toronto, and I like B.C. Think I'll stick around a while longer."

"That's good news," Leith said. And it really was. Bosko was an excellent boss who kept the show running and the stats looking good. Even if he was a philanderer on the side. Leith pointed out the email that was bothering him. "The drug wars are ramping up, Mike. Three bodies in one week. The unit wants me to make a decision. They'll filter me in starting next month, if I say the word. I think I'm going for it."

Bosko nodded. "How does Alison feel about it?"

"She hates the idea. Of course. She's afraid. Maybe more afraid than I am. Did I mention I'm terrified?"

Bosko smiled his understanding. "Lots to consider." He told Leith that they would discuss the move further before any final decisions were made, gave him a reassuring pat on the shoulder, and left.

Soon after Bosko disappeared, Dion arrived, looking better rested than he had in weeks. "I was thinking," he said, settling in over at his desk, switching on his computer. "The prints on the pig were too smudged for lifting, but the only prints on the other lawn ornaments are clear, and all belong to Follick. So the killer comes through the gate, passes five cartoon characters and goes for the pig. Why?"

Leith heard the know-it-all inflection, and said, "Why don't you go ahead and tell us."

JD had swivelled in her chair to listen, including herself in the conversation.

"It's because he was coming from uphill," Dion said. "The pig was the first one in his line of sight as he walked down. He saw it, latched on. He's got a primitive mind, not analytical. Reactive, maybe unstable. If you're right that the pig itself was the source of his anger, it makes sense."

"So now you're on board with my eyesore theory," Leith said, pleased that he had scored a point.

Dion nixed the win. "Not likely. But the pig reminded him of something. Or he didn't like the way it blocked the view, or there was something about the way it looked at him. And how long did Follick have those things on display? Two months. Whoever attacked him doesn't frequent the area, or the pig wouldn't be such a shock that he'd fixate on it like that. He came from uphill heading down, on foot. You can't get to the top of the hill without passing the Follicks, so he lives above and rarely goes to town. A recluse."

Leith stifled a groan. These kinds of problems reminded him of Grade 10 math class, when he was supposed to figure out how far a train travelled if it travelled at a certain speed within a certain time frame. They made his head hurt. "Or he has a morbid hate-on for Porky Pig," he suggested. "Which means direction of travel has nothing to do with it."

JD chimed in. "Cal could be right about the guy's state of mind. Come on down to the case room. I'll show you what I pulled this morning."

In the case room JD spread out a sheaf of autopsy photographs, close-ups of Lawrence Follick's mangled throat. "Look here," she said, as Leith and Dion studied one of several eight-by-tens that had been added to the file after their sign-off last night. "The spike wasn't the first assault. You can see the bruising here. It kind of hides in the trauma, but it's distinct. You can just make it out on this edge. The guy was hit in the windpipe with an object in just about the same area as the rebar, with some force. Enough to leave a mark, not enough to penetrate."

"One and a half inches in diameter," Dion said, examining the pathologist's ruler placed against the half-moon bruise in the photograph. Leith could see that the bruise was cratered to one side by the spike's entry wound. Sure enough, there had been two separate impacts.

"What do we have in the inch-and-a-half diameter range?" JD asked. "Butt end of a gardening tool, say a rake. A flashlight or a screwdriver. Cane or walking stick. Whatever it was, it was on the heavy side."

"Whatever it was, it was taken away after the assault," Dion added.

"Maybe by this guy," JD said, and with a showman's flourish she dropped another photograph for them to check out. An informal shot of a burly man leaning an elbow on a long walking stick while staring warily at the camera.

The man in the photo was about Leith's age, mid-forties. He was possibly about Leith's height and build, as well, though with better muscles and an enviable suntan. He had long sandy-brown hair that coiled down to his shoulders, along with a beard generous enough to house small birds. The man's clothes were about the same hue, shade, and texture as his weathered skin. Cargo pants

cut off mid-calf, tattered T-shirt, unbuttoned safari jacket, heavy socks, and scruffy hiking boots.

Some kind of naturalist, Leith was thinking. "I give
up, JD. Who is he?"

"He's the man with no name who's been seen walking
the foothill roads and trails in the early hours," JD said.
"Near the crime scene. Jim Torr was canvassing houses
along Paradise Road late yesterday and lucked into a
photo journalist named Wing. Mr. Wing lives on the
lower stretch of the road and often walks up to get to
the forest trails. He told Jim he'd first seen The Beard
walking out from the trees at the top of the road. That
was late last spring. He hoped to run into the guy again,
as he thought he'd like to take his picture."

"Why?" Leith said.

"Well, look at him," JD said, tapping the portrait. "If
you were a photo journalist, wouldn't you want to take
his picture?"

Leith put himself in the shoes of a photo journalist
and agreed, yes, he probably would.

"Right. So a couple weeks ago Wing saw him again,
and this time he stopped to talk to him. Not far from the
Follick residence, in fact. After chatting a while, he asked
if he could photograph the guy. This is the photograph."

Leith wasn't thrilled by the photo of the U.M., the
unknown male. "You can't arrest a guy because he car-
ries a walking stick. Got anything more exciting?"

"Yes." JD looked pleased with herself. "We're going to
have to bring Wing in for a full statement, since Jim didn't
get it recorded. Because according to Wing, The Beard
has plenty to say about all kinds of things, environment

wise. A rebel. Too many cars burning too much fuel. Even hinted he'd torched an entire suburb under construction, once, and would do it again if anybody tried putting up another goddamn condo on his land, and by his land he seemed to be referring to the road he was standing on when he was talking to Wing, along with the forest at his back from here to kingdom come."

"His land," Leith echoed, starting to feel the thrill. The Beard sounded like a promisingly entitled bully. And averse to visual pollution, which some might say the whirligig pig was nothing but.

Dion didn't look sold. "Combustion engines and condos," he said. "That's kind of far up the scale from an annoying wind toy."

"It could start an argument," Leith countered. "This is a volatile individual, Cal. And a powerhouse, by the looks of it. Just the kind of guy we're looking for."

JD nodded. "Good luck finding him, though, because our volatile powerhouse also told Wing where he lives."

The sentence made no sense, in Leith's mind, until JD went on to explain. She stood by the Google Earth photo of the crime scene pinned to the cork board, and stuck a pin, seemingly at random, on the green mass of wilderness above Paradise Road. "That's where."

TEN

FLOWN

JD DIDN'T THINK her army of searchers would locate The Beard's den, not today, maybe ever. But by midafternoon she'd heard the news. Two young constables
had been tasked with walking the Old Buck Trail, where
they had spoken to passing hikers. A couple out with
their young sons had pointed the way to a shack the
sons had discovered last fall while exploring off trail.
The constables had employed the kids to help them pinpoint the shack. It had taken several hours, but in the
end the mission had been accomplished, and a report
was handed in to JD late in the afternoon, complete
with GPS coordinates and a snapshot. The snapshot had
been taken from a distance, as the search team had been
warned not to approach the suspect or his accommodations on their own.

A search warrant was obtained, and by late afternoon
the Emergency Response Team had been mustered and
sent on a long hike, bulky in their Kevlar, speaking in
code, hidden behind goggles and doing all the fancy

moves. JD had hiked in, too, and at a safe distance waited with Leith, Dion, Corporal Doug Paley, and Constable Jim Torr, watching the six-member ERT take on the little patchwork cabin like it was a suspicious package in an airport. Unlike bigger operations, this one-roomer was cleared in the time it took to say *come out with your hands up*. Nobody came out, and a few seconds later the team declared the place safe for Leith and the others to enter.

Walking closer, JD admired the building, about ten by twelve, sturdily built, its exterior nicely camouflaged with cut saplings and blowdown. It had a little chimney pipe, and windows made of salvaged fibreglass, walls of plywood, a three-quarter-sized door. Leith went in first, followed by JD, Dion last, while Paley and Torr stayed outside to explore the perimeter.

Three cops in one small, low-ceilinged room made a crowd. There was a bed, folding chair, bookshelf, a jerry-rigged port-a-potty that was thankfully empty, desk, and typewriter. Under the chimney pipe was a counter with a Coleman stove and a set of clean dishes.

The light filtered through rough plexiglass was dim and mottled. The air was icy and fresh. There was no apparent source of heat.

JD thought the place was messy but not too bad. Kind of cozy, actually. She studied the bookshelf while Leith looked through the desk and Dion stood in the corner that could be called a kitchen and examined its contents. The book titles JD read spoke of serious topics. Heavy old volumes on art, philosophy, the environment. A guide to western birds. A weathered old *Concise Oxford English Dictionary*.

"It's pretty tidy," Dion said. "Some tins here but no perishables. Garbage is empty."

JD joined Leith as he donned rubber gloves and went through the bedding. She watched him cautiously turn back blankets, sheets. A human odour drifted up, not as bad as some places JD had explored, but not pleasant, either.

"Want to help me here?" Leith suggested.

"I'm the exhibit officer," JD said, flashing her clipboard. "Exhibit officers don't search."

"In this case, they sure can pitch in."

But JD was called over by Dion. Done with his kitchen forage, he was leaning over to look at the typewriter up close. "I guess he's an author."

JD saw the typewriter was a manual Smith Corona, keys heavily worn. The thing had probably been battered on for decades, producing millions of words. "The next Hemingway, I bet."

Dion experimentally pressed a key and watched the little arm leap.

"Imagine not having a delete button," he said.

"Or a spell checker," JD said. "You'd be doomed."

She heard the stiffness in her voice, even through the banter. He heard it, too. He straightened and looked at her, but she refused to catch his eye. She gazed at the typewriter instead, as if fascinated by its contours. It was the clumsiest kind of avoidance manoeuvre, and she felt herself blushing. She wasn't proud of her conflicted attitude toward him. Cutting him off. Blocking him. She knew he was in some kind of trouble that he was clearly unwilling to share with her. Deep trouble. And instead of throwing him a lifeline, as she should be, she was looking out for number one, keeping her distance so as not to get pulled into his personal vortex. And if he didn't like her attitude, she didn't like his, either. So screw him.

Leith interrupted just as JD's scrutiny of the typewriter was getting a little ridiculous, and she had a feeling Dion was about to tell her so. Leith had found a stack of clean typing paper on a shelf, he pointed out, but no typed documents. Not a single bit of evidence that gave away the identity of the shack dweller. JD heard Torr and Paley outside, talking, and she moved to the doorway to eavesdrop. Sounded like two jaded cops had just been cheered up by an interesting find, and she was torn between going to check it out and staying put and listening to Dion and Leith, who had launched into an argument of sorts. Which could be fun.

"It's just that this guy doesn't look rabid," Dion was saying.

"What does rabid look like?" Leith replied. "Long sharp teeth? Drool? Just because a guy reads books and knows how to type, doesn't mean he can't flip out and kill."

"Over a pig."

"It was just a theory. Something I threw out there, and which, by the way, you agreed with. Somewhat."

"I'm not ready to apply that theory to this man. That's all."

"Okay, well, maybe the pig wasn't the trigger. Maybe it just happened to be attached to the closest sharp object at hand. This guy and Follick got talking about the price of oil, which led to politics, which led to where our tax dollars go. Things got ugly. The pig was there, and Follick ended up on the wrong end of it."

"Except the pig wasn't the closest sharp object at hand, if the stranger had just walked in the gate. It would be the duck, I think."

"We don't know that, though, do we? We don't know where they were standing. Follick could have been giving the guy the grand tour, showing him the whole gamut of whirligigs, and only when they reached the pig did the argument break out."

"Maybe," Dion said. "But whoever lives here has purpose." He gestured out the window at the surrounding forest. "He's happy. He's not going to go out of his way looking for trouble."

Leith's mouth pulled down on one side, and JD could tell he was thinking the same as her, that trouble didn't always need to be looked for. Sometimes a bit of negative chemistry and two overinflated egos was all it took for bloody murder.

"How is burning down construction projects a sign of a happy man not looking for trouble, Cal?" Leith asked, and Dion seemed perfectly ready with a reply, because sometimes the two of them just didn't give up.

From outside came a hoot, distracting JD. She headed for the door. "Sounds like Doug's found something."

The three left the cabin, and not far from its backside their brother officers stood by a small, cold firepit. Paley held up a torn piece of whitish linen, partially burned. The linen was stained with a blackish-brown substance. "That's dried blood or I'm Martha Stewart," Paley declared as he bagged the specimen.

JD charted the find on her clipboard. A smudge of blackish-red and a book on birds, she thought. An iron-clad case this was fast not becoming. But Ident would come in now and lift prints and DNA, and maybe the woodsman with the big stick would be tracked down and convicted. If all went well, the mystery of Lawrence Follick's death would be solved and the perpetrator punished. *If* all went well.

ELEVEN

THE CALM BEFORE

March 18

THE SKY WAS BLUE and the sun shone down. A nice day. Beau had outdone himself taking Justin to town. He wasn't doing it to be nice, but because the boy complained about not having anything new to read, and if new books would shut him up, then that's what he'd get.

Going to town meant a long walk down the hill. It meant ugly memories, too, as he passed the long white fence. But no body lay bleeding, of course, and not a single damned whirligig spoiled the view. The grey-roofed house was clear of junky cartoon crap, just like none of it had ever happened. Beau wished none of it had happened, and would have gladly taken it all back and let the whirligigs whirl, but there was no point crying over what's done and gone.

He still expected to be collared for what he'd done, but for some reason, even though the police had come calling and asked his name, Beau still walked free.

Once he and Justin had made it down the hill, there was a short bus ride to the Parksdale shopping plaza, which had a few stores, a community centre, the Safeway where he got his groceries, and a library.

It was an all-day *excursion*, as he described it to the boy. A lot of hoofing around for a sick man with a cane. "Let it kill me," he had grumbled at Justin. "Just let it."

Beau had never been inside this particular library, or any other in his living memory. Wasn't much for reading, but Justin was, and Beau knew that kind of thing had to be encouraged in kids to make them grow up smart. So he sat waiting at a table with another old goat, who had his nose stuck in a newspaper, while Justin took his time choosing himself a pile of picture books.

Then came the fuss when Beau argued with the librarian about taking the books home. He didn't have a library card, and to get one he'd need ID plus "proof of residency," such as a recent postmarked envelope with his address on it. He had the ID, but not the proof. How could he possibly? Then he found an old hydro bill in his wallet he'd meant to take in and dispute. It was folded and faded and not as *recent* as required, but the librarian made some faces like Beau had farted aloud, and said the bill would suffice, in a voice that said it really shouldn't.

They left the building, Justin carrying his stack of books in his backpack. Then the kid said he was hungry. Beau had forgotten about that, the need to eat when on all-day excursions. Good thing Safeway was nearby. There they did some aisle-by-aisle shopping. Justin was everywhere, covering a mile for Beau's every step. Beau bought a kielbasa ring, and two Kaiser rolls, and some apples. He bought no-name jello, too. Four packs for two bucks, letting Justin choose the flavours.

By the time they were done with the supermarket, Beau's back and shoulders ached. So did his feet. He stood at the bus stop, and the kid munched on the crude sandwich Beau had made using his penknife. A sharp wind blew up and tried to bowl the two of them over. The bus came, and good thing it had a wheelchair lift, because Beau wasn't sure he could hoist a leg to the first step. They boarded, and the bus chugged down the road. Beau sat in the first forward-facing seat behind the driver, holding his silence until he saw they were headed in the wrong goddamn direction, and shouted, "Where we goin'?"

"Deep Cove," the bus driver said over his shoulder, still driving the wrong direction.

"I want to go up Mount Seymour Road," Beau told him.

"Then you're on the wrong bus," the driver told him.

Justin was studying the jello packets, reading the small print. Beau looked down at him. "We're going the wrong damn direction," he said. "We gotta get off, get turned around somehow." He stood, quaking with the effort, cursing time wasted and the expense of two more fares. He and Justin got off the bus at the next stop, even slower than getting on, and stood on the sidewalk. The bus took off leaving a cloud of dust in its wake. Beau clutched and massaged the left side of his chest, which was spasming. "Damn."

"Okay, Gampa?" Justin asked.

"No, I'm not okay," Beau said. "I got one foot in the goddamn grave."

Their backtracking journey brought them to a different bus stop across the road from a park. Another waiting passenger sat on a bench, and Beau asked him when the bus was due. Not for forty-five minutes, he was told. Justin said something that Beau ignored.

Beau stood and closed his eyes. When he opened them the boy was gone. Beau looked left and right. He stared across the road and down a path leading into the green depths of a woodsy park. Noisy machines were at work in the distance, digging and grading. Justin was nowhere in sight. Beau's heart was pounding. He'd heard of children being kidnapped in broad daylight. But before he could start shouting at his fellow waiting passenger to call the police, he refocused and spotted the boy, alive and well. He was far up the park's path, standing on a stone step and drinking from a water fountain. Some lady was talking to him.

Beau frowned, keeping an eye on the lady. Not even women could be trusted when it came to kidnapping. But the lady didn't grab the boy and run, and the boy headed back down the path toward the roadway. He stopped on the far side and looked both ways. When it was safe to cross, he did so. But it was a busy road, and the boy was so small, and Beau waited anxiously, urging Justin in a mutter to move faster. He could see Justin was wearying. No longer skipping along but dragging his feet. His backpack was weighty with books and apples, and he leaned forward like a plough horse, breathing hard. But he seemed pleased, and as he made it safely to the curb he waved a piece of bright green paper. "There's a magic show, Gampa." Speaking in the foreign tongue Beau now understood. The boy took his great-grandfather's outstretched hand. "The lady told me I'm supposed to go. Can I go, please?"

Beau scolded Justin, in as much of a roar as he could muster, for crossing the road alone, and to never do that again. Justin said he was sorry, but he'd been thirsty and he knew how to cross streets by himself. Beau studied the leaflet the kid had given him, an advertisement for something fun looking, with pictures of a lady in a top hat and rabbits and birds and stars scattered all over. "Down here? Here?" He gave it back to the boy. "No power on earth's going to drag me down this way again," he said.

"Please? Pleeeeeeeccceease?"

"No."

The boy sulked. Beau was too sore to care. While they waited, he thought about his body giving out on him, and how he couldn't have run to save Justin if his life depended on it. He remembered running. He'd run after Evvy, swatting her ass, making her laugh. What did she want from him, to be perfect? To not enjoy himself a little? She was supposed to stand by him through thick and thin. She was supposed to honour and obey him till death do them part. Instead, she'd broken up the family and was now snuggling up to her new man. Four-Eyes. Four-Eyes made her happy.

Why couldn't Beau make her happy?

What had she said all those years ago, as she'd thrown his clothes at him, telling him to go. "You're not nice."

"*Nice*," he muttered. He told Justin to never take for granted what he'd got. It's something you only have once, he said, without being able to say exactly what *it* is. In fact he'd never said such a thing before, even to himself, and now he had something to think about for the long wait, the short ride, and then every difficult uphill step back home.

* * *

After a long day's work, Dion was back at Joe's, bolstered by good news. A vacancy had come up at the Harbourview apartments, and he'd jumped in his car and raced over to put down his deposit. The bad news was that he wouldn't be able to move in until April 1.

But now that there was an end in sight, he told himself he could cope with Joe Kent's dream-infested basement. His night at Bianca's had given him the rest he needed. Rest and not much else, he recalled with a grimace.

He sat on the edge of the sofa bed with its sadistic springs and focused on the positive. In two short weeks he would be back where he belonged. As to be expected, the apartment that had come available wasn't ideal. It wasn't up on the tenth floor, like where he'd lived before, but down on the third, with an eastern exposure, and had only one bedroom. But now that his foot was in the door, he'd work his way back up as new vacancies came open. He'd find his way back soon enough.

The red digits on the 1980s clock radio that came gratis with Joe Kent's suite read 8:32. Too late to go out, too early to sleep.

He reflected on the strange night he'd spent in Bianca's attic. She had invited him to stay, but as it turned out, it was an invitation devoid of sexual overtones. Probably she'd asked him because they'd had wine, and talked, and talked some more, and she didn't want the night to end. He didn't, either, and if there *were* sexual overtones in his mind, there were other incentives, as well. Like not having to return to Joe Kent's for another night of horrors.

Bianca's bed was fantastic, a king-sized memory-foam mattress shrouded in crisp cotton sheets and a cloud-like duvet, fairy lights and other fancy stuff strung all over. Dion had to wonder, for a slim little pauper like her, why she'd need such a large and lavish bed. At first sight it had given him hope that she was a sex fiend. But she wasn't. She was honest about what she was, too, letting him know as he unbuttoned his shirt. "I've done this before," she'd said, pretty in her thin pink tank top and panties. She had assumed a relaxed pose by the side of the bed. Her stance was elegant. Model-like. But her words were like a bucket of cold water. "And I kind of liked it at first. But these days, I dunno. I don't like being touched. Just so you know."

Her mouth turned down wistfully. He was too tired to pack up and leave on the spot, as he should have done. It was her place, her rules — her fucking mixed messages — and he would abide by them. "That's okay," he'd said. "We won't do anything you don't want to."

And they hadn't. All she'd done was blab. She'd sat cross-legged beside him, while rain smacked at the leaves of the giant poplar outside. The rain pattern seemed to muddle her words, and at some point he must have slipped into a peaceful, dream-free sleep.

When he woke briefly around midnight she was gone, but probably in the washroom, he'd thought, or in the living room, reading. He well knew the circadian rhythms of night-shift work, having been through it himself.

But in the morning she was still missing, without any indication of where she was or how to get in touch. He'd stood there marvelling at the trust she put in him. She'd stepped into his car, invited him into her home, then her bed, and ultimately left him to clear out her valuables, if that was the kind of person he was. There was nothing worth stealing, however, except for a stereo system that was high quality but outdated. Other than that, nothing but a bunch of thrift store treasures. No computer, no pricey appliances. No wads of cash.

He had almost left a note thanking her for a nice time, but decided against it. In case it encouraged her to stay in touch. He liked her, but this was one relationship that wouldn't lift off. He'd left her rhinestone necklace on the table and departed, locking the door behind him.

If they'd had a chance to talk this morning, he might have told her a few things about trust. He'd let her know that the next man she invited into her bed might have no use for boundaries. She could end up hurt. Or worse.

But did she need lecturing? He didn't think so. She was eccentric, and she had her weaknesses, but she had strengths, too, that he couldn't define. He had a feeling if anyone crossed her boundaries, they'd pay for it.

Anyway, she was no longer his concern. He was back at Joe Kent's, gathering his thoughts, and his plan of action was simple. Get up every morning and go to work. Stay on track for as long as he could before his crime caught up with him.

The room had fallen dark around him as he'd sat thinking. The narrow window across the length of the room let in a glare of street lamp that flickered and flared through the tossing leaves of the maple outside. Dion looked sideways and up, well aware of where the nightmare dwelled. In the hallway leading to the bathroom, where the ceiling rounded a bend and was swallowed in shadow. The thing had grown in size, dream by dream, till it was bigger than himself. Sometimes it spoke.

He shuddered. He should stop avoiding the issue. Should take the nightmare by the lapels and shake it. Except there was nothing to grab hold of, nothing to shake.

A cold chill came over him as darkness fell. He went through the motions of normalcy, undressing, brushing his teeth. He sat in bed with an interesting documentary playing on his iPad. But his mind wandered. He couldn't pace his breathing, sensing all around him an evil presence. He could see the night unfold. First the thing would paralyze him, then it would stomp him. When he didn't show up for work, they'd come looking for him. Find him sliced up and scattered around the room. A mystery for JD to solve.

"Fuck you," he told JD. He spoke through his teeth at the shadow on the ceiling. "You, too. Go fuck yourself."

Swearing didn't help. He was having a panic attack, couldn't fill his lungs. He had to get out of this place. But where to?

He wondered if JD would let him stay over in her very small apartment. He could say he was unwell and crash on her sofa. But he didn't want to beg her for favours, especially since she'd started treating him like a leper. Didn't want to bother Leith, either. Or Paley. They'd all laugh if they knew he was running from bad dreams. They wouldn't get it, even if he explained that these were hyper-evil bad dreams. With claws. Night terrors, they were called. He knew because he'd googled it.

Even knowing the thing *was* a thing didn't help.

He couldn't let his colleagues see him as weak. Scared. Helpless.

Thinking a dream could kill him was a sign of madness. But when he closed his eyes and looked inside, he knew his gut instinct was right.

He didn't want to die. There was one option left. *A hotel.*

Hotels in North Van weren't cheap, but at this time of year one of the budget places wouldn't be too bad. He packed to leave, feigning indifference so the thing wouldn't get the last laugh. With keys and wallet in hand, he gave the dark corner a final glance, then left Joe Kent's house like it was set to blow.

TWELVE

GHOST STORIES

March 18 – 8:00 p.m.

WHILE WAITING AT the front counter of the Travelodge, Dion's phone rang. He didn't recognize the number but answered, anyway. He identified the caller the moment she spoke, but for a moment didn't believe it was her. How could it be? He hadn't given her his number.

"Hey," Bianca said. Her voice was soft and distant. "I'm glad I caught you. Can you come over and talk a bit? Just if you're able. I have something to say."

Dion squeezed his eyes shut and thought, *oh crap.*

Of course, that's what it was all about. She was going to accuse him of things. Try to extort money from him. If you don't pay up I'll take it to the cops, and it'll be your word against mine. An age-old trap, and he'd walked into it without a second thought.

"Why don't you say it now?" he said, coolly.

A pause. "It's just I'd rather see you. I'm out right now, but I'll be there in fifteen minutes, tops. So if you'd like to come by, that would be nice."

Dion told the Travelodge clerk he'd be back in half an hour. He drove to the house on Ridgeway, fingers battering the steering wheel. He climbed the steps and rang the bell marked *Stone*. She came down and let him in. She looked even nicer today, in a long flowery dress. Her face was clean and glowing. And she must have been to the hair salon, as yesterday's chaotic brown curls were trimmed if not tamed.

"I'm so glad you could make it," she said with what looked like a genuine smile.

They walked upstairs. Inside the apartment upbeat Bollywood music was playing. Bianca turned the volume down, explaining it wasn't her CD but Ravina's. Dion didn't care whose CD it was. The only explanation he wanted from her was why he was here.

She nodded at the kitchen table at which they had shared dinner the night before. Dion took a chair, and Bianca set down two badly washed wine glasses, and filled them. "I'm so embarrassed about last night," she said. "I was going on and on about something, I forget what, and all of a sudden I looked at you, because you'd gone very quiet, and that's when I realized, *omigod*, all this time I've been talking you've been fast asleep."

Dion narrowed his eyes at her, even as a doubt niggled that maybe he had leapt to conclusions a tad too swiftly about Bianca and her motives. "Where did you go?" he said. "And how did you get my number?"

Even the way she slumped dejectedly in her chair was graceful. Like she'd taken slumping lessons. She reached for her wine glass and took a dainty sip before answering. "I thought I had the night off, but I got called in at the last moment."

"Called in to what? What do you do for a living? I think I asked you a couple times already and you never answered."

She eyed him, maybe sensing his demeanour had grown chilly since last night. A moment passed, long enough for him to wonder how a woman with such refined manners didn't know how to wash a wine glass properly. Or how an independent hippie living in an attic could be so unworldly. Like she'd been born yesterday. "I'm a server," she said with sudden delight. "I serve."

Dion detected a lie. "Serve what?"

"I'm a maid. I serve drinks and answer the door."

She was making it up as she went along, of course. Dion knew better. She was an escort. And a scam artist. She was a poor girl who'd learned to walk and talk like a rich girl. She'd fogged some old millionaire, pretending she was upper crust. Her client worked during the day and would call her over at night, and she would go running and do his bidding. Dion could guess what that bidding was. *I don't like to be touched*, she had told him. But he'd bet she didn't mind so long as the price was right.

"I asked how you got my number," he said, still expecting the worst.

"I read your mind." She was playing the magician again, giving him the same card-trick smile as that day on the bandstand. *Pick a card, any card.*

When he said nothing, she then admitted with a spurt of anger, like she wasn't accustomed to being challenged, "You were asleep. I wanted to know how to reach you if I had to, so I checked your wallet and found your business card. I'm sorry."

"You could have just asked me."

Already her anger had passed, her moods as fickle as the wind. "It didn't occur to me till it was too late. Plus," she added, and her mood shifted again, and Dion saw in her body language the etchings of anxiety that he now realized were always there. "I had to make sure you were who you said you were." She crossed a palm over her face in a scanner-like gesture that he couldn't interpret.

He thought back to when he'd first knocked on her door, how she'd waited till she thought he'd left before opening it and peeking out. Was she hiding from someone? On the run from the cops? No, not the cops, because he was one, and she knew it. It was the other side she was running from, then. The bad guys. And now he had another epiphany. She had glommed on to him for that very reason. He was a cop, and she needed protection. "Why wouldn't I be who I said I was?"

Instead of answering, she changed the subject, holding up the broken flower necklace. "Also, I wanted to thank you for this. I thought I'd lost it for good. Which would be a *total* disaster. Where did you find it?"

"In my car."

"Well, I can't say I'm sorry," she said. "Because here you are, right?"

Dion wasn't sure he would call their meeting serendipitous, but he smiled in agreement.

"It was *so* good of you to return it," she said. She threw the necklace into a catchall plate on the table, where pocket change and pens had accumulated. "So many people would have just kept the thing. So I wanted to reward you. With money ..."

Keep your five bucks, Dion thought.

"... then I thought of a much better idea," she said. "You told me about that horrible basement that you're stuck in. Why don't you stay here? What do you think? Just for a few days, anyway. You can stay till Wednesday. And this time I promise I won't talk you to death."

Dion wasn't about to become somebody's unpaid bodyguard. "Thanks," he said. "But I'm booking into the Travelodge for now."

Her eyes widened. "It's that bad, the place you're living?"

"It's bad."

"Tell me about it," she said.

And he did.

Sharing private matters like being dogged out the door by nightmares didn't come easily to him, these days, when he thought twice before revealing what troubled him, since what troubled him was a skeleton in the closet. But he felt safe enough with Bianca, who he no longer assumed was out to blackmail him. And if what he told her proved he was nuts, that was okay, because she was worlds nuttier.

He did his best to describe the night terrors and the sense of peril he experienced in the throes of them, and the more he spoke, the sillier he felt. "I guess in the light of day ..." he ended lamely.

Bianca had been following as avidly as a child at a campfire listening to ghost stories. Now her eyes were round and gleaming. "No," she cried. "It's real. They're real. I have them, too, but they're more when I'm awake."

Her words startled him. "What d'you mean?"

She seemed to regret her outburst and covered her face with her hands. "No, forget I said that. I shouldn't have said that. I don't mean anything. Don't listen to me."

Not listening to her wasn't an option, but Dion let it go. He went on to tell her the good news, that in two weeks he'd be moving into a fabulous high-rise apartment and leaving the nightmares behind.

"You're not spending two weeks in a hotel," Bianca said, and reached to refill their scuzzy glasses. "You can stay till Wednesday. You work days and I work nights, so we won't see each other much. But we must meet in between for a glass of wine. Will you stay?" Her smile was as warm and inviting as her words. She left her chair and brought over her bulky shoulder bag. She rummaged inside and held up a small object. She tossed it over, and he caught it on reflex, a little white rabbit attached to a chain, and attached to the chain a shiny gold key.

"Take it," Bianca said. "Seriously. So you can come and go without knocking."

"No way," he said.

"Yes way," she said.

In the end he took the key. Partly he was giving in to natural curiosity, but it had something to do with concern for her well-being, too. And a lot to do with running away from bad dreams. He also felt a brew of affection for Bianca, like a stripped-down infatuation where he expected nothing and owed nothing in return. He turned the gold key over in his hand, and told himself this short-term set-up was harmless. She was lonely, that was all. And so was he. It was nice to have someone to talk to.

And he wouldn't stay till Wednesday — *why Wednesday?* — but take it one step at a time. With a couple nights' reprieve from the nightmares — he still blamed them on Joe Kent's basement — he would gather the strength to kick the dreams to the curb. Then he'd return to the basement and survive till the first of April.

It wasn't like staying at Bianca's was a freebie, either. He'd leave some cash to cover expenses. He lay the key on the table before him. Bollywood still buzzed in the background. Bianca's face was side-lit in the evening rays, her grey eyes hard to read as she studied him. Happy, sad, or indifferent, he wished he knew. He wished she liked being touched.

Was it really harmless, what he was doing? He was pretty sure he heard warning bells ringing, trying to tell him she was more than just a free spirit who had invited him into her home on a whim. She was too deep for whims. Too mesmerizing. She was the undertow.

THIRTEEN

SEARCHLIGHT

March 20

TESTS ON THE BLOODY rag found outside the shack in the woods had come back negative. But a name had been attached to the fingerprints found within the shack: Todd Broadwater. Broadwater's last known address was a recovery house in Deep Cove, and Dion was on his way there, with JD in the passenger seat. JD was recapping aloud what was known about their suspect from her notes while Dion half-listened.

Broadwater was forty-eight, with a long but historical record for a variety of offences, mostly failing to keep the peace, resisting arrest, public nuisance. A protester. Some members at the morning briefing had had a few unflattering things to say about his type, maybe because they'd been egged one time too many in their crowd-control days. Dave Leith had been one of them, prejudging Broadwater as a glory-seeking, troublemaking pain in the ass.

"Save the planet," JD said now, with a sneer, maybe reflecting on Leith's comments. Beyond her still profile, whenever he looked her way, Dion saw the shoreline drifting past, and the boats, the hump of land across the strait, all painted grey by clouds thick with rain. "Eco-nuts, tree huggers, vegetable eaters," she went on. "They should be rounded up and ejected into what's left of their precious ozone."

She was being ironic, of course, because she was something of an eco-nut herself. Dion wanted to say something equally ironic, to get on her side and win back her friendship. But he wasn't going to kowtow, either.

"I was grabbing a coffee at Blenz this morning," he said, after they had travelled a few minutes in not-so-cozy silence. "I overheard part of an interesting conversation when I was standing in line. One old guy said if you die in your dream, you die for real." He grinned. "Ridiculous, right? The other guy said it's just an urban myth. What d'you think?"

"You're asking me if dreaming you die will kill you?"

"Just wondering, just theoretically, 'cause like I said, it's kind of interesting."

She was looking at him, he could sense it, but he was too busy watching the road to meet her eyes. "I have no first-hand experience," she said. "But I do have loads of common sense, and I can tell you flat out, the second old guy was right."

Damn, he wished he could take back the question. She must think him a fool. He was relieved to see their destination approaching, the recovery house. This wasn't the first time he'd come here looking for suspects. He spun the wheel and pulled up in front of the large home with its shrubby lot and shifted to park. "Let's hope he's home. Or if not, that they've kept tabs on him."

The young woman who managed the home was named Pam. Yes, she knew Todd, and yes, he still had a room here. She invited them to sit at a kitchen table, where she told them what she knew about the man.

Todd was free to come and go, and was more often gone than not. She wasn't surprised when JD told her that Todd spent time in a shack in the woods, though he'd never spoken of it. Very private individual. Gruff but gentle.

What had brought him here three years ago was alcohol, but he was now dry, as far as she knew. He was quiet, well-read, fit. She knew he had a bit of a rebellious past, but she didn't think he was a violent man. "On the contrary. He loves animals. Loves the forest."

"Loves people?" JD asked.

Pam hesitated, and only when pressed admitted that Todd didn't have much good to say about humankind. She further admitted there was a time he had come home beet red and riled. He'd seen a dog being whipped, and yes, he had spoken about murder then. But it was just talk.

"Why?" Pam asked. "Is he in some kind of trouble?"

JD told Pam she wasn't sure, that she was just making inquiries at this point and wanted to talk to Todd. She asked Pam if she had any idea where he was now.

Dion was surprised by the answer. Yes, Pam did know. At least she had a general direction kind of idea. "He was going east to visit a friend," she said. "He wouldn't give me her contact info, though. Said it was personal and he wanted to keep it that way. It bothered me somewhat, though, since he doesn't have a phone. But this isn't a jail, you know. And I'm a support worker, not a babysitter."

Mode of transportation to this friend out east? JD asked. Pam wasn't sure, but likely a combination of hiking, hitchhiking, and bus, considering he'd left with a tent and sleeping bag, and not much cash.

When exactly had he left? Pam counted backward and came up with March 16.

Which made it four days ago, one day after the murder of Lawrence Follick. Dion and JD exchanged glances. If they were right about the ex-alcoholic woodsman, he had violently killed a man, and with possibly minor provocation. With a fuse that short, anyone standing in his path was at risk.

JD asked Pam if she had any recent photos of Todd. Pam did not, but did provide a helpful description of him. More particularly, some dramatic changes that had come over him recently in readiness for his trip. "Shaved. Nice haircut. All new clothes. Well, second-hand new, anyway. You wouldn't recognize him, if you'd known him before." She smiled. She couldn't know there was nothing to smile about. She hadn't been told yet what kind of a killer she'd possibly been feeding and nurturing. They would have to warn her before they left. "He looks quite dandy," she said. "Like a country squire."

The warrant allowed for a search of Broadwater's room, but they found the place neat and minimal. No smoking gun. No walking stick that could have been used to club a man, pin him down, and cripple him before the killing blow.

None of the other residents they spoke to following the search could provide clues as to Broadwater's whereabouts, but one housemate did mention that he was quite sure Broadwater actually did have a phone, but was just freaking cagey about it. Probably worried that others would ask to borrow it, use up his minutes.

Dion and JD left the home, talking over what lay ahead. A lot of digital legwork: on the phone, online, posting bulletins, pulling warrants, sniffing out the binary-code footprints that everyone, even a throwback like Todd Broadwater, left in their wake.

And the odds would be so much better, they knew, if the housemate was right about Broadwater being in possession of a cellphone. If they got his number, and if he used it, he'd leave a calling card ping.

* * *

In the early evening Leith heard that Todd Broadwater had been located and arrested as he walked down a street in Lethbridge. Leith was working overtime again, hunched over his computer typing out an email. He wasn't a fast typist, had never learned touch typing, but letter by letter, he was getting down what he was trying to say. Until JD arrived.

"He blipped on our radar," she said, sitting on the edge of his desk. She sounded cheerful. "Better yet, he blipped on the radar using a cellphone that doesn't belong to him. It was a bit of a fluke that we caught it, as we weren't looking in that direction. Our tech team notified me. It's the missing phone. Tracy Hildebrandt's. Looks like Todd is not just our man — *maybe* — but our 911 caller. Isn't that weird?"

"Except he's not, because the 911 caller was female."

She shrugged. "Disguised his voice?"

Leith looked at her with doubt and saw she wasn't kidding. "Anyway," he said, "good work." He was too tired for banter, but JD seemed to be in one of her rare chatty moods. She waited in the periphery of his vision as he finished typing. Only when he had proofed the message and pressed send did he give her his full attention, frowning at her for still being there. "Broadwater won't be shipped back till tomorrow. You might as well go home."

"Why Lethbridge, d'you think?" JD said. "He have connections there? Or was it just a pit stop on his way to somewhere else? He must have hitchhiked. Good thing nobody pissed him off along the way. Or maybe they had, and we just haven't found the bodies."

Leith considered her thin frame, her tightly crossed arms, her unnaturally bright eyes, her unwillingness to leave his company. Lately she'd been peppier than usual. He wasn't sure he trusted the change.

"You have something to say, JD? I'm all ears."

Her mouth flattened into a tight line, but then broke into a sheepish grin. "I can take a hint. Sorry to bug you. 'Night."

Even when she was gone her grin blazed on Leith's retinas. Like the Cheshire Cat's. Except it wasn't a grin, he suspected. It was a grimace. Whatever she wasn't saying was personal, touchy, maybe even perilous.

Kind of how he would describe Dion's perpetual state of being, and maybe he was way off the mark, but he wondered if their two moods were connected.

Maybe something to do with the edginess he'd noticed that had sprung up between them. For a time they had been growing noticeably closer, almost chummy. JD and Dion, often seen sitting together eating lunch. Laughing. Some might even say flirting. But not since around Christmas, when something had shifted.

He thought about the low-level investigation into Dion's crime that was heading inexorably toward a front-page resolution: *Serious Crimes RCMP member indicted for murder.* If not for the setback of one disappearing witness, that headline would already be running. But even if that witness didn't step forward again, Bosko would have no option but to write it up in a report. At which point Leith would be dragged in and forced into a mini cover-up of his own. And there would be no going back. He'd be ducking and dodging for the rest of his career.

Something about the darkening of JD's mood worried him. Not just for Dion's sake but also his own. He'd done a bad thing, sitting on potential evidence. Letting it rot under a ton of gravel, to be exact.

Yes, he had cause for worry. JD was a damn good detective, after all.

FOURTEEN

BROADWATER

March 21

TODD BROADWATER SAT in the interview room, a big man, but not the mountain of muscle Leith had come to expect. The suspect got the conversation off to a bad start by declaring he had nothing to say. Leith took his time considering the mountain man's ruggedly handsome face, clean-shaven and decidedly mean-looking.

Leith tried breaking the ice with a compliment. "I like your jacket."

The jacket he was giving the nod to was a corduroy blazer, brown with contrasting elbow patches. The elbow patches were fashion more than function, Leith knew. Yesterday's fashion, at least. "Where'd you scoop it?"

Broadwater sat up straighter and tugged the lapels. "Sally Ann, ten bucks, not even."

"It's cool. Kind of retro. Kind of, I dunno, country squire. But why the makeover, Todd?"

Broadwater's glower softened almost to a smile. "Met a woman online. Didn't want to show up on Marion's doorstep looking like Grizzly Adams, did I?"

"Grizzly Adams. That's an old wilderness movie, right?"

"Yup. Fugitive from the law. Wrongly accused." The glower was back.

Leith asked Broadwater to tell him about Marion, expecting to be stonewalled. Instead Broadwater offered to provide her contact info, if he'd be allowed access to his notebook.

Leith had the man's notebook brought in, copied down the pertinent information, then asked about the shack in the woods, along with Broadwater's ambles up and down Paradise Road. Broadwater said he preferred to walk and live among the trees. People irritated him. He could put up with society for so long, then needed to retreat, recharge, forget the static and get back to basics. "To most people, life is all about being superior to your surroundings, leaving a mark on it," he said. "To me, none of that matters. If that makes me a misfit, bring it on."

"What's wrong with leaving your mark on your surroundings?" Leith asked, conversationally. "You mean like engraving 'Dave was here' on a park bench? Or are you talking bigger stuff?" Gazebos and whirligigs, he was thinking, hoping Broadwater would tread down that path on his own.

"Graffiti?" Broadwater peered at Leith. "Hell, no, I'm not talking graffiti. I'm talking much larger scale. The need to build, bigger and better. The need to grow, expand, always build, build, build. Advertise, advertise, advertise. And you haven't told me why I'm under arrest."

"You were told, Todd. A couple times. You were read your rights. You refused a lawyer. We're talking about a serious crime, and you could be a material witness. You haven't been charged with anything. I just need answers. The sooner you give them, the sooner you can leave. But I want to hear more about the things that bother you. Buildings, growth, advertising. What's the alternative?"

"I'm not smart enough to offer an alternative. Folks like their lattes in the morning, so nothing change. It gets me down. The volume of it. The noise. I used to like the city. Used to be houses and buildings fit in with the land pretty good. Lots of breathing space in between. Nowadays it's all concrete and glass and people rushing about looking out for number one. I'm watching this world get jackhammered out of shape. It stinks. But I can't stop the wheels. Can't even slow them. Thought I could, for a while, but I was mistaken. So I take to the hills."

"Didn't you tell someone you burned down a condo?"

Broadwater shook with feigned mirth. "I know where you got that, and I think the dude misinterpreted what I was saying. I was speaking figuratively. I wouldn't torch a place. Somebody could get hurt."

An antisocial humanitarian, Leith thought. He offered Broadwater coffee, a sandwich. Once they were both eating and drinking, they talked about off-grid living for a while. The oil sands. Solar and wind power alternatives. To all appearances a civilized conversation between two civilized men. But Leith knew not to trust appearances, knew that killers came in all shapes and sizes. And when he'd had enough of the bonding, he guided the chat back to bloodied whirligig salesmen with spikes in their throats. "I guess it's a part of modern life we've gotten used to," he said. "We're always being told to buy this, buy that. We get bullied into thinking we need stuff. Seems like everything's a commercial. Strip malls to infinity, neon hazing out the stars. Billboards blocking the view, all to make a buck. What would you call it? Eye pollution?"

Broadwater didn't take the bait. He grunted, more interested in the sandwich in his hand. Peanut butter, as requested.

Leith got more direct. "There's a house on Paradise Road with wood sculptures, I guess you'd call them," he said. "Displayed out front along the fence line. Know the place I mean?"

"Sure I do. The spinny things."

Broadwater had said it mildly, with not even a twitch of alarm. Or irritation. In fact, if Leith wasn't mistaken, his suspect had smiled. But maybe it was the peanut butter that was making him mellow. Probably shouldn't have fed the man. Should have kept him hungry.

"Right. The spinny things. Do you know the man's name? Ever talk to him?"

Broadwater washed the last bite of his sandwich down with coffee and dabbed his mouth with a serviette. He looked at Leith inquiringly. "What man?"

"The homeowner."

"No, I don't know the homeowner. What homeowner? Guy who owns the place with the spinny things, that's who you're talking about?"

"Yeah. Somebody attacked him pretty savagely the other day, Todd. Know anything about that?"

Broadwater shook his head. His brow crinkled. "Don't know anything about that. You're saying I'm responsible? Sorry, but you got the wrong guy."

"What do you think about the spinny things he makes?"

"Who makes?" Broadwater was growing sharp, but for all the wrong reasons, as far as Leith could tell. "You're all over the map, man. Speak straight."

"The man who owns the house," Leith said. "The man who was attacked, the man who made those spinny things and put them along the road —"

"Whoa," Broadwater said. "You're saying a grown man made those? I figured it was a kid who done them. Thought they were kind of cute. You know, straight from the heart. But if a grown man made those, wow. That's just weird."

His motive lying in shards, Leith sighed. "Where were you in the early morning hours of the fifteenth of March, Todd?"

"Out and about."

"Out and about where, exactly?"

"Coincidentally and happily for you, I was right smack dab where you want me to be. Heading up Paradise Road. Or not on the road, but just off of it."

"What do you mean just off of it?"

"There's a trail that runs alongside that gets me back to my hut, if I'm going that route. If you give me an aerial shot I can show you."

Leith did so, and Broadwater pointed out where a trail would run behind a greenbelt in the ravine that dipped away from the road to its northeast. Not a groomed trail, barely a deer track, but the one he used often to get from Point A to Point B.

Leith asked Broadwater about the phone that had pinged and led to Broadwater's arrest. The one that belonged to Tracy Hildebrandt. "Where'd you get it, Todd?"

"I found it."

"Where? When?"

Broadwater told him. It was that very same morning, which was in fact how he recalled where he'd been that day. He'd been trudging up the trail at daybreak when he'd seen a figure flitting up ahead, also headed uphill. No, he couldn't describe the figure except it was moving fast. Barely a shadow, maybe just his imagination. "The woods are full of mirages."

Immediately after seeing the figure, the phone had caught his eye, shining in the undergrowth. He'd picked it up and checked it out. It worked. No passcode or anything.

"I thought I'd put it somewhere visible, on a log or something, for the person who lost it to find. But forgot. Later, found it in my pocket, thought it might come in useful, when I reached Lethbridge, to contact Marion. Which I did. Turned it off till then. To preserve battery power."

"Didn't think to turn it in to the police?"

Broadwater shrugged. "Phones are toys for the masses. Even the poor. Cell providers are giving them away these days, to hook you on to their plans. Whoever lost it never even bothered to call it, looking to get it back. Finders keepers."

For an anti-establishmentarian, Broadwater seemed to know a lot about the business of modern tech. The flitting figure went into Leith's notes as another loose thread, while Todd Broadwater continued to diminish in his favour as suspect as he answered further questions. But Leith knew the drill: win some, lose some, and keep gathering the threads till they become rope.

* * *

Broadwater's explanation about the cellphone along with his poor taste in art didn't quite clear his name, but it had taken the edge clean off Leith's admittedly weak theory. He was to learn over the course of the day that the woodman's tryst in Lethbridge was bona fide, and there was an online correspondence chain to prove it. Not to mention the Lethbridge woman's very real anger at the way her new love interest had been snatched off the streets and spirited back to B.C. for questioning.

Leith also was told that the footprint of Broadwater's walking stick wasn't a great fit when laid over the photograph of Follick's throat contusion. Just a tad too big, and lacking a notch in the wood that should have been evident for the impressions to match.

At the end of the day, Broadwater was released, and the suspect count was dialed back, depressingly, to zero.

FIFTEEN

TWISTER

March 22

ON THE MORNING after his fourth night at Bianca's, Dion declared himself officially nightmare free. Mid-week, but he had the next three days off, in compensation for the overtime he'd been putting in. In celebration he had allowed himself to sleep in till eight. And this being the Wednesday deadline Bianca had given him, he would have to head back to Joe's today. But he was okay with that. The distance he had put between himself and the dreams had done the trick, he was sure of it. Even back in Joe's oubliette, he'd get through the next few days without visitations.

Now alone in Bianca's excellent bed, he gazed at the sloped ceiling above. As Bianca had predicted, they had seen little of each other. They were nothing but roomies. Her schedule wasn't so much graveyard as rarely home, he was finding. Yesterday afternoon she had been in the kitchen when he arrived after work. She'd been merrily unloading groceries, and had greeted him like they were an old married couple, but she didn't look well. It seemed she had tried cutting her own hair. The bangs were trimmed high above the brow in an unflattering way, and she had missed some strands. And there was a bruise on her cheek. She explained the bruise away, saying she'd forgotten the cupboard door was open and had walked into it.

How often had Dion heard women blaming their bruises on doors?

She had asked him for help with dinner last night. This time it was rigatoni and mushroom soup, another magazine centrefold. Already she knew how to use measuring cups, the difference between a pecan and a peanut, and how to make a great pot of tea. Their conversation had been relaxed and friendly. It was only when evening fell that he had tripped her switch. She'd been putting on her coat to leave and he had asked her again where she worked, and she'd told him where he could shove his curiosity. "It's not enough I give you a place to stay, you have to know every fucking detail of my life? Am I the only one with secrets? When have you ever said anything in the slightest bit meaningful about yourself? Well? Yeah, exactly, never."

And with that the front door had slammed behind her.

A wiser man would have packed his bags and put some miles between himself and this crazy soap bubble. That's what she was, shiny and pretty but easily popped. But he wasn't wise, and he swore that today, the start of his weekend and the end of his time with her, he'd get to the bottom of who she really was and what kind of trouble she was in. He would wait until she arrived home from wherever she went, and he'd take her out. For breakfast, lunch, dinner, whatever pleased her. And they would talk, for real. He would speak from the heart, and she would trust him, and she'd open up to him in gratitude.

After a shower he made coffee. He had brought over a few essentials from Joe Kent's, an espresso maker being one, along with a bag of dark roast beans. He tried relaxing with coffee and checking the news on his iPad. But who was he kidding? All around him were potential clues, and all he had to do was toss the place. Discreetly. After all, Bianca had done much the same to his privacy, going through his wallet as he slept, which had in fact prompted him to request new credit cards and change all his passwords. So she couldn't complain if he checked out her apartment, could she?

In the bedroom dresser were casual clothes, not many, and nothing of interest. Sweaters, T-shirts, joggers. In the living room, he had a closer look at the bookshelf that held more knick-knacks than reading material. There was a small dictionary and one outdated psychology textbook with a second-hand price sticker on it. A small art deco writing desk had four unlocked drawers and one that required a key. The unlocked drawers held nothing of interest, and the locked one probably did.

He couldn't find a key to the drawer anywhere. There were no bills or any other pieces of correspondence in the unlocked drawers. No notebooks. Not even a stray grocery list.

He was still looking at the locked drawer when he heard steps on the stairs, then a key in the lock. He checked his watch. Not quite nine. Her night shift was over.

"God," Bianca cried, flinging her shoulder bag aside, greeting him with a smile as if they had parted on good terms. "It's so good to be home. I can't wait to get into comfy clothes."

She unzipped pointy-toed heeled boots and kicked them off. Under the belted trench coat she wore skin-tight acid-washed jeans and a soft knit sweater. With barely a glance at Dion, without showing surprise that he was here at this time of morning instead of at work, she ignored his offer to make her a cup of coffee and headed for the bedroom. "Out in a sec," she called, and the door clicked shut.

A minute later she emerged in casuals. Barefoot, black leggings, oversized hoodie. She clicked play on the stereo and a song blared from the speakers, a loud and twangy country-western hit. She whooped at the sound, spun like a leaf in a gale, and rushed over to Dion to throw her arms around his waist and hold him tight. Which was a first. And quite a surprise, coming from a woman who didn't like to be touched.

"Did you say coffee?" she asked him, eyes flashing with manic joy.

He flourished the bag of coffee beans he'd bought for her specially to replace the no-name instant in her cupboard. "Decaf. You must be wiped. You'll want to crash, I'm guessing."

She shook her head, spun away from him, and flopped down on the sofa. She sprawled out and sighed. "What is this music? It's terrible. I love it."

"It's your music, not mine."

She was on something. Too much caffeine. Or drugs. There were dark rings under her eyes that said she wasn't getting enough sleep. "I don't believe you're not tired," he said. "I'm going to the rec centre for an hour. When I'm back, if you're up for it, we'll go for a walk. This is Wednesday, so it's our last day together. I thought I'd take you for lunch. As a thank you. What d'you say?"

She turned her eyes on him, and for a passing moment he thought she looked terrified. But no, it was just her turn to be surprised. "Your last day?"

"Wednesday. You said I could stay till Wednesday."

"Did I? Never mind that. You can stay forever. I don't think she's coming back. I think she's gone for good. And I do so like having you around. It's like being married, but in a good way, if you know what I mean. God, this music is horribly fantastic."

Dion was lost. "Who's gone for good?"

"Pardon me?"

But she was back at his side, hugging him again, distracting him, trying to lure him into a square dance, and he was wondering if he should hug her back, or maybe even kiss her beguiling upturned face. He wondered if this was maybe the turning point in their relationship.

"Lunch?" she said, before he could make up his mind, and sprang away from him. "I would love that! Where to?"

"We'll figure it out. You've got my number. Call me when you're up."

With his gym bag over his shoulder and confusion circling his head, he left the house he now called home.

As always when he stepped out into the world he tuned in on patterns. Sounds, smells, people, and the interplay between all of it. The job had bred attentiveness into him, and the trouble he brought on himself two years ago had given that attentiveness a chronic, even paranoid, slant. People sitting in parked cars piqued his curiosity, for one. Like the individual he noticed in a sedan just down the block from where his own Honda Civic was parked.

People sitting behind steering wheels, if they weren't driving, should be either getting in or getting out. The figure he noticed was doing neither. But on closer scrutiny, he saw the man was looking at an object in his hand. A phone, no doubt. Checking email, answering a call, exchanging texts, or finding the nearest coffee joint. The smartphone was the new good excuse for loitering.

Dion climbed into his own car, forgot the stranger, and headed to the gym.

* * *

Two hours later he and Bianca were walking up Lonsdale. For lunch he had wanted to take her to a fancy bistro with hard-to-pronounce entrees, but she preferred the funky health-food joint they had just passed. They got a snug seat near a window and he ordered the same as her, falafels and mixed baby greens.

Last night, after she had stormed out, Dion had fixed her flower necklace for her, as a kind of make-peace gesture. He pulled it from his pocket now and handed it over, and to his hurt surprise she grimaced as she took it. But it must have been a facial twitch, for she then went overboard in gratitude in her usual way, telling him he was amazing as she clasped it around her throat.

Dion went on to apologize for his nosiness last night. "I just worry about you," he said. "That's all. And I'm a cop. I ask questions for a living. But it's none of my business, and I won't do it again. Unless you want me to."

She hid her face behind her palms, but came out smiling sheepishly. "I guess I yelled at you a bit, didn't I?"

"A little. You were right, though. I ask a lot of questions but don't give anything in return. If we can start over, I'll answer your questions if you answer mine. Just don't yell at me, or we'll get thrown out."

She had to eat a whole falafel and pour a fresh cup of tea before answering. "I despise Q&A games, but tell me one deep dark secret, and I'll tell you one, too," she said.

He shared a childhood secret he had told nobody but Looch: he had once planned on murdering his father. He'd gotten so far as asking other kids on the street where he could get a gun. He'd only been twelve, though, and the plan hadn't gone further than paying a shithead fifty bucks for a Glock that never materialized.

"Oh my god," Bianca said, when his story was done. "Tell me more."

"No. It's your turn."

She leaned to tell him something uber confidential. "Here's a secret you've probably already guessed. I am not me."

Dion considered her words, and only later realized he should have shown patience instead of bewilderment. "What do you mean, you're not you?"

She clammed up. "Oh, forget it," she said, and sulked.

Just like that, they were no longer a happily married couple, but divorcees, lost in their own thoughts. Next to the window, the sunlight underscored Bianca's bad haircut while shadowing her bruised cheekbone. What had driven her to hack at her own beautiful hair, and who had hit her?

Dion paid for the meal and they left the restaurant. The sun was breaking through the clouds, and his mood lifted as he led the way down toward the train tracks and harbour, north along Esplanade, to show off his future home, the Harbourview. At its base he told Bianca to look up. She did, shielding her eyes from the sunlight bouncing off fourteen storeys of glass.

"That's where I'm going to live," he said, telling a little white lie by pointing not to the third floor, to the suite he would be moving into in just over a week, but higher up on the west face of the building, to the tenth floor, which in his mind's eye he would achieve before long.

He wanted Bianca to be awed and pleased. He wanted to protect her from whatever monster was nipping at her heels. He wanted to form a lasting friendship, for once in his life. She would come and visit, and they would stand together on the balcony and marvel at the miniature cars and buses below. The bridge, the sea, the mountains.

But she wasn't looking awed or pleased. She was wincing as she stared upward. "God, that's sick," she said. "What if you fell?" She crossed her arms as if cold. Around her, young cherry trees decorated the plaza, already in bloom, pink and shuddering under grey skies. Dion sighed and turned away, suggesting they visit the Parkgate field instead. They could check how the magic show was shaping up. "It's too far to walk," he said, when she liked the idea. "We'll drive."

Twenty minutes later they were at the park. Workers were finishing the last of the landscaping. What had been a field of weeds was mowed short, like a respectable haircut. New gravel paths led between the venues and all around the circumference. Park benches had been added along the walkways, and a big yellow canteen tent was up, swelling in the wind.

Strolling through the site, taking in the gaily painted structures, Dion could imagine the crowds that would fill the park in a few days. Sun beating down, jugglers and magicians and stilt-walkers, jolly music, puppet shows, strolling families with their kids ripping about. Lawrence Follick would have attended, with his wife and daughter. The man had close friends, it seemed, but no real enemies. No huge life insurance policy as motive, either, and so far nobody to blame for his death. "I hope it doesn't rain," he said.

North Van in late March was unpredictable, weatherwise. The clouds hung over the Lower Mainland now, trapped within the mountain ranges, but maybe the lively wind that was ruffling Dion's hair would also clear the skies. At the bandstand he pointed out to Bianca where she'd sat on the day they'd met following the Svengali act, telling him to pick a card. "Your sleight of hand could use some work," he said, looking down at the bridge of her nose. "But you're definitely a prima ballerina."

He saw blank wonder in her eyes before she laughed. Not laughing like she knew what he was talking about, but like she was pleased by some abstract flattery. "Thanks. And you're the greatest tight-rope walker ever."

He stopped smiling. "You don't remember dancing on this stage? With the guy? That was, like, last week."

"Of course I remember last week, dancing on the stage," she said, too quickly. "A policeman came and told me about a dead man, and I told him I could disappear, and he believed me. That's why I fell in love with him, because nobody believes me, ever. I *know* all that."

Did she know the policeman she was speaking of, that she had purportedly fallen in love with, was him? Was she just being poetic or had she lost track of reality? She was good at ad libbing her memories, piecing them back together, he thought. But not good enough to fool a cop. He took her hand, a knee-jerk grab, like a twister was coming their way and he had to keep her from being swept away.

Maybe he had known all along. It wasn't going to happen overnight, but in months, weeks, maybe even days, Bianca would be leaving for good.

"You'll stay, won't you?" she asked. And though she was looking at him, he felt unseen. Behind her a black squirrel scrambled up a tree trunk, while a small plane droned overhead. All so commonplace and comforting, yet the blustery spring day had become as bleak as midwinter and rife with hazards.

"Let's go home," he told his disappearing girl. And they did.

PART II
MAGIC

SIXTEEN

CLOWNS

March 24

IN THE SOLARIUM of his Forest Hills home, Carey Chance sat luxuriating. Muscular long legs outstretched, coffee cup in hand, and no more wife in the wings to piss him off. If there was a tightness in his chest, it was just the dregs of adrenalin.

"This is so fucking fabulous," he said. He said it again, louder. Shouted it till it resounded within the glassy enclosure.

Simone had left him. Taken her valuables, passport, her favourite jewellery, her best clothes, stuffed them all in her Elantra and driven away to be with her lover, Phillip. She'd cleaned out their joint bank account and stuck a short note on his dresser. A large, lime-green Post-it Note in her unmistakable handwriting. *I'm leaving you, Asshole. Have a happy life.*

The note was real, recent, and undated. He thanked her for taking care of that little detail herself. She had also been setting up the backdrop nicely. For years. Creating testimonials as to her character. Even her best friends would agree she was a hothead, and her parents would attest to her impetuosity. And more recently she'd been letting her social circle know she would leave him on a dime.

Had she been adult about it all and accepted a fast divorce with a reasonable settlement, she'd be alive today. But she wasn't. Greed wasn't her downfall, however, so much as spite. The day she'd found his Achilles heel — his money — was the start of it all. And that had become her anthem. *I'll bankrupt you, dickhead.*

Which in itself wouldn't have gotten her killed, as *empty threat* was her middle name. No. That switch had been thrown the day she'd grown a brain. She went from insults and mood swings to some serious strategizing. Started googling equitable divisions of property, reading case law. Discreetly, but not discreetly enough, and Carey had caught wind of her intentions.

What he had to do was stop her before she got to the point of picking up the phone and calling a lawyer. First step was to curb her anger, mollify her with gifts and attention. Easy enough. Then, when she was in love with him all over again — just this morning, in fact — he had donned the disposable painter's gear, gloves, mask, and goggles, called her into the garage, manhandled her onto the tarp and strangled her, then shoved her into the boot of her own car.

Again, Simone had helped set the stage. Totally her fault for fooling around on him. During one of their more recent fights she'd told him she'd met a guy on-line, way smarter, nicer, and better looking than him. In retrospect, he was glad he'd shared her genuine betrayal with John and Pagg in the way he did. *She's going to leave me, guys. What am I going to do?*

Like he gave a fig if she left him. But he enjoyed bask-ing in sympathy as much as anyone. Of course Pagg and John had offered heartfelt advice that Carey had had to sit through looking like he'd been punched in the gut. If he felt bad about anything, it was deceiving his best bud-dies in the world. But it was in their best interest — not to mention his — that they be kept in the dark.

And now, when it came to police inquiries — and that he could count on, soon as the body was found — his buddies would be there to wholeheartedly back up his story of Simone's pending so-long-John. The cops could go ahead and try to prove she was anything but a cheating wife who'd run off with her lover but met up with foul play along the way. Couldn't tie her death to him. No way. Because she'd been seen by the neigh-bours packing her car and driving off on this very day, when he was most irrefutably occupied. Sure, the out-lines of his plan were borrowed from an old *Columbo* episode, but the alibi he had concocted — or that had concocted itself, more like, when he'd serendipitously lost a bet — gave the perfect crime a unique sparkle. The clown alibi made it memorable. Worthy of a movie. In fact, he'd have to write a book about it someday. *How to Disappear Your Fucking Wife While Riding a Unicycle.*

Just kidding. He wouldn't screw up like so many oth-ers did. Other wannabe masterminds either overthought the cover-up, then got tangled in their own lies, or they wrote a book, so to speak. Bragged. No sir, silence was golden, when it came to the perfect crime. Nobody knew of what he had done but himself and Clarissa. And Clarissa worshipped the ground he walked on. She wouldn't turn on him.

Demeanour was almost as important as alibi. It was imperative that he carry on like an angry, humiliated, betrayed husband. He could be gloomy. *Should* be gloomy. And now and then express worry. *Shouldn't she at least have gotten in touch by now, let me know she's okay?* But he'd soldier on, gradually rebounding from hardship, like he always did. As his friends knew, he was a self-made man who didn't buckle under pressure.

He'd been born poor but had chiselled a path through school, warehouse jobs, the prescription counters, the boss's heart, boom, straight to his position as trainee in Global Health's corporate finance office, climbing the ranks till at thirty-nine years old he was a mostly absentee CEO of the Vancouver branch, working from home and playing the stock market on the side. To all appearances he was morally spick and span, too. Never so much as dabbled in porn or winked at another woman. At least not in public.

He winked now, as something gusting out of the solarium's HVAC system lodged in his eye. In the washroom he tried capfuls of eyewash, but the microscopic piece of crud refused to budge. With vision blurred, he squinted at the mirror and saw Simone behind him. He whirled, spilled the eyewash, cracked his hip against the granite counter.

It wasn't Simone, of course. It was Clarissa, with her hair dyed black, and teased and piled as Simone styled hers. She was also mirroring Simone's anachronistic fashion sense, right down to the cat-eye shades straight out of the '50s.

"How do I look?" she said, striking a pose.

"Christ!" Carey said, trying to catch his breath. "Nearly gave me a heart attack."

He filled a glass of water and swallowed half a pill. Being in the pharmaceutical industry, Carey had access to opioids. Too smart to abuse them, he wouldn't get hooked or thrown off balance. Just indulge in the occasional lift.

Half an hour later, feeling like he was walking on sunshine, he called Pagg and told him he was ready to rock and roll. Little did his buddies know it, it was alibi time, and they were about to help him pull off the perfect crime.

* * *

Carey drove to a sports bar in North Vancouver to meet with John Thorpe and Allan Pagg. The meeting had a seriously silly purpose. Over lunch they would nail down the details of his penance. The thing had begun last week when the three of them had been out drinking. Being tipsy, he had foolishly made a wager, and lost, and as the rules of their long-standing friendship went, he would have to pay up. As agreed in advance of the wager, the loser would have to lark about in a clown outfit, busking for loonies, for however many hours it took to earn twenty-five bucks.

Insane, but insanely fun. And handy, too, as it turned out, for Carey's plan. Because one drawback of working from home was that good, solid alibis that covered several hours were surprisingly hard to manufacture.

Sure, he could have set up something less elaborate and grotesque, and a wiser man might have done so. On the other hand, an alibi couldn't get more solid than being a clown on a unicycle in a crowded park while your wife is being murdered. Could it? And talk about pizzazz. Pizzazz factored big in Carey's life, and he had to confess, there was also a vague notion of immortality. Even if he couldn't write a book about his perfect and colourful crime, he was fairly sure that someday, when he was long gone, somebody would unearth the story in all its colourful audacity and set it to music.

As for the penance itself? Piece of cake. He'd always been a performer, ever since kindergarten, out-twirling all the other snowflakes up on the stage. Then the high-school dramas, then even as an adult, at the mic in karaoke bars and weddings. Wherever he went, he earned laughter and applause.

The items he needed for the day were stuffed in a duffel bag in the car. The goofy hat, oversized sneakers, high-waisted striped trousers. The unicycle he'd had since high school. He even had a rubber fowl to juggle, along with the *pièce de résistance*, the pooter-tooter. Because nothing pleased kids more than adults bending over and making fart noises. And happy kids meant happy parents who would rain coins of gratitude at Carey, filling his hat with twenty-five bucks in no time. Might even need to prolong the gig, alibi-wise. Lose a few coins here and there till he was sure Clarissa had done her deed.

He walked into the sports bar and spotted John and Pagg. He approached with a somber smile that befitted a man whose marriage was in trouble.

"Hey, there he is," Pagg said, more kindly than usual. "We were just wagering whether you'd show up."

The three of them had been making crazy wagers and inventing even crazier penalties since high school, and had vowed as they became respectably employed adults that they'd never stop having fun. As for this particular bet and its consequences, Carey only hazily recalled what had triggered it. They had been at another bar in West Van, sitting at a round table by the dartboards, celebrating Pagg's forty-first birthday with Corona and shooters. At a table nearby were some Jamaican punks with torn jeans and radical T-shirts, hair teased into Medusa worms. Carey and Pagg knew what these guys were: bums. Hacky-sack losers. Probably made their beer money begging on the street corner or soaking the government. John had been more open-minded, saying not to judge a book by its cover. These could be CEOs for all they knew.

To prove they weren't, Carey had pulled out a ten dollar bill. "I'm going to the can," he'd whispered. "I'll let this fall next to Bob Marley there. Bet you anything he puts his foot on it and looks the other way."

John took up the dare. "Bet he won't."

At which point they had giggled as they brainstormed on the prizes and penalties, then Carey had gone to the can, a bit unsteady from the shooters. He had dropped the tenner on cue, and Bob Marley, damn him, had picked it up and called out, "Eh mon, you drop dees."

Should have thought twice, but bets were sacred things — *never be boring, never stop having fun* — and penalties were a foregone conclusion. And again, lady luck had come along and turned his loss to his advantage.

He glanced at his reflection in a mirrored pillar as he took a seat with his friends, and saw a handsome man, fit and firm, with gold chains glinting at the throat and wrist, a neat crew-cut and a sexy, side-parted cowlick. After killing Simone this morning he had tried on the clown outfit as a kind of dress rehearsal, and man, he must have been tripping on something when he'd put it together. It was regretably hideous. But too late to be dialed back.

And pact aside, if he didn't follow through with the clown act, he would have to come up with another plan, quick, to cover his ass while Clarissa did her thing. And as he knew from the business world, plans were best carried out in a linear fashion, and U-turns could be fatal.

No, he would win the day. He'd secure that iron-clad alibi and pay his penance, all in one fell swoop. Because nobody could ever accuse him of backing down from a challenge. He'd get this thing done if it killed him.

* * *

Working together, Beau and Justin had fixed half-a-dozen sandwiches. They had wrestled plastic wrap all around them. They had placed the sandwiches in a paper bag and then into the boy's backpack, along with a thermos of grape juice. This time Beau was ready for the day's challenges. He had a bus schedule, though he'd had a time of it wrestling the pamphlet out of its folds, and once it was flat he couldn't read the tiny print. Ended up spreading the thing on the kitchen table, leaning into it with a magnifying glass and writing the necessary information in ballpoint pen on the back of an old flyer.

Justin had a wristwatch, a huge yellow plastic thing, so they could stick to their schedule. Beau had his bus info, an extra dose of ibuprofen, and he had his wraparound shades, the ones he'd gotten from Dollarama. He had enough cash, he hoped, to buy tickets to some shows for the boy (he had no desire whatsoever to see the acts himself; he would sit on a damn bench and look at the sky, thank you very much), and he had that little card from the library that had caused all the trouble on their last trip.

He wasn't too worried about the trip ahead of him, as he now had experience. He knew about librarians, and the different bus routes, and how to travel with children. He was prepared.

According to Justin's flyer, the festival opened at noon, but even with a departure time of 11:00 they wouldn't arrive until 1:30, what with the slow walk down the long hill and then the wait for the bus, the ride, and another slow walk through the park. Justin would go see the main event at 2:00, then whatever shows followed till the money ran out, and then at 4:00 they would leave the park and go to the library. They would return the old books and pick up some new ones, then catch the 5:15 bus home.

"It's called an itinerary," Beau told the kid as they double-checked the list. "It's what all us seasoned travellers go by. It keeps us on *schedule*."

"Itina-wahwee," said Justin, who liked to mangle new words.

"Itine-*rar*-y," Beau said. "*Rare.* Can you say *rare*?"

"Weahwaw," Justin said.

"Yeah," Beau said. "Like that."

SEVENTEEN

VANISHING ACT

ON THE THIRD DAY of Dion's extended weekend, the sun shone down and the temperature hiked up. He put the idea to Bianca, when she arrived home at nearly 10:00 a.m., that after she'd gotten some rest they would go take in the magic show.

But she didn't want to. She looked tired. Not in the wholesome way that softened her features, but as if whatever hurt within her was wearing her down. She sat on the sofa in an awkward pose, pretending to be relaxed, but the smiles she sent his way were fleeting and pinched.

The distance between them was growing. Dion was so far out of range that he'd slipped off her radar. Even when he sat next to her and asked her what was wrong.

"Nothing," she said, and snuggled against him.

He didn't believe her. "Are you tired of having me around? If you want your space back, just say the word. My move-in date is coming up, but I could easily go back to Joe's place till then."

She snuggled tighter. "Don't be an idiot. I love having you here. You're my darling and I love you very, very much."

Bianca could be flowery one moment, cold and remote the next. He believed her floweriness was false and her silences were real. "So what's wrong?" he asked. "You're not yourself."

"Which is what I told you," she answered, speaking to the wall.

True, she had said exactly that. Dion unsnuggled her and asked if she'd had breakfast. She said she hadn't. He said he'd make toast or something. She said no thanks. He thought she'd lost weight in the short time he'd known her, and had a sudden motherly desire to fatten her up. "I'll make some toast and you'll eat it," he ordered.

In the kitchen he found she had made a pot of tea, but had forgotten to boil the water. He made a fresh pot, added sliced cantaloupe to the plate of toast, put it all on a tray, and brought it to the sofa.

Bianca didn't eat much. Neither did she speak, even when prompted, except to ask why, with a flare of anger, the cantaloupe had peel on it. The room was brilliant with morning light, and Dion tried counting his blessings as he cleared the dishes. Two days, count 'em, he'd be out of here, and for all he cared she could go on being funny weird girl all on her own. From the kitchen sink he risked offending her with a suggestion. "Have you considered getting help?"

Silence.

"Samantha Kerr," he went on. "She's a psychologist. I've seen her myself. She helps all the frontline workers.

Really nice, really helpful. I'm sure I could get her to talk to you. I'll go with you."

Bianca rose from the sofa and headed to the bedroom. "I have a headache," she told him. "I'll see you when I see you."

She was gone, and Dion sat feeling like the last diner at closing time. Not even close to noon and he was thinking about pouring a double of Scotch. Or maybe a triple.

His cellphone buzzed at his belt. It was Leith on the line, sounding hoarse and fed up. "We've got a riot on Lonsdale," he said. "Too many broken skulls to count. Mike said not to bother you, 'cause it's your weekend off, but I know better. You want to be here, okay? All hands on deck. Dress for the field."

Dion holstered the phone. In the dim bedroom he found Bianca curled up on a swirl of sheets, faced away from him, so motionless she had to be asleep. Or dead. She hadn't removed her clothes or pulled up the blankets. He walked around the bed and crouched down and saw that her eyes were open, her hands bunched loosely at her mouth. She didn't look at him.

"I have to go to work," he said. "But I won't be long. We'll spend the rest of the day together. We'll do whatever you want, okay? So work on thinking of something really, really exciting."

She was looking at him now, listening hard. She gave a nod and a smile.

"You won't leave tonight, will you?" he said. "You won't go to work? I mean, you can call in sick, right?" Down on his knees, he placed an arm around her and shifted her so their faces lined up, so she'd have no choice but look at him. "Will you do that?"

She was suddenly with him, completely, sitting up and gripping his hand. "Yes. I'll never go back there. Never!"

Was that joy, terror, or fever he saw in her eyes? "That's great," he told her. "I'll see you soon and we'll figure it out together. Call me if you need me."

She lay back as if comforted, smiling at him. "Yes, I'll phone you," she said.

In the bathroom medicine cabinet Dion found a bottle of antacids, which struck him as poignant. Whatever troubles she had, they went a lot deeper than indigestion. He swallowed one of the pills with water, checked his face in the mirror, and saw worry lines. He forced them away, pulled on his jacket, and headed for the street.

* * *

In the end, the riot was nothing much. Hungover youths at a bus stop arguing about sports, and finally hitting each other with fists, backpacks, and whatever else they could get their hands on.

With Lonsdale restored to peace, Dion returned to his desk to type up his report, where he found a paperback somebody had placed on his keyboard, with a Post-it Note stuck to its face. The handwriting was JD's neat scrawl, as curt as her voice. *Try this.* The book's cover featured a heavy-lidded eye in the clouds, and the title was *Night Fields: A Guide to Lucid Dreaming.* He flipped it onto his desk with a scowl.

"A guide to *what*?" Leith had appeared at his shoulder, face pitted with shadow, and was leaning to grab the book off the desk. "What's this all about?"

Dion was faster and clapped a hand over it. He turned to Leith with a scowl. "That's what *I'd* like to know. It's from JD. I didn't tell her I was having nightmares, so you must have."

Though he supposed JD could have drawn her own conclusions from his question about whether dreams could kill. Anyway, it hardly mattered, and already Leith had lost interest in the book or what it meant. He was preparing to leave, putting on his coat, mismatching the buttons, re-buttoning. "Mike's getting a divorce," he said.

"Bosko's divorcing Sarah?"

"Or she's divorcing him, who knows."

"Why are you telling me?"

Leith looked down at him, seeming at a loss for words. Finally he said with odd gentleness, "There were rumours Mike's transferring out east. But that's not going to happen now. I thought you'd want to know."

Dion was appalled. Bosko was one of the biggest bogeymen in his life, and yes, he wanted the man to go as far east as the map would allow. But just as he would miss Leith and JD, he would miss Bosko, too.

Leith moved away, lifting a hand. "Anyway. Go home. See you Monday."

Dion left the detachment and returned to the attic. Bianca was gone, as he had somehow expected. He stood by the living room window, looking down at the street. Few pedestrians in this neighbourhood; mostly just cars driving by. There was a small park within view, and along either side of the street a mix of modern and older houses. Down at the corner a man stood doing nothing. But no, he'd been waiting, was all. A dog off leash caught up, and man and pet carried on toward the park. No sign of Bianca.

He leaned against the wall as he looked down on the street. A different man appeared on the opposite sidewalk. This guy was dogless, bigger, darker, and seemed to be staring up this way. Maybe he saw his watcher, or maybe he saw nothing but reflections of sky. A moment later he had passed on. Dion took a deep breath and let it out slowly. He unhitched his phone and studied its screen.

He opened his contact list and touched JD's number. He got her voice mail and disconnected without leaving a message. He needed to do something constructive to combat his anxiety. In the bedroom he found the bedding still twirled. In straightening the duvet he saw a necklace lying on the sheet, half hidden by a pillow. The little white flower's chain had snapped again.

Picking it up, he thought he heard a noise. It was soft, sibilant, and all too familiar. He looked behind him and up. He knew what was coming. Not even asleep, and he felt the dread barrelling through his system. He hadn't left the monster behind in Joe Kent's apartment. He'd been foolish to think it would be that easy. The dream was coming back, and with gloves off.

EIGHTEEN

BOZO

CAREY, PAGG, AND JOHN sat at their cluttered table, finalizing plans for the day's adventure. They were all but done with lunch. The nachos had congealed, their beer had gone flat, and dirty dishes sat pushed aside as the three friends schemed. As promised, Pagg handed Carey the busker's licence, fraudulently obtained. "Wasn't easy," he said. "But anything to see you in a fuzzy rainbow wig, CC."

"The wig is not going to happen," Carey said. He looked through the set of documents Pagg handed over, the licence to appear as a performer at the magic festival, along with a flyer advertising the event.

Carey folded the papers into the inner pocket of his blazer. "I'm going to bag twenty-five bucks before I'm even warmed up. Just watch. In fact this gig might be such a gold mine I'll change hats for good."

Carey's other pal, John Thorpe, was the oldest of the group, and at forty-one seemed to be fast approaching the end of adolescence. He'd been unusually quiet, even gloomy. He pushed his quiche around with his fork, but wasn't putting any in his mouth. "Look," he said, abruptly. "This has gone too far, guys. We were drunk. We made a bet. But let's drop it now. Before …"

"Before what?" Pagg said.

"Before it's too late."

Carey and Pagg looked at him. Pagg's mouth hung open in hurt surprise, while Carey felt conflicted. In spite of his bravado, he was wavering. He wondered if his reliance on opioids was getting the better of him. Corroding his decision-making skills. Because wasn't clowning about in public less of an alibi than a blazing hot spotlight? What had felt like a gloriously audacious scheme this morning struck him now as, well, absurd. Maybe agreeing with John would provide him an out, a graceful exit to this big adventure. Hanging around in the bar would be a plenty good alibi, wouldn't it? Except the guys would grow tired of it and want to leave, and he had to remain in their company at least till late afternoon.

"Too late for what?" Pagg said.

John pushed his plate away. "It's idiotic. We're going to make fools of ourselves. My god, how did it get to this? It's not only silly, it's embarrassing, and no, actually, I *don't* want to *carpe* the *diem*. What's worse, we're probably breaking some kind of city ordinance here, even with that licence of yours, which, by the way, isn't even a good counterfeit."

Carey opened his mouth to speak, but Pagg interrupted. "We're not going to make fools of ourselves, John. Not you and me, anyway." He pointed his butter knife at Carey's face. "CC is." He turned the knife blade toward

John. "Don't you go all prim and proper on us now. This is going to be the day of our lives, watching this asshole begging for alms on one wheel. And don't worry, nobody will find out we cut corners. Why would they?"

"Don't worry about it?" John countered. "Humiliation aside, there's probably some kind of clown guild we're not aware of out there. We're going to be stepping on toes."

"Big toes," Carey said. "With polka dots."

Pagg snorted. "We can deal with a few guys in wigs."

Carey snorted, too, no longer conflicted. Perversely, John's cowardice only steeled him to his purpose. Backing down would go against everything they stood for, an insult to their Peter Pan souls.

He looked at the two faces across from him over a landscape of beer bottles and greasy food. The faces were aging. Pagg's was filling out, John's puckering in. In the sharp sunlight streaming through the sports bar windows there were even signs of grey hairs. In a flash of vertigo Carey's world fell away.

He raised his coffee cup to his mates, eying John as he said, "One thing I'm not going to do is turn into an old fart, like some people I won't name."

"Right on. What's the worst that can happen?" Pagg cried. "So you fall off your wheel, hit your head, and end up in diapers, at least you'll never be an old fart." He reached to pat Carey's hand. "And don't worry, buddy. We'll drop by the nursing home now and then. Right, John? We'll bring soft food and funny toys."

John made a noise and threw down his napkin. Probably symbolically. "This is my last gig," he said. "I swear. After this, I'm bidding you dinks adieu. What a joke."

Pagg went on humouring him and John went on griping, but Carey was elsewhere, jolted again by memories
of Simone's face. Mental images of her had been flashing
at him all morning, and with increasing frequency, like
a sound wave seeking the perfect, glass-breaking pitch.
He winced as she flicked at him again. *Flick*, a swirl of
dark hair, *flick*, a cold staring eye. Must get a grip. Under
the table he removed a small pill bottle from his pants
pocket and shook a tablet into his palm. He downed the
pill with lukewarm coffee as he glared sidelong at John.
Already he felt more in control. *We'll see who's the big
joke at the end of the day*, he thought. *Fucking bozo.*

* * *

Two hours into his routine, Carey dipped a bow toward
the ankles of the family that had just flung what turned
out to be a quarter. Once they were gone there came a
lull in foot traffic. Most everyone was in the main venue
now, that spruced-up double-wide trailer, watching the
main event. He spat into the hard-packed gravel pathway and tried to relax. He was sweaty and his rear ached
from the hard unicycle seat. But there was something
else, a bad feeling that wormed its way into his head.
An incompatibility between exertion and happy pills,
maybe, a kind of distant roaring, like an approaching
brush fire. Making faces was an effort, the wacky grins
and grimaces and vaudevillian eye rolls. The roving
knots of humanity that gathered and stared and wandered off again were no longer welcome. They were
cheap. Big people and little people, they kept coming

and coming, much of a muchness, like the replicating hallucinations brought on by fever.

Until now, this welcome lull.

Wind whistled in his ear, and he could hear the ostentatious music blasting from the double-wide. He spat again, and saw the old man was still on his bench, some distance away. The old man was big and knobby looking, and he was leaning forward and supporting both hands on his cane. Seemed to be looking this way, too, with what might be amused interest. Or not.

Sell, sell, sell, Carey told himself, and gave a friendly nod. The old man didn't respond. Carey turned away. He paddled his oversized sneakers on the footpath. He stood straight and tried to relax. The air passing through the red rubber nose stank and was probably carcinogenic. He exhaled slowly through his mouth. He squinted at the sky, and decided it was time. Time to count up the tally, hoping it had miraculously multiplied. He picked up the hat he used for money collection and gave it a shake.

"Shit, shit, shit," he said, and a little girl who'd been creeping closer with a coin in hand scurried back to her mother.

"Sorry, didn't see y'all there," Carey called out. He smiled and did the Mickey Mouse wave, but mother and daughter were departing fast. Taking their fucking coin with them.

Carey pocketed the change and looked at his watch. Thirty-five minutes past four. Only two and a half hours on the job, which left three and a half to go, and he knew he was in trouble. Prime time was over, the crowds had peaked, and he had only gathered about seventeen dollars in quarters and loonies. Mostly quarters, though some schmuck had thrown in a handful of pennies from some past decade.

He was tired. Sore. Not sure he could force another goofy grin or hat-doffing, let alone weave another figure eight or pick up another fallen juggling knife while pretending to trip over his own foot.

I'm losing, he thought. *I can't do this.*

No, he *couldn't* not do it. He'd rather die.

Of course he wouldn't rather die. It was a joke, fun and games, one boys' night out gone too far. And as he reminded himself, the point of the escapade was not to win the bet but to provide himself with an unbreakable alibi. He wasn't losing. He was winning. The critical hour was drawing nigh. Clarissa, in Simone's retro clothes and floppy hat, would wait for her cue, then make a show of hauling Simone's suitcase out to the driveway, along with an armful of garment bags. She would shove it all into the back seat of Simone's white Elantra. It was a nosy neighbourhood, everyone peeking out their window at any noise or movement, and best of all, the neighbours across the street came and went like clockwork, even on weekends. Their minivan would be pulling up at 3:30, give or take five minutes, Mrs. B bringing her kids home from their activities. And Clarissa would be waiting for the van to come rolling down the block before she climbed into Simone's car, slammed the door, and drove away. Never to return. "What are you staring at?" he bellowed suddenly. He clapped his palm to his mouth. There was nobody around but the old man, and he was far enough down the path that he probably hadn't heard. But the yell was a wake-up call for Carey. He'd overdosed. The pills were fermenting in his blood.

He gave a light laugh. "What are you doing, CC? Jesus, get a grip!"

He mounted his unicycle and started wheeling around, arms out for balance, along an invisible tight-rope that looped and undulated. No audience except one old shit on a bench enjoying the show for free. "Must make money, must make money," Carey muttered. He cackled, lost his balance, and almost crashed. Righted himself with a grunt. He went weaving down the path and wheeled a tight circle in front of the old man on the bench. "Hey buddy, why so blue?"

The old man scowled and looked away, toward the main event trailer, as if to say the boxy building was more interesting than Carey and his tricks.

Hovering on the spot, Carey persevered. He ex-tended his artfully squashed bowler hat. "Small token of appreciation, kind sir? Seeing as you got front row seating for the last half-hour?"

"Eh?" the old man said.

"Fellow can't live off adulation alone, y'know."

The old man nodded like he got it, but made a shoo-ing motion with an ugly, misshapen hand.

"Look 'ere, a toonie and we call it even," Carey growled facetiously. God, how unhilarious he felt. "I need CASH!" he shouted. "Okay? A buck? You can't af-ford one lousy buck?"

* * *

Beau Garrett pushed himself up from the bench and started to shuffle away from this unappetizing creature. As he recalled there were benches on the other side of the outdoor stage where another magic show was being put on for the smaller children.

He looked toward the main venue. The gaily painted double doors were closed and the loudspeaker voices that he could hear within were muffled. He worried about Justin alone in there with a mob of strangers. The show was taking too long. He wanted to go up to the doors and peek inside. Would ease his mind if he could just get a glimpse of the boy.

* * *

Carey dismounted the unicycle and stood on the path. He yanked off the red nose and flung it bouncing to the ground. He pulled a coin from his pocket and flipped it a few times. The park was quiet. Only the old man walking away, and in the farther distance some concession standers in their striped aprons stood under the yellow tent, arms crossed. The free agents who had been doing the rounds earlier, the musicians and mime artists and balloon girls and vendors of cheap tricks, had all disappeared now that the main event had sucked up all their customers.

A sharp jolt of anger, physical as a nerve pinch, jagged through Carey's temple. He stared down the pathway at the stooped back of the old man moving off like an arthritic badger. Then he picked up his unicycle and went after him.

* * *

Beau heard a noise and stopped to look back. The sweaty creature was wheeling toward him, calling out what sounded like insults. He went by with arms out wide like an airplane, U-turned and passed again with a metallic whizzing sound, giving Beau a nasty look before zipping off into the distance.

Good riddance. Beau heard a chorus of shrill voices and turned back to see a flock of children streaming from the open doors of the magic show, swarming down the stairs. He smiled and thought, *Justin Time.* He'd come up with that play on words all on his own, and thought it pretty clever, but Justin had told him *everybody* said that. Another noise, a whooping, made him turn once more to see the madman on his wheel careening toward him again, knees cranking double-fast.

"*Goddamn it,*" Beau said.

* * *

Carey had turned to the sound of children's voices. Now that the crowds were back, the sideshows and food stands would resume and the coins would flow. He'd make his quota and get the fuck out of here, to hell with alibis. He'd forgotten his rubber nose and was hurtling down the path toward salvation. He neared the big grey figure of the old man who had antagonized him, and the old man was standing sideways and watching him come. *Screw you*, Carey thought, and beelined to pass, noticing a moment too late that the old man wasn't leaning on his cane so much as balancing on his bandy legs with the stick thrust out at a weird angle, and — *Oh crap, no!* — right into Carey's unalterable path of trajectory.

Swerve, he told himself, leaning sideways. *Swerve!*

He almost made it.

NINETEEN

WHITE RABBITS

A NEW DEATH LANDED on Leith's plate late in the afternoon. Not another murder, by the sounds of it, just good old misadventure. Still, it would have to be looked into.

Leith had Larry Follick on his mind as he took down the details of the new case, and something about the call-out location bothered him. He couldn't put his finger on it. Maybe because this death, too, was set outdoors?

He arrived at the park gate at five fifteen, twenty minutes after the report came in, and the welcoming sign gave him his answer. This was the same magic festival Follick had been involved with. Walking down the path, he saw the first-on-scene police crew was still dealing with the crowd, and it was a big one. A screen was erected around the paramedics working on the injured man, depriving the crowd of the view.

Paley met Leith and broke the news. "Actually, maybe not an accident, Dave," he said. "Least that's how it's looking. People are saying there was a weirdo watching the main show, and others saw him running toward the victim when the show was over. Suspect's long gone though, along with god knows how many witnesses."

Leith was introduced to the magic show's MC, a woman in colourful coattails. He learned she had taken charge when the emergency had been reported to her. She had checked the downed man for a pulse and done her best to preserve the scene, ordering everyone to stay back and wait for emergency services. After his brief words with her, Leith had a brief look behind the screen at the man lying by the path. The deceased was a slim man who looked to be in his late thirties. And strangely attired, to say the least.

Leith rejoined Paley and Torr in the event's office trailer to help with the game plan. The crowds were being herded to one side of the park, to be sorted into categories: those who might have seen something and those who definitely hadn't. Those who hadn't were urged to go home. A team of constables in uniform were busy pegging and stringing lengths of crime scene ribbon around the area.

When JD and Dion arrived, Leith walked with them back to the body. "There's some confusion," he told them. "Some are saying it looked like an accident, others are saying it was a push. But basically they agree a man who was behaving oddly at the show left at a run in this direction. Took off toward the boulevard and disappeared, likely eastbound."

"Any good description of the guy?" JD asked.

"Doug's trying to drill down into people's memories for details."

The coroner was done, and the body was being photographed. Leith tilted his head and tried to analyze the scene. Didn't take a master of physics to figure out what had happened here. The body lay prone on the grass, sprawled like he was making snow angels, feet angled back toward the walkway, while the crown of his bloodied head rested near a concrete drinking fountain. There was blood on the fountain, too, a great splat on its uppermost edge. An old felt bowler hat lay on the path. The hat looked squashed, which made sense. Most telling, a unicycle lay not far from the dead man's feet, tilting forlornly off the edge of the path where gravel merged with turf.

So the cyclist had been charging along, probably at some speed, going that way, had lost it, for whatever reason, pitched forward, cracked his head on the upper edge of the water fountain, and dropped, his machine skittering into its resting position behind him. Leith looked at the cyclist's likely path of travel and tried to gauge where exactly the capsize had commenced. No potential trip hazards were visible. The path was groomed and clear.

Dion was staring at the dead man's striped pants. "So, no ID on him?"

Leith shook his head. "Just a busker's licence. It says 'C.C. Chance.' Sounds like a stage name. His nose was found over there." He pointed far down the path to where the red rubber ball remained, an exhibit marker next to it. "Strange," he added, though more to himself. The nose didn't fit in with his physics-based theory.

"A lot of these buskers live on the fringes and abandon their identities," JD said. "Drift on the wind, live from hostel to hostel, handout to handout."

"He looks rich," Dion said. "He's got one of those suntans."

"You can get a damn good suntan picking cherries in the Okanagan," JD told him.

"Or hitchhiking," Leith put in.

JD nodded. "Or sitting on the curb with your hat out."

"It's not cherry-picking season, and that's no beggar's tan," Dion said. "It's too even. And followed up with moisturizer. And look at the haircut. That's a high-priced trim."

Dion knew a thing or two about haircuts, Leith had to admit. He never came to work looking unkempt. Or at least until he had moved into Joe's basement suite, when he showed up some days looking like he'd ridden to work on a bucking bronco.

Glancing away and across the turf, Leith saw a massive TV camera trained on his face, BCTV trawling for footage. He drew up his shoulders and said, "God, don't let this be another broad daylight murder we can't solve."

A group approached, Paley escorting two men. The men were in their late thirties or early forties, clean-cut and wearing expensive parkas. Either wealthy mountaineers or urban yuppies, Leith guessed.

Paley left the men standing at some distance and took Leith aside to explain. These guys were looking for a friend of theirs. Said he was in the park doing a clown act on a unicycle.

"Pretty sure we've found him," Leith muttered. "I'll talk to them." He had to jump to it, too, as the men in their bright jackets were disobeying Paley's instructions to stay where he'd left them and were inching forward, trying to see the body behind the screen.

"Allan Pagg," one of the men introduced himself to Leith as he halted them. This was the shorter one in Day-Glo blue with black shoulder flashings. "What's going on here? Where's CC?"

"There's been an accident. You say your friend was performing on a unicycle?"

The other stranger nodded. He was John Thorpe, he said, with a thrust-out hand. Leith shook the hand briefly, and Thorpe said, "Carey doesn't do this for a living, officer. He was just doing it for a lark. I tried to tell him —"

"Look," Pagg interrupted, pointing past Leith at the screen. "Is that him? I'm not an idiot. There's an ambulance back there, and they're packing up to go. Somebody said someone was killed. Is that CC in there? Is he dead? Can we see our friend or not?"

Leith had to break it to them that the cyclist was dead. "There's no picture ID on him, so your identification will be helpful. Appears he lost balance and struck his head against that water fountain. There's quite a lot of blood, just so you're aware. Just hold tight for a moment."

The two men waited in shocked silence as the body removal people got to work, transferring the dead man from lawn to shroud, and then onto a gurney. Only then were they allowed to see his face.

"Oh no," Pagg cried.

"Poor Simone," Thorpe whispered.

JD, who was standing close enough to hear, asked, "Who's Simone?"

"His wife," Pagg said. He had gone pale. "Who's going to break it to her?"

"They were on the rocks," Thorpe said. "But they still love each other. She's going to be devastated." He turned to Leith and nodded. "Yes, that's Carey. Carey Chance. It's not at all what it seems. He's a CEO."

* * *

At just before 6:00 p.m., while Leith focused on the eastbound suspect, Dion and JD were tasked with the hardest part, notifying the wife. They drove to the Forest Hills address they had been given. A stiff breeze was blowing as they drew close, and the trees along the avenue surged and settled.

"That must be her," JD said as they approached the home in question, her eyes on a woman in the driveway.

"Looks like she's going somewhere," Dion said.

The full-bodied young woman in a pastel pantsuit and sunhat was standing next to a huge wheeled suitcase at the side of a white Elantra. The car's rear door was wide open as if to accept the luggage, but the woman wasn't loading it. She was standing, apparently oblivious to their presence as she stared in the opposite direction. Shielding her eyes, looking down the block, waiting for something or somebody to appear.

Dion parked curbside and he and JD stepped out and walked toward the woman. "Simone Chance?" Dion called out.

She spun to stare at them. "Yes," she exclaimed, and clapped the sunglasses she was holding over her eyes. "Why?"

The curtains twitched at the house next door. Down at the end of the block a minivan turned a corner. The woman's chiffony sunhat blew off in the breeze, and she grabbed at it, but it was gone, rolling along the sidewalk like a pink tumbleweed. The wind had given the suitcase a nudge, as well, and it crept off down the slant of the driveway.

The woman ignored the suitcase's departure. Visibly flustered, she grasped the Elantra's door handle. "Listen," she shouted at Dion and JD, who were still a stone's throw away, JD advising her that they had to talk, that it was important. "I'm in a hurry. You'll have to come back later."

With that she dropped in behind the wheel, revved the engine and reversed so crookedly that her visitors had to jump clear. The tires squealed, rear fender crunching into the minivan as it approached. The minivan jerked to a stop, but the Elantra straightened and peeled out, fishtailing down the block.

While Dion got on his radio and JD called out to the minivan's occupants, checking that all were okay, they ran to their car. With emergency light attached and flashing, Dion breached the speed limit in pursuit of Simone Chance. He didn't think she would get far, the way she was driving, and he was right. Four blocks down she had overshot a slight curve and landed nose-first in somebody's front yard, splintering a fence and setting off an angry-dog alarm. The Elantra's front tires spun, caught in ruts in the lawn, and the driver abandoned her car and fled on foot. Dion sprinted after her, and as JD told him later, the takedown wasn't pretty.

* * *

JD was still spiritually uplifted by what she had witnessed, the feisty woman in her retro pantsuit trying to fight off a detective in suit and tie. Dion was scuffed and scratched as he and JD joined Leith at the cramped table in the crime-scene van. He had brushed off most of the vegetation he'd picked up while rolling around with his arrestee in somebody's flowerbed. "Did I get it all?" he'd asked JD, doing a full turn. Yes, all clear, she'd told him, when in fact there was a tiny blue flower caught in his hair, just behind the right ear.

A forget-me-not she wouldn't soon forget.

The exercise seemed to have done him good. Put colour in his cheeks and a shine in his eye. Leith, on the other hand, was looking bagged. In it for the long haul, with sandwich and coffee before him, along with paperwork, a pen, a bottle of Tylenol, and his cellphone. He confirmed he'd heard about the arrest, the neatly parcelled body found in the Elantra's trunk, and the imposter's full confession. He was only glad the case was a wrap before it had even actually opened. Carey Chance had killed his wife, and a quick death had spared him from answering for his sins in a Canadian court of law.

Which only left the killer's killer to be apprehended.

"Got a pretty good description," he said about the man who had allegedly fled the crime scene. "Had to do some reading between the lines, but we've got a loose sequence of events. Witnesses say this guy was in the audience at the magic show, being obnoxious, shouting out inappropriate comments. Almost got himself kicked out. Soon as the show's over he boots it, goes racing toward the clown on the unicycle. Nobody actually saw him knock Chance over, but it's a good bet that's what happened. I don't have a name for this man, but he's in his late thirties, long blond hair, tattoos all over his neck and some on his face."

A face and name came to JD. "*Bad* tattoos?" she asked Leith.

"I wouldn't know."

"Brando Reese," she suggested to Dion.

He shook his head. "Reese is inside."

"On probation since last week," she informed him. She described Reese to Leith, who hadn't been on the North Shore long enough to know its regulars. "I don't know how many times we've booked him," she said. "He's always finding Jesus and getting out early. I'll talk to probation, for starters. We'll find him fast enough."

"We always do," Dion added.

"Clowns," Leith reflected, shaking a Tylenol into his palm. "There's got to be some connection here. A whirligig guy goes down. He was working on the magic show. Then ten days later a clown goes down. Same magic show. The clown had just killed his wife and managed to convince his girlfriend to pose as her to put him in the clear."

"*Columbo*," JD said. "My favourite show. Did you see the one where he murders his wife and gets the young actress —"

"No," Leith said, killing the small talk. "What this clown has to do with Larry Follick, I can't imagine." He downed the pill with coffee. "Have to see if there's any kind of relationship between the two victims. And Brando Reese, what's his connection to the magic show, aside from watching it? I'm drawing a blank here. What d'you know about him?"

JD answered, ticking off the facts on her fingers. "He's a serial inmate, his last stay was for beating up his girlfriend, he's an alcoholic, and he's a shitty liar. He's a drunk and a bully, but lucky for us he belongs in the dumb-criminal hall of fame. I arrested him once, told him what he was being charged with, and asked if he had anything I should add to the list of charges. And you know what?" She waited a beat before delivering the punchline. "He *did*."

She stopped laughing under Leith's withering gaze. For Carey and Simone Chance, his eyes were saying, there was nothing funny in this situation. Nothing funny at all.

He had a point. But wait till he saw their cruiser's dash-cam footage, which had just captured, almost off-frame, Cal Dion tackling an Elizabeth Taylor lookalike to the sidewalk.

If that didn't bring a smile to Leith's face, nothing would.

* * *

Bianca still wasn't home when Dion stepped through the door. The note he had left for her appeared untouched. He told himself it didn't matter. He hadn't seen her since he'd left her dozing this morning, but he didn't know her routine well enough to say it was anything to worry about. Maybe it was her pattern, coming home five days a week, staying elsewhere for two.

He went to the little wooden desk and tried the larger bottom drawer again, the one that maybe held hanging files and possibly some answers to the mystery that was Bianca Stone. It was still locked, of course, and he stood and gave the top a thump with his fist. The thump rattled the pretty crap on the desk's surface but advanced him nowhere.

He stretched out on the sofa and studied the ceiling as he tried to work out a plan of action. He had to keep moving, or he'd sink. He studied the hook that suspended the empty birdcage near the open window. Something about the hook depressed him. Or not the hook, but the cage. Or not the cage but its emptiness. A missing canary and a missing girl named Bianca.

One facet of his job was to track down missing people, so it was crazy that he couldn't keep this one in his sights. He couldn't hold onto anybody. As far back as his mother, who had disappeared from his life when he was too young to ask the right questions. *Where is she? Why did she leave me here?* Only years later he had learned the truth, that she'd been sick, institutionalized, and had died without knowing her own name. He'd been left with a new understanding of an old sorrow, but the understanding didn't ease the pain.

He'd tromped through life ever since, burning bridges. He'd split up with Kate and alienated JD. And he'd lost Looch, his best friend, a vibrant and vital man who should be here, alive and well, but instead was fading, his face losing definition and his voice thinning to silence. All the things he'd said and done that were so brave, so smart, so stupid, so kind, and so funny, vanishing from Dion's memory.

He squeezed his eyes shut and tried to conjure up his dead friend in 3-D and stereo sound. It had been so easy, till lately. Now all he saw was mist.

TWENTY

PHANTASM

March 26

BRANDO REESE SAT in the interview room, unshackled and sulking. JD sat across from him and said, "Wow, this is just like old times. How's it going, Brando?"

"Good," Brando said. Because that was the kind of guy he was, JD knew. Not one to weigh his words so well before speaking. "I mean not good," he revised. "This is bullshit. I didn't do what you guys are saying I done, no way, never in a million years."

"Nobody's saying you did anything," JD said. "But you were placed at the scene by a whole bunch of witnesses, so of course we have to talk to you. You understand that, right?"

"I run by the guy," Reese said, with a sigh. He had said it a few times before. "That's all I done. I stopped, I looked at him, he's a bleeding mess, but I figured there's other people around who can help him out, it's not my problem, and I kept going."

"You were in a hurry?"

Reese had a good excuse for running. He was due at his mother's house for dinner, and it was her birthday, and he hadn't yet got her a present. He was heading to the Quay for flowers and chocolate. Paley, who had questioned him earlier, thought it was a bald-faced lie. JD didn't. As she had told the others, Reese was a lot of things, but he wasn't a liar. Still, goading him further wouldn't hurt. "There's a whole bunch of problems with your story, Brando, like why you'd go all the way out to Parkgate to attend a magic show, then bolt like your life depended on it."

"I've always liked magic, so I went. It sucked. Lousiest magic I've ever seen. Like it was aimed at five-year-olds."

"It *was* aimed at five-year-olds," JD said. "But what did you have against the man on the unicycle? Were you taking out your disappointment on him? Did he offend you somehow? What happened?"

"I noticed the time. I was jogging down the path, and the clown was coming at me like a bat out of hell, then all of a sudden he was lying by the water fountain. I stopped to look is all I did."

"He got in your way, did he?"

"He what?"

"He was panhandling. You didn't have the time for his B.S., told him to go screw himself. He kept pestering you, so you shoved him. Is that what happened?"

"I never shoved the guy," Reese shouted. He was quiet for a moment then shouted again. "The old man musta done it. He stuck out his foot or something."

"What old man?"

JD peered into Reese's not-so-bright eyes. There was no old man in his earlier account. And nobody else had reported seeing one on scene. Which was significant, considering there had been a lot of witnesses to *not* see that old man. And what old man would be stupid enough to stick his foot into the path of anything on wheels, even something as compact as a unicycle? And if he'd done so, he would have been knocked on his ass. He wouldn't just up and vanish. The old man was Brando's oddly convincing invention, is what he was, and JD was having second thoughts about her suspect's inability to tell a lie.

"Describe this guy for me."

Reese shrugged. "Just another old man. I wasn't looking at him exactly. I was looking at the guy on the wheelie thing."

"Describe him for me. The old man who stuck out his foot."

"White guy."

"Tall, short, fat, thin?"

Reese looked exasperated. "I don't know. Just some old man. Big. A big old man."

"Big as in tall or wide?"

"Tall." With a palm Reese indicated a good twelve inches over his own head, which topped out at six foot two, according to his stats.

"So he's seven feet tall?" JD said.

"At least."

"When you say old, is that fifty, ninety?"

Reese guessed ninety. "Stiff," he added. "He was moving stiff."

"Okay. And what was he wearing?"

"A long coat, I think. Greyish, or brownish."

"A hat?" JD said. "Wings?"

"What?"

"I'm kidding. Of course he didn't have wings. But he somehow managed to vanish from the scene, this stiff, seven-foot-tall ninety-year-old badass who stuck his foot in front of a moving unicycle."

Reese gave her a suspicious scowl. "Maybe a hat," he said. "I don't know."

"What about his face? Can you fill that in at all?"

"I never looked at his face."

"Maybe he didn't stick out his foot, but pushed the cyclist. Is that possible?"

"No, I would have seen him push him if he'd pushed him. He didn't push him."

"Maybe the unicycle veered to avoid him?"

Reese gave the question careful consideration. "No," he said. "There was plenty room to get by."

"Did the old man say anything, make any noise at all?"

"Didn't hear nothing."

"After the incident, did you confront the old man? Say 'Hey, mister, what in hell did you do that for?'"

"No. It was none of my business."

JD was struck by inspiration. "Maybe he stuck out a cane or something, not his foot."

Reese disappointed her. "He didn't have a cane."

"You sound sure about that. I thought you weren't looking at the old man."

Reese was growing mutinous, as he had done in his earlier interview with Paley. "I told you all I know.

Maybe he had a cane, maybe not. What's with you? Why are you always biting my ass? Jesus Christ."

"Maybe if you stopped getting in trouble, Brando, I'd stop biting your ass."

Reese's voice rose an octave. "I didn't do a single goddam fucking thing, though, this time, did I? Can I go now?"

"That's what I'm trying to find out," JD answered. "And not quite yet."

* * *

Dion thought Brando Reese's statement was interesting. He agreed with JD that Reese wasn't much of a liar, so the story he'd given added a ghost to the mix, a looming old man in grey who wasn't quite there. He believed the ghost at least had bones, and got into an argument with Leith, Torr, and Paley about it. "We can't assume Reese made it up," he told them. "We'll have to re-interview everyone we've got listed at the park, put it to them directly, ask if an old man was present. If just one person remembers him, we've got a real avenue to explore."

Paley snorted. "Reese made it up on the spot. A seven-foot ninety-year-old. With wings. You believe everything you're told? And you know how many people we interviewed?"

"A hundred and two."

"A hundred and two," Paley repeated. "None of whom mentioned an old man on or near the path at the time of the murder."

Leith joined in, reluctantly taking Dion's side. "We can't just write it off. Besides, if Reese was going to invent a scapegoat, he'd have invented someone more likely. A punk. A young punk, somebody on legs who could disappear in a flash."

"But let's not forget Brando's dumber than duck-weed," Paley said. "So we're going to spend the next twenty-four hours re-interviewing a hundred and two people, only to find out there *was* an old man in the park, because there's always at least one in a crowd, and what happened is Reese *did* see this guy, and even he's smart enough to take a fact and work it into his fiction. Thanks, Cal. You're one fine fucking make-work fairy."

Leith told Paley to stop whining, gather up his team, and get to work.

Alone at his desk when the briefing ended, Dion went over Reese's statement and the pile of witness reports once more. He was still riffling pages when JD joined him and took a chair. "How's my little make-work fairy?" she said, coolly.

"Paley's taking Reese's observations too literally," Dion told her. "Reese got his measurement and age estimate wrong. So what? A lot of people do." He flipped the witness statements folder shut, discouraged. "Though I guess it's strange nobody else seemed to have seen any old man where it mattered."

"That's because he's old," JD said. "A weird thing happens to old people. They go invisible. Unless they do something to get noticed or make a scene. The only reason Reese saw this particular old man is because he made a scene. Sticking out your foot and causing a fatal crash is one way of doing it."

"So you're agreeing with me."

"I'm seeing your point and improving on it, is all," she said, and rose to leave.

Dion stopped her, pointing at the chair she had just vacated. "Sit down a moment," he demanded, and once she was doing so, he faced her squarely. "So what did I do? Why are you pissed off at me?"

"Am I pissed off at you?"

"You have been for months."

She studied him with what he saw as contempt. "I've got my reasons."

"Which are what?"

"Maybe it's 'cause you never talk about Looch," she said. "You never talk about Brooke. You never talk about Ken. Three major deaths in not only your life but mine. Maybe you're taking stoic to an extreme, but what it does, this stoicism of yours, is put a wall between us. That's your choice, not mine. I'm fine. It makes my life simpler. But don't expect me to try climbing your walls. You've made it clear you don't trust me, and that pisses me off. Simple."

"I trust you," he said, and reflected. "You're the only one I do trust." On further reflection he said, "Who told you I'm having bad dreams?"

"You did," she said. "I can read between the lines, you know. It's my job. Did the book help?"

He shrugged. "I flipped through it. Won't work. Not with the kind of nightmares I'm having."

"They're that bad?"

"They're terrible. It's like they're trying to kill me."

JD suggested he read the book instead of flipping through it, then steered him back to his original question. "And how do you figure I'm pissed off? I thought I was doing a good job of just being me."

"You're being you more than usual, I guess," he said. They sat in silence for another long moment before she rose and walked away, leaving plenty unsaid.

Dion wondered if JD was angry at him because she had some idea of the trouble he was in. Maybe it was self-preservation on her part. If that was the case, he couldn't blame her. She was smart to keep her distance. He should let it lie.

Except he couldn't. Not without getting the last word in. He joined her at her desk, took a chair without invitation and said, "You want me to tell you how I feel about Looch and Brooke and Ken? How long do you have? And what'll you do when you're tired of hearing me spill my heart? Careful what you wish for, JD."

He saw he had scored a point, as she looked nervous. She said, darkly, "No, you're so right. Go away."

A photo in a small frame next to her monitor caught Dion's eye. He picked it up. Featured in the snapshot was an attractive thirty-something man with windblown brown hair and smiling blue eyes. "Who's this?"

"A pilot with Pacific Coastal," JD said. "Put that down."

He put it down. "What's he doing on your desk?"

"He's my boyfriend, is what."

Dion tried to hide his surprise. One thing JD was good at, it was being single. "What's his name?"

"Why? You're going to look up his bona fides? Just because your love life is in the pits, don't go messing with mine."

"Mine isn't in the pits," he told her. "I'm with somebody, too. I've moved in with her."

He regretted his words with boomerang speed. Why had he mentioned Bianca, his crazy roomie, their relationship nothing but a joke? He rose, determined to do no more damage, but now it was JD stopping him in his tracks, taking him off guard. "I'm thinking Ken Poole's suicide wasn't a suicide," she said, so quietly he almost didn't hear. "I'm thinking someone silenced him."

Her words were loaded, and she was skewering him with a stare. Fear danced a powwow in his gut. She would see right through him, see him quaking.

"You're thinking you know who did it?" he asked.

She didn't reply.

Dion pulled a face and walked away. In the men's room he leaned over a sink, necktie over his shoulder, thinking he would spew out his anxiety and feel better for it. He did neither.

Back at his desk he found a message from Paley. Several other witnesses at the magic show had seen an old man in the park, maybe walking with a small boy. Yes, the old guy was tall, and didn't look too spritely. Nobody could place him in proximity to the unicycle crash, and for sure nobody could pin a name or any other lead on him.

Paley was right about one thing. The possibility remained that Reese was lying. He'd seen an old man in the park, and later used him as a scapegoat for his own crime. For all the work Dion had created, he'd moved the case ahead not even an inch.

PART III
DAY'S END

TWENTY-ONE

GONE

March 27

BEAU IGNORED THE NOISE of knuckle-rapping, since it came from the front door where he'd posted the sign telling visitors to go around back. Let whoever it was figure it out for themselves. He was stirring porridge on the stove. Through trial and error he had figured out Justin put up with oatmeal so long as it had lots of raisins. And cinnamon sprinkled on top, and a swamping of brown sugar and milk.

The oats were thickening nicely when there came a second rapping, more of a double thud, this time at the back door, just two feet from where he stood. Through the yellowed lace he could see two shapes blocking the light and shifting this way and that. "Go away," he muttered.

But they didn't, and he knew they wouldn't. He shut off the flame and shuffled over, opened the door, frowned at the two people standing there. A youngish man and an older woman, both neatly dressed. The man was short and thin and the woman was pear-shaped, nearly as tall as Beau, with a flat smiling face.

They were missionaries, he could tell at a glance. With their proper clothes and their know-it-all stares they were everything he'd come to hate in the world. As the woman opened her mouth to start saving his soul, Beau said, "Don't want it, already got it," and tried to shut them out.

"Hey, hey," the young man said, and wedged the door open with his elbow. "*Excuse me*, sir," he said, peeking around. "We're not selling anything. We're with the Ministry of Children and Family Development. May we come in and speak to you for a moment?"

Them being government was even worse than missionaries. Missionaries could be told to go to hell, but the government couldn't. Beau let the door swing as wide as it wished, and stood back and let his chin sink to his chest as he continued to eye them. Experience told him people backed off when he stood like this. It said if he was a bull, he'd butt them over the fence.

The woman closed the door behind her, shutting out the chill. She said, "I'm Anne Mills and this is Curtis Vandermeer." A business card was extended. "You're Mr. Garrett?"

"Beau," Beau said. "Beau Garrett."

The woman named Mills got right to it, chatty like they were a bunch of friends having a chinwag. She told Beau she had called him up a few times, but received no answer, so she and Curt had decided to drop by, and hoped he didn't mind.

The man named Vandermeer stood beside her, being her backup. He was looking around and trying not to be obvious about it. Looking at the stove, the furniture, the ceiling.

Mills asked Beau about Justin. "I take it the little boy who lives here is related to you? Is he your grandson? Is he here now?"

"Great-grandson. He's in his room. Reading. He reads."

"May we talk to him?"

Beau barked out Justin's name, and the boy scuffled into the room with an open picture book balanced on his head. The workers looked at the boy, and the boy looked at Beau.

"Hi there." Vandermeer was hunkered down by the boy, introducing himself, asking in a sugary way that raised Beau's hackles, "And what's *your* name?"

"Justin time for tea," Justin said. Just yesterday he had taken Beau's joke and made it even better.

"Justin time for tea." Mills was laughing like it was the funniest thing she'd ever heard. She caught Beau's eye and tried to make him laugh along with her. "So cute."

Vandermeer kept talking to the boy. "So, my name's Curtis, and this is Anne. We've come to chat with your great-grandfather. How old are you, Justin?"

While the man and boy talked, Mills said to Beau, "Why isn't he with his parents, Mr. Garrett?"

It was vague in Beau's mind, Sharla's visit last month, the things she had left behind and why she had left them: a small boy, an aquarium, a bunch of suitcases. He couldn't remember what she'd said. Had assumed it would be an hour or so, but it had turned out to be forever. "She's gone away for a while," he said. "She'll be back."

"That's your daughter? What's her name?"

Beau gave Sharla's name, first and last. Grandmother to Justin, not mother. The mother was dead. Sharla hadn't left a phone number, and he couldn't think of her address, or even whether it was Surrey or Richmond or where the hell, so Mills said in a kind voice, "No fixed address?" and Beau nodded. She nodded, too. "When is she planning to return?"

Beau thought about lying, making up a date, but somehow couldn't settle on a number. "Soon."

Mills finally got to the point, telling him she'd received concerns about Justin's welfare, and said why she and her sidekick were here, and talked about some process and procedures that might have to be followed. She said how nobody wanted to take his great-grandson away from him, and she knew this had to be upsetting, but that every report of concern for a child's welfare had to be investigated. She asked if he understood. He said he did.

Then she asked, like she was giving last rites to a dying man, "Do you feel you're capable of looking after a small boy, Mr. Garrett? It seems your daughter didn't give you much warning, leaving her grandson with you. A place has to be childproofed, for starters. Right? And it doesn't reflect on you," she was quick to add, putting a hand on his arm. "Not at all, but small children aren't like us. They bounce around, hurt themselves. A couple things jump out at me here." She tilted her head toward Lucky. "That aquarium looks just a bit tipsy. And have you given some thought to taping up that exposed wire?"

"That what?" Beau said.

"Would you mind if we had a look at his room?" she asked.

Before he could answer properly, she was gone, moving down the dim hall, looking into each of the three rooms. She disappeared not into the boy's bedroom but the patched-up little bathroom.

Vandermeer was still squatting next to Justin, asking him about school. Justin was putting on his terrified face, which was a gag of his, no doubt learned off all the horror films his grandmother had no doubt let him watch. Vandermeer looked up and around. "Mr. Garrett, how did Justin get this big bruise on his arm?"

"Ask *him*," Beau said. The bruise was Justin's fault, the kid sitting down on the road and refusing to budge the day Sharla had dumped him, having to be picked up bodily by the arm and airlifted to safety. Beau had since learned that arguing and bribery, or some combination of the two, worked better than manhandling, when it came to Justin. But that was then and this is now, and bruises heal, and the kid didn't seem to hold it against him in the end, and that was what mattered.

Mills came back from her snooping and started talking about furniture. Or lack of it. She talked about options, the services Beau could resort to for help, the funding he could apply for to get the place better equipped.

"What's wrong with that goddamn perfectly good mattress he's got?" Beau fired at her.

Vandermeer was standing now, looking at Garrett. Hard to say if he was smiling or sneering, he had that kind of face.

"And who sent you, anyway?" Beau asked. "That damned busybody Louise down the road?"

They didn't seem to hear him. Vandermeer was pointing out something to Mills when he thought Beau wasn't looking. The bruise on Justin's arm. She was pretending not to notice. And it all went downhill from there. With a lot more words than necessary, the lady made it clear she wanted to either plant someone in the home to supervise Beau's care of Justin, or else take the boy away for a day or two, all the while promising she wouldn't separate the family in the long run. She asked Beau how he felt about it all, but seemed to be telling him how he *should* feel about it all.

She seemed to think that whatever she did, she was doing him a favour by stepping in, insulting his wiring, taking control of his life. A buzzing was starting up in Beau's ears, like angry bees. Embarrassing to have his grubby bathroom looked at, being told he was a bad caretaker. He hated their soft talk, their sharp eyes. Most of all he hated how they seemed to think they loved Justin more than he did.

What he wanted was to have these two vanish and leave him and Justin to their life, which wasn't fancy but good enough, thank you. Better get his act together, though. Order a proper bed and dresser for the boy, stop swearing in front of him, be nicer. When Sharla came back she'd see Justin was better off with Beau. She could come visit, if she wanted, but this would be the kid's home.

But the more he argued with Vandermeer and Mills, the more they talked back. They buried him in words, and their long words began to make him feel ugly and unfit and small. He hated the sound of his own voice as he tried to talk back. He hated not knowing what half the words they used meant. He waved his huge arms as he argued, and he knew that his temper was only making things worse. He saw himself through their eyes, a cranky old man in a shitty old house who had no place taking care of a sweet little kid like Justin.

In a fit of anger he gave in. He told them they could take the boy and give him back to Sharla, if they could find her. Or Evvy, whose address he couldn't provide either. Or put him in foster care, if they thought someone else could do a better job of raising the kid than him. Because maybe she was right, and maybe they could. "Take his damn fish, too," he said.

They didn't take the fish, but paperwork was filled out and Beau signed what he had to sign. They told him about follow-up visits and how he would be kept informed every step of the way, none of which he believed. Finally, the boy's bags were packed as Beau stood outside on the back porch, preferring not to see it happen. The door opened and Justin went uncomplaining out and down the steps, holding Vandermeer's hand, looking back at Beau with big eyes. Vandermeer paused and said something to Justin about waving goodbye to his great-grandpa.

The boy waved. Beau couldn't bring himself to wave back. Then they were gone, and Beau remained on the porch a while. Already the doubts flooded in. Why hadn't he put up more of a fight? He went back to his stove, and found the porridge was cold. Two clean bowls sat waiting on the counter. He put them both away with a clatter.

* * *

By late afternoon Dion was still waiting for Bianca. He had checked his phone and gone through its call log, retrieving the number she had used to call him that day when he'd been checking into the Travelodge and she had invited him over. He called the number, expecting her voice, and instead got a man. The man's name was Bill Richmond, and once Bill heard Dion's question, he explained that this was his own phone, that he'd been sitting at Starbucks one evening when a pretty girl had asked to borrow it to make a call, as hers was out of juice. Yes, she matched Bianca's description, and no, Richmond knew nothing else about her.

Irritated by his own anxiety, Dion made up his mind that when Bianca returned, he would tell her he was going back to Joe Kent's for the remainder of March, a mere few days. He couldn't take the uncertainty of living with her. She had asked him why her coming and going mattered to him, and all he could say in answer was that he worried about her. And speaking of worry, here he was at the window again, scanning the street below, willing her to appear. The emptiness of the street got on his nerves, and he was struck by a chilling new thought. What if she didn't return at all, and he became a suspect in her disappearance?

Probably best to cut all ties with this nutcase. Pack his bags and go, erase all evidence of his ever having been here. Nobody knew of his live-in presence except the guy downstairs, Brad Gillespie. He didn't know Dion by name, and probably wasn't sharp enough to pick him out of a line-up, after their one brief meeting, if it ever came to that.

His notion about becoming a suspect wasn't altogether serious, but he wiped down the most obvious surfaces in the place, anyway. He left three hundred-dollar bills in an envelope under Bianca's pillow. He packed his bags in the car and went upstairs for a final look around. He placed the key she'd given him on the table, white rabbit and all. He wouldn't leave a goodbye note, as the key said it all. If Bianca really wanted closure, she had his number and could call him.

Coat on, he headed down the creaky attic stairs, leaving the house for the last time like a thief in the night. But on the bottom step he froze. Through the glass front door he saw two people talking on the porch. Brad Gillespie and a twiggy old woman. He considered retreating before they spied him, but too late. Their eyes had fixed on him through the glass.

"Crap," he muttered, and stepped outside.

The woman, who had to be at least eighty, was white-haired, dark-skinned, and wore faded jeans and an oversized flannel work shirt. He gave a friendly nod and tried to pass wordlessly by, but the woman stopped him with a grin. "Well, you must be Ms. Stone's beau!"

"No," he said, paused on the top step. "We're just friends. You haven't seen her around lately, have you?"

They hadn't. The woman said, "I'm the landlady, Fanny Riddle. I live down here on the main floor. I've seen you coming and going, but never got a chance to say hello."

He was done. Brad Gillespie might not be able to pick him out of a line-up, but this woman had his face memorized. He could see it in her eyes.

"Are you staying long, Mr. …?" she said.

"Dion," he said. "Cal."

This was about money, he was thinking. About the local tenancy laws, and his breaking of them by living here without her permission. But before he could explain that he had only stayed over a few nights, and was actually leaving today, she interrupted with a mystifying statement. "Brad here says he's not good with hammers," she said, placing a hand on Gillespie's narrow chest like he was a family pet while directing a bright smile at Dion. "So I was just hoping, you know, the lattice here. But that's all right. I had to ask." Apparently forgiven, Dion thanked his lucky stars and turned to go. "There's also the weeds," the landlady said. "A hell of a lot of weeds, and the girl isn't up for it, either."

He murmured an apology, gave the politest nod he could manage, and went on his way.

He needed groceries for the next few days. He thought about Bianca as he drove to the supermarket, the photo he'd snapped of her the day they'd walked through the park. Just a sidelong shot of her turning away, but he should frame it and stick it on his desk for all the world to see. Especially JD. Thoughts of JD distracted him as he shopped. He'd been replaying their last conversation since he'd walked away from it, her insinuation that he was responsible for the death of Kenny Poole.

She was right, he was. Even if he hadn't personally squeezed the trigger, he had ended that man's life. Back in his car, pulling away from the curb, he sensed something dark on the periphery of his vision. The something came dangerously close to becoming a fender-bender. He cursed himself for letting his mind wander, pulling out without shoulder checking to see the grey sedan approaching.

Not that he was fully at fault, as the sedan must have been speeding. There was a moment of awkwardness as he waited for the car to shoot by and the car waited for him to pull out. He steered into traffic and lifted a hand in thanks as the driver fell in behind him. The evening sun glared as he turned down Lonsdale facing the waterfront. Hard to see. Even with the visor slapped down and sunglasses slipped on he felt like he was running blind, and that, for sure, couldn't be good.

TWENTY-TWO

STICKS AND STONES

March 29

THE DAY AFTER BEAU had been hoodwinked into letting the Ministry kidnap his grandson, his foolish decision wouldn't leave him be. It was all he could think about. How could he have let perfect strangers take the kid? Hadn't he heard the horror stories? Fake ID, children going to the highest bidder? He almost called the cops but then thought better of it. He would do some investigations of his own first. He picked up his phone receiver and made a call.

The call didn't go well. The machine on the Ministry's end started gabbing instructions at him, saying press this for this and that for that, and when he'd pressed this or that there were only more instructions, and finally he hung up in anger.

He went for a walk down Paradise Road, heavy and slow. It was all for the best, he figured, not having Justin to worry about all the time. His fears were silly. There was no fake ID, no highest bidder. They were real government types, and Vandermeer would track down Sharla or Evvy, stick the kid back into their care, and Beau could dust his hands of it all. Never see any of them again, and good riddance.

He came to the view that had once been his goal, and found the white fence was still there, but all the whirly garbage was gone. There was a real estate sign up instead. The place was nothing but bad memories, but he told himself to stop fretting about it.

What was done was done.

He looked at the distant ocean and tried to call up the best days of his life. Hot sand and the smell of suntan lotion on Evvy's skin. But it wouldn't come back to him. Everything was different. The view looked flat. Dull. The air smelled dirty.

He returned to the house, finding the road had grown steeper since he'd last walked it. At home the answering machine was blinking, but he had never cottoned on to the gizmo and how it worked. He pressed a button and heard nothing but a hiss.

He tried phoning the Ministry again. This time he paid attention better, and pressed the right buttons at the right time, and somehow got Mills on the line. Except it wasn't really her, just her recorded voice telling him to leave a message and she'd get right back to him.

He spoke loud and clear into the phone. "I want to know where my goddamn grandson is. Call me."

He hung up hard, damp with the effort.

She didn't call back, and as an hour ticked by, he made up his mind to take the bus downtown, find the building, and prove to himself that Mills and Vandermeer were real people. And once there he'd talk to Mills and tell her he'd changed his mind. He wanted Justin back.

He found the bus schedule, and with shaking hands packed a sandwich and set out. It was a cold, cloudy day. He made it down the long hill without Justin tagging along. He stood at the bus stop without Justin yapping gibberish at his side. He climbed aboard the bus, and paid his fare, and sat down, without Justin yelling that he wanted the window seat. He rode downtown without Justin talking about every dog, car, cloud, and pedestrian that passed.

The bus driver had looked at the address on Mills's business card, and promised to tell Beau which stop to get off at. When the stop came the driver opened the door and pointed the way for Beau. That building there, across the street.

Beau got off the bus and crossed the street in the middle of the block, cane out to bring the cars to a squealing stop to left and right. He entered the large building, and with some work got directions from a lady in the lobby who pointed out the elevator he needed to take for the fourth floor. Once there Beau walked down a hall to a threshold with the Ministry's long title printed on it. Inside was another desk, and he told the woman who sat there that he wanted to see Anne Mills.

He was told Mills wasn't available, but the other worker on the file, Curtis Vandermeer, was in. "What time is your appointment?" she asked.

"Now," he told her.

She blinked at him. She tapped at her machine, saying, "Your name, sir?"

"Beauregard," Beau said. "Garrett."

"I don't have you down for an appointment, Mr. Garrett. But one moment."

It took a lot longer than a moment for her to return with Vandermeer. The man looked pleased to see Beau, saying, "This is kind of a surprise, sir. We've been trying to reach you. Well, come on down to my office, then. Let's talk."

Beau wasn't as pleased to see Vandermeer as Vandermeer seemed pleased to see him. They walked into a boxy little space made up of half walls. Vandermeer offered Beau a chair, but Beau wasn't here to sit and talk about the weather. "I come to see my grandson," he said, in his most reasonable voice. Low and respectful, fit for church.

Vandermeer put on a sad face and started to talk in figure eights, much like yesterday. "And, Mr. Garrett, let me say that your concerns are perfectly valid," he finished. There had been a lot of words thrown at him, but Beau got the gist. He was being told no. "I can assure you," Vandermeer said, "... scrupulously screened ... give you some of the particulars ... put your mind at ease ... was trying to get in touch ... interim order ... until such time ... place him with his family ... can't at this exact time release —"

"I don't care about your interim orders," Beau shouted. "He's *my* great-grandson. I want to see him. I want to make sure he's *safe*. You hear me?"

Vandermeer's hands patted the air. "Would you please sit down and not shout, sir?"

Beau wasn't going to sit. He folded his hands on his cane and said, slowly and carefully, to make himself clear for the wart, "Where. Is. My. Great. *Grandson*?"

"As I've *just* said, Justin is in the very capable hands of foster parents, whose names I *cannot* divulge at this point. We do respect your bond with the child, but I have to reiterate …"

And reiterate Vandermeer did. The same words, but switched around fast like a fairground shyster. Beau raised his cane in warning. *Slow down and speak straight, or I'll swat you.* Vandermeer cowered, and Beau lowered the cane again quickly. Must cap his temper. Must stay reasonable.

But too late. Vandermeer's eyes were hard and his voice was dry and tight as he asked, "Are you threatening me, sir?"

He didn't wait for an answer but moved to the opening in the half wall, calling down the hall, "Janet, stand by, would you? We may have a problem here."

"I'm not *threatening* anyone," Beau grumbled. "All I want —"

"I think you should leave, Mr. Garrett. Now."

The lady from the desk and another man showed up, asking if everything was all right, if they should call security.

"I just want to see Justin," Beau said, reasonably. "Why can't you goddam people just bloody —"

"That's it, Janet, call security," the other man said. "Back off, Curt. He's obviously agitated."

"Put down your stick," Vandermeer said.

The demand was an outrage, as Beau's cane was planted firmly on the carpet. "How about I put it down on your backside," he suggested, lifting the cane and giving it a little nonthreatening shake. He was speaking nicely, and all he was doing was making a point, but he had to admit, later, it had been a bad choice of words.

The police showed up. Mills showed up. There was a lot of fuss and everyone treated him like he was a hornet's nest instead of a man looking for justice.

In the end he was driven home in a police car. The two cops in uniform who had brought him to his front door also went inside with him, whether he liked it or not, and the young blond cop who said her name was Constable Hart sat him down and lectured him for a bit.

Beau didn't listen, but sat with head hanging and pain raging through his marrow. His rescue mission had failed, and Justin was still out there, living with strangers. Probably scared out of his little wits.

Justin, Beau thought. What was this sick feeling in his belly that was just as bad as the pain in his joints? A flood of sour anger. He'd never been allowed to keep anything, ever. Pets, toys, friends, wife. Even his great-grandson, taken from him just when he was starting to feel all right. *You're not nice*, Evvy had said, like he was at fault for their break-up.

Why should I be nice? He almost said it aloud, as Constable Hart finished what she had to say and turned to leave. And the answer came to him as he closed the door behind her: *Because.*

In the silence of solitude Beau sat at his kitchen table, mouth wobbling at the corners like a big crybaby. What's done is done. No point crying over spilled milk. *Must try to be nicer*, he thought, but for the first time the idea had depth. He would see the boy again, some day, and he'd do better. He was starting to understand something. It was large and airy-fairy, but within his grasp. Something about cause and effect, and what goes around comes around. He was starting to take some of the blame, for once in his life. And just in time, too.

TWENTY-THREE

RIDDLES

March 31

DION WAS PLEASED to have put distance between himself and Bianca, even if it meant staying at Joe's for five more nights. The girl was out of sight and out of mind, he hoped. And now that he understood the nightmares weren't location based, but inside him, he had nowhere to run and might as well stay at Joe's as anywhere.

Now, at just past midnight, he was back on the lumpy basement sofa bed. The lights were out and the house was silent, Joe away at his bartending job. Dion expected the full-blown nightmare would be back soon. He was resigned to the dreams. He waited for them with sullen fatalism. Wherever he went and whatever he did, they would get him in the end. They'd dog him to the Harbourview and sleep walk him off the balcony to his death.

He switched on the light, picked up JD's lucid dreaming book again, and read through another chapter before tossing it aside. The writer was trying to tell him that he could wake up inside his dream, be aware he was dreaming, and take control. Fly, or whatever else he fancied. Even tackle his demons. Even win the fight. *As if.*

* * *

In the morning, back at work and between tasks, Dion punched Bianca Stone into PRIME, the police database, and other online inquiry systems. He'd given it a shot before, but now he included every spelling variation he could think of. Still no hits. He searched her name on the web. Nothing relevant at all.

He tried the online phone directories, narrowing down the regions to North Shore first, then West Vancouver. Then the Lower Mainland, with all the outlying districts. He went as far afield as Mission to the south and Squamish to the north before giving up.

Lot of Stones, but no Biancas. Lot of B. Stones, but none of the numbers he called gave him a Bianca, and calling them all would be impractical. He photocopied the "Stones" pages as a last resort and kept them in a folder in his desk.

He tried the local hospitals, asking about recent admittances. He didn't go so far as the morgue. Not yet. He sighed. He told himself it wasn't his concern. He could report her as a missing person, but they'd just file it under loopy and flag him for another fitness hearing.

He pushed her out of his thoughts and got back to his real job. But she just pushed her way back in, and he would see her gripping his hand, telling him she would never go back there. Yet she had.

When his workday was over he decided to swing around to her place once more. Likely she would have returned, and would either be there or would have left signs of being there. Maybe she'd left a note pinned to the door. Apologizing.

He parked on the street and climbed the steps of the Ridgeway home, and as he no longer had a key, he rang her doorbell. No answer. He tried Brad Gillespie's buzzer next. The man came down, again in his socks, and allowed him entry.

"Any sign of Bianca lately?" Dion asked as they climbed in tandem.

"Who?"

"Bianca," Dion said. "Upstairs. Bianca Stone."

Jesus, the distance between neighbours could be brutal. It was the same in high-rises, in Dion's experience. In the several years he had lived on the tenth floor of the Harbourview — his best years ever — he'd known most of the other tenants on that floor by sight, but had he ever said more than a brief hello, let alone learned their names?

"Oh," Gillespie replied, stopped by his door. "Her. No. Why?"

Dion explained how Bianca had taken off some days ago and hadn't returned, and that he was starting to worry. He went up and banged on the girl's door. No answer. He saw that Gillespie remained standing on the second floor landing, looking up. Hooked by mystery. Looking at him, Dion had to wonder. Whatever Bianca's troubles were elsewhere, maybe there was a more immediate threat within these very walls.

He called down, "Could we talk for a minute?"

Gillespie looked frightened. "In here? No. My place is a mess."

How many murders and abductions turned out to have been perpetrated by neighbours, friends, acquaintances? Too many. Dion pictured Bianca trussed and gagged in that man's closet. He would have to dig deeper, if only to cover off a possibility. But first he had to get through the edgy man's doorway. He tried putting Gillespie at ease with a boy's club grin as he joined him on the landing. "No problem. You should see my place."

You should see my place implied Dion's own place was even more of a mess. Which it wasn't. He kept his world neat as a pin. Always had, always would. With a reluctant not, Gillespie bought the roundabout lie and allowed him in.

The flat was bigger than Bianca's. Not so whimsically furnished, but nice enough, with music playing, something jazzy. There was no mess that he could see, so Gillespie had been bending the truth, too. "Please have a seat," he said.

Dion sat at the kitchen table. Centred on its surface were salt and pepper shakers and a small sprig of fake flowers in a vase and a plate of Peek Freans. He could hear nothing that set off alarm bells, no muffled thumps or cries. He couldn't smell bleach or blood or decay. Nothing but maybe a recently grilled cheese sandwich. "I was wondering if you could tell me what you know about Bianca," he began. "Have you spoken to her much? Has she ever told you where she works, where she's from, where her parents live? Anything like that, Brad?"

Gillespie's head tilted as though listening between the lines for an ulterior motive. "I don't know her at all," he said. "Just to see her. I keep to myself, basically. As does she."

"How long have you lived here?"

"Seven years."

"And how long has she lived upstairs?"

"She moved in last fall, I think. You should ask Mrs. Riddle. She's the landlady."

Dion gave himself a slap on the forehead. The landlady, of course. He'd wasted all morning searching the databanks when he should have headed straight to the one person who was sure to have Bianca's contact information on file. "Great idea," he said. "Thanks."

"You're welcome," Gillespie said.

But so coldly spoken that Dion sensed he wasn't welcome at all. "Is there a problem?"

"Yes, there's a problem." Gillespie's voice rose. "Weird things have been happening since you showed up. People lurking about, watching me. I don't like it. I feel vulnerable enough as it is."

Dion blinked. Lurkers? He scrolled back through the days and recalled the man on the opposite sidewalk, glancing up before walking past. The man in the parked car, too, supposedly checking his phone. And maybe other glimpses he had dismissed too readily.

He asked Gillespie about the stalker. Description, any theories about who he was, what he wanted? But Gillespie knew nothing. Dion suggested how to deal with further incidences, thanked him for his time, and went downstairs to talk to the landlady.

Luck was with him, and she was home. She was a lot friendlier than Gillespie, too.

"I'm with the North Shore RCMP," Dion told her, once invited inside. The ground floor was luxuriously large, compared to the upstairs units. But cluttered, as Mrs. Riddle had an evident fondness for *things*. Figurines on display stands, books overloading shelves, sprawling houseplants hogging space. Lacing the air was the sweet aroma of something baking. "Cinnamon buns," she told him, inviting him to have a seat on the sofa.

He didn't take up the offer, in part because the sofa was occupied by a calico cat on one end and a small brown dog on the other. The cat dozed but the dog was sitting upright, visibly alert, showing its teeth in what was by no means a smile.

Dion turned back to the landlady. "No, I'll just be a moment. I'm not here on police business, but am just hoping you could help me figure out how to contact Bianca, as she left without warning a few days ago, and I have no way to get in touch."

"Oh, yes?"

"As I told you before, I stayed with her for a few days. I was waiting for a vacancy to come up. But I've left now, back to other accommodations." A long story, but he felt he owed her an explanation. He told her as briefly as he could why he had been staying upstairs, leaving out the nightmare bits. "It was very generous of Bianca," he finished.

"Oh, yes," Mrs. Riddle repeated.

Dion was having trouble reading her. She seemed puzzled, and he wasn't sure why. Was it wariness? No, he was quite sure it wasn't that. "We should have asked your permission," he added. "I hope you don't mind."

Her brows arched up along with her smile. "You stay as long as you like," she said. "Long as there's no trouble in my house, I'm good with that. I don't know if you have much experience with hot water tanks?"

He hesitated. There it was again, another disconnected thought stream. Seemed everyone in the place was a little off-key. "Not much," he said. "I'm sure there's a simple explanation to where she's gone. Bianca, I mean. She seemed to be living part-time elsewhere, so there's that. But I can't help worrying, and I'm hoping you can help me out. When she moved in — I think Brad said last Fall — did Bianca fill in a tenant's agreement?"

Mrs. Riddle's puzzlement was back. Maybe it *was* wariness, which would hardly be surprising. As a land-lady she'd know all about privacy rights and the import-ance of not trampling them. He produced his wallet, showed his ID, proved he was with the police, and hoped she wouldn't know that frankly, without a warrant, who he was meant little. "If you could provide anything that gave some kind of contact number ..."

"I'm not keen on paperwork, myself," she said. "I've got a lifetime supply of documents, but could I find one particular piece of paper if you asked? No, sir, but you're welcome to wade through the boxes. For what

I need close at hand, I rely on this perfectly good filing cabinet." She tapped her temple. "As for tenancy agreements and such, my tenants and I are fine with the verbal. How do I end up with such good people? I post a big *For Rent* sign on the porch. I get a lot of inquiries, but no good fits. Then Brad comes along, and he's very nice, and I like him, and so he moves in. Same with Ms. Stone."

"Might lead to problems, I'd think," Dion said, recalling a few verbal contracts he'd seen dragged through court at no small cost to all parties.

"No problems at all," she declared. "Bit of a thing with the rock and roll at first, as Ms. Stone liked to play it loud, leaving Brad a little bit upset, but I spoke to her about it and she's kept it down since."

Dion could well imagine Bianca, in one of her manic phases, playing her music too loud. And her not-so-elegant ballerina moves across the floorboards would have resounded. "Have you talked to her much?" he asked, more or less fishing for information by now without high hopes of catching anything. Bianca had not once mentioned her landlady or how they got along.

"We haven't talked much at all," Mrs. Riddle said. "She's much like Brad upstairs, keeps to herself. Brad is mostly home, though, while Ms. Stone is forever out and about. I tried asking her to help out by raking up a few leaves in the yard when she first moved in, and she did her best, but soon flitted off. That's fine. She had better things to do, and I understand that. I'm old, you know. Not so interesting to young people. Nearly invisible, I sometimes feel."

She smiled good-naturedly, not invisible at all.

Dion remembered JD saying much the same thing last week when talking about the supposed old man in the park, and it occurred to him that the two of them would get along. And when it came to JD, that was saying a lot. "Any chance you can give me her actual move-in date?" he asked.

"Must have been October, November, somewhere in there. I remember because there were leaves everywhere. She took the rake and just tossed them from one place to another. Didn't get the concept much."

"How does she pay her rent? Cash, cheque?"

"She's paid up till end of April. Paid cash when she moved in."

Dion tried not to look shocked. "She paid in advance?"

"Otherwise she'd forget, she told me. And she didn't want to make me climb the steps to remind her, is what she said."

Hmm. "Is there anything else you can tell me, Mrs. Riddle? She didn't give you a contact number for friends, family, parents?"

The landlady pointed around at the mess of books, papers, plants, not a clear surface in sight. "I'm sure she did, and I'm sure it's in here somewhere. My daughters always come around wanting to tidy up, but I don't want them misplacing anything. If you give me your name and phone number, I'll call as soon as I find it."

Dion had little faith in her promise. "I'd appreciate that," he said, and gave her his card, thanking her for her time. While he was making his way to the door, there came a loud ping from down the hall. "That's my oven timer," she said. "Just you wait here a moment."

He waited as she fussed about in the kitchen, barred from following her by the little dog with the bared teeth. Mrs. Riddle returned and handed over a paper bag that Dion guessed contained fresh baked cinnamon rolls. He looked inside, saw he was correct, and gave her a polite if uncertain smile. "That's very kind of you."

"It's probably not difficult," she said. "Adjusting the temperature, I mean. I just keep scalding myself! Who needs water coming out of the tap hot enough to boil an egg? I'd do it myself, but I can't get down on my hands and knees so easy these days, and the instructions are so small."

Maybe her thoughts weren't so disconnected as Dion had believed. She had been leading up to this moment with planning and precision, and the baked goods were only to seal the deal. He followed her to the basement and spent some minutes figuring out how to adjust the temperature on her hot water tank.

"Don't make it ice cold, either," she said, standing nearby with the dog at her heels.

"That should be about right." He stood, dusting off his hands. "You've got my number. Just let me know if you need it tweaked."

On leaving the house — to the small dog's victory yap — he noticed a dark-grey sedan idling by the curb, several vehicles down from his own. The same car as before, no doubt about it. Gillespie's spook, maybe. Nothing to do with him. He headed over with intentions of checking out the driver and getting the tag number, for Brad's sake, but the car pulled out and cruised away as he approached. A *4* and an *X* was all he caught of the plate, and the driver was little but a silhouette and an essence: a large man with hair in a ponytail.

Back in Joe Kent's basement, Dion pulled a cinnamon bun in half, stuffed in a mouthful, and sat down to read chapter three on lucid dreaming.

* * *

Constable Lil Hart approached Leith at his desk. "Hey, Dave," she said. "Something I should bring to your attention."

She dropped into a chair, weighty in patrol gear. "Yesterday I was called to a disturbance in the government building. Old guy upset about his great-grandson being taken into custody, making threats at social workers, shouting and waving his fists. Wasn't a big deal. We took him home, gave him a good talk. He seemed compliant. We warned him that his name's on file, so he'd better be good, and left. I'm just telling you because he lives on Paradise Road, a couple kilometres up from where Lawrence Follick was killed. Thought I'd point it out."

"Name?" Leith said.

"Garrett. Here's his ID."

Leith looked at the printout of the personal identification card Hart had supplied. The name was spelled G-a-r-r-e-t-t, and there was nobody on the Follick homicide file by that name. There was, however, Leith seemed to recall, a *Garrod*.

The man's face on the page was jowly and age-battered. People having their ID shots taken were told not to smile for the camera. Didn't look like that would be a huge challenge for Beauregard Garrett.

"Unlikely he's your guy, though," Hart was saying. "He's quite disabled. Walks with a cane."

"Thanks, Lil," Leith said, and waved her away. Only when she'd left the room and he was reaching for his coffee cup did her last words sink in. He grabbed the printout and stared at the grainy black-and-white image, hardly larger than a postage stamp. "Holy crap."

Maybe — just maybe — their U.M. finally had a face.

TWENTY-FOUR

BLUR

March 31

LEITH SHARED WITH the team the news Hart had dropped on him. He also produced Beauregard Garrett's criminal record from way back in the '70s. Just one conviction, but it showed what kind of guy he was. Assault causing bodily harm. Reading between the lines of the file, Leith had learned that Garrett had lost patience with his daughter, Sharla Garrett, and smacked her across the room, causing bruises and a dislocated wrist.

Impatience. Anger. Lashing out. The connections were there.

Mike Bosko was consulted. He agreed that Garrett should be brought in, but not before a thorough review of the file. Interview Ministry staff about the disturbance and get it down in detail. Try to get Garrett's photo ID enhanced and enlarged, and show it to Brando Reese, see if it rings a bell. Once all that was done, then coordinate an arrest. Make double sure Garrett under-stands his rights. Then see what he has to say for himself.

* * *

Dion drew the Ministry short stick. He drove to the government building on Esplanade and took statements from several social workers and support staff. They told him about the elderly client, Beauregard Garrett, who had come in without an appointment and thrown his weight around. They answered Dion's questions about Garrett's size and apparent physical condition. Did they feel he was capable of doing serious injury if it came to a fight? What exactly had stopped the man from lashing out? What did Garrett say during the incident, as best they could recall?

With answers in hand, he drove back toward the de-tachment. On the way he suspected he was being fol-lowed. A dark sedan, a newer model Ford. He pulled over on Esplanade and idled. The Ford, several cars behind him, did likewise. Dion signalled and rejoined traffic. The Ford did, too.

He thought of the dark-grey sedan he'd nearly side-swiped. And the other dark-grey sedan parked outside Bianca's place. And the man on the street he'd seen look-ing up before walking on by. Maybe Gillespie was only half right; there was a lurker on Ridgeway, but that lurk-er wasn't interested in him.

Turning north on Lonsdale, Dion pulled into a paral-lel parking slot. The sedan zipped past without slowing, and the driver, that familiar profile of a stocky male with a ponytail, didn't glance his way. Dion squinted at the plate and managed to add a nine to his previous capture of 4 and X, enough to try a VIN search.

But why bother? He swore out loud. He knew an undercover cop when he saw one. Had they been watching him at Bianca's place, too? Was this about her disappearance, or was this about his own crime? Or neither? He sat thinking about his only real enemy, the team of internal investigators he believed were piece by piece constructing a case against him, with tips fed to them by Dave Leith and Mike Bosko.

He watched the Ford proceed up Lonsdale until it was lost in traffic. As it disappeared he noticed the time. Past noon, and even fugitives had to eat. A text blinged on his phone clipped to the dashboard, and he glanced at the message. JD: Want to do lunch? And a dinosaur emoji.

The initial spike of relief he felt flattened into doubt. Since when did JD send emojis? And when was the last time she had invited him for lunch? Why was she being so nice all of a sudden, and moments after a surveillance car had been nipping at his heels? He could map out the progression of her attitude toward him. She'd gone cold as she'd learned of his crime, keeping him at arm's length. But now she had been recruited to chum up to him.

As if he'd fall for it.

He left the text unanswered.

He was still thinking about Bianca, mining his memory for clues as to who she was and where she'd gone. For such an independent woman, she still needed lessons on basic kitchen skills. She must have been living alone for a short while, then. Maybe recently sprung from a bad relationship that she didn't want to talk about. Maybe her night shift was really just her going back to her ex, trying to make it work. He thought about her affection and her anger, her moods swivelling like a weather vane in a storm. There were at least two Biancas, he decided. And he'd managed to lose them both.

* * *

After lunch in a downtown bistro, he was on his way back to work, forgetting to watch for lurking sedans. In the office he sought help from a colleague, received a tutorial on the department's latest facial composite software, and was left alone to try bringing Bianca to life on the screen. But though she remained vivid in his mind, she was impossible to digitally reproduce. Too flighty, too mobile for the program to handle.

Back at his desk, he tried his hand at capturing her with pencil and paper. Time slipped by, and he was busy sketching a third try when somebody behind him hooted a laugh and said, "What the hell is *that*?"

He rotated his chair to block JD's view, but she rotated with him. He misjudged, rotated the wrong way, and found her waiting to seize the drawing. She held the picture at arm's length for viewing, and laughed again.

He knew she was laughing at his artistic skills, and could hardly blame her. Instead of his lovely Bianca, he had drawn the Pillsbury Doughboy's evil twin, with wild curly hair and a demonic grin.

He rose and seized the paper back from her, balled it up, and dunked it into the waste bin. He started to explain his reason for the sketch, but JD stopped him. "No more bull-shit," she said. "I don't know what's going on with you, but I've had enough. Get your coat. It's walk-and-talk time."

* * *

The only photograph Dion had of Bianca he had snapped with his phone as she'd been turning away. It seemed he was good at taking pictures of people's backsides or shoes, and not much more. He wasn't sure why he both-ered, but he had a collection of such fails on his comput-er. A few of Kate, one of Leith, one of Mike Bosko way down at the end of the hall, just a blurry blob talking to some other blobs. He also had a couple of JD that she never knew he'd taken and he prayed she never would.

Should delete the whole folder, but he couldn't bring himself to do it.

"No, I don't have a good shot of her," he said, as he and JD walked and talked. "That's why I was trying to sketch a composite."

"I get that. But really? A mysterious girl you hardly know, who slips in and out of your life without warning and tells you nothing of her background, takes off for a day or two? Aren't you being a little antsy?"

"It's a lot more than a day or two," he said. "It's been over a week. And sure, she's an adult, but if you ask me, she's more like a missing child. So yes, I'm antsy."

"Then why not make a report?"

"Because they'd laugh at me. Just like you are."

"So what? You have something against being laughed at? Laughter is good. The only reason I'm not laughing right now is I have a toothache."

Dion saw it was true; she'd been rubbing her lower jaw all morning. "Then go to a dentist."

"I don't like dentists."

"You prefer pain?"

She was silent a moment, as if seriously considering the question. She seemed to also be considering his face, as if making some connection he wasn't sure he liked. "Which pain is worse, that's the thing," she said. "But yes, Mom, I'll make an appointment. Anyway, I bet you're worrying your head for nothing, and she's home right now, waiting for you. You say it's on Ridgeway? That's an easy walk. Let's go say hi."

"No. Like I told you, I no longer live there. I left my key on her table."

"Then we'll get the key from the landlady. You said she's nice."

"Still no."

"Why?"

"We're on duty."

"We're investigating a missing person."

* * *

They walked to the house on Ridgeway and climbed the stairs. "I like this place," JD said. "And look at you, pretty boy."

The last was directed at the cat she was stopping to pet, the landlady's calico.

"You'd like Mrs. Riddle," Dion told her. "You'd get along."

"Mrs. Riddle?"

"She owns the place. That's her cat."

"Speaking of landlords," JD said, as they stepped onto the porch. "Tomorrow's April first. Rent day. From what you've said, sounds like your girlfriend isn't computerized, so no e-transfers, so she'll pay cash or cheque. You can lie in wait and pounce on her when she comes to pay."

"Mrs. Riddle said she's paid up till the end of April," Dion said. He had rung Bianca's doorbell, received no answer, and now tried the landlady's.

JD raised her brows. "Who pays their rent in advance except millionaires?"

"Bianca is no millionaire, but she's got connections of some sort. I just can't figure out what they are. I'm thinking she meets up with a married guy. For pay. She wants out of the arrangement, though. She's miserable. That's what worries me."

From behind the door came the yapping of a dog. The door opened and the landlady stood there with the yapper in her arms, telling the animal to shush. The dog growled at Dion but listened up as JD scolded it. "You be nice, now. We're the good guys."

Mrs. Riddle smiled at Dion first, then JD, then Dion again, and told him the water was perfect now, not too hot, not too cold, and he ought to be a plumber. He told her the cinnamon buns were fabulous, best he'd ever had. She asked if he wanted more. He thanked her and said no, he was just here to check on Bianca. Was there any chance he could borrow the key and have a look around upstairs?

Mrs. Riddle, who probably should have refused entry, went and got the key.

"Thanks," Dion said. "Just a quick look, and I'll bring it right back."

JD remarked that he seemed awfully cozy with the landlady, as he unlocked the front door to the upstairs suites. "That's all her doing," he assured her. "Not mine." They climbed to the third floor, and he let himself into Bianca's empty flat. A quick look around the bathroom and bedroom told him nothing had been touched. He checked the fridge and found the same carton of milk, near empty and now gone sour, the same green onions wilting in the crisper.

"So did you sleep with her?" JD called, as she snooped around the bedroom.

"Yes," he called back. It was only true in the literal sense, but he wasn't about to tell her so. She leaned against the kitchen door jamb as he poured the milk down the drain and rinsed the container. "What's funny?" she said.

He was still smirking at the ingenuity of his half-truth. And since she'd taken the liberty of asking him, he directed the question back at her. "Are you sleeping with the pilot?"

"Yes," she said, and when he glanced over he saw the *yes* was no half-truth. She was sleeping with the pilot in every sense of the word.

He became suddenly irate. He was tired of JD, tired of Bianca, tired of himself. He turned on her so they were eye to eye and said, "You always look at me like that. Like I've done something wrong. What are you thinking I've done, JD? You really think I killed Ken? Maybe Brooke, too?"

In February Looch's widow, Brooke, had been found dead along the banks of the Fraser, apparently a drug overdose. Soon afterward Constable Ken Poole had killed himself. Two deaths that seemed unrelated but that Dion knew were linked to his own crime in a way he could only guess at. It all sourced back to his killing of Kelley Stouffer that night in Surrey. Maybe Brooke knew, and maybe she'd talked, and maybe that was why undercovers were circling like a lariat.

Or could be the loose end was finally tied, and the girl with pink hair had spoken up. The memory of her would haunt him to his deathbed. In the darkness he had looked up and seen her straddling her dirt bike on the dunes above. She'd been watching him struggle to bury Stouffer in that dreadful makeshift grave while Looch stood by, probably crying to Brooke on his phone, because for all his street smarts, Looch could be such a baby.

Should have cut their losses right then, when they knew they'd been made. Should have let the dirt biker go her way. Should have fessed up and faced the consequences. They would have been treated with relative leniency, he knew. Compared to what had befallen them both.

Instead of surrender, he had chased after the girl in his car, and in an unlit intersection on the lonely, pitch-black backroads of Surrey — what were the chances? — he had been T-boned by a kid in a hotrod. Instant karma. A blast from God for what he'd done to Stouffer and what he planned to do to the pink-haired girl when he caught her. The hot-rodder and Looch both died on the scene. There were days Dion wished he hadn't survived.

Two years later, it seemed the pink-haired girl had never spoken up. But neither had she gone away. All she'd done was mutate. She had become the grit in his eye, the cocoon in his nightmares, and every young woman with pink hair he passed on the street.

He realized now, standing in this empty apartment with dust motes swimming in the sunlight and his own question hanging in the air, that he was tired of the whole stinking charade. He was tired of faking it every moment of every day, and he believed that all JD had to do was say the word, and he would break down and tell her everything. All she had to do was ask.

* * *

JD absorbed his question without betraying surprise. Masking surprise no matter what a suspect sprang on her was a skill she'd mastered on the job. At the moment she was trying to mask her admiration, too. For his parkour moves — so to speak — the way he bounded from ledge to ledge to avoid the spotlight, until when she least expected it he landed square on his feet before her and asked point blank if she thought he had committed murder.

Well, yes, she reflected. *I think maybe you killed Ken, and Brooke, too. Why? To protect your secrets.* She supposed she should be afraid of him, if she believed him capable of tracking down and murdering his dead friend's widow, and of then visiting Ken Poole in his apartment, shooting Ken's brains out and contriving to make it look like a suicide. If she wasn't afraid of someone who would go to those lengths to protect his secrets, what was she afraid of?

"Well," he said. He looked feverish and shaky as he pressed her for a verdict. "You think I'm a killer?"

"Well," she said, when the silence had drawn out too long. "Are you?"

TWENTY-FIVE

SHELTER

April 1

BEAU WAS MIGHTY uncomfortable. Interrogation rooms hadn't changed much over the years. And neither had the interrogators. Still big, still dense, still thinking they could get you to talk by pretending to be nice. This one, a blond and bearded guy who called himself Dave, sat hunched over across from him and spoke slowly, seriously, as though Beau was brick stupid, saying this was about inquiries into a homicide on Paradise Road.

Homicide, Beau knew, was just a dressed-up word for murder.

"If you have any worries about talking to me, any at all," said Dave, "you can walk out that door. You're not being charged with anything, but I'd just like to fill in your background a little bit. It's a process of elimination that we go through with everybody. First of all, you're retired, Mr. Garrett?"

"Look at me," Beau said. "'Course I'm retired."

"What's your skill set? What did you do for a living before retirement, sir?"

Beau didn't like questions. He didn't like talking about himself or his rotten past. He let the cop named Dave drag it out of him in bits and pieces, the different labouring jobs he'd done over the years, his marriage, his kid, his divorce. Dave finagled him into speaking about the trouble he'd gotten into when younger, but it hardly mattered. It was all on record, anyway, time served, damage done.

Dave asked him about his arthritis and how it affected his day-to-day living.

"Not good," Garrett said.

Now Dave was full of sympathy, like the funeral home director who'd put Beau's parents to rest so many years ago, staring Beau down with false sorrow on both occasions, as Beau, self-sufficient by then, dry-eyed and just wanting to get the thing over with, handed across the cheques. Now Dave was asking about Justin and the hullabaloo at the Ministry office, wanting to hear Beau's side of the story.

"Thought this was about some homicide," Beau said.

"It's the big picture," Dave said, and made a globe shape in the air with his hands.

Beau wondered if telling Dave his side of the story, about the trickery on the part of the Ministry, might help him get Justin back. He decided he had nothing to lose, and went about setting the record straight. He hadn't attacked anybody, he told Dave. There was no call for the cops to come around like they did and lecture him like he was a four-year-old. Vandermeer was a coward who had no right taking Justin in the first place, an action that amounted to kidnapping, in Beau's books. And now they wouldn't let him see Justin. That's all he wanted, just to see him, make sure he's okay.

Dave told him he'd do his best to arrange for a visit with the boy, but Beau didn't believe a word of it. Not from that man, not in this room.

There were no more questions about Justin. Now Dave was asking Beau about the dead man and his whirligigs, the pink house, Paradise Road.

Beau was good at lying. He had lied and stepped around the truth and stayed mum ever since he was a tot, just like his parents did. At first it was just the way of the world. Then it became survival. Then as he got older it was the easiest path to getting things he wanted. Nowadays he lied just to stay clear of complications. He lied like he breathed, without thought or shame or fear. He told this grave-faced policeman that he didn't know any Follick and hadn't paid heed to any pink house or whirly-whatevers, and of course he knew the road. He lived on the road. He used to walk that road all the time, before the arthritis made it damn near impossible. Now he walked the road only if he had to get down to the bus stop to go fetch his groceries or pills, is all, and didn't want to pay for a taxi.

"Well, you heard about Mr. Follick's murder, didn't you?" Dave asked.

"No."

"You don't watch the TV, read the paper, listen to the radio?"

"I listen to the radio," Beau said. "Hear all kinds of murder. Don't pay much attention."

The big blond cop was getting a sore back from hunching forward. He sat back and rolled his shoulders, saying, "You want some coffee, Mr. Garrett? We could take a bit of a break."

"No," Beau said. And as an afterthought, "Thank you anyhow."

So the questions continued. "Did you and Justin go see the magic show, the one last week at Parkgate?"

"Magic what?"

"The magic show in the park, Mr. Garrett. Tricks, acts. You didn't go?"

"Didn't go," Beau said. "Don't know what you're talking about."

Dave ignored him for a bit, fooling around on his phone as everyone did these days. Then he gazed at Beau for a long moment. Then started all over again, same questions but not so nice. Beau knew this tactic, too. Dave was getting pushy, trying to rile him. But Beau was too smart to be riled. He knew how to look clueless, pretend like he didn't know what the hell the guy was going on about.

Must have been an hour later or so he was released. He was given a ride home, which was good, as his body was hurting all over. More than likely they'd piss off and leave him alone now, he expected. He said so, more or less, to the cop who dropped him off, watched the car launch away, and turned to haul himself inside. A handful of pills and his easy chair were about all he could face right now. Maybe a whole bottle of pills would be best.

But no. Everyone was giving him the runaround when it came to Justin, like they were hiding something. He couldn't die in peace till he knew the brat was okay, because as much as he wanted not to give a damn about any of it, he did just that. Gave a damn.

* * *

JD received Leith's text, advising that Beau Garrett would not admit to being at the magic show, and that she should go interview the great-grandson, Justin. Hopefully, the kid would put a lie to Garrett's denial.

"Talk about guilty until proven innocent," she said to Dion, who had volunteered to join her. As they made their way to the parkade, she was wondering if and when they would talk further about his bombshell disclosure. Neither of them had spoken much since then. Awkward, like workmates after a drunken staff party where they'd both made fools of themselves.

She had asked him, yesterday, standing there in his girlfriend's apartment, *Well, are you?*

At first he had looked bewildered, then angry, then ragged, like he'd been beaten up and kicked to the curb. He'd also looked so close to tears that JD's heart had melted, and he'd gone on to tell her in a broken voice that he hadn't killed Brooke, hadn't killed Ken, but he had taken part in a murder.

"What do you mean, you took part?" JD had asked.

And they'd sat down so he could tell her a story about driving home from a barbecue at Looch Ferraro's parents' place in Abbotsford. Two years ago, Canada Day, coming through Surrey on the border with Cloverdale at sometime past midnight, seeing Kelley Stouffer standing on the side of the road, talking to a kid. Kelley Stouffer, who had gone off the radar and was thought to be living in the States. JD knew who Stouffer was. A man who had gotten away with the rape and murder of his young stepdaughter. Stouffer, who everyone knew was guilty without being able to prove it. A man who had walked.

Dion explained how he and Looch had circled back, checking out the situation. Saw the kid was gone but confronted the man, anyway. The argument took place in the driveway of a rural property Dion wouldn't be able to locate now for the life of him. Near an old shed or garage. Things had gotten out of hand pretty fast, he admitted, and yes, Stouffer ended up dead in the brawl. They had driven him to a nearby gravel pit, and they might have buried their troubles along with the body, except there was a witness. A girl with pink hair on a dirt bike. In chasing after her, there had been the crash, the coma.

Without filling in the details, Dion fast-forwarded his story to how he guessed Brooke and Ken had gotten involved. Once the body was in the gravel pit and while he was working hard at burying it, Looch had made a furtive call to Brooke, telling her what had happened. "Is my guess," Dion had clarified, keeping the record straight. "Because I looked back and saw his face was lit up, just for a second. Like he'd been checking his phone. I asked him what he was doing. 'Nothing,' he says."

JD had interrupted. "Why do you think he called her?"

"Why did Looch call Brooke and tell her something we'd sworn to keep to ourselves? Because he was scared and Brooke always made him feel better, and he's a fucking idiot."

Was a fucking idiot, JD had silently corrected.

The grim story went on. For some reason, if Brooke had knowledge that Looch and Dion had committed a murder, she'd kept that knowledge to herself for nearly two years after Looch's funeral. Maybe some residual loyalty, wanting to protect Looch's closest friend who had so unfairly survived the rollover. For whatever reason — maybe it was the unfairness itself — she'd changed her mind around Christmas time and decided to rat out Dion. And would have done so except Kenny Poole had got wind of the threat and took steps to cut it off at the pass. Drastic steps.

Dion had closed with a caveat, that how and why Brooke and Kenny had died was only guesswork on his part. "But I'm pretty sure that's how it all went down."

JD thought the theory sounded credible, except for one sticking point. "So Kenny would *kill* for you?"

The blush that crept up Dion's neck confirmed what she had guessed for years. Kenny had never admitted to being gay, but he was. And maybe he had loved Cal in the most tragic, unrequited way. Maybe he'd even given up his life for him.

With his terrible story told, Dion had not seemed set free by the truth. He was still in the ring and clinging to the ropes, but he looked like he was about to buckle.

"You wanted the truth," he told her, bitterly. "You got it. What are you going to do about it?"

JD considered pressing him on the all-important piece he had left out entirely: which of them, himself or Looch, had actually physically killed Kelley Stouffer. But maybe she would leave it for another day.

"What do you *want* me to do about it?"

"The only thing you can do now," he answered, chin up in challenge. "Take it to Bosko. Go ahead. I'm ready."

"Not now," she'd said. "I'll think about it. I'll let you know what I decide before I do anything."

She saw it wasn't the answer he'd been expecting. She saw as well that it worried him. "Don't think too long," he had warned. She understood his concern, and was touched. The longer she wavered, the more of an aider and abettor she'd become.

A day later she still hadn't turned him in. And though they hadn't referred back to yesterday's conversation and were avoiding eye contact, they tended to stand a little closer, as if sharing an umbrella.

The foster home they arrived at looked to JD like a good, safe place. The little boy they met there was cute and outwardly happy, but as she chatted with him, JD found Justin was not hugely coherent. Arrangements were made then to take him to the site of the now-shuttered magic show, in hopes that being on location would prove helpful.

With a woman from the Ministry accompanying them, they drove to the park. They left the car and as a group walked down the path, under overcast skies, toward where the magic show had been so bright and lively just days ago. With the Ministry staffer trailing out of earshot, it occurred to JD with a wave of melancholy that anyone seeing her and Dion and the child from afar would think they were just an ordinary family out for a walk. But no, they were two cops, with a very small witness, doing their best to throw an old man in jail.

The park was a crime scene, but all signs of the crime were gone, not a flutter of perimeter tape remaining. The drinking fountain had been sanitized to pristine condition and was once again gaily offering water to passersby. JD glanced at Dion and saw he was probably thinking the same as her; he'd walk a mile rather than drink that water.

Building rapport with Justin was JD's job. She held the boy's hand and chatted with him about the last time he'd visited this place, and soon enough she got what she was looking for, as he pointed out what he couldn't express so clearly in words. That's where the trailer had been, where he'd seen a woman sawed in half, and then she had a big snake that the kids were allowed to come up and touch if they wanted. No, he hadn't been with anybody he knew in the trailer during the show. So who had he come to the park with? "Gampa," he said. *Grandpa.* Where had Grandpa been when Justin was watching the magic unfold? Justin shrugged, but the extrapolation was a cinch. Grandpa had been waiting outside. Outside in the relatively quiet park, where he had every chance to assault a unicycle clown as the show was coming to an end.

When Justin had been delivered back to his foster home, JD and Dion returned to the detachment in time for the four o'clock briefing, where JD described to the team the walk in the park and how their suspect had been caught in a serious fib. Now all they had to do was nail him with murder.

* * *

Leith led the briefing, which was more of a brainstorming session. Beau Garrett hadn't admitted to anything, but Justin had supplied the ammunition they needed to keep hounding the man. Not the greatest ammunition, Leith realized, since Garrett would likely just shrug and say he'd forgotten. He was that kind of guy.

With no useful forensic evidence at hand, the team discussed ways to get Garrett to confess. What did they know about the man? He was anti-social, so they couldn't schmooze. Didn't seem susceptible to female charms, so he wouldn't be seduced with one of the prettier interrogators. His conscience seemed lacklustre and unmalleable, so guilt-tripping him wouldn't go far. He had no close siblings or parents to plead with him to come clean. The only carrot they could dangle would be Justin, but that would be unethical.

"What are this guy's vulnerabilities?" Leith had asked, open to suggestions.

Age, they came up with. Rheumatism. An inability to sprint if it came to a takedown. A marked abhorrence of folk art, clowns, and government employees. It was Jim Torr who finally put his finger on it, and it was so obvious, once said aloud, that Leith blushed that he hadn't thought of it himself.

"If he done what we think he done," Torr said, "That means he's one cranky dude. Freakin' easy to piss off, anyway."

Leith considered Torr's flash of brilliance. Garrett's crankiness was obvious enough, but taking advantage of it was the epiphany. "Close your notebooks," he told his team, trusted members who didn't need to be told twice. So far these were just loose thoughts, and he didn't want the strategy he had in mind going down in black and white until he could couch it in some kind of safe phraseology. "What we need to do," he mused, "is tickle that hair-trigger temper. Irk him. Get him to show his true colours. What if we sent someone over to question him again? It's got to be in a place he's comfortable. His own home, where he'll feel free to get nasty."

"Operation Aggravation," Paley said.

"Awesome," JD said. "Can I do it?"

Leith looked at her. Aside from her dark brows that could gather into a terrifying scowl, she wasn't much of a physical threat. "No. We need someone more Garrett's size."

Torr would have fit the bill, a big guy with muscles all over, but Leith suspected he was a tad too big and strong, even for a giant like Garrett to dare tackle. "I need someone who can piss him off enough to make him lash out. Someone he might feel is his match. I'm not saying we start a fistfight, but hopefully in anger he'll let something slip. Once he slips up we can maybe get a search warrant. I could talk to him again myself, but I've already played Mr. Nice Guy with him. He wouldn't buy it."

"What you need is somebody super irritating," JD said, and her thumb indicated Dion at her side. He seemed lost in a moody daydream, and either ignored or didn't notice the endorsement.

Leith eyed him and thought it over. From the day they'd met, in the backroom of a rustic coffee shop up north, irritation had festered between them. And followed through to this day.

Yes, he thought, in all truthfulness. *You're perfect.*

* * *

It took Dion a moment to put it together, why Leith was assigning him the star role. It should have been funny, but it wasn't. Might have been considered an honour, but it wasn't that, either. If anything, it was embarrassing. In his mind's eye he could see the guys joking about it afterward behind his back. *Cal the Human Irritant always gets his man.*

Stifling his depression, he spent the remainder of the day working out the logistics with Leith and the team. Tomorrow afternoon, wearing a wire, he would go pay Beau Garrett a visit. He would confront Garrett about his attendance at the magic show, and take it from there, needling and pissing off the suspect however he saw fit. Ad lib to your heart's content, as Leith put it.

But that was tomorrow. He signed off work now feeling edgy after what he'd stupidly, recklessly, self-destructively, done yesterday. He'd broken his own rule and talked. Only to JD, and not quite the whole truth, but enough to jail him, if she so chose. After his confession they had sat together in Bianca's attic, heads bowed, like mourners at a funeral. She had said she wasn't going to rat him out. Not yet, anyway.

What had he been thinking? And where was the sense of release he'd been hoping for, telling a friend? All he'd done was given JD the gift of guilty knowledge.

With a sigh he pushed the thoughts away. Tonight he would get drunk and celebrate being in his new apartment. It was move-in day at the Harbourview. Down on the third floor and on the shady side of the building, but it was still better than any other digs he'd had since his return from the north.

He had arranged a moving van to bring his furniture from storage, but not until the weekend. For now he would have nothing but a camping mattress and folding lawn chair, a portable stereo, and a bottle of Scotch. But he would make the most of it. Order pizza, play music, forget about the world and all its troubles in his clean, empty apartment.

He drove toward his new home, fully aware of the dark car that followed him. "See if I care," he told the car in his rear-view mirror. Same big undercover moron with a ponytail. What they expected to learn from all this tailing was beyond him. Maybe they had him bugged, too. Maybe they'd even bugged his new apartment. Fine, they could listen to his boom box all they wanted.

He parallel parked on the street and jogged across the plaza to the lobby entrance, duffel bag over his shoulder, stereo in hand, camping gear under an arm. He buzzed the resident manager and whistled a cheerful tune while he waited.

Key in hand, he rode the elevator up to third and walked down the quiet carpeted hallway to the door marked 313. Unlocked it for the first time and walked inside. Set down his gear and had a good look around. Empty little entrance hall, closet on one side with the accordion doors ajar. Bunch of free coat hangers. There was a bit of déjà vu of the first time he had moved in, up on the tenth floor, when he'd been a little bit younger and a whole lot happier. He stepped into the living room, a big open space smelling of lemon cleanser. The wall-to-wall carpet was nubby dark grey. Sliding glass doors onto a balcony let in muted light from an overcast sky. Kitchenette to one side, hallway to the other. Down the hall was a good-sized bedroom and a windowless bathroom.

He leaned against the bedroom doorway, looking at the floor and walls, imagining his furniture installed. Looking out the window, he found the view hardly spectacular, as it had been on the tenth, but nice enough.

He uncapped the whisky bottle he had brought and realized he'd forgotten to bring a glass. Drank straight from the bottle as he stood on the little balcony and thought about Bianca's horror at the idea of living in a high-rise. What if he fell? Maybe she was right. He thought how she seemed to love her attic flat, how she seemed to belong there. Yet didn't belong at all. What was that all about? He worried, too, about her losing the space. Rent was paid up till May, but after that how long would Mrs. Riddle wait before getting rid of all her things and letting the place out to somebody else? What if Bianca surfaced a month down the road and found the apartment she loved was gone?

The annoying thing about free spirits like Bianca was the chaos they left behind them as they went their merry way.

He phoned Mrs. Riddle. "I hate to be a pest, but has Bianca been around at all, do you know?"

Her answer disappointed him. "I haven't seen Ms. Stone at all."

Was it his imagination, or did the woman always say *Ms. Stone* with an uncalled-for emphasis? He plugged in his stereo and selected music with a driving beat to keep the thoughts from circling like black flies. Still, he couldn't shake the feeling that he was missing something fundamental when it came to the mystery of Bianca Stone.

TWENTY-SIX

PAIN

April 2

DION WAS RIGHT about his teammates finding humour in his assignment, but he was wrong thinking they'd only laugh behind his back. He put up with their ribbing as he got wired for sound, along with some last-minute advice on how to go about riling Beau Garrett. JD tossed a pack of Bubbalicious at him. "Nothing more aggravating that a gum-chewing butthead cop prying into your life."

Torr agreed. "And just when you've got him this close to punching you out, blow a bubble. The bubble will take him over the edge, guaranteed."

"I'm not blowing bubbles," Dion said, and turned to Leith, who was fussing over safety concerns and insisting he wear Kevlar.

"His MO is a *cane*," Dion objected.

"I don't care. You're wearing the vest."

Much of the conversation was lost in the din, though Dion caught snatches. Like Paley saying in an aside to Leith, "Remind me, Dave. Even if Garrett gets nasty and starts waving his cane around, what does it prove, besides our unfettered willingness to entrap senior citizens?"

"Like I mentioned a few times, I think, if nothing else, it'll give us leverage," Leith answered. "And don't forget Justin. We don't want Garrett getting custody of the boy. Best case, we get a full confession. It's the symptomatology of a blown gasket, Doug. One truth leads to another. And what do we risk, really?"

"Just one tin soldier," JD said.

Or maybe Dion had misheard her. The room was noisy and he was overheated, wearing the weighty Kevlar under his black leather car coat. But they were ready to move. He double-checked his audio, and they went over the game plan once more. There would be a support unit up the road, and the monitoring van below, both out of sight but ready to move in at any sign of distress. And all of it, in Dion's opinion, was overkill.

JD summed up the operation as "another of Dave's best laid plans," while slapping Leith on the shoulder. She was laughing and Leith was looking offended as Dion climbed into his car and slammed the door. He was to go in alone, giving Garrett the impression that it would be a fair fight, if a fight was what he wanted.

The support team was in place well before he arrived, so his appearance wouldn't coincide with an unusual spate of traffic on this remote hillside. It was eight forty-five in the morning, misty and cool. Garrett's house was a nice little bungalow with a glassed-in front porch. No fence, a gravelled driveway leading up to an old garage that was leaning slightly. Garage door open, no vehicle inside. The lot had been landscaped once, maybe, but the lilacs had gone leggy and the lawn had reverted to a wildflower meadow bisected by crumbly paving stones. Dion parked in the driveway and climbed the front steps. In his distraction earlier he had pocketted JD's Bubblicious, and now popped a piece in his mouth as he read the badly printed note taped to the front door's murky pane. Obeying, he walked around to the back of the house, stepped up onto the little wooden porch, and knocked once.

The man who opened the door must have been born with haywire genes. He stood a good three inches taller than Dion, and his hands were huge and knobby, his features ponderous. He seemed horrified, but Dion soon understood it wasn't horror and had nothing to do with his own presence. It was simple physical distress. The man was hurting.

"Beau Garrett? I'm Constable Dion. I'm with the RCMP. I have some questions for you, if that's okay. It's optional, but I'd appreciate just a few minutes of your time. We can talk here or we can go down to the detachment, it's up to you."

Garrett apparently had a third option in mind — that Dion could take himself straight to hell — but instead of saying so, the door widened and Dion was allowed to step inside.

It was a poor man's house. Old appliances, tatty wallpaper, everything practical and loveless. Orderly but dusty, and with an unpleasant smell of ripe garbage.

Garrett sat down heavily at a kitchen table, waving a hand at the other chair. "What's this all about? I already answered all his questions. Constable Dave's."

Dion sat and flipped open a notebook, then set a digital recorder on the table. "Are you okay with me taping this conversation, Beau? Can I call you Beau?"

"Please yourself," Garrett said. He grimaced, but the face he pulled had nothing to do with the cop or his recorder. "Bad day," he said, when Dion asked what was wrong. He rubbed a forearm as if trying to massage out an ache. "Just a damn bad day."

"How so? Did you hurt yourself?"

"Rheumatoid arthritis. Degenerative. Those are my pills there. Didn't do bugger-all last night."

Keeping an eye on the man, in case this was one of those *hey, look behind you* tricks, Dion went to the kitchen and picked up a bottle of over-the-counter anti-inflammatories. "This is all you take? Don't you have some kind of prescription?"

"Don't like doctors."

Well, pain was good. It would shorten Garrett's patience. Pelt him with questions, maybe throw in some snide remarks about this home being no place for a four-year-old, and Dion would have Garrett brandishing his cane in no time.

He got down to business. "So you told Corporal Dave Leith that you didn't go to the magic show down at the Parkside field on the twenty-fifth of March. We've got proof that that's not true. You were there with your great-grandson. So what's that all about?"

"Was I?" Garrett said. "Guess I must have forgot."

"You forgot? How many magic shows do you attend, Beau? So many that they all kind of blend together in your mind?"

Snarky, gum-chewing cop, giving his suspect the cold-eyed sneer.

"Maybe I didn't forget," Garrett said, with crushing indifference. "Maybe I just didn't want to fucking talk about it."

Listening and watching, already Dion knew the plan was going to fail. This old guy was immune to sarcasm and everything that went with it. He was in a kind of cold bubble of depression, and probably had been for years. "Why wouldn't you want to talk about it?"

A moment of silence before Garrett blared, "'Cause it hurts to talk. It hurts to draw breath and spit out the words. It hurts to goddam think. The less said, the sooner I was out of there."

"Got a garbage?" Dion asked.

"Under the sink."

Dion got rid of his chewing gum, then sat again. "What d'you know about the guy in the park who got pushed into a water fountain and died?"

Garrett shook his head, sign language for *no clue and who cares*.

"What d'you know about a man down the road here back in March who got the crap kicked out of him and died?"

Shrug.

"You lied about being at the magic show, and it was a pretty lame excuse. What else are you lying about? How am I going to trust anything you say, Beau?"

"I'm tired," Garrett said, and shut his eyes tight. His grimace deepened.

"You have quite a temper," Dion went on. "Showed up at the Ministry office and threatened a worker there 'cause he wouldn't give you what you wanted. Why did you do that? You really expect to get custody of a four-year-old by push and shove? You expect to get anywhere with the government with that kind of attitude? Just the opposite, Beau. You're proving you're the worst custodian on the planet."

Garrett's head swung back and forth. Eyes still closed, the words were doing nothing but bouncing off him like mild sleet. "Don't expect nothing," he said. "Nothing except death. Death will be a blessing, so why am I so afraid of dying?"

From one squeezed eyelid a tear sprang and coursed its way down the creases of the oversized face. Then the lids opened and Garrett was glaring across the table with what looked like surprise and anger. "You still here?"

Dion considered his options. From what little he knew of Garrett, he guessed the great-grandson was the best button to push. "I mean, forget about the fact that you fly off the handle without provocation," he scolded. "Look at this place." Cobwebs above, grime on the windows, an almost palpable layer of dust underfoot. "Ever hear of a vacuum cleaner?"

Garrett seemed to be listening with an effort, as if the nagging was distorted through a filter. Finally, he said, "Yes, I've heard of a vacuum cleaner. It's broken, like everything else around here. Clogged. I could fix it, but my hands hurt. You know what it's like to have hurtin' hands? Have you got any idea, you smarmy little shit?"

Progress. Still, the conversation wasn't gathering the momentum Dion had hoped for. He looked toward the kitchen sink, and it was dripping. All quiet here but for that irregular *plop, plop*. He could see how a four-year-old would brighten the place, bring life indoors. He could also see the vacuum cleaner in question. It was parked in a corner of the living room, an old Electrolux, and with nothing better to do, he went and brought it to the kitchen where he could inspect the problem, as he had unclogged a few vacuums in his lifetime. A dirty and tedious job, but no big deal with pain-free hands.

He felt Garrett's eyes on him as he unhooked the hose and bent it this way and that, feeling down its length till he found the blockage. He suspended the hose, gave it a hard shake, then winkled it till the problem splatted out the end, an unsightly wad of hair and fluff. He noticed Garrett's heavy mouth turn up at both corners. The old man was smiling, but not in a pleasant way.

"Make you a deal," Garrett said. "Fix another thing or two around here, and I'll tell you some stories."

"Like what?"

"Goldilocks and the Three Bears," Garrett said, and a painful noise spurted out of him, wheezy laughter or an aborted cough.

Irked, Dion plugged in the vacuum, reattached the hose, and flicked it on.

* * *

In the surveillance van Leith sat listening to the conversation, his hopes rising as Garrett called Dion a smarmy little shit. But then came a long stretch of silence, followed by this near-friendly chat. "What's he doing?" he complained to Paley. "They're not battling it out. They're *hobnobbing*. About fairy tales. Guess Cal's specialty is antagonizing his superiors, not suspects. I'm calling this off."

Which was when the explosion in his headphones made him jump from his seat.

* * *

Beau watched the young cop test out the vacuum and seem satisfied with the suction. More than satisfied, he looked like he was about to start vacuuming the whole godforsaken living room. But no, after a few passes he turned the machine off and placed it back in its corner.

Beau regretted having laughed at the Goldilocks joke. Laughing was a bad idea at his age. Felt like he'd inhaled the clog that had spat out of the vacuum hose, and the strain it had put on his body left him feeling weak. The cop had swept up the vaccum clog, meanwhile, and thrown it in the waste bin under the sink, and was now dusting his hands and looking like he didn't know where to catch the bus.

Beau tried to get up to make himself a cup of instant coffee, thinking maybe that would unclog his own old airways, but found himself grounded in his chair, sweating, spasms coursing through his chest. Eyes closed again, the world going dark. Another lightning rod of pain wrung the breath from him, and he must have groaned aloud because when he opened his eyes the cop was leaning over him, asking questions. "It's getting worse, is it?"

"It'll pass."

"Is it your heart? You can't breathe?" The cop sounded angry. "Damn. That's it. We're getting you to the hospital."

"It's not a heart attack," Garrett bellowed at him. "Happens all the time." He hated hospitals and doctors and nurses and all the other meddlers in the world. Half the time they only made things worse. "It's passing. It always does. What the hell's the matter with you? I answered your questions. I appreciate what you did there, but I want you to leave. Now."

The cop gave him a long look, then opened the back door and stepped out. But he'd be back, Beau knew. Like every other pain in the ass, he'd be back.

TWENTY-SEVEN

MAGENTA

A LIGHT RAIN WAS pattering down in the weedy backyard, not a patch of blue above. Dion shut off his body mic and phoned Leith in the surveillance van. The problem with any wired conversation was it was bound to be played back in court, in full, and defence lawyers could do amazing tricks with stray words. The cellphone call would also be on the record, but only in the paraphrased longhand notes of its participants, in this case himself and Leith.

"You heard it," he told Leith. "He's too sick to stand up, let alone attack me."

"Mostly what I heard was a sonic boom. Next time warn me, if you would."

"Like I'm saying, Garrett's pale and sweaty. Seems to be having some serious chest pain. He says it's not his heart, but I'm not so sure. I have to get him to the hospital."

"Ambulance?"

"I could just drive him down. The thing is, I fixed his vac. He smiled. Maybe even laughed. I think we have a kind of rapport going. I could use this. Get him help. He'll like me. If it comes down to it, he'll talk to me."

Leith's doubt rumbled across the line. "'Cause he offered to tell you stories? Sounds to me like he's just yanking your chain."

"Maybe. But he's tired of it all. What he wants is relief. I give it to him, he feels better, I talk to him again, we're best friends. He'll tell me everything. But you have to clear off. No tails on us."

"No dice," Leith said.

"Why? He's no threat. The worst he can do is shout at me."

"I'm not cutting transmission. We're not rigged for a travelling circus here, Cal."

"Then hang far back. We'll be in cellphone contact if necessary. I'll take him downtown. Twenty minutes, max."

Leith was silent a moment before giving in. "Okay. Play it how you think best. I'll get Yee and Wiseman to follow at a distance. Call me if there's any change to the plan. Got that?"

"Of course," Dion said, and disconnected.

Back in the house, body mic back on, he told Garrett what was going to happen, and that it wasn't an option. Garrett would go to the hospital, get his heart checked out, maybe see to getting some proper meds for that arthritis. And an inhaler.

Garrett started to argue, but seemed to change his mind mid-profanity. Not without a grumble, he allowed himself to be helped up from his chair and assisted down the hallway to the bathroom, where he could gather the things he might need for an overnight stay in privacy.

In the living room as he waited, Dion looked out the street-facing window. He couldn't see the monitoring van, but he watched the first backup unit roll down past the house and disappear. The second would remain and follow him, keep him safe from a helpless old man who could barely lift his cane. Ridiculous.

After an inordinate amount of time, Garrett came from the bathroom with his overnight kit, but he was looking around, as if hunting for a good excuse to delay the trip. Dion could guess why. At a certain age, trips to the hospital could end up being forever.

"Lucky," Garrett said. "Gotta feed Lucky."

Lucky turned out to be the lone goldfish in the tank by the bookshelf. Garrett went about unscrewing the lid of a little plastic container, then shaking some of its contents into his palm, then pinching flakes and dropping them one by one into the tank. Each flake took an eternity, and Dion knew the man was playing for time. But he didn't blame him, and waited with forced patience at the threshold between kitchen and living room.

"What if I'm in overnight?" Garrett asked as another flake landed and swirled. "What about two nights? What if I die in hospital? Who's going to look after Lucky?"

"I don't know," Dion snapped. Maybe Garrett's pain was contagious, because this visit was starting to hurt. "Don't you have a neighbour who could deal with it?"

"Louise, I guess." Garrett pointed through the lace of the living room window. "If she's not out cruising the world again."

Looking out past the lace, Dion could see a blue house across the road and uphill a ways. It was the only other building in sight. Bed linens flapped from a line, and a woman stood on the porch, apparently attentive, but idle. Attentive to what? Probably had noticed all the covert activity, that's what. He said, "I can see her there. Phone her up and ask."

"Don't know her number. Don't know her last name, either."

Dion looked at his watch. "D'you have a spare key? I'll go talk to her, ask if she can look after your fish for you."

Garrett pointed out the spare key on its hook. Dion took the key and stepped outside. He spent a few moments looking up Wiseman's number and calling him to let him know he'd be a few minutes more, just had to deal with this goldfish problem. Sorry for the wait.

Wiseman said, "Ten-four."

Dion crossed the road and greeted the woman on the porch. She seemed to know he was a cop before he said so, and asked what all the fuss was about.

"Beau Garrett's going to the hospital for a checkup," he told her, climbing the steps to her porch. "He might be away for a few days, and wants to know if you can feed his goldfish while he's gone."

"Impossible," she said. "I'm flying to Reno tomorrow for five days. Has he done something? Couple of RCMP were up here asking questions last week about that man who got attacked and murdered down the road. How awful! And just now there was a van up the road full of police, but it's gone. Oh, there goes another." She waved.

"Just inquiries," Dion said, turning to watch an unmarked sedan roll down Paradise Road. Wasn't that Wiseman in the passenger seat? Strange, but maybe Yee was moving them into an alternate position down the road to wait.

"I can't help thinking you're investigating Beau for something serious," Louise went on. "Bet it's about the little boy. His grandson, I assume, though he never mentioned him in all the time I've known him. But then he never mentions anything much. Be lucky if I can get him to agree it's a nice day. Well, I'm sorry, but I had no choice but call the Ministry when I saw him nearly rip that boy's arm off yanking him up the stairs. I just feel bad I didn't call right away, but I've been keeping an eye on things, and see the little boy's face popping up in the window sometimes, and he seems okay. Still, I worried. Because what an awful place for a child. I didn't mean for them to take the boy away, just make sure he's being taken care of properly."

"He's been removed," Dion said. "Into a foster home."

"Well, that's for the best, I suppose. Beau is not your nice old grandfather. Never seen him smile. Like I said, he can barely even muster up the good manners to say good day. But I'd never wish ill on anyone, especially not a long hospital stay. Poor Beau. If you give me his key, I could get my niece Zoey to look in on his goldfish for him. She'll come by most days to feed my cat. She's old and cranky and needs her meds, so I hate to leave her, but I can hardly take her with me, can I?" She saw Dion's confusion, and said, "My cat, I mean. Anyway, I'll be back on Friday, so then I can take over doing whatever that fish needs."

Something about the conversation had pinged a warning in Dion's mind, but he couldn't source it. And he had a more immediate concern, whether he should be handing over Garrett's key to an unknown entity, or even the necessity of it. How long could a fish live without food? Probably a while. Also, when Garrett was released from care, precautions would have to be taken that the niece didn't find herself alone with the man. "Your niece, does Beau know her?"

"He must have seen her around, as she helps me out from time to time. But I doubt they've spoken."

"I'm not sure —"

"Zoey's a good girl," Louise said, bristling, maybe misreading his doubts. "If you're worried about her stealing his whatevers, no need. Will we be much longer here? I need to dash out and get a few things for my trip tomorrow."

Dion took down Zoey's full name and address, gave Louise the key, thanked her, and re-crossed the road. When he looked back, her car was reversing out. She gave a friendly nod his way before booting off downhill. He headed up Beau Garrett's bushily hedged driveway, passed the nose of his own sedan, heard the crunch of gravel behind him, and in a flash of understanding knew the crunch wasn't Garrett, and it wouldn't be a team member, which left only danger. He was turning to face the threat but didn't make it as an arm in leather whipped around his throat and pulled him off balance, and he knew even as panic struck that the arm within the jacket was solid with muscle. He toppled backward against a mass that he knew had to be bigger than himself, his hands flying to the crook of the arm that was cinching his airway with steady force.

He gripped and tugged, but the arm was iron. He couldn't cry out, and wouldn't even if he could because every breath was precious. He inhaled through his nostrils, trying to keep a clear head, trying to understand the arm's intent. He leaned back, trying to throw the man off balance, leaned forward, trying to break the hold, twisted sideways hoping to slip out and down.

Nothing worked. He was fighting for air, inhaling too hard through his nostrils, smelling liquor. And leather. And rain. The sky was starting to blur.

"Where is she?" a gravelly voice said, close to his ear. "Where's my Ryvita?"

Crackers. He must have misheard, but it hardly mattered. Nothing mattered but grabbing a lungful of air.

"Wha've you done to my girl?" the voice said.

Dion tugged at the choking arm. He tried to lift a leg for a backward kick to the shin but lost power. Another five seconds and he'd black out. He'd die.

The pressure released slightly. He sucked air and tried to cough, still trapped in the man's killing embrace, seeing his fate written in the stars that were sparkling behind his lids. He wasn't dead yet, but only because the man wanted him alive to answer questions.

"She didn't want you, is that it?" the voice continued, blasts of sweet and sour breath hitting Dion's face. "So you forced yourself on her. Where'd you put her, y'creep? Where you keeping her?"

There was something else now, a pressure just below his ribcage. The sky wasn't just blurry but colourful and quivering. The pressure on his throat was excruciating but the pressure on his abdomen was terrifying. He knew it was a knife tip, and he knew the grade of Kevlar he wore wasn't so great when it came to knife-point penetration, and there was no pain but a freezing flood of dread as the spike came through and pushed into his flesh.

"But you know what? If I find out she let you fuck her, I'm gonna hunt her down, and I'm gonna cut out her gorgeous eyes and make her eat them. You can have each other in hell."

The pain came like a branding iron. The words blended into a slurring drum roll. Dion kept his left hand hooked around the throttling bicep and with his right groped for the arm that was shoving the blade into his abdomen. His right hand found leather, gripped it, pushed against it. He could hear the man breathing in his ear. He could feel the knife entering, angling inward. He resisted the push of steel and maybe slowed the puncture but couldn't stop it. His left hand gave up tugging at the arm and joined his right in defence against the greater threat, the knife that was slicing him in half. He felt the wet stain of his own blood, felt his knees juddering, and he watched the sky turn electric blue, then muddy magenta, then black as the darkest night.

TWENTY-EIGHT

SEEING RED

TIRED OF WAITING, Beau gathered his overnight bag and left the house. He made his way down the stairs and scuffed around the corner of the building. As much as he griped, and as much as he'd never admit it, he was glad the cop was pushing him to seek medical attention.

He just hoped the cop's car was one of the full-sized old-fashioned ones, not one of those compacts that Beau would have to pretzel himself to fit inside. And there it was, gleaming black in the driveway, plenty big. But what Beau saw on the other side of the car made him drop his bag and call out, "Hey!" He made his way over as fast as his good-for-nothing legs would take him toward the stranger, big as Beau himself, long ponytail and short beard, his arm wrapped tight around the young cop's throat.

The attacker gave Beau barely a glance and kept on doing what he was doing, strangling the life out of the cop, who was maybe dead already, by the looks of it.

Beau planted himself behind the stranger, reversed his cane and raised it in both hands, crook side down, and swung hard, like a big league hitter going for a fly ball. The blow landed and the stranger staggered and fell. Beau staggered, too, splaying a hand on the roof of the cop car to save himself from a fall. He saw the cop hit the gravel and lie dead still. The stranger was getting to his feet, and Beau raised his cane again, and he must have looked more of a contender than he felt, because the stranger stepped unsteadily out of range. Beau knew the look on that face: the high colour, the floppy eyelids, the flabby wet mouth. Mean as a snake but drunk as a skunk.

It took all of Beau's energy to keep his cane lifted high as he shouted at the stranger, "Get the hell outta here. Get!"

The stranger seemed to take stock of the situation, and after a tense moment gave a snort that said Beau wasn't worth the effort. He gave the downed cop a kick in the gut before pulling back his shoulders and carrying on his way.

Beau watched the man till he was out of sight behind the big old rhododendron that had become a forest on the downhill corner of the house and shrouded an old road spur where he must have parked his wheels.

A car door slammed and an engine roared. That would be him now, driving past in a newer sedan, heading uphill. Beau waited, because there was no exit uphill, and the driver would have to come back down sooner than later. And he wasn't going to breathe easy till that car had shown its tail lights and those tail lights were gone for good.

Sure enough, the car reappeared, coming this way, pelting fast. Beau wondered if it was aiming to smash through the fence, maybe try to knock him over or crush the downed cop, but it sailed by and kept going. Grey car, shiny bumper, and a sticker with a red heart on it.

Beau leaned on his cane and lowered himself into a one-legged kneel beside the cop, whose eyes were open but weirdly dark and blind. Probably he wasn't seeing anything but angels or devils fluttering around waiting to take him off. Not dead but not alive, mouth hanging open and drool spilling to the gravel.

"Damn," Beau said. He saw blood oozing from the cop's midriff, and reached to place a palm over his shirt, underneath which he could feel a tough vest. Bulletproof, no doubt. He tried to stop the flow, but knew he wouldn't manage. What he needed to do was call 119.

He used his cane to clamber to his feet, wiped blood on his trousers, and shuffled back to the house. In his living room he dropped into his armchair with the phone dragged onto his lap. He lifted the receiver and looked down at the push buttons. His eyes were watery from exhaustion, and he could hardly see the buttons to punch them. He did his best, then held the receiver to his ear. The thing beeped, then a recorded voice came on and told him the number could not be completed as dialed. He hung up, tried again. Same thing. Did he have the number wrong? Was it 999? He tried that. No luck. Would have to find the telephone directory book. And reading glasses. He could see from where he sat that the phone book wasn't where it was supposed to be on the bookshelf. That little rotter Justin had taken it off somewhere. Finding the thing would be a chore in itself.

Beau sat rubbing his chest till the spasms eased. He sat back in the chair and closed his eyes. In a minute, he would have to get off his lazy butt and see about getting help. In a minute. Goddamn it all, how beat he felt.

* * *

In his superior's office, Leith was breaking the news that the operation hadn't gone so well. "If Garrett had any fight in him," he told Bosko, "it's shot. He's sick as a dog. But neither is he admitting to anything. Cal thinks he's having heart failure or something, and I gave him the okay to take him in to the ER. But he thinks the guy might be close to confession. I left Wiseman and Yee to cover him. Somebody should have reported in by now." He frowned at his watch.

"Let's hope Cal's right about a confession," Bosko said. "Without it we're stuck. No fibres. No DNA. No witnesses. You'd think this Garrett fellow was some kind of elite hitman instead of a pensioner with a stick."

"I can just see this hitting the news, if we ever get him," Leith replied. "Two killings in broad daylight, one in a crowded park. We'll never live it down."

He looked at his watch again. "Not that Cal ever takes a simple task and turns it into a living disaster," he joked. "But I'm starting to wonder. I'll go makes some calls."

He returned to his desk and did so. Dion's number went to voice mail. Leith called the hospital and learned that Beau Garrett hadn't been checked in. Next he called the cover team and spoke to Barry Wiseman. The constable sounded like he was working at swallowing food, and Leith guessed where he was, but asked, anyway.

"Denny's," Wiseman answered. Seemed cheerful enough, through his stuffed mouth. Cheerfulness was a good sign. There had been some breakdown in communication, then, nothing worse. Probably Garrett was still being processed and the guys had all gone for lunch, Cal included.

Relief didn't improve Leith's mood. "You guys ducked out for lunch without reporting in? What did you do with Garrett? He hasn't been checked into the ER."

"Garrett, sir?" Wiseman said. "I dunno."

"Is Cal with you? Would you just tell him his phone's not picking up. Better yet —"

"Cal?" Wiseman interrupted. "What d'you mean tell Cal —"

"His phone keeps going to voice mail," Leith blared. "Forget it, just give him the phone."

A stretch of silence twanged at Leith's nerves before Wiseman gave the answer that Leith was, frankly, more than half expecting.

"Sir, I don't follow."

"He's with you, isn't he, at Denny's?"

No, he realized even as he asked it. Dion wouldn't change plans, wouldn't not report in, and even if there was some kind of misunderstanding, he was unlikely to go for lunch with a couple of general duty cops on the spur of the moment. A social butterfly he was not.

"No," he answered himself. "He's not with you. So where is he? Because he's not here, and he's not at the hospital."

The inaptly named Wiseman said he didn't know where Cal was. He and Yee had left him up on the hill there, sorting stuff out, after Cal had called and given them the okay to leave. Why? Was there a problem?

"He gave you the okay to leave? What did he say?"

"He said, 'You don't have to wait.'" Now doubt crept into Wiseman's voice. "I'm *sure* that's what he said."

Leith tried Dion's number once more, and once more it rang four times before Dion's cool, deep voice suggested Leith leave a message after the tone. It wasn't Dion himself speaking, as his real body was up on a remote hillside with a homicidal maniac, but his recorded self.

With Doug Paley in tow, Leith hurried down to the police garage, climbed into an unmarked SUV, and set off toward Paradise Road, dodging through traffic, siren wailing. And fifteen grueling minutes later he was up on the breezy heights, where he found Garrett's house just as he'd seen it from the surveillance van this morning. And there was Dion's black Crown Vic parked in the driveway, and down beside the car, being rained on, was a man's body.

No sign of Beau Garrett.

Leith left the car at a sprint. Behind him Paley was calling for an ambulance, talking in code, demanding double-quick service.

Down on his knees, Leith checked Dion's face. He thumbed an eyelid open and saw only white. He saw blood. "Cal," he said. "Talk to me." He placed two shaking fingers against the throat and felt no pulse.

No heartbeat, no life, while his own heart was knocking hard enough to sustain two. Back on his feet he shoved his trembling hands up under his armpits to still them.

"He's dead," he told Paley.

"I'll believe it when I see it," Paley growled as he crouched, folding open a first aid kit and pointing out a buck knife, gored to the hilt, lying in the grasses nearby. Leith stared at the knife, his nerves buzzing. Cal had been gutted. They were fools, every last one of them on the team. Laughing. Thinking Garrett's deadliest weapon was a cane. "Get his vest off," he ordered. "Stop the bleeding. I'm going in."

Firearm drawn, he walked around to the back of the house because back doors were usually easier to bust open. Up the stairs. Shoved the door wide with his shoulder and saw the killer, either asleep or dead in his armchair, blood on hands and trousers.

Leith hoped he was alive, if only so he could finish him off himself. "Garrett," he said, with soft vehemence. Then again, loud enough to shake the rafters. "Garrett! Open your fucking eyes and look at me."

* * *

The words slapped Beau awake from an exhausted half-doze. He opened his eyes to see the blond cop, Dave, who had questioned him not so long ago in a buddy-buddy way, staring down at him.

Dave's eyes were flashing, and the black gun in his hand floated at his side like it itched to take aim. Dave told Beau to get up, then holstered his gun, grasped him by the arm, and helped him do just that, bullying him out of the armchair and letting him know that he was under arrest for assault of a peace officer, and that he had the right to call a lawyer of his choice, and that anything he said could be used against him in court. Seemed Dave no longer considered Beau a buddy.

Big surprise.

TWENTY-NINE

HALO

BOSKO DIDN'T GET the news until Dion was in surgery. Alive, though barely, he was told. It was Paley who brought him further scant details.

"Dave's booking in Beau Garrett," Paley said. "Then he's running him over to the hospital, 'cause the bastard's complaining of chest pains."

"Garrett did this?" Bosko asked.

"Seems so." Paley looked shaken. "None of us thought this could happen. Dave's ready to jump off a bridge. I might follow."

Bosko called the hospital for an update and learned there was no news to get. He asked to be notified on his direct line as soon as anything changed. It was past four when he learned Dion had made it through the surgery and was being moved to the ICU. Though not conveyed in so many words, he understood the odds of survival weren't good.

With his office door closed, he used his personal phone to call Kate and let her know. He tried to give the news a positive spin, but she knew him too well and guessed the truth.

"He's going to die, isn't he?" she said.

She sounded shredded.

"There's a chance," Bosko admitted, as there was no point in sweetening the news. Kate still loved Cal. Of course she did, after their many on-again, off-again years together. Even though following their final break-up, Cal had frozen her out. *He's erased me*, Kate had told Bosko on their first night together at her place, after that chance meeting on the street, the spontaneous decision to go for dinner, the long talk into the evening, and the mutual unwillingness to part ways.

"I'll let you know as soon as anything changes," he told her. "I'll be home soon."

"Home" was Kate's condo, where he was living part-time in discreet fashion until his divorce from Sarah was finalized. Then Sarah would move east, Kate would move in with him, and their relationship would be out in the open at last.

The hospital was just across the street. He left the detachment and walked over to meet with the surgeon, Casselmann. He had dealt with the doctor before, and knew not to jump to conclusions when Casselmann said with a long face, "We have Cal stabilized, Mike. But I can't give you any odds at this point."

"I don't want the odds," Bosko said. "Can you tell me what happened? Any injuries besides the stabbing?"

Casselmann told him that it looked like Dion had been incapacitated in a sleeper hold. He mimed a demonstration on an invisible victim, in case Bosko didn't know the move. Bosko knew the move, and knew as well that a few moments of that kind of pressure would disable a man. A minute more would kill him. It was maybe fortunate that the assailant had unlocked one arm in order to employ the knife.

Casselmann went on to fill in the particulars of the post-surgical treatment, and ended by asking if Bosko had managed to notify next of kin.

"I'm probably as close as he's got, at the moment," Bosko said. He was still trying to picture the assault, old Beau Garrett versus young Cal Dion. "You'd have to be pretty powerful to pull off a chokehold like that," he said. "And drive a knife through Kevlar at the same time. Agreed?"

"Agreed," Casselmann said, and declaring he was needed in post-op, he strode off with the same long face he had arrived with.

Bosko stood a moment longer, wondering about the assailant's lack of follow-through. Once the knife pierced the body armour, why not plunge it deeper, angle it around, hit a vital organ, finish the job? Or if meeting the resistance of metal, why not pull the blade and go for the throat instead?

In another section of the ICU, he spoke with another doctor about a prisoner brought in under tight security, one Beauregard Garrett.

Dr. Hui told Bosko that Garrett had a stable form of angina, signs of pulmonary disease, and advanced rheumatoid arthritis. Hui had elicited from Garrett that the man had never seen a specialist, and was presently on the most pathetic regimen of over-the-counter anti-inflammatories and extra-strength Tylenol. "Ridiculous," he said. "I've given him something for the pain, and I've got a rheumatologist coming over to take a look at him. Because Mr. Garrett needs more than medicine. He needs a plan. I also tried to speak to his last known family doctor, but the guy's long since retired."

Bosko asked Hui if a person in Garrett's condition could place a fit young man in a chokehold with one arm and stab him in the abdomen with the other.

"Of course not," Hui said. "Unless maybe the healthy young man put up no struggle and maybe assisted with plunging the knife in."

"Sure," Bosko said. "Thanks, doctor."

＊ ＊ ＊

Leith sat at his desk, his face in his hands. What if Dion didn't pull through? And even if he did, would he ever be fit to return to work? Losing the job would be as good as dead for a one-track soul like Dion. And Leith had let it all happen. Practically condoned it. *Sure, Cal, go ahead and change the script.*

Beau Garrett, who they'd all underestimated so abysmally, was now in hospital, and wasn't going to say anything until he spoke to counsel.

Leith groaned. He should be busy consulting with IHIT about Garrett's upcoming interrogation, but he couldn't seem to pick up the phone. Couldn't leave his chair.

His own career was probably finished, too, all because he'd handed over the controls to Cal, assuming he could look after himself. Of course he couldn't look after himself. He was a walking minefield, and Leith should have known better.

"Headache, Dave?"

Leith glanced up. For a man who seemed to know a lot about everything, Mike Bosko could be as dumb as doughnuts. "Headache? No. I'm feeling just fucking fantastic!"

Bosko took the visitor's chair and said, "You've heard, haven't you? They've got Cal stabilized and moved to the ICU."

Leith's head was spinning, maybe with too much oxygen pulled in too fast. Was he dreaming, or was Bosko droning on in his usual measured, all-is-well way, like they were dealing with a scraped shin here instead of a gored detective. "What does that mean?" he rasped. "He's just fine? Up and about? Back on the job next week?"

"Only time will tell. Another thing you should know," Bosko went on. "Beau Garrett isn't the one who attacked him. Dr. Hui says it's impossible. A man in Beau's condition doesn't have the strength. He couldn't inflict that kind of damage without Cal's cooperation. And I doubt Cal was in a cooperative mood. Any news on your end?"

Leith was still blinking. "Not Garrett? How do you figure?"

"Quite a different form of attack, and quite a different victim."

The guilt riding Leith's shoulders lifted slightly. "So if not Garrett, then who?"

"That's the question."

The news absorbed, the battle plan rejigged, Leith went on to report on the team's progress. "Ground search is ongoing. We've pulled a warrant to toss Garrett's house. And canvassing the neighbourhood for witnesses is underway."

"Yes, well," Bosko said. "Your best witness might be your heretofore prime suspect. I'll see if he's willing to talk on that basis." He stood, but paused for a last word. "Doug told me you insisted Cal wear his vest this morning. Good thing you're looking out for him. He needs all the guardian angels he can get. And don't worry. He'll pull through."

With that the supersized harbinger walked off.

Leith rotated in his chair, staring blindly at the window overlooking high-rises, mountains, and a hazy grey sky. He swore aloud at Dion, who he cared about more than he wished to admit. "Guardian angel, my ass," he muttered. "Soon as you're out of hospital, you're going to need a whole team of much bigger angels to keep me from stomping you."

Is this what it came down to? Making sure Dion didn't get himself killed?

The crisis of Dion's attack had jolted Leith and left him questioning his own role in life. His career plans, whether he even belonged in the RCMP. And Bosko's last words had raised a troubling new question. If Dion made it out of the ICU alive, and if he returned to the job — two big ifs — who would be his guardian angel then, should Leith leave the North Shore behind?

* * *

The big man who approached Beau in his hospital bed looked like a middle-aged salesmen of some kind. He wore glasses, a tan suit, a white shirt, and a brownish tie that hung off to one side. He said he was RCMP Sergeant Mike something-or-other with the General Investigations Section, Serious Crimes. He asked Beau how he was doing.

Beau had been asked that same question by all kinds of people all morning. "Not so bad," he said. And it was true, he wasn't so bad. Dr. Hui had given him something to help the heart twinges and the breathing. Even the motley pains in Beau's bones had eased off. And Hui said that those pains, too, would improve with time.

"Excellent," Sergeant Mike said. "Because I'm afraid I have a bunch of questions for you about what happened up at your house this morning."

Beau had been waiting for this. They were going to blame him for that as they blamed him for everything. He answered angrily. "There was a man, a stranger. Built like a wrestler, all in black clothes, leather jacket. Long hair, tied back. And one of those half-ass beards."

"A goatee, you mean?"

"Right. He was choking your cop there, so I just sent him packing. Then tried calling 911." He stopped cold, realizing only now that he'd been so tired after the battle that he hadn't been thinking straight and had got the numbers flipped. 119. Still, no point in saying so. "Didn't go through," he said. "Must have punched the numbers in wrong. I lost steam."

The sergeant listened, nodding. He didn't say Beau was full of shit, as Beau expected. Just listened and nodded and seemed to believe every word of it.

"I lost steam," Beau repeated. He considered apologizing, but why should he? Nobody had asked the young cop to come around and get himself throttled. "So did he die?"

"No," Mike said. "It's serious, but we have faith that he'll pull through."

"Well, I hope so. Not a bad fellow. Seemed a bit confused. Fixed my vacuum for me. Then made me come here, to the hospital, except that ponytailed son of a bitch got to him first."

Sergeant Mike surprised Beau by thanking him for chasing off the attacker and saving the constable's life. Seemed to mean it, too. No sugar on top. No rush to get up and go once that was done, either.

Mike wasn't like the other cops. Wasn't like Dave or the constable who'd got himself stabbed whose name he couldn't remember. And not like the young lady cop who had brought Beau home from the Ministry office and lectured him. For that matter, Mike was unlike the Ministry staff, Dr. Hui, all the nurses, paramedics, and the lady librarian. They were lofty, all of them. Lofty, tense, snoopy, watching Beau, expecting the worst from him.

Even on his feet at the foot of the bed, asking questions and trying to solve a murder, Mike was more like a man on holiday, asking a local for directions to a good restaurant. Looking across at Beau, eye to eye, man to man.

"So go through it for me, what happened in your driveway there," Mike said. "What happened to Constable Dion?"

"Dion," Beau said. He didn't snap his fingers, but thanks to the new meds he felt he could at least try. "That's his name. I sent him off to get Louise to feed

Lucky while I'm in hospital. Louise is my neighbour. Lucky's my great-grandson's goldfish. Dumb name for a fish, but like Justin said, it fits his face." Thinking of Justin distracted him, but when Mike told him to go on, he made the effort. "So I waited, and Officer Dion never came back to fetch me. I don't like doctors, and I sure don't like hospitals, but he made up my mind for me. Said I'm going and that was that. I wanted to get it over with. So I come out looking for him, and see he's in trouble. This brick shithouse of a wrestler type has him in a chokehold in the driveway. I told you all the rest. Guy drove off. It was a grey or silver car, regular four-door."

"The man with the ponytail, what nationality was he, as far as you could tell?"

"White. Kind of pale, even. Dark hair, kind of stringy."

"Good." Mike was opening a notebook, clicking a pen. "I'm going to make some notes, so just throw as much detail as you can at me, about this guy. His face, age, build, voice, what he said, what he wore. What he was driving, make, model, year. Even the smallest thing that comes to mind, okay? Let's start with his face."

Beau did so, but there wasn't much he could add to what he'd said already. He hadn't had a good look at the stranger's ugly mug. He was oddly disappointed with himself, wishing he could prove to Mike that he was sharper than anyone knew.

"No, that's good," Mike said. "We'll get a sketch artist in. That often helps solid up the features. Now, age?"

They went through the list, one by one, and Beau was able to fill in more than he expected. When Mike got to a description of the car, pressing for any distinguishing characteristics, as he put it, an image came to Beau. "The sticker," he said. "Back bumper. I saw it as it took off. A red heart, something written across it. Couldn't read what it said."

As the meeting came to an end, Mike was looking pleased, and Beau was feeling pleased, too. It wasn't every day he assisted in a police investigation. Better yet, it gave him leverage. "Now that I helped you out," he said. "What about my great-grandson, Justin? I don't want him back. I know I can't take care of him. I just want to know he's okay."

Mike had listened and was nodding agreeably. "I can tell you my people have talked to Justin. They've been to his place, and he's in a really good home. He misses you, but he's doing well. Now, I'll have more to ask you shortly, and meantime I'll see if I can arrange a visit for you two. All right? I'll see you later, sir."

Beau decided he wouldn't hold his breath about getting to see Justin, but he somehow believed Mike would at least try. He clamped his mouth shut and watched the big man with the crooked tie take his leave. There was something else that talking with Mike had winkled out of his conscience. For the first time he thought back to his argument with the whirligig man, and he had to admit that it wasn't all that classless bastard's fault for what had happened. Most of it was Beau's own.

His heart thumped in his chest like he'd seen a ghost, just thinking about the whirligig man, because admitting that he himself had been the problem opened the door to a bigger question, one that stretched far back in

time. All the way back to Evvy turning red and screaming at him to get out of the house. She was just a cold-
hearted bitch who had taken a good thing and ruined
it, he'd been telling himself for all these years. But he no
longer believed it.

THIRTY

KIN

April 3

JD STUDIED THE MESSY board of collected evidence in the case room. She was on a new file, investigating the blitz attack of a man she had worked with for years. Cal. Her mind was numb, her heart sore, and it was only with concerted effort that she focused on the facts before her. Tire tracks had been found in the dust of a little plateau or pull-off near Beau Garrett's house. From the tire tracks a tire brand had been identified, and from the distance between the tracks a list of possible chassis makes was being assembled. But other than those few clues and Garrett's description of the man who had knifed Dion, nothing.

As she propped her rear against the conference room table and gazed at the board, playing at being productive, Leith came along and assigned her a new task. She needed to track down Cal's next of kin.

"What do you mean, track them down?" she said.

"The contact numbers on file are defunct is what I mean," he told her.

"You're just too lazy to do it yourself," she said. Being snarky was almost the same as being nice, to JD, but she saw he was too depressed for repartee. She felt bad. "I'm sorry, Dave. I was kidding. You're the least lazy human being on the planet. I just don't want to do it. Get somebody else to tell the guy's parents their only son is dead."

"Don't tell them he's dead, because he's not. And he's not their only son, because he has a brother. Apparently. Just do it, JD. Please."

JD took Dion's personnel file and found out Leith was right. Cal's mother was dead, and now she seemed to remember him saying so once, long ago, and that what he had left was a father and a brother. But for his file he had only supplied contact info for two sets of grandparents, all four of whom, Leith had already confirmed, had passed on. Cal was making it abundantly clear, through omission, that he identified as an orphan, and now she could either spend however many hours or days looking for the disowned family, or elect an alternative next of kin.

A last resort, she supposed, was Dion's long-time girlfriend, now ex. Kate Ballentyne would have to be given the news in person, not over the phone. But where did she live?

Paley would know. If anyone kept in touch with old friends, it was Doug. He was the class clown but he was also tender-hearted. JD went to his desk and asked whether he had Kate's address at hand.

Oddly, the question seemed to make him uncomfortable. As though he knew very well where Kate lived but didn't want to say. "Leave it with me," he said, hands pretending to be busy shuffling papers on his desk. "I'll contact her, let her know."

JD's patience was firecracker short, and she pressed him, hard. "You seem to know where she is. Why won't you tell me? What are you hiding?"

"I'm not hiding anything," Paley objected. "But no worries. Kate's getting updated on Cal's condition as fast as anybody."

"You didn't tell her yourself. You'd have said so right away. So who told her? Who's updating her?"

"Mike," Paley snapped. "Mike told her."

"Mike Bosko? Why Mike?"

Paley's answer was unusually snippy. "'Cause he knows Kate, naturally enough, as Kate's been to social events and whatnot, and so he's taken it upon himself to pass on the news to her as it comes in. I'm sure she's been to the hospital already. So relax. If you can't find blood relatives, Kate's as good as it gets. We've got notification covered."

"Why didn't you just say so?" JD asked. One thing she couldn't stand was being taken for a ride. Especially by a friend. "And why did you then say so in so many words? What's going on?"

"Nothing's going on."

"Something's going on. You're blushing."

Paley sighed. "Sit down."

JD sat.

"Katie and Mike," Paley said. "They're … seeing each other. It was bound to come out sooner or later, so it's not the end of the world if I tell you. Mike just wanted it kept on the lowdown, for a while."

"Oh," JD said, layering fire with ice. "Uh-huh. How long have they been an item?"

"I don't know."

JD let the betrayal sink in. Why was she so upset? Kate and Cal were a lousy match, and so what if Kate latched on to the next male who hoofed into view? Power to her. From JD's experience, relationships were false constructs. Like her short-lived affair with the Coastal Pacific pilot, who had turned out to be just another handsome jerk trying to expand his harem. Nope. She knew what so-called *love* was. Just a round-about path to loneliness. As for herself, she'd stick to the more direct route.

Paley was correctly interpreting her grimace. "It's one of those things," he explained. "Kate and Mike just clicked. She feels bad about it. They both do. But it's destiny, JD. And probably for the best, in the end. Kate and Cal were great before the crash. But since then, well, he's changed. *I* sure wouldn't want to date him, for one. You can't blame her for moving on."

"So now Bosko's fast-tracked his divorce to get himself a younger model, is that it?"

Paley's blush deepened to anger. "Don't talk about Kate like she's packaged meat."

"She is packaged meat. And the two of them are planning to sneak around behind Cal's back for how long?"

"Don't oversimplify things. And don't look at me like I'm the fuckin' cupid who shot them full of arrows. I had nothing to do with it."

"Kate's a scuzzy slut," JD said, with maybe more deep satisfaction than the woman deserved. She saw Leith approaching and asked Paley without bothering with discretion, "I suppose *he* knows, too?"

"I doubt it," Paley said. "But at this point, who cares?"

"You suppose I know what?" Leith asked.

"Nothing," Paley said.

Leith was clearly too distracted to care that he apparently knew nothing. He asked JD if she'd had any luck with the next of kin task, and she told him she hadn't, but that Kate would suffice, and she had been duly notified and no doubt comforted by a superior she wouldn't name.

She was being snarky again, this time with no niceness intended. She knew she shouldn't be taking it out on Leith, who was wretched enough. He'd taken full responsibility for Dion's death — or pending death, rather — though he shouldn't, because whatever had happened on Paradise Road had been beyond his control. Some trouble Cal had gotten himself into on the side, or maybe just a random attack. Like a bolt of lightning. She wanted to remind him of all these mitigating factors but sadly, showing kindness didn't come naturally to her.

He handed her a cellphone. The phone was in a plastic evidence baggie, and labelled, but the label had been broken. "It's Cal's work phone," he said. "No prints on it but his own. Five minutes ago it rang. I breached the seal and answered. It was a hang-up. See if you can find out who the caller is and what they want. And what are you two doing, standing around like there's no work to do? Jump to it."

His order given, he walked away like something weighty was not only riding his shoulders but yanking at his hair.

JD sighed and looked at the phone. Probably the girl-friend from the attic had surfaced and wanted to whisper sweet nothings into Cal's ear. The girl had heard Leith's voice instead and hung up. Now it was up to JD to track her down and let her know there wouldn't be any sweet nothings to exchange for a while. Probably ever. Dave and all these guys around her could be as optimistic as they pleased about Cal's chances. She knew better. "Fuck me," she said.

"I was about to give you the same advice," Paley said.

JD fucked off to her own desk to call back the number. But the woman who answered sounded like she was in her sixties, and with a heavy accent. "D'Souza residence."

JD introduced herself. "I'm calling from RCMP Constable Cal Dion's phone," she said. "Did you just call this number and hang up?"

The woman, who sounded South Asian, said it must have been a mistake, and she was sorry to be a bother. JD said it was no bother at all and rang off. Just some wrong number telephone tag. Happens.

* * *

Up in the ICU, JD gave a vague excuse at the desk and was allowed entry. She stood in Dion's room, a section reserved for special cases. He had his own guard, too. And a tent over his bed. He was visible only through rippled plastic, intubated and masked and monitored by the monolithic life support systems that were as mysterious to JD as her own physiology. The room was too bright, and silent but for the machinery. She checked her phone and found no messages. But she shouldn't be here, wasting time. Had work to do. Should rush back to the detachment, jump on the investigation train that was charging ahead without her.

But she couldn't seem to move. She took a chair at Dion's bedside and stayed a while, listening to the breathing of his machines.

THIRTY-ONE

UP

April 4

DION WAS IN HIS new apartment. Tenth floor! The sunlight hurt his eyes, even though his eyes were closed, but the light was all wrong because he knew without seeing that the patch of sky through the window was midnight black.

Then he knew exactly where he was. Back in the dream. And he knew where he was going. Back to hell.

Don't look up, he told himself. But he looked up, anyway, and saw the thing out in the hallway, up in the corner above the laundry nook. Not moving. Just sitting there, a seething bag of evil. The breath caught in his lungs and the paralysis bolted through his system. His heart began to pound, and he knew with frustration and fear and anger that even here at the Harbourview there would be no escape. He'd known all along, from the day two years ago he'd stood staggering from the heady exertion of pummelling a man he despised to mince-meat, that the thing would take shape and come after him until he paid with his life or his sanity for what he'd done, murdering a man — whatever kind of lowlife that man was — and burying him in a shallow grave, then lying through his teeth to the people he loved like family.

The thing was here to out the lie. It would show up night after night till it got inside and punctured holes in his body from the inside out. Though bodily trapped in a dream he was vividly aware of who he was, where he was, and what an ironic fate would befall him tonight. He'd come home to the Harbourview only to die. That's what.

Also vivid in his mind were a strange set of words. *Eat ginko biloba. Keep a dream journal. This is not real. You're in control.*

JD's how-to book, that was the source. Or not a how-to book but a fucking fairy tale, because the thing *was* real, and he *wasn't* in control.

It's all in your head. Become unparalyzed.

The thing had shifted into view. It was on the wall, bits of it dropping to the floor.

Dion tried to shout for help, tried calling out Looch's name.

But Looch didn't come to his rescue. Of course he didn't. Looch was dead.

He doesn't have to be dead.

Dion wanted to believe in JD's instruction manual. He wanted to be in control. He tried willing Looch to not be dead, but again failed. Instead, the smell of the ocean came to him, sharp and melancholy, linked with memories of weekends and friendship. "I can't do this anymore," he told Looch, staring at the thing coming down the wall. It was making a noise, like static electricity mingled with words he couldn't make out.

"Just say I did it," somebody said.

Clear as day.

Was it Looch speaking, or was it himself? He saw a shovel leaning against the wall, not too far from the thing, and he decided he should grab it. Should start digging in dirt and weeds and gravel to unbury the corpse and bring it to the North Shore and throw it at Bosko's feet.

It was all so incredibly sad. Looch, the ocean, the shovel, and a sudden fierce yearning to talk to JD. He lifted a hand toward the thing on the wall, not sure if he was trying to fend it off or still trying to reach for the shovel. Or was he looking for his phone to call JD?

He stared at his raised hand in amazement.

Progress.

But how could he see when his eyes were glued shut?

The thing on the ceiling was gone, which was not good news. His lungs were pumping fear. The disappearance of the thing meant it could be on the floor now, behind him, or under him, or on the other side of him, the side he couldn't turn to see because he couldn't move. His heart was beating so fast he knew it would shatter, but his fear had forked. Strange. The thing was terrifying, but some more practical anxiety was nagging, too.

Unfinished business. He had to give a statement. To Leith. About getting stabbed. Because without his input, the case could go unsolved.

Opening his eyes took huge effort, but his lids lifted. At least one did. Slowly. Then the other. He blinked into a brightly lit room, saw machinery and a window with a view of night skies, and knew it was real. He was fuzzy-headed but awake. His chest was tight, like all his ribs had been crushed and taped back together. Vague pains all over. Logy, and his throat hurt like something was locked around it and squeezing.

But with pain came an incoming tide of relief. The physical angst displaced what was left of the dream, goading him awake. He was alive. In bed. In a hospital. He remembered being in Beau Garrett's driveway. The ambush, an arm like steel cables cutting off his air. Not a lot of detail other than that. Not a face. Not even skin colour. But he had to tell Leith what little he could.

Again he tried speaking, but he made only a wispy exhalation. He clenched his fist and tried giving the mattress a pounding. Not a tight fist and not a real pounding, but if nothing else, the effort would spur the monitor somewhere above to blip faster. He heard the door swing open and a nurse's voice.

THIRTY-TWO

RAVINA

THE BLEATING OF LEITH'S work phone woke him at 4:00 a.m. It was the hospital, which could mean only one thing. In spite of Bosko's unqualified optimism, Leith knew as he answered the call that it was time to unshroud his funeral suit and buff his funeral shoes. Should probably start writing a eulogy, too. Think of some nice things to say about Cal Dion. Which wouldn't be easy.

But after his gloomily muttered *yes*, he was shocked and delighted by what the hospital had to say. The patient had not only pulled through, but he was talking. Well, rasping, anyway. Not making much sense, though.

Worried all over again, Leith asked if there were signs of brain damage from the choking. He was told no, just pain. The patient would be groggy from sedatives, but likely able to answer a few questions.

Leith was thrilled enough to shake Alison awake and pass on the news. He then got dressed and hurried over to the hospital. Stepping into the room, he saw that the tent was gone and the oxygen mask was off. Dion was awake, but looking like human wreckage. Bruised, wired to machines, and visibly bewildered.

"Well, hello," Leith said. Hardly a ceremonious couple of words, considering the man had just stepped back from the brink of death, but he let the broadness of his smile express what he wanted to say about relief and brotherly love and a continuing concern about recuperation. Besides, Dion wouldn't want hugs and flowers. He would just want to get on with it. Which he proved now by pointing to an object that lay on the bedside table. A clipboard. He indicated his mouth, too, with a frown that said, *I can't speak.* He mimed writing. *Ready to give a statement.* And finally pulled a grimace that said, *I hurt all over.*

Leith commiserated as he gave Dion the clipboard and a pen. "Do you know who did this?"

Dion shook his head. He wrote, "Hoped you got him already."

"No. We don't have much of a lead," Leith told him. "We thought Garrett was responsible, but it seems he wouldn't be physically capable. In fact we're pretty sure he saved your life. Chased the guy off."

Dion raised his brows. He then wrote in point form that the man who had attacked him was probably taller than himself, wore leather, and reeked of liquor. It was all he knew. Then he wrote, *Grey 4 door maybe newer mod Taurus follg me last wk.* The sentence ended in a big sloping question mark.

"There was a car following you?" Leith exclaimed, and his feelings of brotherly love cooled a degree.

"And you didn't report it?" They exchanged a brief glare. "Sounds like the car Garrett described," Leith said. "But you have no idea who that was? You can't even guess?"

No.

"Did the grey car have any signs or marks, bumper stickers, anything like that, that you noticed?"

Don't know.

"Did you see the grey car up on Paradise Road yesterday, before or after he attacked you?"

No.

"Did the man say anything?"

Yes. Dion worked at his clipboard again. A series of unreadable scribbles, along with one word that was clear enough, but puzzling and wildly out of context. *Ryvita.*

"Ryvita?" Leith said. "The cracker?"

Dion took the board, circled *Ryvita* and attached another question mark to the circle with a line, which supposedly meant the word was only a phonetic guess. Leith said he couldn't read the rest, and Dion rewrote it, not in cursive this time, but laborious block letters. *Said I took his girl Ryvita. No clue.*

He was sweating from either physical exertion or pain. He could answer no further questions or even pick up the pen. His eyes fell shut.

Leith gave him a grateful pat on the shoulder. "This is a good start, Cal. Let staff know if you think of anything else. Now just focus on getting better, 'cause we need you back quick as you can make it. Okay?"

Turning to leave, he was struck in the back with a small projectile. He turned and saw the pen on the floor, and Dion, with a wince of exhaustion, was motioning for him to return.

With pen back in hand, Dion wrote a simple final message: *Send JD.*

"Now?" Leith said.

Dion nodded.

* * *

The note Dion wrote for JD an hour later was more like a letter, and the effort took the wind out of his sails all over again. He watched her read, knowing he must seem obsessed. But the worry nagged him, wouldn't fade, kept him awake, even overrode his pain. His letter asked her to go to the house on Ridgeway as soon as she could and ask Mrs. Riddle if she had any news of Bianca, and if not, had she found a contact number yet, and if she had a contact number, to bring it back here so he could try to reach the girl.

JD read the note and looked at him quizzically. "This is your priority? You've just been jumped and stabbed, you're hardly out of the woods, and whoever did this is on the loose. We all spent the night thinking of the last thing we'd said to you and wishing we'd been nicer. But hey, fine, top of your list, you're still checking up on this person you keep calling a lost cause. Sure, I'll do this for you, but at some point you've got to let go. She's not one of your files."

Dion flicked a finger at her to go and do as told. Instead she leaned close and said, "I'm glad you're alive. You know I hate you, right? And hate is a feeling, too."

He mouthed *what?* at her. His throat hurt, his head ached, his eyelids were heavy, and there was a creepy numbness around his midriff that he feared meant he would spend the rest of his days in a wheelchair. He wanted JD to shove off. For one thing, he wanted Bianca found. For another, he didn't want JD seeing him like this, laid out flat and unsightly, catheter bag no doubt hung somewhere on the bed frame.

She leaned even closer and gave his forehead a swift kiss.

"Never mind," she whispered. "I'll find your lost cause for you and all will be well. See you later."

* * *

Beau Garrett was home at last, up on Paradise Road, with the sunlight dancing in a blurry way through the window grime. He felt like a stranger in his own body. He sat at his kitchen table crying, and for no good reason, a hollow noise that belched up from his chest and out through his mouth.

He didn't know why he was crying, and couldn't recall the last time he had.

He had stuff to inhale, and his lungs no longer felt like smoke-filled bellows. Even the chest spasms were easier to take, and didn't grab hold so much. Some people had come to the house this morning, not to nag him about his sins, or what a lousy grandfather he was, or what a dump his house was, but to see how he was living, and how he could live better. Nice people, who smiled at his grumblings and told him nothing was impossible, and went on to talk about ramps and rails, and breathing techniques, and a different kind of faucet on his kitchen sink, and telephones with big buttons.

They annoyed him with their youthful busyness, and their cheeriness that he couldn't trust as real, but when they left the loneliness came back, bigger than ever.

What was this?

He had always been hard like granite. Always been poor, never been praised. He'd hardly had a childhood, hardly knew what it meant, had gone through a string of back-breaking labour jobs without much pay, a marriage that ended badly, ending up on Paradise Road with a body racked with aches and pains. Now he felt better than he had in years, but he was no longer a rock. And to add insult to injury, Lucky the goldfish, who he'd placed in Louise's care, was thin as an anchovy.

Beau went across the road to fetch his key from Louise. She pulled open the door and said, "Oh, Mr. Garrett, welcome home. I heard you were in hospital. You're looking well. Ten years younger!"

"Thanks," Beau said. "Came for my key. Thought you were supposed to feed my fish. He's half dead."

She gave him one of her faces, all puckered in except the lower lip stuck out. "I was away, but Zoey fed your fish. I'll get your key."

When she gave him the key, he said, "Zoey?"

"My niece, who you've seen around, I'm sure. She was looking after my place for me and I asked her to check in on your fish for you while she was at it, like the officer asked me to. If your fish is dead, it's nothing to do with Zoey. Fish die all the time. And hey, some people say *thank you* when you do them a favour."

Beau returned home. He burrowed through his closet, found the Oriental tea tin with his cash in it. Counted it. Okay. Then he checked his sock drawer for the Pot of Gold chocolate box where he kept his personal valuables collected over the years. He pawed through watches and tie pins and cufflinks. And it was all there, except the locket. The ornate silver locket with his wife's face in it. Evvy, captured young and smiling. It was gone.

* * *

The woman who owned the house on Ridgeway Avenue, Mrs. Riddle, told JD she hadn't seen Ms. Stone in days. And neither had she found the contact number that Cal had asked for, though she'd had a good search.

JD thought it was cute, the older woman calling Dion by his first name. "Cal says Bianca's paid up to the end of April," she told the landlady, doing a little sleuthing of her own. "Did you ask for her to do that, or she offered? I'm just curious."

Mrs. Riddle shrugged. "Ms. Stone just pulled out her wallet … it was a beautiful wallet, sparkly like it was covered in gold leaf. Just pulled it out and counted out the money like it was pocket change. I didn't argue, though my sons are mad at me. They think I'm getting ripped off charging five hundred dollars a month for each suite. But it's plenty for my needs. And I like my tenants to have peace of mind. I want them to like where they're at, because then they stay longer, and we're all civil to each other."

"Good policy," JD said, marvelling at the rate. Five hundred was crazy good for a suite in North Vancouver. The landlady could easily charge double that, even triple. No wonder her sons were miffed. "I saw the attic," she added. "It's a gem for that kind of rent."

Mrs. Riddle invited JD inside and served her a cup of tea at the dining room table. "I started out with a plan that in lieu of higher rent the tenants would help me out around the property," she admitted. "You know, lift heavier items, some minor repairs. And Brad, who's been living just above me for a few years now, you know, JD, he genuinely did his best ..."

JD nodded sympathetically. She had seen the man picking up his mail as she'd arrived, and he didn't strike her as the hammer-hefting type.

"... and Ms. Stone put an hour or so into the garden before losing interest," Mrs. Riddle went on, with cheerful resignation. "Let's face it, I'm not a good foreman. Five years later and my flower beds have all gone feral and my trellis is *still* falling down." She frowned at JD. "But you say Cal is hurt? I hope it's not too bad. He fixed my hot water tank, you know. Got that finicky temperature control just right, too."

JD smiled. So Cal was turning out to be a regular amateur repairman. Vacuums and hot water tanks, what next? Maybe if and when he served his time and got out of jail he could get himself a van and advertise. "He's in bad condition, but I have a feeling he'll be okay."

She also had a feeling Mrs. Riddle was genuinely concerned about Cal, a man she hardly knew. This was a generous individual, then. A humanitarian. Someone who jumped into intimacy and called everyone by their first names. Even herself, introduced as Constable JD Temple, was instantly *JD*.

All except Bianca, who was consistently *Ms. Stone.*

"Like I say, Cal's quite worried about Bianca's whereabouts," JD said. She still had half a cup of tea to finish, and a growing curiosity to satisfy. "Can you tell me something about her, anything, conversations you had, say while she was out here gardening, what you thought of her, how often she drops by."

"I really haven't seen Ms. Stone much since she moved in," Mrs. Riddle said. "As I told Cal, she comes and goes. I actually can't remember the last time I saw her."

"Is she always alone? I mean, other than with Cal? Any other friends or visitors that you've seen?"

Mrs. Riddle nodded, then seemed to grow reticent. "Used to have friends come over."

"Men, women?"

"Maybe some of each."

"Mrs. Riddle," JD said. "Sorry for being nosy, but you seem to have doubts about Bianca. Like you're not sure what kind of person she is, or maybe you don't even trust her. And I haven't heard you refer to her by her first name at all."

Mrs. Riddle smiled. "That must be because I'm actually not sure she goes by Bianca. But I could be wrong. It's been a long time since we've talked, but I could have *sworn* her name started with an *R.*"

Inspiration hit JD. "You don't have a photo of Ms. Stone, do you?"

Of course Mrs. Riddle didn't.

"Then can you describe her for me?"

The verbal description JD received was nothing like the hilarious sketch Dion had crumpled up in anger. Ms. Stone was beautiful, according to Mrs. Riddle. Long black hair, sloping black eyes. Dark skin. East Indian descent for sure, though she spoke without even a lilt and was likely born and brought up in Canada.

"Ravina," Mrs. Riddle said, in an *aha* moment that lit up her face. "That's her name. I *knew* 'Bianca' was wrong."

JD blinked. "Ravina," she echoed, and the name ricocheted off another puzzle that Leith had so recently shared with her, the patchy statement Dion had transmitted via notepad.

"There's something seriously strange going on here," she told the older woman over the steam from their teacups. "We're going to need to see Ravina's apartment right away. Is that okay?"

* * *

The attic suite Leith observed had a slanted ceiling and was somewhat run down, but it was airy and bright and decorated with feminine flair. "Cal was living here?" he asked JD, mystified. "I thought he was staying with a pal of mine, Joe. How did he end up here? Run that by me again."

JD reran the convoluted story about a girl Cal had met. That her name was Bianca seemed to be all Dion knew about her. After a few days together, she had failed to show up, and Cal feared she was in some kind of trouble.

But JD had also discovered — hence the search warrant — that the Bianca who had been staying here was some kind of imposter. Neither the landlady nor the second floor tenant had met her. And the apparently legitimate tenant, one Ravina Stone, was also missing.

"Well, there must be names and numbers attached to the tenancy agreement," Leith said.

"Mrs. Riddle is a bit lax with the paperwork," JD said. "She lets people come and go on the strength of a handshake."

"God," Leith said.

"And there's something else," JD said. "Remember Cal's *Ryvita*? Not too far off from *Ravina*, is it? Especially if you're being throttled when you're hearing it."

"Huh," Leith said.

"So Cal starts getting stalked not long after starting to stay with Bianca in what's actually Ravina's apartment," JD said. "When he's attacked, he's accused of fooling around with this guy's girl. Put it together. Cal was seen coming and going from Ravina's apartment, and this guy jumps to the wrong conclusion. He starts hunting Cal, maybe hoping to catch him and Ravina together. In the end he blows a fuse and attacks Cal in revenge."

"And Bianca was living here without the landlady's knowledge. That's all we know about her?"

"She's an unknown. A will-o'-the-wisp. That's why Cal can't even report her missing. She comes and goes, stays out all night. Doesn't use a computer, phone, or receive mail. He's thinking she may be a call girl or some guy's private geisha. And she wants out. So he's worried about her and wants to track her down."

They were interrupted by the arrival of the forensics team, and Leith looked out the window, down at the street below, while JD gave instructions to Ident. Along with other likely items in the pad, they were to jimmy that locked drawer, seize what's inside, try to lift prints from the items within. If the contents belonged to the real Ms. Stone, they could provide the answers they needed. Who was the missing Ravina, and who was obsessed with her to the point of murder?

JD joined him by the window. "Maybe Bianca was an informal sublet? Maybe she took over from Ms. Stone, and neither of them bothered asking the landlady if that was acceptable."

Leith thought about the lack of mail, the lack of a phone, computer, TV. The place was a hangout, not a home. A no-tell-motel setup for one or both of the girls. Maybe Dion's attacker was their pimp.

From the other side of the room someone said, "Whoo-hoo!" It seemed one of the forensics people had found something worth looking at. Leith and JD went to check out what lay in the pried-open drawer. A stash of vibrators, condom packets, lube, and other fun things, along with a baggie of what looked like weed.

The items gave Leith hope. If Ryvita was Ravina, and if Ravina's jilted lover was the man who had jumped Dion, there was a good chance his prints were on those toys and the dope. And having a violent streak, the brute likely had a record, meaning the lifted prints would be in the database, and an arrest was just steps away.

THIRTY-THREE

TAKEDOWN

April 5

BOSKO FULLY BELIEVED that Beau Garrett had killed Lawrence Follick up on Paradise Road, and that he had then killed the clown on the unicycle, Carey Chance. But without a confession, and no physical evidence, with nothing to suggest charges be laid, his only course of action was to leave the lines of communication open with the suspect, hoping that through chance or persistence, proof of some kind would emerge.

With open lines of communication in mind, he applied for a court order, the order was granted, and he collected Justin from his foster home and took him for a short visit to see Garrett at his home on Paradise Road. Once invited inside, Bosko watched the reunion with interest, the small boy and his oversized great-grandfather greeting each other with an easy familiarity that required few words. Garrett ruffled Justin's hair, and the boy went to say hi to his goldfish.

"Not as peppy as he was," Garrett said in a worried aside to Bosko. "But I do appreciate it," he added. "You bringing him around, I mean. And maybe that's a good thing, him being not so peppy. It's called growing up."

"He'll be okay," Bosko told him. "He's a resilient kid."

"Did you track down Sharla?" Garrett asked. "Or Evvy?"

"Both, in fact. There's some negotiations going on, but there seems to be a mutual agreement that he's better off in the foster home for now. It's a good place for him."

"Hey, kid," Garrett called out. "What's that goddam fish telling you?"

Justin replied, maybe quoting the goldfish, but Bosko didn't catch a word of it.

After the visit, Garrett saw his guests to the door to say goodbye. He had some last words for Bosko, as well, another complaint. Not about the boy but the fish. "Lucky near died when I was in hospital," he said. "The niece never fed him. And she stole my locket, my locket with my wife Evvy in it."

"Niece?"

"Louise sent her niece over, the one with tattoos. I never gave that key to the niece. I gave it to Louise. I want that locket back."

"I'll go talk to Louise," Bosko said.

He did as promised, but all he got from the neighbour were assurances that Zoey had fed the fish, and would never steal from anybody, that Beau Garrett was an old crank, and that was the last time Louise would do him any favours.

Bosko added the info to the growing file, a short report about a missing locket and a girl named Zoey. Incidental, and not much more, but sometimes it was the smallest flaw that crashed the largest machine.

* * *

Leith coordinated the evidence that came in fast and furious once the desk drawer in the attic suite was broken open and the contents had been processed on an expedited basis. Fingerprints were found, one set un-identified, the other attached to a name: Brian Kaeck.

Unexpectedly, Kaeck's slim criminal record showed no history of violence. Just a recent narcotics charge for which he'd done negligible jail time and a bit of pro-bation. His mugshot showed a burly, male-model type with long brown hair, disappointed pale blue eyes, neat goatee. Six foot three and 260 pounds, with the weighty look of a wrecking ball. Heavy but trim, because muscle weighed more than fat, Leith knew, regretfully placing a hand over his own flab.

"We got him," JD announced to the crew, as the second day of the evidence gathering wound down. "Looks like we're going to have our Kaeck and eat him, too."

In a conference call with Delta the arrest script was cobbled together, the takedown planned for tonight. Leith received word that Kaeck would be at his place of employment, the low-volume bar of an upscale chain hotel. It wasn't a busy lounge, and customers would be turned away at the door until the place was empty, after which he would be cuffed and read his rights.

In the early evening Leith and JD drove across the Second Narrows and made the long drive through city, suburbia, and marshy flatlands toward the Tsawwassen ferry terminal. At a muster point a kilometre past the hotel where Kaeck worked they met up with the Delta team leader and IHIT members. Here they waited as a group until word came through that the bar was cleared but for the target. IHIT members proceeded with the takedown, while Leith and JD moved to the hotel's parking lot and waited, eavesdropping on the live feed transmissions with the team leader.

In the end Kaeck didn't go down without a fight. Leith couldn't help smiling as he listened to the shouts of IHIT members approaching their target. He couldn't be sure, but it sounded like Kaeck had vaulted a counter and made a dash for the rear exit before being tackled, brought down with a crash, and handcuffed. Lot of noise. Lot of swearing from both sides of the law.

"Epic," JD cried, more like a kid at a parade than a cop on the job, as the arrestee was pushed and pulled outside to the waiting vehicles. She grinned at Leith. "I can't wait to meet this guy."

Vengeful glee was highly unprofessional, Leith knew. But in this case he would let it slide. "Oh, you bet," he said. "Me, too."

* * *

Leith and JD got to meet the icy-eyed Brian Kaeck, but they didn't get to question him, as it was an IHIT member from a dedicated interview team who did the talking. Which was second best. Instead they sat in an adjoining room and watched.

Kaeck was tense and sweaty. He denied everything. He'd never been to North Vancouver, didn't know a girl named Ravina. He hadn't stalked a man all over North Van for the love of any woman or attacked him on Paradise Road. He was a happily married man, so no way, man, had he done any of it.

Placed before Kaeck was a photograph of the grey Ford Taurus registered in his name, complete with a rear bumper sticker that featured a red heart and a stylized paw print, a pictogram for *I love my dog*. Seemed the car and sticker were a darn good match to the one seen fleeing the scene of the stabbing on Paradise Road.

Kaeck said he was being framed.

Fingerprint evidence was put before him, suggesting his fingers had been all over some hash pipes, condom packets, lube bottles, and other specialty items found in the locked drawer of an apartment rented by an attractive young woman named Ravina Stone.

Ravina. The name gave him a visible jolt. It showed in the pulsing of the carotid, the flare of the nostrils, the beads of sweat, the narrowing of the eyes. In Kaeck's case, bodily actions spoke louder than words. And before he could recover, next came evidence from the ether, the cellphone tower pings attached to his cell number, the records having been obtained through warrant, along with credit card transactions at some high-end North Vancouver restaurants, gift shops, lingerie boutiques. One of the gift shops had been able to supply video surveillance from December that matched the credit card purchase of a man buying a bouquet of red roses. The buyer looked a lot like Kaeck.

Those were for his wife, Shelley, he said.

Would Shelley attest to receiving a dozen red roses in December?

Of course she would, Kaeck answered. But he didn't look too sure about it.

Changing topics, the interrogator shared some good news with Kaeck. The cop who'd been stabbed was recovering, and in the next day or so would be able to confirm that Kaeck wasn't the stabber. Or otherwise.

Kaeck changed course from defence to offence and suggested the interrogator could go fuck himself up the ass, along with all his faggot cop friends.

But in the end it was Kaeck's burning infatuation with Ravina Stone that felled him. The interrogator had noticed Kaeck's physical reaction to the name, and so he wielded it frequently. And toward the end he both wielded and twisted, driving it in deep, saying it again and again, in morbid refrain, that Ravina was missing, had disappeared, was maybe dead, and what did Kaeck know about it?

Grief undermined what was left of Kaeck's composure, and he broke down and cried. An angry confession followed the tears, Kaeck stating that the man he had stabbed up on Paradise Road had not only taken Ravina from him but had killed her, and that's why she hadn't been answering his calls. She was dead, that's why. And for that the man deserved to burn in hell.

After Kaeck's emotional admission, he and his interrogator had a good talk about right and wrong, truth, guilt, redemption, and other stuff cops apparently knew so much about. Leith listened to every word. There was value in this talk, he knew. A kind of win-win conversation. The prisoner ends up with a sense of absolution, while the interrogator manages to plug any holes in the confession, hopefully offsetting any second thoughts the prisoner will no doubt have by morning.

Now for one loose end named Ravina Stone, and another known only as Bianca. Dead or alive, the two young women had be to tracked down.

THIRTY-FOUR

EPHEMERA

April 15

AFTER TWO LONG weeks in hospital, Dion was picked up by JD and driven to his apartment. They left the car and he looked up at the tower, the new home he'd had barely one day to enjoy before being laid flat by a crazed ape up on Paradise Road. "It feels like I've been gone a year," he said, as he and JD rode the elevator up. "I feel like an alien."

Yet in the elevator mirror he looked human enough. He felt good, too. He'd been told by the physician at the hospital that he would be off work for a while, at least a couple of months. But he wasn't too worried, because every physician he'd ever met was a pessimist, always delivering the worst case scenario. By his own prognosis, he would be back on light duties in no more than a week or so.

In the apartment, JD set down the paper bag of groceries they had picked up on their way over. Dion moved with care, like he was made of glass, as he took a seat on the lawn chair he'd brought to the place on move-in day, his one piece of furniture. "Well, what d'you think?" he asked, as JD looked around.

"It's not as spacious," she said. "Or as nice. But it's not bad."

It took Dion a moment to recall that back in the good old days, when he'd lived on the tenth floor, he'd thrown some great house parties, and JD would have been to at least a few. He saw that she saw that he had forgotten about her presence back then, and saw as well that she expected to have been forgotten. He wasn't sure if that meant she held herself in low esteem, or him. Maybe both.

"Anyway," she said. "Look what I got you!" She lifted two bottles from a bag she was carrying, one of Scotch and one of bubble bath. "You're going to have a lot of time to kill."

He looked at the Scotch bottle wistfully. "I can't mix drink and meds."

"A sip won't hurt."

"What if one sip leads to another?"

She started putting the bottle back in its bag, grumbling about people who lacked self-discipline, but he stopped her, getting up to grab the gift. "You're right, one sip won't hurt."

"Now, tomorrow," she said. "If you're feeling up to it, I'll pick you up and we'll go to the Ridgeway house. I've got a few questions for you. But ciao for now."

"Questions about what?" he asked her.

But she was gone.

* * *

As darkness fell, Dion lay in a bubbly, lavender scented tub, liquor scorching his veins, moodily rhythmic music on the boom box. He was thinking about JD, how he had told her about his criminal act and how she had received the confession. Apparently, she had done nothing with it. Two weeks had passed since then, with no sign from above that she'd shared the info with a superior and that an investigation was underway.

But then he'd spent some time at death's door, and maybe she'd been waiting for the outcome. Or she'd given him a little reprieve while he recuperated. Maybe the bottom was about to fall out, now that she knew he was going to live.

He tried to remember exactly what he'd told her that day. He'd been talking on autopilot, the adrenalin roaring through his system so he could hardly hear himself speak. All he could be sure of was he'd given away enough that if she had decided to turn around and share it with the force, the force would get to work on it, and as soon as they had a plan of action, they'd collar him.

The more he thought about it, the more he was sure she had turned him in. Because of her attitude. She was being nicer than usual. Kind of soft, when she should be freezing him out. Maybe this was all about revenge, and tomorrow she was going to tell him the game was up, that she'd either given her statement or would do so shortly. Stick it to him with a smile.

But why in Bianca's attic?

* * *

April 16

The following evening was unseasonably cold. Dion waited on the sidewalk till JD pulled up, as promised, for their supposed interview. He sat in the passenger seat, checking her expression for clues. "You said you have questions," he said. "About what? And why at Bianca's place?"

"Buckle up," she said.

She drove toward the detachment, which wasn't the route he would have taken to get to Ridgeway. In fact, the direction she was taking confirmed his worst fears, that she had only used Bianca as a ruse. A way to get him in the car. In his mind's eye he saw the hall leading to the interrogation room, saw Leith and Bosko and the set of shadowy IHIT members he imagined had him under surveillance all lined up to coldly watch him go by. But there was nothing he could do about it now. There was nowhere to run.

He was so sure of JD's ulterior motive that when she cruised past the detachment instead of turning toward its parking entrance, he almost pointed out that she'd missed the turn. She signalled a left at St. Georges instead, back toward the hospital, then down Ridgeway, and finally parked outside of Bianca's house.

She shut off the engine and frowned at him. "Looks like you've seen a ghost. My driving's that bad?"

"What are we doing here?"

"You're going to tell me all you know about Bianca. She's not what we're calling an open file, but the boss is concerned enough about both her and Ravina that he wants to get your narrative about your dealings with either woman. I thought the attic would be the best place to talk."

Dion's pulse shot up again as the truth struck him — this wasn't about a past crime but a current one. "I didn't do anything to Bianca," he cried. His throat was still healing, and shouting was painful. He grasped the door latch as if he might bail and go pelting down the block.

JD clicked the lock to ensure he wouldn't. "Calm down," she snapped. "What's the matter with you? How much Scotch did you swallow with your meds?"

"Who's up there?" He stared through the windshield, up the face of the house to the attic, imagining a twitch of curtains. "What's this about?"

"Nobody's up there. This isn't about anything except filling in some gaps. Breathe, Cal. Inhale. Exhale."

Her teasing reassured him. "Sorry. I can't think too straight."

"No shit."

"I was the last person to see Bianca," he explained. "I mean, as far as I know." He worried that JD would see the slamming of his heart against his shirt, and clapped a palm over it. He worried he was suffering a heart attack. He wished he hadn't had so much to drink last night. "They already suspect me of all kinds of other things. So why not say I did away with her, too?"

"They suspect you of all kinds of things because they have every right to," JD reminded him. "But not Bianca. Though the way you're carrying on, I'm having doubts. Are you okay now? Seriously? Can we get on with this?"

They got on with it.

Setting foot in the attic filled Dion with a mixed brew of emotions. All the affection and frustration Bianca had stirred in him came back afresh, distilled now into sadness.

The place was dark and chilly, no longer somebody's home sweet home. Some of Bianca's things had been removed, he saw, in the course of the investigation, but plenty remained. Or not hers, but the other mystery girl's, Ravina. JD had filled him in on that new mystery, too.

They sat on either end of the sofa. JD switched on a table lamp and set up her gear, explaining that she would record his statement plus take a few notes. With the recorder on, she asked him how he had met Bianca.

He gave the abridged version. He described speaking to the stage crew at the magic show and having ended up talking to Bianca. How he'd given her a ride home. How she'd dropped her necklace in his cruiser, how when he tried to return it to her, she had invited him in for dinner. The next day she had phoned him and invited him over, this time to stay. And things had gone from there.

"She called you," JD said. "So her number would be on your phone. I bet you didn't think to follow up."

"Of course I followed up. Some guy answered. Said a girl had borrowed his phone to make a quick call as he was sitting at Starbucks. He didn't know who the girl was. A stranger."

"Aha," JD said. "The mystery thickens."

It occurred to Dion that a good mystery brightened JD's eyes and made her pretty. In fact everything about her was pretty, even in her darkest moods, and maybe that was why he found himself staring at her at times as though soaking her up. Why had he never seen it till now? Why had he always thought of her as just another brother officer? "So either she doesn't have a phone," she went on. "Or didn't want to be traced. I'd bet the latter. Did Bianca mention a roommate?"

"Never."

"Or the name Ravina?"

"She did say something about Ravina. I wasn't paying attention. I didn't follow up. I didn't think it mattered."

"Not everything in life is a vital clue. Give yourself a break."

Wrapping up the story, he told her how on the day he'd left the attic for the last time he had slung the girl's glittery bit of junk jewellery on a bedpost for her to find. Curious, he went to see if the necklace was still there. It was. He brought it to show JD.

"Seemed to mean something to her," he said, as he handed it over. "But it was weird how she treated it, now that I think about it. Like it was important to her but not in a sentimental way."

JD took the necklace and squinted at it up close, front and back. She whistled. "One thing you're not is a gemologist. This isn't junk. These emeralds look to me like the real McCoy."

"So *you're* the gemologist all of a sudden."

"No. Just observant. And they're set in platinum. There's a mark on the back here. We can look it up." She seemed lost in thought for a moment, then told Dion to drill down into his memories and tell her more about Bianca, every little thing he could remember.

"We were just friends," he said. Not even friends, more acquaintances. The girl had never given him any background info that he could dig into. She had told him about crashing a Maserati, which was either a joke or a tall tale, coming from a girl who seemed to be living on a shoestring budget. "Oh, and she couldn't cook worth a damn," he said. "She seemed a little out of it, most of the time. The longer I knew her, the more out of it she seemed."

He gave JD an account of the few days he had spent with Bianca, a decidedly touch-and-go relationship. Wherever she went at night, it was something she didn't want to talk about. A bad situation she couldn't seem to free herself from. He should have pried more when he had the chance, but he'd thought there would be time. As it turned out, there wasn't. She had disappeared. A simple story with no end.

JD shut off the recorder and looked at him closely. "You're sure she's living on a shoestring? We've got a fancy piece of jewellery. Maybe one crashed Maserati. What did she wear?"

He shrugged. "Clothes."

"High end or bargain basement? Did she darn her own socks or throw them out after every use? Designer labels or Joe Fresh?"

Dion was beginning to doubt his own detective skills. He was fairly sharp in his observations of the world at large, but when it came to Bianca, he seemed to have a filter over his eyes, blurring out the truth. "Sometimes she was dressed really nicely, sometimes not so much. Doesn't mean anything. Whoever she spent her nights with, I'm guessing he showered her with gifts, so she had some pricey things. One time it seemed like she got her hair done, but the next day it looked like she hacked it off herself. If you're right about the value of the necklace, it was probably from her boyfriend."

"How do you figure?"

"She was relieved to get it back, but then she tossed it aside and didn't give it a second glance. I thought I'd do her a favour and fix it for her. Same reaction. She was grateful on one level, indifferent on another. So it's a gift from a man, and it's a man she doesn't care for."

He sat back, pleased that his detective skills were sharpening up.

"And how did she talk?" JD asked.

"What d'you mean, how did she talk?"

JD gave him one of her evil know-it-all smiles. "I think you've been duped," she said. "And funny thing is, I don't think she even *tried* to dupe you. How did she talk? Like us proles, or like a rich girl?"

"And how does a rich girl talk?"

"Like this," JD said, drawing out the words in a lazy lilt. "Don't you know *anything*."

Dion sat straighter. She had mimicked Bianca to a *T*.

"Though let's not jump to conclusions," JD continued. "Poor girls can learn to talk like rich girls easily enough. But put it all together, Cal. This necklace. The Maserati. The nice clothes. And you say she can't slice a lemon without cutting off her fingers. I think she's a thoroughbred. Rich. All her life, people have been slicing lemons for her."

"So what's she doing in an attic on Ridgeway?"

"It's a getaway. Rich people have more time to worry about the meaning of life than you or I, and they get restless, and they blame their dissatisfaction on their wealth. Maybe that's Bianca. She started rooming with her buddy Ravina, thinking playing a pauper would make her real. But then it got too difficult, or boring, or she learned being rich wasn't such a drag after all, and she ditched the whole charade and went back to her mansion where the kitchen staff would serve her breakfast in bed. Crusts trimmed off and whipped butter on the side."

Considering her theory, Dion looked around the funky little flat, thinking back, rewriting the strange girl in his mind. Bianca being a fraud fit, and yet it didn't.

JD said, "You know what else I think? I think if you'd really wanted the answers, you'd have asked the questions. Bianca was a mystery to you, and you liked her that way. It gave you something in common."

"Stop playing the shrink with me," Dion told her. But maybe she'd hit the nail on the head, and he'd preferred Bianca being ephemeral. He took in JD's face, marvelling that she seemed to know him better than he knew himself. And now she knew far more than she should. On impulse he grabbed her recorder and made sure it was turned off, then gave it back and said in a low voice that wouldn't carry beyond her ear, "I shouldn't have told you what I did. If it came out that you were withholding information, you'd be in big trouble."

JD imitated his whisper. "I know that."

"So I want you to do what's right," he said.

"Believe me, I'll do my best. And while we're on the subject, I'm super pissed at you for taking your perfectly good life and screwing it up. And now I'm a party to it, and it's scary and keeps me up at night. But I'll be okay. Don't worry about it."

"Do what you want, JD. But I promise you that if it all comes out, if I'm arrested, I'll never let them know what I told you. I'm erasing it from my memory that we ever talked."

"Ever talked about what?"

She was joking, but neither of them laughed. "To tell the truth, I'm not sure what I did tell you," he added. "I've gone over that night so much in my own head that it's hard to figure out what I've said and what I haven't."

"Want me to remind you?"

God no, he didn't.

"Anyway," she said. "Whatever happens, happens. If we both lose our jobs or do time, we'll just find a better gig once we get out. Join the circus or whatever."

Her flippancy was chilling. Maybe she didn't care about losing the job. Maybe she was halfway to quitting, anyway, like she'd threatened often enough. But to him, the job was everything. He couldn't imagine not being a cop. Leaving this world behind was like the edge of a precipice he couldn't bear to look over.

"Back to Bianca," JD said, recorder rolling again. "You say she talked a lot."

"At times."

"But you can't remember anything she said?"

"Not much. I asked about her family, and her work, and whatever, but she had a way of not answering straight. Never spoke about friends or workmates." He tried replaying their conversations in his mind, but drew a blank. "I think she was a vegetarian."

"Tell me about the last time you saw her."

"Something was bothering her. She went silent. I thought she had a headache or something. She lay down for a nap. I promised we'd do something fun when I got back, then I left. When I returned a couple hours later, she was gone."

"Okay. Let's see if we can get a picture of her for the bulletin board." JD took up a notepad and a pencil she had brought along, and told him to describe Bianca while she tried her hand as a police sketch artist. "Just like the pros do it."

Dion described Bianca's features and JD put them to paper, adjusting the slant of the eyes, the width of the mouth to his specifications. The end result they looked at together was a better likeness than the kindergarten-level drawing Dion had produced, but not by far.

"Maybe not just like the pros," JD admitted.

"But it's not bad. You like to draw?"

"Sure. Though I haven't had much practice at portraits. Here, let's try this." She switched off the recorder once more, angled herself toward Dion on the sofa and flipped to a clean sheet of paper. "Just for fun, I'm going to draw you."

"No chance," he said, and wrestled pad and pencil from her grip.

"Okay, so you draw me."

"You're kidding."

"I'm not kidding. Draw me."

He humoured her, dashing off a cartoon. A smiley face, minus the smile, a circle with two dots for eyes and a downturned mouth that he thought was a good likeness.

JD wasn't fazed. "I'm serious. You clearly need to get in touch with your inner artist, so here's your chance. Draw me. What have you got to lose?"

"Face."

"I won't laugh. Promise."

She seemed sincere, and he tried to draw her. Half-heartedly at first, but pulled in by the process. JD sat patiently as his model, and he realized that this was what he longed for, a good excuse to study her. He sketched carefully, doing his best. He forgot about Bianca and his own troubles. He etched her dark eyes, her brows, nose, mouth, the shock of hair coursing over one eye and wisping out from behind one ear. Shaded in the side of her face. He forgot the pain in his side as he drew. He forgot the crime he had committed and the door that was closing on his world. Over the next ten minutes, capturing JD to paper became all that mattered.

Yet the end result was terrible, not like JD at all. He growled and threw aside the pad, then immediately wished he hadn't. He wanted to keep the drawing, but re-claiming it now would be awkward. And JD had scooped it up to take a look, and as he watched her smile in de-light he came close to asking her if she was still seeing the good-looking pilot. But just as he wouldn't admit to want-ing to hoard images of her, he couldn't ask such a personal question. How could he, without letting on that he cared?

* * *

JD had fallen in love once, in her teens. She remembered the headiness, the drama, the heartbreak. The first time must have left her inoculated against lovesickness — thank god — as her next romance had been more a merry-go-round than a rollercoaster. Or maybe a House of Mirrors, like with the pilot, who had since moved on, as pilots do.

Falling in love with Dion was different. It was more of a controlled fall that had probably started the day she'd laid eyes on him, to be honest, since she wasn't immune to beauty. But back then, on a scale of one to ten, personality-wise, he'd hovered around a two, in her opinion.

But then the accident happened. In their conversation the other day, on the heels of his confession, they had talked about how the crash had affected him. No, he had suffered no amnesia around the hours leading up to the collision, as he had claimed to investigators — blackout being the oldest trick in the book, when it came to trying to get away with murder. He had gone on to tell her that though he had been knocked out of orbit for a while, he was back to normal. No brain damage. Good to go.

She wasn't sure if he believed his own claim that he was back to normal. She sure didn't. He'd gone into the crash a handsome, cocky bastard and come out a handsome, pensive bastard. Maybe it was brain damage or maybe it was a cosmic slap upside the head, but she preferred the pensive version, if only because he seemed to have gained some degree of introspection, and introspection made him real. And now her feelings for him had deepened into what she supposed was a crush. A one-sided crush, because she knew she wasn't his type. What was his type? The flawless human Barbie doll, probably, a transcendency she couldn't possibly aspire to.

Don't worry, she told herself as she studied him. *It will die a natural death.*

She watched him draw, his lashes downturned as he worked, his troubled expression clearing and a more peaceful seriousness setting in as he scanned her face and tried to transfer it to paper. His peace was short-lived. He lost his temper and threw the drawing aside. He'd forgotten that drawing her was all in fun.

She rescued the picture he had thrown aside and gave it a look. *Whoo.* The image was so bad and so beautiful, even if he'd made her look a bit like a girl version of E.T., with nice black hair and crooked eyes. He'd also missed her cleft upper lip. Was he just trying to be diplomatic, or did he no longer see the deformity? She would have to tell him someday that she wasn't ashamed of it, and she wouldn't reverse it even if the world's top cosmetic surgeon offered to fix it for free.

They left Bianca's apartment and walked downstairs. JD cherished her memento from this strange moment in a missing girl's attic, when Cal had focused on her face with such intensity and made her heart go pitter-pat.

What a fool she was to fall for such a lost cause. But at least she knew it.

THIRTY-FIVE

FLAW

April 17

THE CREW INVITED Dion to a welcome-back-to-the-planet party at Rainey's. The gathering happened around dinnertime, and he was touched to find it a bigger turnout than usual. Leith and JD were present, along with Doug Paley and Mike Bosko. Sean Urbanski had made it in from Surrey. Jimmy Torr, Lil Hart, even some civilian staff were there. Even a lawyer from the Crown counsel's office had dropped by, all adding up to enough of a crowd that the servers had to hustle about, shifting tables and chairs to make room.

The place of honour had been saved for Dion at the head of the table. The jokes he'd expected about how many lives he had left were made as he took his seat and accepted a stein of light beer.

He was updated on the arrest of Brian Kaeck, now in remand, and the Bianca/Ravina case. Even with what

Kaeck had told investigators about Ravina, she couldn't be tracked down, and it was likely the last name she had been handing out, Stone, was an alias. Bianca remained even more of a ghost. Some team members suggested, tongue-in-cheek, that she was maybe only a figment of Dion's imagination. He was starting to think the same.

The Lawrence Follick case had stalled, as well, meaning all he had managed to accomplish with his mission to Garrett's was to convert their prime suspect into the hero of the day. Garrett saving his life could even prove a mitigating factor at sentencing, taking time off the old man's ultimate jail term.

But failures and dead ends aside, Dion was feeling good to be alive and back with the people he knew so well and missed so terribly, and he raised a toast to Beau Garrett for making it all possible.

Bosko met the raised glass with his own, and to the team at large said, "Do you know what I'm thinking about Mr. Garrett?"

The team gave a near-audible sigh of resignation, as Bosko was known to go on at length. Dion listened to his superior against the noise of the pub and only partially registered the words.

"In some way the operation was a success," Bosko was saying. "I mean, in the sense that Garrett's quality of life has improved. He's got some pain relief at the same time as his mind's been put at ease regarding the welfare of his great-grandson. Hopefully, he's seeing that it's not as much him against the world as he might have believed. Maybe, just maybe, he'll see the light and come forward on his own."

Dion's drink had gone to his head, inspiring him to argue. "That's not going to happen. Beau Garrett is stubborn. He won't give till he's pushed into a corner."

"And if he's pushed into a corner, he'll hit you with his cane," Leith put in, raising a toast to something unspoken. "So I guess we're at a standoff with the pig-wielding old bastard."

Clearly, Leith had had too much to drink, but as he'd told everyone every time he accepted a refill, his car keys were with his wife.

As Leith drunkenly went on bad-mouthing Garrett to his half of the table, opining that his saving of Cal was probably as much of a whim as his putting a spike through Larry Follick, on the other half Bosko said something that caught Dion's attention. Something about a missing locket. He tuned in with an effort. "Garrett what?"

Bosko told him a convoluted story about one of Beau Garrett's possessions going missing, a silver locket, and the accusations the man had lobbed against a neighbour, Louise. Or more specifically, Louise's niece, who house-sat sometimes and had been delegated the task of feeding Beau's goldfish while Beau was in hospital. Happily, the stolen locket file had closed before it had a chance to open, as Garrett had decided not to give a formal statement and only wanted the whole thing dropped.

In the din of their surroundings, Dion watched Bosko speak. Galvanized, though he wasn't sure why. He heard the others chime in, making light of Garrett's accusations and the neighbour's pithy reaction. It was a neighbour he had spoken to himself, standing on her doorstep discussing Beau Garrett's goldfish.

"Louise," he said. "Isn't her last name Maxwell?"

Nobody at the table within earshot could say for sure, but the surname kept pinging in his mind. "Louise Maxwell," he said. "We were canvassing the neighbourhood the day of Follick's murder, and she wasn't home. She went on a shortlist for follow-up. When she got home she was questioned but had nothing useful to say."

Of the crew only Bosko seemed briefly interested in his recap. It then struck Dion why Louise Maxwell mattered. "Zoey," he said, addressing Bosko, who sat kitty-corner. "Her niece. Zoey's the name."

Bosko leaned closer to hear more.

"She house-sits *sometimes*?" Dion asked. "Louise said that? So her niece had housesat in the past? I had thought …"

His words were drowned out by pub noise, and even Bosko rejoined the more interesting conversation to his left. Dion sat thinking over the revelation. The house-sitting the niece had done for her aunt, he had assumed when he'd spoken to Louise Maxwell, was just a one-off arrangement. Before being distracted by his cover team cruising by, he recalled the question that had been teasing at his mind, only to be sideswiped by Brian Kaeck's ambush. Had Zoey been house-sitting on the morning of Follick's murder?

But he was obsessing over a moot point, he realized, because the team would have covered off that particular loose end in his absence. "So Zoey's been interviewed?" he asked, to reassure himself.

Somewhere in the pub someone was having a birthday, or maybe getting stagged, and there was a surge in distant rowdiness that drummed out his question. Paley noticed him struggling to get his point across, and pinged a glass with a teaspoon until all around the table were listening up. Dion repeated his question. To his surprise, nobody could confirm that the niece had been tracked down and questioned, to find out if maybe she was witness to anything suspicious on the day of Follick's murder, maybe even the off-chance that she was the anonymous 911 caller who had reported a man lying on a lawn early that morning. Only JD could safely say that no, there was nothing in the file about any such follow-up.

Dion slapped the table. *Unbelievable.*

THIRTY-SIX

ALMOST GOLD

April 18

LEITH HAD A BAD HANGOVER, along with a new lead to follow. Cal Dion, bless his officious heart, had provided the lead at last night's celebration at Rainey's, and Leith's task force had spent the morning tracking down Zoey Maxwell. She was delivered to an interview room in midafternoon, a slim, respectable looking girl in her twenties, who if not for the tattoos covering both arms from wrist to shoulder might have been a church mouse stepping in for a cup of tea.

Her eyes wide, she sat across from Leith and told him categorically no, she had not been on Paradise Road on the day of Lawrence Follick's murder, ergo she hadn't witnessed anything hinky, and certainly hadn't called 911.

Leith said that was kind of strange, since Louise Maxwell said otherwise. It had taken some jogging of Louise's memory this morning, but some landline phone records had done the job. Yes, Louise had indeed spoken to Zoey from her Vegas hotel room at 8:10 a.m. on the day in question.

"Memory sometimes works domino fashion, don't you find?" Leith put to Zoey. "Your aunt checked her phone records and saw she'd made a nine-minute call to her own home that day, which reminded her she was anxious to confirm you knew what to do about the cat. Something about the medicine it's supposed to be given. For parasites. Ring a bell? She knew you didn't have a cellphone, so she was trying to catch you while you were at her place, watering the plants and so on. She knows you're an early bird, knew more or less the time you'd show up, and remembered being relieved that she'd managed to catch you, just as you were leaving."

"Oh, was *that* the day you're asking about?" Zoey eyed the phone records in question that Leith had placed next to his folded hands. "Okay, now I remember talking to her about the meds for her cat. But doesn't mean I saw anything on my way up, and I sure didn't call 911 from any cellphone. How could I, since I don't have one?"

Leith smiled. "You must be the last person on the planet who doesn't."

"They're ridiculously expensive. The phone companies hook you with a fancy phone for zero down, then gouge you for the rest of your life on their stupid plans. Anyway, I wouldn't want one even if it were free. What for? So I can become another phone zombie?"

Leith chatted with Zoey about the worldwide phenomenon of interconnectedness for a while before guiding her back to Paradise Road. "Your aunt pays you to house-sit?"

"Yes. She's quite generous, too. She knows I'm a pauper. Perpetually between jobs."

Zoey talked about the economy for a while, and Leith sympathized. Then he said, "So I guess you do what I'd do at your age, if I had a house to myself. Invite friends over, throw a party, spend the night?"

Zoey looked almost offended. "No way. It's dead dull up there. I go in, pick up the mail, water the plants, feed the cat, then I'm out. Back home fast as I can. I like the boonies, but I like New West a whole lot more."

"Right, you live all the way out in New Westminster. So you bus it to North Van? That's a long ride. SkyTrain, SeaBus, and once you hit North Van, the local bus runs are pretty limited, aren't they?"

"Yeah, it's quite an odyssey. But I don't mind."

"Why head over there so early?"

"Beat the rush."

"Smart. How long do your tasks at the house take you? An hour at most?"

Zoey opened her mouth, closed it, and stared at him through narrowed eyes. Doing the math, no doubt, and realizing that all told, with the earliest possible North Shore bus schedules taken into account, the time frame would place her trudging up the road from the bus stop at around 7:00 a.m., which lined up nicely with when the 911 call had come in.

Checkmate, Leith thought.

"Look," Zoey said. "I found the phone when I was waiting at the SeaBus terminal. It was just sitting there.

I was going to turn it in, but after I made the call, I lost my nerve and threw it away."

Leith nodded. When the file was closed he would return the phone to its rightful owner, old Mrs. Hildebrandt, whether she wanted it back or not. "Tell me about making the call."

"I didn't think it was a dead body, honestly. But I saw this shape lying there on a lawn, in the dark, behind a fence. I stepped closer to have a look. The fence had these really ugly cartoon things all along it, like some kind of satirical art installation, who knows, so I figured that guy was probably part of the show, a sculpture or a dummy symbolizing god knows what. But then he twitched."

"He twitched?" Leith echoed.

"Or maybe not. It was darkish out. Maybe a trick of the light. But I thought I'd better call it in, anyway. On the phone I'd found. So I did."

Leith was quite sure she'd "found" the phone in a stranger's handbag when the stranger was looking the other way. But he would leave the question of petty theft for another time. "You must have heard on the news that it wasn't a dummy. You'd have saved us a lot of trouble if you'd come in and talked to us."

"Why? Wasn't anything I could add to *Hey, 911, seems to be a guy lying on a lawn up here.* Right? I'd done my duty. Police stations give me the willies."

"Sadly for us, we give a lot of people the willies, without even trying." Leith was wondering how this girl had slipped past unnoticed, either heading up or heading down the road that early morning. "When you left your aunt's house and were returning to town, didn't you see all the police activity?"

"I avoided it."

"How?"

"Don't you know? Wow, investigate much? There's a path that runs through the woods behind all those homes along there, on the ravine side. Soon as I saw that body and knew there might be cops all over the place, I decided to take a detour. Takes a bit longer, and it's kind of creepy in the middle of the woods, but that's what I did. Because, believe me, I had regrets about making that call soon as I'd disconnected. Had a bad feeling you'd pin whatever happened to that guy on me, just 'cause I was there."

She had a point. Until eventually cleared, she would have been at the top of the suspect board, just for being at the wrong place at the wrong time.

"And you saw nothing, before, during, after your 911 call, that might point to who'd done this?"

She shook her head. "I got to Auntie's place and did what I had to do, and I got out of there again. Took the same detour on my way down."

Leith dug out the Google Maps printout from the file and showed her. "Where's this path of yours?"

She traced it with her finger, delineating the same path Todd Broadwater used. The same path where he'd found the phone that had made the 911 call. Which all added up. "There are entry points in a few places along here," she said. "But you gotta know what you're looking for."

Leith made a note and thanked her, disappointed. A few outstanding questions had been answered, but the most important remaining hanging. He tackled the issue now, expecting more disappointment. "Did you see anybody out and about when you were either approaching or leaving your aunt's place, whether on the road or on the trail?"

"Your killer, you mean? No, I sure didn't. You don't think I'd have told you first thing if I did?"

"Do you know Beau Garrett?"

"Beau who?"

"Garrett. Your aunt's neighbour. She asked you to look in on his goldfish while you were up there."

"The old guy across the road who thinks I took his locket? No, I don't know him, except to see him. Auntie's pointed him out before, said he's a grumpy son of a bitch. Yes, I looked in on his fish. Didn't feed it. It was like a golf ball with fins. What that fish needs is a serious diet."

"The locket is of sentimental value to him."

"No doubt. What's of sentimental value to *me* is my freedom. I'm not going to jail for stealing some guy's trinkets."

Again her eyes went narrow, maybe with spite. "I saw him, you know. That day I called 911. I was just leaving Auntie's, looked out the window, and saw him coming up the road. Coming out of the mist like a scary old tortoise."

Leith blinked at her, and she read his expression and snorted a laugh. "Much as I'd like to say he could be your killer, no, he isn't," she said. "About all he could murder is a beetle, if he managed to step on it just so."

"You're saying your aunt's neighbour, Beau Garrett, was walking up the road?"

"Inching, more like. Leaning on his cane. Huffing and puffing."

Leith again referred Zoey to the map and got her to pinpoint where she'd seen Beau Garrett that morning, as best as she could remember.

She pointed to a spot about a hundred metres from Garrett's front gate. He was coming up the hill, and it was about 8:00 a.m.

From Follick's to Garrett's would be a twenty-minute walk for someone like Zoey, Leith estimated. But it could take up to an hour for someone moving along at Garrett's pace.

He arranged to have Zoey delivered back to the SeaBus terminal, then sat thinking. What she'd given him wasn't much, but it was maybe all he needed to back Garrett into the proverbial corner. If Garrett knew an eyewitness had placed him where he shouldn't have been on the morning of the North Shore's cruelest killing act of the decade, maybe then he would fold, and the case could be put to rest.

Victory was twinkling on the horizon. It was almost gold.

THIRTY-SEVEN

RED SKY AT NIGHT

April 19

THE SUN WAS SETTING, the sky ablaze, the day's heat dispersing. Beau had cut his finger while opening a tin can. He flicked on the light in the bathroom and searched for a band-aid, and in the process he found the locket on its silver chain. So it wasn't where it was supposed to be, in his sock drawer, but in the top drawer in the bathroom cabinet, mixed up with the flotsam of old thermometers, cough-drops, burn ointments. He clicked the locket open and checked, and sure enough Evvy's face was still in there. She'd been snipped from a snapshot, years ago, back when he knew how to act the part of a husband.

Funny, he couldn't remember moving the locket from the chocolate box where he kept all his valuables to here. But at some point he must have. The way it was all tangled and covered in dust proved that it had been in that drawer a while.

So it seemed he had wasted a lot of breath cursing that niece of Louise's for a thief. Made him think, what other stuff had he wasted his breath on over the course of his life? Probably a lot.

Clasping it around his throat was a chore, the kind of work best left for dainty fingers, but he managed. Then checked in the mirror and snorted. He looked damned silly, a big old gnarled stump like himself wearing fine jewellery. But he liked the sensation of having Evvy so close. Made him think of a time they'd truly liked each other. She was now cruising the world with that boyfriend of hers, but it was time to stop blaming her. Maybe if she dropped by again one of these days, he'd say something nice. Start them off on the right foot again.

There came a rap on the door as Beau made coffee.

Two policemen were standing there. They told him they were arresting him on suspicion of murder. One of them listed all his rights faster than he could understand, then asked if he understood. He nodded. They then let him know he had to go with them.

He told them he wasn't ready. For a moment he even considered fighting them off and shutting the door. But he knew that wasn't going to happen. It would just be a big fuss and noise, and he'd end up covered in bruises. He went to put on his boots.

* * *

While at his desk working late that night, Leith was notified of a hotline tip that brought Ravina Stone back into the spotlight. The tip was a response to the media release about both missing women, put out since the two cases were going nowhere. No AFIS hits had come back on any of the female prints lifted from the attic and no missing person reports matching either Ravina or Bianca's descriptions had surfaced. There being no evidence that either woman was in danger, the files dropped down to the low priority shelf. Still, they nagged at Leith's conscience, so when the tip came in, he sat up and paid attention.

The tipster's recorded voice — female, middle-aged, with a trace of a mid-east accent — intoned, "You police are maybe looking for Ravina *Patel*, not Stone. She lives in Port Coquitlam with her poor fool of a husband, Anwar."

That was all. The tipster rang off, not leaving a name.

Leith made a note in the skinny file and placed some calls to the Coquitlam detachment, arranging to have Ms. Patel brought in, hopefully this afternoon. On his high priority case, meanwhile, he went to let Bosko know that Beau Garrett had spoken to counsel and was ready in the interview room. Leith would be on the outside looking in, monitoring the interview from behind glass. Bosko had chosen to speak to Garrett himself. Maybe because the suspect had made it clear on facing Leith upon arrival that he just plain disliked him.

Fine, Leith had reflected. *I don't like you, either.*

* * *

The interrogation was atypical. From the monitor room Leith watched and scoffed, with JD at his side. There was no bullying that he could detect, or even cajoling, on Bosko's part. No talk of God or morality. In an unhurried and respectful fashion, Bosko told Garrett how an eyewitness had seen him, Garrett, walking up Paradise Road on the morning of Lawrence Follick's death, and how the sighting fit into the time frame of the assault.

Focus on the sighting, Leith was thinking, almost mouthing as he watched. Dance with it, lean into it, skewer the suspect as the suspect had skewered poor Larry Follick. And for heaven's sake, don't let Garrett know how far from ironclad the evidence is. A distant circumstantial, at best.

But Bosko didn't dance or skewer. He plodded. Leaving Leith tearing out his hair — or at least tugging at his beard. JD was suffering, too, he could tell. The way her crossed arms tightened defensively. And sure enough, it was clear Garrett was going to maintain his innocence.

But an odd thing happened. Bosko and Garrett left Paradise Road behind and talked about life. They talked about the suspect's great-grandson. Bosko mentioned his own divorce, and the fact he'd never had kids, something he was starting to regret at the age of forty-three. They talked about the locket around Garrett's throat. *Hey, you found it!* And Garrett's wife and daughter. Alcohol. Violence.

Regret.

And somehow in the course of that serious but comfortable chat, slow as a Sunday afternoon, Garrett confessed. It slipped out when Leith was on the verge of dozing off, and it popped his eyes wide open.

Later he would have to analyze the transcript, figure out exactly when the tables had turned, but for now he uttered an under-the-breath *hallelujah* of delight. JD's eyes had widened, too, and her arms uncrossed and fell loose at her sides.

Garrett went on to tell Bosko that it had been an accident. That morning — just days after Evvy had dropped by, showing off her new man and their car that was long as a boat and waxed to a sheen — he had gone for his walk down Paradise Road, coming upon those damned eyesores that were grinning and spinning and blocking the view.

Leith pumped a childish fist in self-congratulation. He'd got it right from the start. If the whirligigs weren't entirely the inciting event, they were at least the last straw.

Garrett went on to tell Bosko how he'd been in a foul mood that morning, so when a man had come from the house with the view spoiled by cartoon characters, a push and shove kind of argument had struck up. The pushing and shoving had left the homeowner rolling around on the ground, injured. Must have got struck in the throat, by mistake. Not knowing what else to do, Beau had put Follick out of his misery with the object he had closest at hand, the whirligig he had pulled from the lawn in demonstration of what should be done with all of them.

Yes, Garrett admitted. Some days later, down at the festival in the park by the shopping mall, while waiting for Justin to come out of the trailer where some abracadabra show was happening, he had been pestered by a clown on a unicycle. Yes, when the clown kept pestering him, he had stuck out his cane. Just wanted the man to go around him, go away, leave him alone. Hadn't intended for the clown to lose his balance. He wasn't sure how bad the clown was hurt, as he hadn't stayed around to see. He'd gathered Justin and headed to the library.

"Shouldn't have done either of those things," Garrett grumbled at the end of his story, presumably referring to both killings.

"Wow," Leith exclaimed, in the privacy of the monitor room. "You don't say."

JD was hanging on Garrett's every word, and flapped a hand at Leith to be quiet.

Garrett went on to tell Bosko he had no plans to contest the charges. He'd plead guilty in court, he said. He also said he was sorry.

He didn't sound sorry to Leith. But actions spoke louder than words, and he was in there, confessing, bringing at least some closure to the families of the victims, while sparing the province the cost of a full-blown trial that could run for months.

Minutes after Garrett was taken away for booking, JD answered a call on her cell, and relayed the message to Leith. Ravina Patel had been tracked down at her Port Coquitlam home. She had agreed to come to the detachment there first thing tomorrow for questioning, and Leith and JD could come by and finally meet the woman who had caused so much havoc.

THIRTY-EIGHT

WAYWARD

April 20

ON FIRST SIGHT, Leith knew at least this piece of the puzzle was snapping nicely into place. Ravina Patel perfectly fit the description he had of Ravina Stone, who he saw at a glance possessed the kind of otherworldly beauty that could drive many a man into a jealous rage.

She had been arrested on charges of obstruction, and seemed ready to carry that behaviour forward. As she took her seat before Leith, JD, and a Port Coquitlam detective, she looked at the photograph of the Ridgeway Avenue house presented to her and replied that no way was she the Ravina Stone who had rented that suite in North Vancouver over the last half year or so.

Her voice was lazy and bold, a girl who was used to getting her way. Unfortunately for her, she wasn't going to get it this time. Leith told her there was fingerprint evidence that would settle the identity question soon enough. Without apology, she changed her story. Yes, she had rented the place, she admitted, but it was her private business and hardly against the law.

No, she was adamant it had nothing to do with an extramarital affair. She simply had wished to secure a home away from home, where she could get a break from her big, noisy family, and a ton of friends, who sometimes became a total headache. She needed time alone. To find herself, as it were.

Leith didn't believe her. She was a charming liar but transparent as hell. "There's this married guy, Brian Kaeck," he put to her. "He tells us he fell for a girl named Ravina. He was so smitten that he got her to set up an apartment, which he'd pay for, cash. A place she could furnish to her heart's content, on his dime. A place where they could meet up whenever her engineer husband was out of town. Brian was married, too. He told the girl to find a place in North Van, far from their own hoods. He didn't want to be seen with her. Didn't want word getting back to his wife. This is the place she found for that purpose." Leith tapped the photo.

"What an interesting story," Patel said, her dark eyes twinkling merrily. "But this guy Brian of yours is a big fat liar, because I never dated anyone by that name."

"Really? We have his text history. A lot of raunchy back-and-forths. It's your number."

"Wow. Awesome. Fake news."

"And all went well, Brian says, till one day this girl, who isn't you, stopped answering his texts, and when he went around repeatedly to find her, nobody answered the bell. She was gone. It was like, I don't know, she'd maybe got tired of him and wanted to vanish off his radar."

For whatever reason, probably boredom, Patel abruptly dropped the charade and heaved a sigh. "It was nothing. It's over. We met at the gym, and he was quite a looker, and all flowers and gifts, so how could I resist? But it turned out he was nothing but a pig. Wanted it too much, like *all the fucking time*. I was smart, didn't let him know my real name or my address. I dumped him. Are you going to go and tell my husband now? Break his heart and destroy my life?"

Leith had no desire to destroy her life, which she could manage well enough on her own, it seemed. After nailing down more particulars about her relationship with Brian, to add to Kaeck's prosecution file, he moved on to another mystery he was hoping to solve. He told Patel he was interested in the identity of a young woman who had apparently shared the flat on Ridgeway Avenue for some period of time.

Patel answered without hesitation and in the same lazy drawl that was starting to get up Leith's nose. "Bianca. What about her?"

JD took over then, as she was lead on Bianca's case. "She's kind of gone missing," she told Patel. "We'd like to find her, and we can't seem to pin down an identity, so we're hoping you can help out."

Without breaking stride, Patel tossed them a bribe. "If you don't tell my husband about any of this, I'll tell you what I know about that girl. Whose last name I actually forget."

Leith was tempted to reject the offer. How much could she tell them, if she couldn't even dig up a surname? But he gave the nod; her husband could carry on being hoodwinked, and Patel could go on and tell them about Bianca.

"We met at some political fundraiser dinner and dance thing long ago, when we were kids," she said. "Dragged along by our parents. So we kind of knew each other a bit. Then last year we met again at a Christmas charity soiree. I was there with my husband and she was with her fiancé. I didn't like him. Jared, I think his name was. What a prick. The son of a car salesman. Well, luxury car salesman, I guess. Her parents are rich. I mean, even more so than mine, like super rich, and she is super sheltered. She's always been super timid, too, so when we were at the soiree, which was a big yawn, I snuck her off and talked her into sharing a joint. Her first, apparently. One toke and we were best friends. I never tell anybody about all my private shit, but I trusted her somehow, and I ended up telling her about my husband and my affair and my North Shore love nest, and she told me she thought getting married was the right thing to do, but was getting cold feet. I told her don't tie the knot, then. Like, what, is it some kind of arranged marriage thing where you get no say? Well, apparently it was pretty much that. She also seemed to think they were fast-tracking the wedding because she wasn't well. In the head. I was wondering the same. I mean, that there was something wrong with her, mentally. Just something about her demeanour, you know, wasn't quite right. I tried asking her more about Jared and she clammed up.

But I had it figured. Auto-King's dad wants his son to marry royalty, and quick, before she grows a brain and says fuck off from my horizon. Which she should do, I told her. But she didn't have the guts."

Patel rolled her eyes and sighed. "Anyway, I had myself a mission of mercy, get this girl out of jail for a while. What she needed was some time away from her mother and father where she could learn to think independently. Because that wasn't part of her homeschooling curriculum, apparently. Wasn't a whole lot of time to do it, either, as they were already fitting her up for the long white dress. I think the wedding is supposed to be next month. Well, I soon found out she's even more sheltered than I thought, to the point of cruel and unusual. Would they let her take off for the day on her own? No way. I bet if she tried, they'd dope her and lock her in her room. But we figured it would be acceptable if she had a best friend from a respectable family to go shopping with now and then. That was me. Overnight I became her designated buddy, an excuse to take off, say we're shopping together or taking pottery classes or whatever. Wasn't easy. I had to attend their mansion and get the once-over. Imagine me, a chaperone? But it worked in the end. Handy for me, too, as we could alibi each other. We only went shopping together once, actually. She was *not* a fun shopper. She didn't like malls, didn't like crowds, didn't want to go clubbing. In fact the whole set-up turned out to be a pain in the ass, and I wished I'd never been so nice. Frankly, she's a drip. Doesn't drink, doesn't party, doesn't gossip. And she's the first to admit, she's not right in the head. Schizo, I think. Anyway, after our shopping trip she wanted to see my place in North Van, so we drove over, and oh my god, she was floored. Loved it there. Said she wanted to stay forever. If you ask me, it wasn't the place she fell in love with but the concept. Her own fucking place, where she could be whatever she wanted to be. So stay, I said. She couldn't, she said. If her parents found out, blah, blah, blah. So we rigged an alibi. We'd tell them she was staying over at my place in Port Coquitlam, if it came to an interrogation, because unlike her, I'm not monitored 24/7. And I handed her the spare keys, said there you go, sugar. Have some alone time. We'll take alternate weeks or something. And grow a spine for god's sake and dump Jared. I picked her up the next day and took her home. She was so depressed the closer we got to her parents' gates. She knew her days were numbered, I think. How sad. Like a dead woman walking. And she said she wanted to come to Ridgeway and pretend she was a free agent as much as she could before they caught on and she'd be reined in and forced to be the goose that laid Jared's golden egg, or whatnot. I said fine, but I wasn't going to become her chauffeur. I'd still be her alibi, if she needed one, but she'd have to find her own way there and back. She doesn't have a driver's licence, believe it or not. Not for lack of trying. Jared tried to teach her, but as soon as she touched the gas pedal, she banged into a tree. It was a Maserati, too. Candy-apple red. So nobody was very happy with her.

"Anyway. She came up with a plan of getting her driver to drop her at my place, then soon as he was out of sight she'd grab the bus from there to North Van. Our overnight alibi thing wasn't going to work out in the long run, too much trouble for me, so she'd have to head home in the evening. Same thing. Get to my place, call her driver, get picked up, as though she'd spent the day with me. Nobody knew better. But like I say, we both knew it wasn't going to last."

"So you stopped meeting Brian and more or less abandoned the place," JD said. "What about all your belongings?"

Patel wafted a hand. "Much of the furniture was already there when I moved in. An ugly old sofa, a bed frame. I think I ordered the eight-inch memory foam and Brian paid, and I also bought a nice knock-off Persian carpet and got some fairy lights, put some pictures on the wall. I brought over an old compact stereo and a bunch of CDs, for ambience. But the stereo is yesterday's technology and the CDs are garbage, 'cause I'm on the cloud now. There's also a cool birdcage I wouldn't mind getting back. Gift from Brian, complete with canary. And Bianca went and released it. I'm like, bitch, don't you know birds born in cages can't survive in the wild? She didn't even say sorry. Anyway, that's about all I can think of, as far as belongings."

"There are some items in a drawer ..."

"Oh, oops. Forgot about that. You can keep it all." Patel grinned.

JD sat thinking, and Leith could see her thoughts ran to something more profound than the girl's weed and dildos. "I don't understand why Bianca couldn't just say no to the marriage, if she was so against it," she said.

Patel's smile cooled. "Maybe you don't understand gilded cages."

"And you don't know her last name?"

"D'Souza," Patel said. It popped out of her without effort, and Leith suspected she had known all along. She stretched her gorgeous back, rolled her beautiful shoulders. "Am I done here?"

"In a moment," he told her. "What's Bianca's cell number?"

Patel checked her phone and read out a number.

"But she won't answer," she said. "I've tried. She used to be addicted to her cellphone just like you and me, but last time we talked she'd decided the phone was a tracking device, used to spy on her every move and record everything she was doing and thinking. Which it probably is, frankly. But that's modern living, right? You can't fight it. But she was such a fucked-up little girl, I wouldn't be surprised if she wrapped the thing in tinfoil and threw it in the ocean. Bad idea, because once her parents found she'd gone incommunicado, so much for her day trips. And how was she going to call her driver to get picked up? I was there to make the call for her the last time, but I told her I'm not going to be there to help out at the drop of a hat. Anyway, you'll be wanting her address, I suppose. I don't have it on me, but I can tell you generally where the D'Souzas live. You can't miss it. It's the biggest house on the block — actually it *is* a block — and you'll need to use the intercom to get through the gates."

On the drive home JD said, "Bianca D'Souza. Poor little rich girl."

She tried the phone number that Patel had supplied. She listened a moment before confirming to Leith, "Not in service." Then snapped her fingers. "D'Souza residence. Remember that phone call to Cal's phone, the one I called back, and an older woman answered, seemed confused, said it must have been a mistake? I thought it was just a wrong number. But it wasn't. Bianca used the palace landline to call Cal. She heard your voice instead and hung up."

The image Leith was forming of the mystery girl was starting to firm up. A runaway who couldn't run far enough or fast enough, who probably didn't even know what she was running from. Losing her mind, losing her will, losing hope. One day she had returned home and the cage door had clicked shut, once and for all.

He couldn't wait to meet her jailers.

* * *

The jailers, as it turned out, were gracious people, and the cage was as beautiful a castle as Leith had expected, though without the turrets his imagination had tacked on. John and Ana D'Souza apologized that their daughter had caused so much furor. She was being treated, and the prognosis was uncertain, but all the specialists agreed there was some form of early-onset dementia at play in her young and fragile mind.

"The medication seems to be helping," Ana said. "But it makes her sleepy."

Invited onto a vast covered patio shaded by grapevines, Leith and JD were allowed a short visit with the mystery girl. No longer a mystery, just ill. She struck Leith as friendly but remote. Her eyelids fell between her slow and somewhat nonsensical responses to his questions. She recalled her North Vancouver attic. Her parents had gone crazy when they found out. But for a few beautiful days she had lived there with a ghost. No, not a ghost. A policeman.

Bianca became suddenly lucid and present. "His name was Cal. He was having these horrible nightmares, and I let him stay till Wednesday."

"Why Wednesday?"

"Because Ravina is there on Thursdays sometimes. It's something to do with her husband going out of town for work, I think. I loved Cal. I hope his nightmares have gone away. He found my necklace, and I've gone and lost it again. It cost a fortune and Jared's pretending like it doesn't matter, but he's so angry." She gave a demonstrative shiver.

JD told her that the necklace had been found, and would be returned as soon as some detachment paperwork was dealt with.

Bianca nodded, but she was sailing away again to unknown shores. "Oh, yes, paperwork. It's becoming official, all of it. Me, Jared. We're becoming official."

"When's your wedding date?" JD asked.

"When I burn in hell," the girl murmured. Her curly brown hair blew in the breeze, obscuring her eyes. She suddenly struck Leith as beautiful and wild, and in a moment of clarity that passed before he could quite put the thought to words, he wondered if madness could be a kind of freedom in itself. Bianca was leaning toward JD, voice lowered to a whisper. "I'm going to run away with the gardener's son. Don't tell anyone!"

En route back to North Vancouver, Leith remarked that he should have warned the D'Souzas about the gardener's son, and would do so soon as he got back to his desk.

JD snorted. "Get real. You saw the way her eyeballs were spinning. It's a fantasy. There's a gardener's son in every rich girl's daydream. Let her have *at least* that."

And like the fool he was, Leith decided JD was probably right.

THIRTY-NINE

BARE

April 29

BEAU HAD DONE some jail time, long ago, and it was strange being back. Not like some might take it, a punishment, but a homecoming of sorts. He hadn't thought about it much, then, when he was young, about what jail was to him. It was just where he'd landed for whatever he'd done. It was different now that he had come here to die.

Though he wasn't up to dying yet. Felt not bad. Got regular treatment now. They had given him some exercises to do. The meds had seemed to kick in, and the inhaler was, well, nothing short of a miracle.

He went through his days in remand. Didn't like the noise, but even got used to that pretty quick. There was plenty to see, in the common areas. Almost in a way it could be a kind of entertainment, if a man had the guts for it.

He didn't even mind the food. Nothing worse than what he made at home. There were a few guys his own age he shared a table with at most meal times.

"Some kind of punishment," he'd said to the guys when they had their poker cards out.

"Sort of an all-inclusive vacation," one of the guys said to him.

Goddamn true, Beau thought. They'd stuck his useless carcass in jail to punish him for what he'd done to that man on Paradise Road, and now they'd have to feed him, do his laundry, supply him with meds he needed till the day he croaked. If this was penance, give him more.

He'd thought since everyone had found out what he'd done, he wouldn't be allowed to talk to his great-grandson ever again. But he'd had a surprise visitor. Not Justin but Evvy. Came by, sat there. They'd looked at each other, talked about the weather. The apology he'd planned for being such a bastard all his life didn't come out, but instead he asked if she was doing okay. She'd said yes. *That new boyfriend of yours treating you right?* he'd asked. Turned out her new boyfriend was actually her husband for the last fifteen years. Yes, he was a good guy. *Good*, Beau had said. Evvy had smiled then. Said she was sorry he was in jail. She told him neither she nor Sharla had custody of Justin, in the end. She was too old, she had to admit, and Sharla didn't have the attention span, and since the foster home was a good one, and Justin was doing well, they had come to a mutual agreement that he would stay. Evvy told Beau that he could talk with Justin on the phone, if he wanted. He didn't really, but did in the end, and the kid sounded like his usual peppy self. Talked about his foster parents a bit, who didn't sound like monsters after all.

Funny, too, that Justin was speaking more clearly, enunciating his Rs. But that's what kids do. They change. Learn. Grow. Move on.

It was nice talking to his great-grandson, but Beau had kept the call short, as he wasn't a great conversationalist. Last thing he told Justin was to be good.

Unlike his great-grandfather.

He opted out of tonight's card game, as he had something else to do. He looked at the sheet of notepaper he'd requested, wrapped his heavy-knuckled hand around the pen, and started to write out his letter of apology to Brenda Follick.

* * *

Midnight rolled past and became 1:00 a.m. The bad dreams had come creeping back, tentacle by slithering tentacle. Dion felt himself falling apart like the shittiest car in a demolition derby. Physical pain and emotional jitters persisted during the day and wouldn't let him sleep at night. Being here in the new apartment hadn't helped an iota. Homecoming didn't feel like the first step to redemption, as he had for some reason imagined it would. Plus the doctor wasn't giving him the okay to return to work, and he was finally accepting that the doctor had a point.

Why wouldn't the pain in his gut go away? Maybe because the knife's blade had come close to hitting an old wound, from the time he'd fallen downslope through snow and been gored by a tree branch. That was a while back, when he'd been working in the north, when he'd been close to suicidal. That had been night time, as well, pitch black, just him and his flashlight chasing some theory along a mountainside. He'd come full circle to the depression that had wrapped around him then and had never completely faded. The end result was he was physically and mentally unfit for police work.

"It's 'cause I'm a criminal," he said aloud. Unable to sleep, he poured himself a drink and stepped through the sliding door onto his patio, a six-by-eight space three floors over concrete. The air was cold and lively tonight, singing through the balcony rungs. Probably the drop wouldn't kill him, he decided, looking down. It would just mangle him further, leaving him a silently screaming invalid in a long-term care home with no access to a gun to finish the job. "I'm a criminal, and my badge is my disguise."

He turned the thought over, surprised that the simple truth had eluded him till now. Self-analysis 101. Maybe what he needed was a better disguise. Just had to work harder. Become indispensable to the force. He gazed at the sidewalk below, the neat landscaping that surrounded the tower, the cherry trees that had blown off all their pink petals. Cars skimmed past, and a few insomniacs loitered. Behind him the vertical blinds clattered in the wind. He was drunk enough to not care that he was crying, but not too drunk to understand what he'd lost. He was bare, and he couldn't find where he'd put his mask.

FORTY

FLOWERS IN THEIR HAIR ...

July 4

THREE MONTHS AFTER Bianca D'Souza had been tracked down to her parents' chateau, alive and unwell, JD learned she had packed her bag one night and slipped out. She was now officially a missing person.

Leith had been angry and anxious when he found out, because he had listened to JD and failed to warn the D'Souzas that their daughter was planning to run off with the gardener's son, something he was now obliged to report.

Although the D'Souzas were upset with him, they accepted his apology, and since their gardener didn't have a son, they suspected Bianca was merely deluded. Bianca couldn't drive, and there was no evidence of her being picked up by a cab, so they feared the worst. Their daughter had been kidnapped, and all they wanted was her safe return.

Ironically, now that Bianca had vanished, JD no longer thought her deluded when she'd whispered of stealing away with the gardener's son. Just mistaken. If it was a typical estate, it would be crawling with gardeners and contractors and hired hands who came and went, and it wasn't so far-fetched to imagine that she had bewitched one of them and they had helped her get away.

But JD had put Bianca and all other work worries aside. She was on vacation — at least staycation, enjoying life in her new attic suite, and there were other, more personal matters to occupy her. Like today's dentist appointment. She sat in the waiting room, listening to the awful distant whine of a drill. She wasn't here to fill a cavity, this time, because that had been dealt with some time ago at Dion's suggestion. What brought her back was vanity. On her last visit, as she'd stood griping to the receptionist about her toothache, she had happened to peruse a leaflet on teeth whitening, which promised a Hollywood smile in a couple of weeks.

JD had smirked at the concept then, but certain things had happened since that prompted her to spend more time in front of the mirror, contemplating her own tomboy haircut, her uninspired wardrobe, and, yes, the tinge of yellow on her teeth. She was trying out a longer, softer hair style. She was giving her cargo trousers a pass and choosing more fitted clothes that showed off her physique. She had once vowed never to get too hung up on any man, not to the point where she fussed over her looks. But maybe she could fuss just a little. As her mother had always said, *You could be so pretty, JD. Why not try harder? Be more like your sister.*

Just wait till she flashed her bright white teeth at them at the next family dinner. Maybe she'd even flash a genuine boyfriend who was drop-dead gorgeous. She smiled to herself thinking of her sister's eyes, which would glow downright green with envy when she got a load of Cal.

She knew she was getting ahead of herself. She told herself to just stick to the program. Don't look too far into the future. Just whiten your damn teeth and hope the relationship lasts more than a month.

With nothing better to do for the next five minutes, she opened her phone to check the world news. She'd already scoured the bad and now focused on the good. Another cute cat video going viral. And here was a cool article about an outdoor music festival that had gone down in San Francisco last weekend. A raving success, apparently. A throwback to the '60s, nothing but love and peace and groovy music.

The '60s were before JD's time, but she knew of the era from movies and documentaries. She'd heard of Woodstock. Flower power. Like every bright thing, flower power would have its dark side, she would bet. But in the final analsysis, light always wins.

A video clip was embedded in the article, one advantage digital news had over paper. With earbuds in, she played the clip. It was lovely. Singers singing, guitars twanging, colours shifting. People dancing in sunlight or sitting cross-legged on the grass. The vibe was much the same as in bygone days, JD supposed. People of all ages getting high, grooving to the music. *Make love, not war.* She pictured herself within the video, reclined on a blanket, warm in the sun, Cal at her side leaning in for a kiss.

"Hey, whoa," she said, back in the dentist's waiting room. She paused the video. Replayed. Paused again. Snapped a screenshot and expanded the image, zeroing in on the face of the girl reclining on a blanket, warm in the sun, the young man next to her leaning in for a kiss. "Damn!"

The receptionist peeked at her from behind her counter.

"Sorry," JD said. "I just solved a missing person case. And I bet you anything that's the so-to-speak gardener's son beside her. Damn!"

* * *

In the afternoon JD was repairing the trellis that supported her landlady's wild roses. The roses sprawled sideways, perfuming the air and snagging passersby. Dion sat on the front steps leading up to the porch, keeping her company while she worked. Mostly he was listening, ball cap on, brim pulled low against the hot afternoon sun beating down.

JD was telling him about her morning's adventure, about killing time at the dentist's office, chancing on the news clip, catching Bianca's face in the crowd, and doing her duty by ratting out the runaway to the distressed parents. Dion looked at the screenshot and agreed, with a gasp, that that was the Bianca he had known so briefly.

"Cruel, turning her in," JD said. "But just as cruel to leave her parents in the dark. How's this trellis looking?"

"Looks good," Dion said, in a strange mood. Quiet.

JD, up on a stepstool, looked down at him. Tonight she was throwing a belated party. She had moved into the

Ridgeway flat on May 1, but held off on the housewarming party for two months. One, so she could do a few renovations to the suite and furnish it nicely, and two, so that Leith could attend. His schedule had been tight. He'd been away periodically, getting trained for his upcoming stint with Special E, an undercover assignment that JD had tried talking him out of, in vain. "Promise you'll come back alive, then," she'd told him. He had promised.

JD put away Mrs. Riddle's carpentry tools and dusted off her hands. The front porch was looking spiffy, the buffet-type food upstairs was all prepared and plated, the fridge stocked with beer. It was time to chill. She sat on the step next to Dion, and they leaned shoulder to shoulder. The guests would be arriving around five and staying till around ten. Not a rowdy bash, just a casual, collegial get-together. Bosko and Leith, Doug, Jim, Lil, and whoever else decided to show up.

JD gazed down at Mrs. Riddle's wildflower garden. Mrs. Riddle had named the flowers for JD, who had known only dandelions till then. She was now a bit of an expert. Black-eyed Susans and buttercups, columbine and yarrow and phlox and bachelor's buttons, she could put names to all the perennials growing below. The flowers swayed, backlit and lively with bees. Some plants were just budding, others gone to seed. Not quite bucolic, with the noise of traffic in the not-so-far distance. But close. She went to gather a bouquet to adorn the apartment and found herself thinking again of Bianca and her own role in foiling the girl's escape.

"Her parents will find her," she told Dion, with regret. She was back on the step beside him, bouquet picked, twirling a bachelor's button between thumb and finger. "They'll bring her home and put her back on her meds, and her condition will worsen, till she's committed to some psych ward."

"But it's good you found her," Dion said. "She needs care."

"I guess so. At least she had a kick at life in the wild."

He nodded. Holding his hand, JD felt his strength and was comforted. She sensed too the undercurrent of his sadness, though he wouldn't talk about it, and she wouldn't ask. They weren't great talkers, yet, either of them, and even togetherness was going to involve a learning curve. But she had a feeling they would make it, whatever storm was on the horizon. As he had told her last night, they were made for each other. Sometimes a cliché was lovelier than a dozen red roses.

FORTY-ONE

DAY'S END

DION WAS GLAD that JD's party had been a success. Mrs. Riddle had been entertaining, breaking up the cop talk with snippets of a life story that stretched back longer than anyone else in the room could remember. Even Brad Gillespie seemed to have enjoyed himself, in an anxious way. But night was falling, and one by one the guests had said goodnight and departed. All but one straggler, who was now collecting his windbreaker. Dion waited till Leith had given JD a hug, saying not only goodnight but goodbye, promising never to be a stranger.

Dion joined him at the door. "I'll walk you out."

The jazz faded behind them as they took the stairs down and strolled along the path to Leith's pickup, parked curbside.

"Funny how things turn out," Leith said. "JD ends up living in your crime scene. Well, not really a crime scene, but close enough."

Dion didn't think it was funny. Nothing was funny right now. Leith leaving on an undercover mission was far from funny, and his own resolution was farther still. Everything was grim, tragic, frightening. But he had thought it over and knew what he had to do. He had also listened to Looch Ferraro, speaking to him through a dream, giving him a piece of advice that only last night he had decided to follow.

Just say I did it.

Dion was sure it had been Looch speaking, as he would never have thought up the strategy on his own. Brilliant, because nobody knew it was Dion who had delivered the killing blows to Stouffer that night in Surrey. Not even JD knew. He had told her a lot, but he hadn't spilled that one damning detail.

If the courts believed that Looch was the killer and Dion the accessory, his sentence would be lower than if it were the other way around. He'd be out before he was too old to start living again. And Looch would forgive him. Hell, he'd be honoured. *Give me full credit for slamming Kelley Stouffer into the mud, bro. Lay it on thick as you want.*

But even with Looch taking the worst of the heat, he was giving up and he was going to jail. He was doing it for JD, stripping her of her guilty knowledge, and better sooner than later, because the longer she kept it to herself, the more trouble she'd be in when it surfaced that she knew what she knew.

He was doing it for himself, too. Giving up was the only way to banish the girl with pink hair. He realized she was no real threat. If she hadn't come forward two years ago, why would she now? But she'd grown into a banshee who would follow him around till the end of his days, if he didn't do what he was going to do.

And giving up was the only way to bring the creeping bag of bones down off the ceiling and into the light, where he could deal with it.

He was standing next to the passenger door of Leith's truck. Leith, in off-duty denims and plaid, leaned against the driver's door, elbow on the hood, squinting at the blood-red sky. He had quit making small talk but seemed in no hurry to leave. Maybe because this was his last day on the North Shore for the foreseeable future, so this was goodbye, and saying goodbye was never easy. Or maybe he just knew what was coming from Dion's side of the vehicle, that the chase was over. He looked across at Dion with a silent invitation. *Go on. Say what you want to say. I'm listening.*

But Dion couldn't say what he wanted to say. Like the paralysis that came in the throes of a nightmare, he was frozen in place, fists in pockets, heart slamming against his ribcage and a knot of fear writhing in his stomach. He was afraid of the jail cell and the shame. Afraid Leith would be killed in the field and they'd never see each other again. He was afraid JD wouldn't or couldn't stand by him. But most of all he was afraid of disappearing, and he'd be sure to do so if he turned back now and went on pretending to be something he wasn't.

He heard himself say it, as if from a distance, and felt a caving in with every word, like his insides were made of sand. "Something I have to tell you."

The world was coming to an end, and it was just beginning, and how could that be? He'd said the opening line he'd been holding back for so long, and he hadn't crumbled to dust. Still standing upright and still breathing on Ridgeway Avenue, looking straight across the hood of a pickup truck at the man who would soon be putting him under arrest.

Leith showed no surprise, but gave a nod toward the passenger door, with the gentleness he reserved for the worst of the bruised and beaten he dealt with in his day-to-day life. "Sure," he said. "Let's talk."

Acknowledgements

I WISH TO THANK my writer friend Judy Toews, who once again read the first draft and pointed out which parts shone and which parts needed a sledgehammer. But most of all she made me laugh, at the business of writing — which sometimes gets too serious — at us, at myself.

I wish to thank those at Dundurn Press for their hard work, especially my excellent editing team: Allister Thompson, for his crucial substantive advice, Jenny McWha, for her oversight and patience (again), and Mary Ann Blair, who dug into the details with such care and attention.

I've said it before but I'll say it again, I owe a special debt of gratitude to two brilliant writers, the late Holley Rubinsky, and fellow Nelsonite, novelist, mentor, friend, Deryn Collier. After all, it was their faith in me that sent me on this grand adventure.

And as always, thank you, reader!

Note: I have fictionalized some parts of North Vancouver, especially when it comes to crime scenes. There is no Paradise Road, and the magic field is only in my head.

About the Author

R.M. GREENAWAY has worked in darkrooms, nightclubs, and probation offices, along with her travels across B.C. as an independent court reporter. In 2014, she won the Unhanged Arthur Award for best unpublished novel for the first B.C. Blues Crime, *Cold Girl*. Her short stories have been published in the anthologies *Voices from the Valleys* (2016), *The Dame Was Trouble* (2018), and *Vancouver Noir* (2018). R.M. is a member of the Crime Writers of Canada and lives in Nelson, B.C.

Mystery and Crime Fiction from Dundurn Press

Victor Lessard Thrillers
by Martin Michaud
(Quebec Thriller, Police Procedural)
Never Forget
Without Blood

The Day She Died
by S.M. Freedman
(Domestic Thriller, Psychological)

Amanda Doucette Mysteries
by Barbara Fradkin
(Female Sleuth, Wilderness)
Fire in the Stars
The Trickster's Lullaby
Prisoners of Hope
The Ancient Dead

The Candace Starr Series
by C.S. O'Cinneide
(Noir, Hitwoman, Dark Humour)
The Starr Sting Scale
Starr Sign

Stonechild & Rouleau Mysteries
by Brenda Chapman
(Indigenous Sleuth, Kingston, Police Procedural)
Cold Mourning
Butterfly Kills
Tumbled Graves
Shallow End
Bleeding Darkness
Turning Secrets
Closing Time

Tell Me My Name
by Erin Ruddy
(Domestic Thriller, Dark Secrets)

The Walking Shadows
by Brenden Carlson
(Alternate History, Robots)
Night Call
Coming soon: *Midnight*

Creature X Mysteries
by J.J. Dupuis
(Cryptozoology, Female Sleuth)
Roanoke Ridge
Coming soon: *Lake Crescent*

Birder Murder Mysteries
by Steve Burrows
(Birding, British Coastal Town)
A Siege of Bitterns
A Pitying of Doves
A Cast of Falcons
A Shimmer of Hummingbirds
A Tiding of Magpies
A Dance of Cranes

B.C. Blues Crime
by R.M. Greenaway
(British Columbia, Police Procedural)
Cold Girl
Undertow
Creep
Flights and Falls
River of Lies
Five Ways to Disappear

Jenny Willson Mysteries
by Dave Butler
(National Parks, Animal Protection)
Full Curl
No Place for Wolverines
In Rhino We Trust

Jack Palace Series
by A.G. Pasquella
(Noir, Toronto, Mob)
Yard Dog
Carve the Heart
Season of Smoke

The Falls Mysteries
by J.E. Barnard
(Rural Alberta, Female Sleuth)
When the Flood Falls
Where the Ice Falls
Why the Rock Falls